PERCEPTION

Also by LIANNE DOWNEY

∞

Cosmic Dancer

*Speed Your Evolution:
Become the Star Being You Are Meant to Be*

∞

*The Liberator:
A Psychic-Spiritual History of the Orion Empire*

*Biography of an Archangel:
The Accomplishments of Uriel*

∞

PERCEPTION

Lianne Downey

Jolibro Publishing
La Mesa, California
www.jolibro.com

PERCEPTION. Copyright 2024 by Lianne Downey.
All rights reserved.

No part of this book may be used or reproduced in any manner whatsoever without written permission except in the case of brief quotations embodied in critical articles and reviews. For information, contact Jolibro Publishing, www.jolibro.com; info@jolibro.com

Visit the author on social media or at
www.liannedowney.com

Hardcover: ISBN 978-1-953474-07-0
Paperback: ISBN 978-1-953474-08-7
eBook: ISBN 978-1-953474-09-4

Library of Congress Control Number: 2024934004

This is a work of fiction. Names, characters, places, and incidents are the products of the author's imagination or are used fictitiously and are not to be construed as real. Any resemblance to actual events, locales, organizations, or persons, living or dead, is entirely coincidental.

TO THE GOLDEN ONES, AND THE BLUE ONES,
AND THE SHIMMERING WHITE ONES,
AND THE RAINBOW, BLUE/PURPLE,
RED, AND GREEN ONES.
I'd be lost without you.

CONTENTS

1 Moral Injury 11
2 Lifeless 23
3 Pulled Pork 30
4 Haunted 45
5 Vanished 57
6 Misperception 63
7 Devotion 68
8 Marooned 73
9 Compassion 82
10 Whiteout 89
11 Blue Light 97
12 Evidence 103
13 Confession 111
14 A Broken Oath 123
15 Breakout 136
16 Blackthorn 144
17 Church 148
18 Soonika 163
19 Trackers 176
20 Rescue 184
21 The Basement 195
22 Common Enemies 199
23 The Posse 211
24 The Cabin 221

25 Ocean Blue   227
26 The Green Drink   234
27 Suspended   250
28 Perception   259
29 Orders   271
30 Truth and Lies   275
31 Friends   279
32 Loyalty   288
33 Flight   297
34 Fallen Trout   304
35 The Agreement   310
36 The Third Man Factor   314
37 Remote   319
38 In the Aethers   324
39 What Does Not Glitter   330
40 Too Far   338
41 Authority   344
42 Rose   347
43 Connection   358
44 Elevation   365
45 Clarity   371
46 Luminosity   379
47 Alien   386
Acknowledgments
About the Author

1

Moral Injury

∞

All her training said she must protect this lie.

All her patriotic oaths and vows, spoken and written and sworn, told Minda Blake that she must keep this secret, that it would save lives, including her own.

But that was not true. The lie was already killing her. So said Blackthorn's company doctor.

He had no idea what she did for the government contractor. That was classified. But he said she had the symptoms of a new disease he called "moral injury."

"Kind of like PTSD but with a less tangible cause. It's what happens when, day after day, you violate your inner sense of what's right."

When he rattled off the symptoms, she had them all: sleepless nights, headaches, nausea. Suicidal reveries.

"Military drone pilots. They're the first ones who brought it to our attention."

She stared at him blankly.

"See, they watch a guy halfway across the planet, maybe for weeks. Watch him eat, pray, play with his kids. The technology is so refined now they can see a fly land on his nose. Once our pilot confirms that this is the guy they're after, *bam.*"

He fluttered his hands to mimic oblivion.

"But our pilot, safe and sound in his little cubicle somewhere in North America—*he's the one who gave the confirmation.* And he's the guy—or gal, sorry."

He focused on her for a moment before he returned to the scene in his mind, clearly clocking that she was a woman with enough curves to prove it. The scrutiny made her blush.

"Our *pilot,*" he amended, "is the one who's still watching the screen when the guy gets blown to bits. Literally. Everyone screaming, wife and kids running to where he'd been standing moments before."

He looped the stethoscope back over his neck, shaking his gray head in disgust.

"Drone assassination," he spat as he pulled off his gloves. "It violates centuries of the warrior's code, that of mutual risk."

He ran a hand through the spiky Marine cut that probably reminded him of back in the day—before he retired to work for her mercenary bosses.

"Moral injury. Slow-motion spiritual suicide—self-imposed. It blows them apart just like the bodies they obliterate on command. Karma's a bitch, so some try to get it over with. The quick way."

He looked at her significantly and Min knew what he meant. She'd found herself studying her mother's bathtub one day, wondering how long it would take to bleed out.

This doctor was a real bouquet of lollipops.

She had never killed anyone—directly. But over the years she worked for Blackthorn, she'd come to believe that her job was taking life from people merely by keeping the truth a secret. If they knew what she knew, the world might gather in its wrongs and release all its delayed goodness into society.

The doctor didn't ask her what she did every day; he knew she'd have to lie. Instead he offered her drugs, which she refused. Remote viewers can't take psychotropic substances. They would impair her psychic clarity, never mind the potential for ugly side effects, including addiction. He gave her a business card for the company shrink, which she promptly threw away.

She never went back to him. Couldn't risk Blackthorn finding out. The black ops government contractor she worked for wasn't one to coddle the infirm. But Blackthorn's doctor had answered her most pressing question.

Thanks to him, she knew what she had to do. She just didn't know how yet.

"Blake, you're on rotation to accompany the retrieval team. The rest of the remote viewers will begin reconnaissance immediately to provide general search locations. Once the team's on site in Michigan, Blake will narrow down the parameters to ping specific targets. Questions?"

Blackthorn's Commander was a former Navy Seal who'd seen too many tours in bad places. If he had another name, Min didn't know it. He ran his teams with rigid formality, and he always kept these San Diego briefings short. Tonight he seemed especially eager to finish up.

Irish Alex raised a hand. "I heard they call this the 'Dutch Triangle—where liberals go to die.'"

She laughed with the others but the Commander, long accustomed to Alex, turned to a projected map.

"The Dutch Triangle. It stretches from Holland on Lake Michigan's eastern shore, north to Muskegon, then east to Grand Rapids near the center of the state, and back again to Holland. In between, you've got a shit ton of bump-in-the-road towns where Dutch descendants practice their religion with rigorous devotion. Their unwritten motto? 'If you're not Dutch, you're not much.' Their churches discourage fraternization with outsiders, or 'Americans,' as they've called everyone who isn't Dutch since the pioneer days."

"So they kicked these fanatics out of the Netherlands?" Alex asked. "Because I spent a week in Amsterdam once. Can't remember it, though," he winked.

The team laughed again but the boss maintained his scowl. "These are *Michigan* Dutch. They're highly conservative, and their pastors, called *dominees,* exert a powerful influence over the region's politics and commerce. That influence goes up the chain of command to DC. Prominent locals have even figured as President's Cabinet members."

"Wait—you mean like Betsy DeVos?" Wren interrupted. "Who told *60 Minutes* that Black kids deserve more severe punishments than White kids?" Wren could hack into any system they needed, so no one cared that he always looked like he'd just gotten out of bed.

"Yeah, the one who tried to take money from public schools to fund private schools for rich kids," prim-brilliant Susan the rule-follower agreed.

"'The most hated Secretary of Education ever,'" Luther quoted the old headlines. The less said about Luther, the better.

"*De*-Vos," the Commander droned in agreement, "wealthiest Dutch family in the Triangle, founders of Amway and military mercenary companies giving us a bad name, and yes, that's the kind of influence they have." His muscular shoulders heaved with a deep, controlled breath.

She read it as a clear effort to maintain professional neutrality. That other soldier-for-hire company had shared a name too close to Blackthorn's. She knew how much their screw-ups in Iraq irked him, even after they changed their name to protect the guilty.

"Now, certain elements of local government are aware and sympathetic to our mission. If anyone spots your caravan rolling in tonight, you can count on official cover. The locals aren't likely to embrace touchy-feely tourism like Sedona has, which would make our job tougher. Your objective here is to make sure no one sees, knows, or remembers that anything unusual has ever happened in the area. And that not a single piece of evidence remains." He glared at Minda.

Minda—Min to her friends—used to brag that she'd been a patriot for all of her thirty-six years, starting in the crib under her father's influence, rest his soul, and rising up through Naval Intelligence. Then Blackthorn caught wind of what her mind could do and influenced her discharge from the Navy so they could "recruit" her to their cause.

These days her patriotism was tougher to justify. Working for Blackthorn was as if she'd joined a gang, and everyone knows that to leave a gang could cost your life. But what did that matter now, if even her doctor thought she was headed for self-annihilation?

∞

A long charter flight later, her team infiltrated a section of Rosy Dunes Natural Area—towering, protected sand dunes along Lake Michigan's wooded eastern shoreline. Boardwalk trails threaded through the public park, which lay smack in the heart of West Michigan's Dutch Triangle. As usual, they'd come in under cover of darkness in two unmarked SUVs, ignoring the park's deserted pay stations.

Min struggled with her hazmat suit, which she detested despite its sleek-fitting, state-of-the-art "smart fabric." Supposedly it kept artificial pores open to release heat and moisture for comfort, but would automatically clamp them shut in the presence of toxins. The suits always felt like overkill to her, and worse, they gave her a rash. As usual, she had to ask Susan for help to adjust her respirator.

"At least you didn't break the radio or fog the night goggles this time."

"I'm a psychic, okay? I don't do tech."

"Right. Perfect qualifications for retrieving the most sophisticated technology we'll ever hide."

Was that a note of sarcasm from the team's most dedicated member? Min flipped her off as they spread out with the others to reach coordinates indicated by the remote-viewing team back at headquarters.

An hour later, they'd only bagged three out of twelve designated targets. "Where's your enthusiasm, Blake?" her radio squawked. "You're laggin'."

Wade. New team leader, Southern drawl, fan of his own muscles, transferred from another division. Rumor had it they'd gotten themselves into what Blackthorn euphemistically termed, "legal jeopardy." The dirtier jobs. Collateral damage was the general rationale; they were fighting a kind of war. That's why Min and the others had been carefully trained at a Blackthorn facility in the dry foothills outside San Diego for all potential challenges. They traveled the world—never knew what might come up.

She didn't need that training to handle this guy. Now that she'd made up her mind, no one was going to stop her bid for liberation tonight. She kept quiet. Let him rant.

"Nothing here, Blake. Get your shit together!"

Oh, there's something here, Jock-itch. You just don't know about it.

After the briefing in San Diego, when she'd hung around waiting for the other remote viewers to complete their assessments, the object had risen up in her inner eye, completely unbidden. She wasn't supposed to start her psychic chores until they were on location. But there it was, clear as day.

Magic, some called this finding ability of hers. She knew that was only a term for science we didn't understand yet. Or that we'd forgotten.

To her surprise, none of the other viewers marked this object on their maps. The remote viewers worked in isolation from one another to avoid cross-influence. When they met to compile results and her object was missing from the consensus, Min kept her mouth shut.

So Wade was entirely correct. She'd been throwing out false cues all night to slow the team's progress. She needed them to stay in one spot for a while, tangled up with multiple misdirections.

She had never dared anything so bold in her entire career. Her fingers trembled, knees lost tension, palms like a dead woman—the whole package, including a stomach that wanted to throw off a week's worth of dinners. But this was her moment, her one chance in a million. A fluke of an opportunity.

Seize it, Minda! It might never happen again.

"Hey guys, I gotta take a pee." No one could argue with that.

Routine was, get well clear of the identified danger zone before dealing with the suit. And no one would expect super speed. She ignored Wade's colorful expletives about pampered psychic pains-in-the-ass and plunged into the dark woods. Her night vision apparatus cast everything in eerie green light as she wound her way down among fragrant pines and wide, autumn-stripped beeches to a narrow dip between two of the massive dunes. She reached the spot she'd seen in her vision. Put her gloved hands down.

She felt it immediately, mere inches beneath the sand. Flat, about the size of an iPad mini, ragged edges where it had broken from the rest. When she lifted it, gently as if it were a holy relic, the sand fell away to reveal a glowing, polished-gold surface.

How long had it been here? Dunes shifted constantly, burying and revealing, claiming and releasing. Rain, snow, ice, fallen leaves, streams of thawing winter, scorching sunlight—nothing would mar this substance. It could have been here for days, months—or thousands of centuries. Maybe it arrived before the Odawa and Ojibwe tribes who once shared this hunting ground before they fled the Dutch settlers. If that were true, it might explain why the other viewers hadn't seen this one. They'd been asked to target a *recent* event.

According to the Commander, neither Blackthorn nor anyone else had been able to date fragments like this one. Even the San Diego company that built their highly-classified SQUID detectors—their *superconducting quantum interference devices*—had to engineer portable, cryogenic technology in order to create a tool that could detect the faintest magnetic signals emitted by the only recognizable components in this mysterious alloy. The same alloy they'd been finding for years by scouring beneath certain unidentified anomalous phenomena, UAPs, all over the world—"UFO sightings" to the uninformed.

Still, the SQUID was less effective than trained viewers. They only used the device when the humans' accuracy failed.

If she didn't hurry, Wade might order their use and that could be a problem.

Ordinarily, Min was not permitted to handle the artifacts despite the suits, which came with dire warnings to protect the team from accidental exposure. She'd heard stories: bubbling skin, festering wounds, zombie-worthy descriptions of rotting limbs. The on-site remote viewer's role was to guide the team to the targets, where one of the others would retrieve the object and deposit it into a secure container. She wasn't privy to what happened after that. Need to know. Destruction, she assumed. No one ever explained why they only found fragments, never a whole ship, although newbies always asked the question. Again, need to know. Or maybe Blackthorn didn't have that answer.

Heart pounding—she'd never broken protocol before—she carried her treasure through the darkness up a steep, wooded slope of sand, north of the team's current location. The slipping grains beneath her feet had her panting by the time she reached a high clearing with a view out over the big lake, although all she could see of it now was an endless dark plain, unmarred by the lights of civilization.

Behind her, a circle of trees provided protection. If anyone came looking for her they would have to crash up through the branches. She felt confident she would hear them, despite the steady bluster blowing up off the frigid lake. Right now her ears picked out only distant waves thrashing around a deserted beach, dozens of feet below where she stood. Odd, how the fresh water sounded different than the ocean surf back in San Diego. Maybe it was the absence of shells and crabs and kelp, or the way the rocks here rolled back and forth, grinding into small shiny gravel.

When she was about twelve, her family had spent a couple of weeks visiting a Michigan uncle and his family. They lived south of where she stood but still close enough to Lake Michigan to take them all for a day at the beach. She had trouble believing that this ocean-like body of water—where she couldn't see the other side—was actually fresh water. Until she dipped a toe in and felt the biting cold try to nip it off.

Her male cousins delighted in telling her scary stories about climbing over ice mountains in the winter, about blow holes and drowned babies, and about the haunted shipwrecks that littered the Great Lakes basin. Their favorite way to torment her was to describe the "giant eels" that would latch on and suck the life out of you if you didn't swim fast enough. Their stories never dissuaded her from enjoying their excursions in the chilly lake that year, but she always kept an eye out for those eels, just in case they weren't a lie.

She felt that same mix of exhilaration and anxiety now, as she crouched in the moonlight to lay her forbidden fragment on a patch of fallen leaves, still soggy from an autumn storm. The object's golden radiance lit the dark air around her but didn't travel as far as the trees.

She took a deep breath and pulled off her gloves. Another violation.

Over the years she'd developed a theory about their ridiculous suits. The recovery teams were like mothers who aren't allowed to hold their babies before they give them up for adoption, she decided. The less contact, the easier for them to destroy this astounding truth. Defiantly, she slipped out of her hood and night scope so she could see the broken shard with naked eyes. Overkill respirator be damned; how could anything so magnificent be harmful? Her deep inner self told her it wasn't, and she'd learned to trust that voice.

At first glance, the object mimicked solid gold. As she stared, living swirls of luminous color blossomed beneath its surface. Always the same mystical material—which was the only reason she could find it. She'd seen others like it, one or two of them in dawn light, which was when she first noticed the kaleidoscopic interior. She felt in her soul, in her heart of hearts, that this artifact could not hurt her. She held her breath and reached out a finger to touch.

Cold, though not painfully so like the waters of Lake Michigan. Shivers of sheer delight traveled into her palm, trailed up her arm, crossed all the way to her heart. Her mind filled with mysteries, questions she had never been allowed to ask of anyone who might know. The biggest, of course, was who built this ship, a piece of which she now held cupped in her bare hands, with the wind blowing wisps of sand in her face. For this moment, all hers.

What if the famous wrecks at the bottom of Lake Michigan weren't only seafaring vessels?

Mt. Shasta, people speculated. Or Sedona. Or possibly Egypt, South Africa, Peru, Turkey, England even, in the northern regions—or India, with its rich religious aura. And what of Somalia, or Lebanon's Beqaa valley, inhospitable places that prohibited the kind of purging the company was now conducting? In those cases, they usually didn't bother. A little kindling thrown on the fires of conflict kept discovery at bay in countless hot spots around the globe. Sheer destruction of buildings and landscape—not to mention people—could keep the curious away. She thought of Beirut, once the "Paris of the Middle East," turned to bullet-ridden rubble, split down its belly by the Green Line in the seventies, the result of so-called religious conflict. Frequent destruction ever since, by forces unidentified. She knew the truth, and it wasn't a bit religious.

The builders of this starship—what were their lives like?

More reasonable than ours, she decided. How else would they have the time and freedom of mind to create something this stunning?

She stroked the surface, coaxed it to send that tingle up her arms again. Her imagination conjured a world for these mysterious builders: exquisite yet bizarre, with crystal trees and palaces of glass and people wearing brilliant colors in shades and hues she'd never seen before. The vision was so distinct, she believed for a moment that she'd remote-viewed it and her heart thumped with panicky excitement. Was that even possible? Frightened, she laid the piece down again. The vision faded.

If that's where they lived, then why come here?

Maybe it wasn't intentional. Maybe an accident—or an act of desperation. Or this might have been a drone, she considered.

But she'd heard rumors about crew members, that some even lived here for a time. No one knew exactly when, before the Ice Age or after. Only the craziest believed they might still be here, and they usually kept that to themselves—unless it was Alex, teasing a new recruit.

She felt a sudden cramp and stood to stretch her legs. Though small enough to hold in her hands, this mesmerizing item could obliterate centuries of ignorance. When people know…they might wise up, do things differently. That's what had agitated her doubt and finally blew open the trap door of her "moral injury." What could these so-called aliens teach us? How to solve wars, pandemics, global warming? Systemic racism? Incurable diseases? What if they've already overcome these things and know the key, found the solutions?

Who are we to decide what people should know?

Broken it might be, but the oscillating colors told her this material lived on. That was the thing. It might be Ice-Age old, this fragment, but…she'd seen things. Things that were *now*.

A familiar pain lanced across her chest. *Grief,* an energy healer had once told her, rippling through her acupuncture Lung meridian. "You have to find the source of it or you'll keep getting these pains," the woman advised.

Was she grieving the loss of her own moral compass? They had convinced her that this was her patriotic duty, this job she'd sworn to carry out. But was it "what's right"?

The world deserves to know, she would argue with herself when she woke at four a.m. unable to go back to sleep. This poor, trembling world, full of trivial cruelties, where selfish men and women make others suffer. *What if these visitors hold answers?* If they wanted to invade and conquer, they could have done so long ago. *They've certainly been here often enough.*

What if all the patriotic justification she'd once believed (people will panic; we're protecting them; it's too much of a shock; global instability; economic destruction, starvation, hardship, blah blah blah) had caused her superiors to make a horrible mistake?

She couldn't be part of it any longer. Tonight she would sneak this unclaimed fragment out of here and take it straight to the media. They'd find scientists. The scientists would confirm its authenticity and the world would spin differently. Because nothing else on earth functioned like this stuff.

Nothing else on earth…

She hadn't used the SQUID! Like a rotted tree struck by a hurricane, her narrow plan ripped apart with sudden, devastating finality.

She'd used her mind to find this. What if the fragment sent out a detectable ray? A *trackable* ray?

Is this a truth worth dying for? Because Blackthorn would make sure...

The doubts rained down like debris. Even if she tried to keep this specimen private, a personal talisman, Blackthorn would find out somehow. They would have her arrested as a thief, lock her away. No...her brain churned like a waterwheel...they would "secure the evidence" like they had with everything—and everyone—else. She would disappear in some accident.

You're no Ed Snowden. You don't have the skills, Minda. You don't know how to evade Blackthorn's network of operatives. It takes a tactical mind and you don't have one.

What was I thinking?

Wiser minds than hers had made this choice. They might be right.

Maybe they'd give her some kind of reward for finding this solo object, so far out of their search parameters. *Yeah, that's it—the only remote viewer to see it.* That thought did nothing to restore her broken heart.

A few feet to her right, a branch snapped.

She froze. Then tensed, ready for them to burst into her clearing.

Nothing happened.

In a frenzy, she crouched to bury her treasure beneath the leaves, down deep, where her secret might survive. She shoved sand over it and leaped up, breathing hard. She tried to compose her face and posture to look calm, disinterested, as if she'd climbed up here merely to enjoy the first rays of sunrise now painting the lake with hues of madder and violet. She grabbed the gear she'd left lying. Then dropped it again. Of course she wouldn't need it if she were merely sight-seeing, right?

No sound except her rasping breath and the distant *thrush* of waves grinding rock.

No one emerged.

Were they watching? Waiting?

She slowly turned toward the trees at her back, mentally rehearsing her cover story.

All the while, another part of her wondered if she could come back for the artifact. This had been her chance...maybe her only chance... maybe the world's opportunity to learn the truth at last...

A fat opossum lumbered out from behind a tree, as startled to see her as she was to see it. Bulging black eyes glittered at her for a long moment. The pale nose twitched. Appeased, it snuffled the ground for scraps from park visitors. Finding none, the animal turned its white-furred face away and ambled out of sight.

Pretend, Minda. Play 'possum.

She let out a breath, brushed sand off her hands, stared out over the water.

Bow to superior wisdom about the right moral choice. Carry on like you've done for years, Minda. No one will fault you, if you turn this in now. Who are you to defy the hierarchy that keeps this secret from the world? Play dead to your conscience and keep your job. It takes more than you've got to pull off the stunt you had in mind! What on earth were you thinking?

She was already sailing face-first down the dune when she realized she'd taken a blow to the back. Instinct made her fold into a ball.

"You're slippin,' Blake! I never shoulda gotten the jump on you!"

Wade! That's three times he's pranked me! Dung-brained, rat kissing—

She'd nearly finished planning her revenge by the time she slammed into the broken cement block half-buried beneath a patch of beach grass, remnant from an old snow fence.

2

Lifeless

∞

When Min's eyes opened, she couldn't see a thing. Black as night. *What happened to sunrise?* She tried to rise up on an elbow but couldn't feel the dune beneath it. *Broken?* Odd, that she felt no pain.

I must be in shock. That idiot Wade's in for it. Soon as I get back up this blasted dune.

She figured he didn't intend to hurt her, only hurl her down a relatively harmless slope of sand, the kind kids loved to roll down at these dune parks. But this bullying had to stop.

If she complained, management would tell her to suck it up and be a man, just like the Navy had. So she'd get her revenge. Might take months to find the right moment but they were always working in locations that provided opportunity. Always sneaking around in the dark of night.

She plotted the twists and turns of his payback even as she tried to stand on the steeply angled dune. Slipping a little in the sand, she finally regained a semblance of upright: downslope foot buried to the ankle, upslope foot at the end of a bent knee which was close to her chest. She yanked hard at her buried back foot—and landed on her elbows again when it sank deeper, her face inches from the grating crystals.

By the time she was thirteen, she'd already spent years ignoring her mother and grandmother's pleas and punishments to clean up her language. But that was the year her older brother Cale opened her eyes to reality.

"Boys don't like girls who swear," he said. "They don't respect them."

That motivated her. She started to make up her own words, the kind nobody could blame you for using. She rarely said them aloud, especially around schoolmates, but she quickly discovered that they took the edge off pain as well as the real ones did. It wasn't the word itself that carried the power. It was the energy she thrust into it.

She spat out a few of her favorites, *farfnoodles* among the worst. That caused more sandy grit to lodge between her teeth.

"Okay, you…you sand-burr infested monster," she spat. "So I'll crawl."

After falling more than crawling, Min stood at last atop the dune, only to realize that she couldn't hear the steady thrum of waves on the lake behind her. The blow must've taken her hearing, too. Worse: it was still black as night up here and Wade, the team—no one in sight. And the trees were moving. Not in the wind but with limber branches and once she noticed, they started to move faster, undulating like Egyptian belly dancers, rippling in sinuous motions all around her. Her skin registered this with electric shocks and she tried to run, stumbling and dizzy, back toward the trail that led to the park's exit. All around her, trees moved like they shouldn't and the ground beneath her feet felt…absent. Maybe it was, because now the nightmare fully enveloped her fleeing body.

Nightmare! That's what this is. Hah! I've got you now. I'll just wake up.
She tried. She'd done this before. But it didn't happen this time.

The darkness felt like a blanket over her face and she sucked for a breath that wouldn't come. Tried to scream but no sound emerged from her throat. She panicked.

Wake up, Minda! Wake up now! Dear Lord Jesus Christ, wake me up!!
He didn't. Instead she saw a light ahead of her and she ran toward the sharp golden pinpoint that danced behind the twisting pines. Each time she thought she'd reach it, it vanished and appeared again, further away, twinkling in tantalizing mystery.

Suddenly exhausted, she gave up the chase and sank to her knees, panting in useless attempts to fully aerate her lungs. The ground called to her and she fell to her side, still heaving in pointless breaths. This was a dream, after all. No need to breathe. But she felt so airless as the night closed around her and she lost consciousness again.

This time the dream took her higher.

"Minda, wake up, honey," her grandmother pleaded. "Everything's going to be okay now. Your mama is worried but I'm here with you."

She patted Min's limp hand. "Just open your eyes, sweetie."

No, she resisted. *Why should I? It's all dark anyway. And I don't want to go to school! The boys on the bus are mean to me…*

"Don't you wanna to see your Gramma again? It's been a long time, honey."

Her soft rich voice, like butter on pancakes, wrapped itself around and through Min's consciousness. She opened one eye, expecting to see her grandmother in the flowered mu-mu she favored on mornings when her mother went to work and Gramma Julene made breakfast.

"That's my girl," she soothed. Gramma Julene lived with them until Minda was twelve, and then …

Wait! She died of a heart attack that year…

Min tried to sit up and failed.

Her grandmother patted her hand again, "That's okay, now, you just lie there for a minute while I catch you up on things. It's been so long …" A confused look flickered over her shining face for a moment, then cleared. "You know, I don't think I've talked to your mama for a while, either. But I've been so busy here! I'm going to a new church now and they've got me doing all kinds of things I didn't before. Praise the Lord, I'm singing in the choir, Minda! Can you believe it?" Her eyes lit up with pleasure and she laughed that joyous jingle of hers. "And by golly if I'm not singing in tune now. There are a lot of new people at this church but old Belinda is there, and Freddy—you remember Freddy, don't you? That boy! Ran off to play music all his life…"

The look passed over her eyes again but tumbled quickly away, as if she'd flicked it off like a speck of custard from her old blue apron. She smiled down at her granddaughter with so much love, Min nearly passed out again from the intensity of it.

Warmth filled Min's chest and she stopped trying to make sense of things. She closed her eyes for a minute to better soak up the beloved sound of her grandmother's warm voice. Gramma Julene always loved to tell her tales after school, and when she was little, she often took her on her lap to comfort and instruct. "You just pay those boys no never mind," she would say when Min came in with tears streaming. "Listen to your old granny. They're never gonna learn, so don't you give 'em any of your life, you hear me? Just let 'em be."

But sure enough, one of those "boys" had sent her here. And she wasn't certain where "here" was.

"You know, I'm going to take you with me to church! You'll like this new pastor. There's something about him—don't know what it is, but he's got a feeling about him. Somethin' different. Somethin' special."

"Gramma Julene—where are we?"

"Well, honey, that's hard to say. I learned not to question it much. Reverend Ben—he can tell you more than I can."

"But Gramma—"

Min stopped herself. How could she say those words, *You're dead?* That sounded ridiculous because clearly she was not. Here they both were, talking as if her grandmother had simply moved to a new town. And if her grandmother were dead, what did that make her?

She suddenly felt a sense of urgency, something she'd forgotten. Something she had to do. This time when she tried, she sat up easily.

"Gramma, there's somewhere I need to go now."

"Yes, honey, I know, and I'm taking you to him right now."

"Who? No, I mean, someplace else—"

But they were already standing in a church, a beautiful church. The windows soared up out of sight, ablaze with glorious stained glass in every rainbow color, and the peace she felt here quelled the sense of urgency that had grown in her belly. She gasped as she looked around and couldn't see where the church left off, as if it were an endless meadow of church-like majesty.

"Well, greetings to you, dear friend," a voice boomed behind her.

Min whirled to see a tall Black man—basketball-player tall—with a wide smile spread across his handsome face. He stuck out a hand.

"I am Reverend Ben, and your grandmother tells me you are new to us. Welcome!"

She found herself putting her hand inside his huge fingers before she could stop the automatic gesture. Warmth flooded up her arm and straight into her heart, soothing the frantic beating which had begun when she realized she might be…you know…*dead*.

The reverend chuckled. "No, you're not," he answered her thought. "But you are in danger. Or rather, not you but your body. You're here with us because your body is lying in a hospital bed where doctors have induced a medical coma. They believe that's the best way for your injuries to heal. You suffered quite a blow to the head, young lady. Your brain is in danger of swelling, perhaps bleeding, which they hope the coma will quell."

The golden fragment! It all gushed back to her awareness at once: the alien artifact, Wade, the sand, her job with Blackthorn—all of it, along with a lot of other mental detritus that followed quickly after, everything from failed love relationships to how her teacher treated her in third grade and all the blessings she'd ever received, the sunrises and sunsets and candlelit moments…

"You had better sit here with me for a moment," Reverend Ben suggested, guiding her to a smooth crystal bench that felt like silky gossamer when she sat.

"My grandmother," she blurted. "Does she know? That she's dead, I mean."

"Well, that's complicated. She does and she doesn't. Most of my congregation here are folks who had a certain belief about where they'd go after death. When things didn't line up accurately, they found themselves here. We are taking our time with them, gently urging them along until the day when they can accept a, um, let us say a more complete story. We try to provide something familiar and comforting until that day comes."

"What about me? Why do I know this isn't right? I mean, am I dying? Will I die? Or am I already dead, and that's why I'm here with you and Gramma Julene? Tell me the truth!"

"I could not do otherwise," he answered smoothly. "You are an older soul. You have been around the block a time or two, I'll admit. You are not dead; not entirely. The induced coma in which your body rests mimics death but your body is still functioning, with machine help."

"But this feels so—*real*. I feel so real…"

"Yes, my child. This is more real than anything you've experienced on Earth, which is at best only a temporary condition. Now your grandmother told me, through her thoughts, that you had something urgent on your mind. Would you like to talk about it? Perhaps I can help relieve some of your concerns."

"Holy shit—" Realizing what she'd said, she blanched, then quickly blushed. "Sorry. I mean yes, please."

"No need to apologize. We are not the church we appear to be, as you may have realized by now. Language to us, the kind you use on Earth, is merely a means for communication, albeit a primitive one," he added.

She could agree with that. She'd never be able to describe this place with words, it was so…so…*sparkly* was all she could come up with.

"Words carry power, Minda, but they also carry meaning and connection. The word itself gives me no offense whatsoever, in whichever language you speak. I read your mind and your heart and, most importantly, the energy of your intentions. That doesn't lie; it neither conceals nor distorts. So please, carry on with no concern for proprieties of Earth language or religious convention."

Yes! That's what she'd always believed! That was why her personal cuss words worked so well, although it slowly dawned on her that he meant they could be as destructive as she intended them to be, as harmful as the real ones. Or as harmless, if that were her intention…

But this was her chance to ask the questions she'd always wanted to ask. *What about God?* No, too big to start with. *The ships—where did they come from?* Were they friendly? Was her work with Blackthorn to conceal their existence wrong, or right? Was the government right, that people couldn't handle the truth? That it would destroy all social and commercial structures and lead to chaos and anarchy, maybe even war among countries competing to own the ships' technology?

The moment she thought of her work, she felt the wet ground beneath her again as she knelt before that glowing fragment, the one that sent a thrill up her fingers every time she touched it. Indecision wracked her. Take it public, take it home—would it matter? Tell the media and die a martyr to truth?

Sweat trickled down her face and she reached to wipe it away. Soon Wade and the others would come looking for her and she had to do something. She heard a rustle and shoved the fragment deep into the sand, leaping up to look casual, as if enjoying the view of the lake down below …

Wait, I've done this before.

Then it burst into her sluggish brain: *He saw it! Wade saw me with the fragment and he tried to kill me because—but why would he yell after me like he did?*

She felt something pierce through her like a weapon and wanted to scream but her mouth was clogged by tubes and tape and the lights stabbed at her eyes. She quickly squeezed them shut again.

"Minda," her mother cried out. "Honey, I'm here!"

A stench of chemicals filled her nostrils and she struggled to bat them away.

"Nurse!" her mother shouted. "She's awake! Praise the Lord!"

But before the nurse arrived she drifted off again, away from the terrible tortures wracking her body. She floated in space for a time, wondering how to get back to where she'd been, where the reverend was going to answer her questions.

Then she was yanked back into her body with a force she couldn't resist. Machines were beeping—no, *screaming* to her sensitive ears. Panicked people flustered around her.

"Clear!" someone shouted, and again the sword shot through her but she was taped and shackled and powerless to fend it off. She sucked air intuitively and it coursed into her lungs with a vengeance, bringing endless pain with it.

She was back, blast it. And not a single question answered.

3

Pulled Pork

∞

Susan, Wren, her best friend Amrita, even the Commander texted her in the hospital, but Wade didn't offer so much as a *Hi*, let alone an apology. And no one mentioned the artifact. She wasn't about to ask, either. Wade shoved her down that dune seconds before she decided whether to radio the team—or not. If he saw her bury the fragment… she wasn't wearing gloves; she hadn't told them about it; she was in deep molasses. She might not have it in her hands but technically, she'd stolen Blackthorn's artifact.

Since she still lived, that meant they might be waiting for her to recover before they hit her with consequences. All she could do was lie here and fret, while doctors and nurses and needles and noises tormented her—though nothing tortured her more than her own conscience.

She'd seen them. Whole starships. For instance on her first job for Blackthorn, in New Jersey, right before 9/11.

That's not a secret I should have to keep, she fretted—all through the doctor-talk about brain injuries, how lucky she was, *blah blah blah,* how she'd overcome the drug that was supposed to keep her in a coma and they couldn't understand why but here she was, no brain hemorrhage, no bone fragments as far as they could see, and, "Plastic surgery later can fix that scar right up."

Yeah, yeah, great.

"Later" actually meant, "After we're sure we don't have to open you up again if something else emerges."

There was no way she'd let anyone put her under until she knew whether her employer wanted her dead or not. But what about the people dying in the hospital all around her? She couldn't forget about Amrita's husband, Sourav. *How many cures are out there, waiting for us, if we let Earth surge ahead? Take its place in a populated cosmos? They must know things we don't.*

Amrita nagged her to rest, to sleep, to let everything else go. While she ruminated in a Michigan hospital, her best friend was back at their shared apartment in San Diego watering their plants. She was on a break from a rigorous training schedule that, like Min, kept her traveling around the world.

The two had met during their training with Blackthorn, though Amrita's unique talents quickly put her on a different path in the organization. Amrita had been struggling with the remote viewing during those first days, and Min kept trying to encourage her, keep her spirits up. She herself had been quick to catch on but she knew the typical viewer required weeks of training and practice before their gifts blossomed into what Blackthorn needed.

Then one day out of the blue, Amrita suddenly clutched at her own arm and let out a yelp. "That's going to be a big one," she grimaced, clearly in a lot of pain.

"What are you talking about? Are you hurt?"

Min had been sitting in the Quiet Room with her. They were supposed to be relaxing silently so they could tune in to a remote site, then sketch dominant details for their handlers to compare with information provided by a Blackthorn employee who was physically at the site. This early training was old-school, originated as the first fumbling methods the military and its subcontractors developed after they realized they had to keep up with the Russians and Chinese, before modern technology seemed to make remote viewing irrelevant.

For a time, that is. Not anymore.

"It will happen in the next forty-eight hours," Amrita mumbled, rubbing a palm over her elbow. "Too bad I can never predict where."

"Amrita, *what* will happen? And what's it got to do with your arm?"

"Earthquake. I've always been able to predict them because I get these pains. My family detests it, so I usually keep it to myself. Sorry."

Sure enough, a major quake hit Turkey the very next day, destroying buildings and taking lives. Amrita simply nodded knowingly when they heard the news. "Told you. Useless talent."

"Are you crazy? It's priceless!"

That was the trouble with psychics. They were all so highly sensitive to so many things above and beyond their sought-after skills, it seemed like only other psychics could understand. And they tended to take their abilities for granted. In ordinary working environments, they quickly developed reputations as "difficult" or "snowflakes," or worse. So they tended to stick together, leaving the rest of the population clueless about their actual value to society. Or how they did what they did. Min knew many who, like Amrita, undervalued their rare sensitivities because to them it was no big deal. Some grew up assuming, for instance, that *everyone* could see colors swirling around people and simply didn't mention it. Or they were frightened by stuff their families believed, so they suppressed any glimmers of intuition that couldn't be explained away.

And yet, for those who tried to advance their talents, countless charlatans with ridiculous promises awaited them in the public marketplace. They offered elaborate, nonsensical, but serial "training" schemes that fed off the general ignorance and kept their students paying for that "next level" that would finally help them break through. Min hated to see the gullible sucked in like that, but she understood why they were so vulnerable. Their talents were rarely praised or acknowledged by the people who mattered in their lives, so anything that flattered their needy egos was likely to lure them in and keep them stuck.

The U.S. military, however, had reluctantly followed their Cold War enemies into the realm of the invisible mind, eventually tripped over its own prejudices, and then rallied behind the scenes with the help of companies like Blackthorn who found profit in the skills others had shunned.

That day in the Quiet Room, Min convinced her friend to explain this earthquake phenomenon to their team leader, who took it up the ladder, and next thing she knew, they whisked Amrita into a new training program she could only describe to Min in general terms because of the company's codes of secrecy.

Basically, if Amrita could discover a way to connect her pain to a particular place on a map—it was always different in character and body location, and yet similar enough to identify as an earthquake warning—her contributions to humanity would be incalculable. Something like, if her elbow hurt, then the quake might be happening around the Black Sea, say, in Turkey. Blackthorn never gave her an opportunity to decline—just like when they snatched Minda out of Naval Intelligence.

Problem was, they were working Amrita too hard now. She would come back from her frequent trips to unknown locations pale, exhausted, barely any appetite. She'd fall into bed without another word, which was not at all like the chattery friend Min had known. She worried about her at first, then convinced herself that at least this new training distracted Amrita from mourning the loss of her husband, which is how Min wound up sharing an apartment with her. Amrita and her beau had finally agreed to a massive wedding in India to please both sets of parents after years of living together, and then, six months later, Sourav dropped dead from a rare form of brain cancer.

It was one of those vicious, merciless diseases that Min's aliens might have been able to cure, and that made her furious. In fact, that was the trigger that first set her thinking about how to tell the world the truth.

Ugh. Min chided herself for going down that bitter thought-trail again.

When they found an apartment to share in Bay Park, Min had to adjust to the pungent smell of frying cumin, chili, turmeric, and coriander, but thankfully she fell in love with Indian food. They also discovered a shared passion for dance movies, no matter how simplistic the plot, as long as the dancing was good. And for scrounging used bookstores to find arcane tomes that explained more about their talents than one could find on the Internet. That is, whenever Blackthorn allowed a moment when both were in town. Most of the time they traveled in opposite directions, chasing after UAPs or bizarre methods for mapping the pain sites on Amrita's body. Some would say they had the perfect recipe for roommates: they rarely landed at the apartment at the same time.

And now Min was about to betray their friendship.

To quell her guilt, she turned her thoughts back to the problem at hand: what to do about the artifact she'd buried on the dune. By now she'd had plenty of down-time to nurture her doubts. Yeah, okay, if she tried to take that golden object to the media, Blackthorn might hunt her down and silence her before she managed it. She knew they were capable of it. But from what the company doctor told her about moral injury, she might die anyway, and by her own hand. What if her death could mean something to humanity?

She was convinced now that she had glimpsed the afterlife with her Gramma Julene and the Reverend Ben. It didn't appear to be the kind of numb silence that meant you could forget what you'd failed to accomplish during your time on Earth. *Some things are worse than dying*, she concluded, like failing to carry out a mission for humanity that oddly felt like something she'd been born to do.

∞

Four weeks out of the hospital, Min told Amrita a lie.

She didn't buy it.

"Yeah right. I am sure they 'asked you to visit that site in Michigan again to see if you missed something.' What are you hiding?"

Psychics. "I'm not hiding anything. I'm protecting, you know that."

"*Hmpf.* I know the difference between a security protocol and a bold-faced lie, my dear. And besides, you're still on official leave until you finish healing. Why are you going to Michigan?"

"I can't tell you."

"You already have. What did you leave behind?"

Dammit. "Nothing you need to be concerned about."

"I am concerned about you, and if you're about to do what I think you're about to do, I want to know about it."

"You can't help me and you could get hurt."

"So? I should wait until you disappear from the planet and then I won't feel guilty, like I haven't let my best friend down in her time of need? What would you do if our roles were reversed?"

Min rolled her eyes. This was not part of her plan.

Only because of her injury were her mother and her roommate informed of the location of the hospital where she was first taken, so Michigan wasn't news to Amrita, although they weren't told precisely where Min's team had been working. Min's mother believed she did some kind of government consulting job that, yes, involved a security clearance but no, did not involve scrounging up alien artifacts around the world. Whenever anyone asked what she did, Min could demur with, "I work for the federal government." Indirectly, that was true. And if they probed further, she'd wink, "Need to know." Ha! Half of them believed she worked for the CIA.

Actually, she might. Things were siloed in such a way, it was difficult to surmise who pulled the strings at the top. Blackthorn recruits quickly learned not to ask questions. They were like the British codebreakers working at Bletchley Park during WWII, who never shared their work details, even with one another. Some took their wartime secrets all the way to the grave.

Amrita knew not to ask more of her that morning. Although they worked for the same company, their oaths of secrecy meant they didn't speak about specifics. For instance, she knew about Amrita's training objectives, but nothing about the how. Amrita knew Min worked with a remote viewing team that aided Blackthorn's reconnaissance and retrieval services, but nothing about alien artifacts. For all her friend knew, Min could be helping important prisoners escape, or finding classified military equipment lost in dangerous locations. Min couldn't drag her friend into this; the risk was too great that she'd fail, and her friend's life wasn't hers to gamble. If things didn't go well, Amrita could proclaim total innocence of Min's intentions.

"If our roles were reversed, I would politely shut up and let you do whatever you needed to do to keep your job," Min lied again. "You know the rules."

Amrita crossed her arms and squinted at her for a long moment. "Have it your way, then. But at least let me drop you at the airport."

"Only if you promise no more questions."

"*Hmphf.*"

"I'll let you drive my Tesla while I'm gone."

She didn't relent but Min detected a spark in her eyes.

"And if anyone asks, which I doubt since I'm cleared for two more weeks of medical leave," she added, "tell them I'm going to visit my cousin's family in Berrien Springs for some R&R."

∞

Min's red-eye landed at Chicago's O'Hare in the wee hours of a cold November day—colder than she'd expected. She threw her overnight case into the rental car, tugged her chic little San Diego jacket tight around her shoulders, and floored it as soon as she hit the toll road that curved around the bottom of Lake Michigan.

It was too soon for her to make this trip and she knew it. She couldn't wait, though. She had to put her hands on that artifact again. What she'd do after that, she hadn't fully mapped out but already her sleep had improved and her stomach was behaving normally because she'd decided to do "what's right." Maybe she wouldn't have found the guts to follow through out on that dune, she could never know for sure, but on leave she'd had time to think.

Follow the money. Who profits from keeping this secret?

Weapons manufacturers. When they decide to make trillions of dollars building massive interstellar weapons, they'll simply terrify the people they've kept in the dark all these years into agreeing to pour more taxpayer money into the Space Force to purchase weapons to fight imaginary foes. She couldn't let that happen.

If it weren't for the strange flashes of places she'd never seen before—some kind of static in her remote viewing—and the dizzy spells, she wouldn't be worried that someone might slam her back in the ICU before she could retrieve the artifact. So she told no one about her lingering symptoms, especially her mother or her nosy roommate. She needed her freedom.

The rental car was nothing like her Tesla. She wasn't used to the noise or stink of gasoline, and the darn thing wouldn't accelerate for beans. *Why do people still drive these beasts?* she wondered as she tried to pass one of the big truck rigs that clogged three of the right lanes.

She knew, of course. She had been willing to pay a small fortune for her electric luxury car because it reminded her of how she dreamed the world would be one day, *could be,* if we allowed it. Driving the Tesla was like piloting a starship to her. Besides, she lived a very frugal lifestyle on a salary that could well afford more.

She didn't like the word mercenary, but truthfully that's who she worked for. She could be wearing designer clothes and dating lawyers and doctors, or buying whatever male company she liked, if her job had given her time enough.

Well, that's what she told herself.

Honestly, she didn't want the complications a romantic relationship would bring, having to lie like her co-workers did in order to keep their families safe and unburdened by this terrible secret. The last time she dated it hadn't ended well. He thought she was hiding things. He was right. Except that he thought it was another man, and that brought out an ugly side that completely turned her off. She'd tried marriage once. Briefly. That was enough.

If they wanted to know, Blackthorn could easily pinpoint her location at this moment. Even their remote viewers were fitted out with microchips. The tech who inserted the rice-sized capsule into her back, just inside her shoulder blade where she couldn't reach to scratch, told her it was a miniature ELT, an emergency locator transmitter like they install in airplanes. It was supposed to protect her during ops in dangerous places. If necessary, the company's powerful mobile receivers could activate the chip's radio transmission remotely to pinpoint her exact location.

"Kind of like remote viewing, only without the fallible human," he said as he jabbed it in.

"Great. So glad they care."

What else could she say? She'd been taught to follow the rules and this was a requirement of her lucrative employment.

So her first priorities this morning were a burner phone to replace the iPhone she left in San Diego, and a way to shut down the chip. (Naturally, Blackthorn wouldn't install them in the forearm, where they'd be easy to cut out like in the movies. Nope. This was exactly the kind of dark, strategic thinking at which the company excelled.) So far, if they wanted to check up on her, she was on a path to her cousin's house in Berrien Springs—where she had no intention of going.

She knew she wouldn't have made it out of that hospital alive if they'd wanted her dead. But that didn't prove they were ignorant of her attempted treachery. Maybe they were waiting for her to retrieve the artifact to catch her in the act. She would take no chances.

She sighed as she wheeled the white Ford into a sprawling truck stop just off the toll road in northern Indiana. She definitely wasn't practiced at this sort of high-stakes deception. All she could trust was the inner voice that led her one step at a time, though in her humble opinion it sometimes waited too long to offer its advice.

As hoped, she found overpriced rolls of Reynolds Wrap and first-aid tape in the incidentals section, near the pay showers that served the truckers rolling through this busy, dirty, shipping corridor. She grabbed those, a pay-as-you-go phone, and a bear claw for her breakfast, paid cash at the grimy counter, then slipped into a stall in the Ladies, sidestepping puddles. Not glamorous, but after a lot of wriggling and twisting, she managed to tape a square of foil to her back, large enough, she hoped, to block radio signals. She slipped back into her sweater and short jacket and headed out to her car in the biting autumn wind. No snow yet, merely bleak and bitterly cold south of the big lake.

A niggling thought at the back of her mind wanted to say something about why movie characters cut the thing out, if they could just wrap their arms in foil, but she shoved it away before it fully formed.

Blood makes better drama, right?

Two hours later, her eyes blurred and her stomach rumbled. The bear claw was long gone, washed down with some bitter black brew they called coffee back at the truck stop, and she had long before passed the exit that would have taken her to her cousin's house. She pulled over somewhere between South Haven and Saugatuck to use the skill her co-workers liked best.

Forget Google. As with the wild strawberries and morels she located so easily in the woods when she visited Michigan as a kid, she could remote-view the best eats in any locale, anywhere in the world except Japan. Most of her colleagues didn't realize how essential food could be for her. None of the other remote viewers seemed to have her problem.

Taking careful note that no mysterious vehicles pulled over behind her—no one following her, thank goodness—she closed her eyes, sucked in a deep breath, and let it out through her mouth. Again. As her body calmed and she tuned out the roar of cars and trucks whizzing by, she settled into herself in a familiar, peaceful way. This was where she felt most comfortable, floating in a safe sphere of mental communion with the universe. Gradually, a map took shape in her mind. Then she saw a glassed-in façade and a clean, upscale design, classier than expected in rural West Michigan. Just inside the door, a signboard featured a chalk sketch of something that made her mouth water. Odd, that she could see so much detail, especially as hungry as she was.

"Good enough for me," she muttered and started back up the tree-lined *Gerald R. Ford Freeway*.

Minutes later, she was driving straight east across flat farmland. No one following her here, either. She passed a sign for Ichabod's U-pick Orchards, then mom-and-pop fruit stands, gray and deserted, all the pretty autumn colors blown and drenched into oblivion. Miles of bare orchards and church billboards later, she passed another sign, "Welcome to Veenlanden, Population 1,385."

The town didn't have much else to recommend it. She passed a pristine, white-sided, colonial-style building tucked behind the roadside pines with a sign for an Inn, then a compact public library, and then the county highway became Main Street, a drab display of weather-beaten, nineteenth-century brick that had long ago lost any charm. A single, glamorous window stood out, glistening with enticement and a chalkboard that promised freshly baked breads, farm-to-table delicacies, and friendly folks enjoying liquid libations. *Avery's Cafe,* the sign proclaimed.

A thrill passed through her when she saw it in living color. Occasionally she saw details of places she hadn't been before, but rarely so accurate as this. Something more flickered through her senses—a flash of dense jungle—which she quickly forgot as hunger drove her through the front door, just in time for the weekday lunch rush: she was the only customer at half past eleven on a bleak Wednesday in mid-November. The pierced and tattooed girl at the front gave her a snooty vibe. Min didn't care. As usual, her stomach won out over social discomfort.

She let herself be led to a corner table in the back, directly across from a red brick arch that offered a partial view of the kitchen, from which emanated the sounds of rattling pans and calling voices and a heavenly scent of baking bread that wafted over to dazzle her senses. She settled in against red brick walls warmed by the midday sunlight that poured in and bounced off a restored tin ceiling to illuminate the small room. Any other day, a place like this would invite her to kick off her boots, tuck up her feet, and enjoy a good book with her lunch. The scene lacked only a blazing fireplace—and time. Time she no longer possessed.

Pulled Local Pork with Organic Fennel and Rosemary on Homemade Ciabatta. Yes, and never mind the steep big-city prices. This could be her last meal—although she hoped that was an exaggeration. In such a cozy place, it was hard to believe that anyone could be willing to actually terminate her life. Ex-military she might be, but she'd spent her Navy years indoors, wrangling classified information.

She slipped out of her cropped jacket and stretched her legs under the rough table, ignoring the wide-eyed gaze of the young waitress who lingered at the deli counter after taking her order all the way, by hand, into the kitchen. She was close enough to hear the voices and whispers, and thought she saw a face peeking at her from around a brick column.

Guess they don't see strangers here very often.

She tried to ignore the itchy foil beneath her sweater as she pulled off chunks of chewy, sunflower-seed bread from the generous basket the girl brought to her table. She dipped them into a miniature dish of garlic-infused olive oil, chased flavorful wisps from the swirl of dark balsamic vinegar floating on top as her newly manicured nails glistened in the reflected sunlight. (One of the perks of being on leave for weeks with nothing of substance to occupy her time.) The bread dissolved into luscious masses of starch on her tongue.

"Eat like a lady, Minda," her grandmother would scold.

Delicate. Right. She exerted an effort not to gorge herself on the freshly baked rosemary, or the honey whole-grain slices she also found in the basket. Good thing she'd be hiking later.

"You're here for Garritt, aren't you?" The plainly-dressed young waitress in her green *Avery's Café* apron stood poised with a water pitcher to fill her glass.

"Who the heck is Garritt?"

"Aren't you a reporter? This place has been crawling with them ever since he got back. Not that he's saying much. He usually refuses to see them, I should warn you. My name is Agnes, by the way." The round-cheeked young woman held out a welcoming hand, clean but rough in a way that spelled manual labor.

Min indicated her pork-sandwich greased hands but responded as politely as possible around a full mouth, "Pleased to meet you." She didn't offer her own name, a defensive reflex honed during her tenure with Blackthorn. Need to know. "So who is this Garritt person everyone wants to talk to—or about?"

She kept chewing; she was eager to get back on the road as soon as possible.

"You haven't heard? Garritt Vanderhoeven?" The waitress seemed completely astonished. "I thought that's why you came in today, you know, undercover-like. Thinking maybe you could get a scoop by spying on him indirectly. We don't usually see…I mean…" She stuttered, looked suddenly down at her clunky shoes.

Min realized that her dark denim, neat sweater, and high-heeled boots probably made her stand out like the city girl she was. She hadn't thought of that; she liked to dress up when she flew, an old habit from her father who always insisted that he got better service when he wore his best. That certainly proved itself out in her life, as well. Except this was a situation where she should have been dressing to blend in.

"No, you're right. I'm not from around here," she admitted, silently cursing her mistake. If anyone asked, these people would remember her now. But she found the girl's bluntness sweet, and all too rare. Although she was dead accurate about Min being undercover.

"And I'm not a reporter, though now you've got my attention. Who is this Garritt Vander-whatsits?"

"Vanderhoeven."

Agnes pointed toward the open kitchen, at a guy in a white chef's toque visible through the arch. He was looking down, engrossed in his work. A few days' stubble spread across what she could see of his pale face. He looked ordinary enough, except for the long strands of light brown hair that had slipped out to tease at his cheeks, draping as far as his chin. *Rebel,* that hair said. Most of the male creatures she'd seen here sported buzz cuts or fades.

"What's he done?" She took another bite of ciabatta. Orgasmic perfection. She'd been sooo hungry! A good sign of healing.

"You don't recognize him? Gosh, he was even on *Good Morning America* when he flew back six weeks ago. You'd have to be in a coma to miss all the fuss."

Ah, too true. She stifled a wry chuckle with another mouthful of pork. Whatever his fame—and how famous could he be, working in a place like this?—she could at least vouch for his cooking. She licked delectable bits of fat from her fingers. Delicately, of course.

"Wait one minute." Agnes dashed away to take an order from the other solitary customer who wandered in, and then she was back in her bland gray skirt and plain ivory blouse. Even the grass-green apron did little for her mousy hair and faint blue eyes. But her aura reflected something pure—like the farm-to-fork produce the restaurant served. Min found that very appealing. And she wouldn't have to probe. Clearly this girl longed to tell the famous Garritt's tale.

"People call him Tarzan now, after what he did." Agnes whispered, because after all, the man was standing just beyond the kitchen arch. "He was on his way to visit Machu Picchu when his plane crashed."

She raised a curious eyebrow. Famous because he survived?

"People were dying." Agnes's eyes widened, "A lot of them were already dead. The plane broke in half when it crashed—wind sheer, the pilot claimed. But secretly," she moved in closer, "he told Garritt they hadn't sent any distress calls and the, um, some other thing broke that sends a signal after a plane crashes."

"The ELT?"

"Yeah, that's it. Anyway, Garritt knew rescuers would never find them. But the pilot insisted they stay put. So all on his own, Garritt got up and ran through the Peruvian rainforest for help."

"That was brave." Or was it stupid?

She didn't mind the conversation but her thoughts were churning about her next destination, so she only half-listened.

"Oh, that's not unusual for Garritt."

"It's not?"

"No, he's like that—always looking out for others." The waitress glanced over at him admiringly. "No, the weird thing is that no one can figure out how he got across this deep canyon—a *pongo,* they called it. He should have been killed—I mean—you know what I mean," she fumbled, blushing again.

"Right. I do." *Interesting.* "Did he find a bridge or something?"

"No. That's what's so weird. At first, he said he leaped across. Then when they told him the distance along that canyon was wider than the Olympic record, that nobody could jump that far, he stopped talking."

She glanced quickly back at him, then dropped her voice again. "Then he got up and ran about another twenty-five miles through the rainforest until he found a village."

Min stopped eating because suddenly she could see it: the village on the riverbank, the thick vegetation, and something…something else that wasn't coming clear. It was the same jungle scene she'd flashed on earlier.

Misunderstanding, Agnes nodded at her expression. "Yeah, I saw the pilot on the news. The man looked guilty to me. I mean, some people died anyway in the crash but Garritt saved about a hundred of them. And the weirdest part?" She leaned a little closer. "His feet. They weren't cut or bruised or anything! Doctors couldn't believe it. It's not like he's a young man in his twenties or anything. He didn't even have a machete!" She stood up straight, hands on her hips. "And he's not a runner. Dropped out of high school track."

Min was ready to ask how she knew that when the girl added, "Reporters came to interview his old coach in Holland." By now she was fairly glowing with pride. "Yeah, they've been interviewing everyone because Garritt won't talk. People call it a miracle." She shrugged. "He'll only say he was grateful he could help."

Some things cannot be explained by Newtonian physics. Min should know. She wondered what the guy was hiding.

"Anyway, I shouldn't bother you while you're eating," Agnes apologized, belatedly. "Sorry. I thought that's what you'd come for."

"Not a problem," she reassured the young woman as she took a sip of water and asked for her bill. "It's a great story. I wonder why he won't talk about it."

"If you ask me, something very unusual happened in that rainforest. He's Dutch and they're old-school religious."

Min suppressed a smile. As if this country girl weren't old-fashioned herself.

"His father is big in the Dutch Reformed community, you know." She said it as if Min actually should know.

She mumbled some agreement, pretending that this might indeed be a huge dilemma. In her world, of course, such beliefs were long outmoded. God, Devil—those were pagan beliefs carried over from antiquity and pressed into service as Christianity took root. (But don't say that around Gramma Julene!)

"Hmmm, well, it is a puzzle. If I see any reporters out front—wait, is that why the other girl threw shade when I came in?"

"Sam? She feels guilty. She's the one talked him into going, although he went alone. But she's a traveler. Saving money for her next trip. Sometimes she pairs up with people. Although that last guy left her stranded." She looked genuinely sad for her co-worker, which made Min's heart go out to Agnes, not Sam.

Min turned to take another look at the hostess. Embroidered tunic, patterned leggings, shaved side of dyed hair, ample tattoos. A style that never seemed to go out of style in some quarters. She and Agnes must be about the same age—late twenties, maybe—though they certainly seemed worlds apart.

"I'm sure that was a good lesson for her and she's grateful for it now," she offered.

"Oh yes. She'll be off again in a couple of months." Agnes sighed with obvious envy, then hurried away to pick up an order called out from the kitchen.

When Min heard the voice, she glanced over involuntarily. For a flicker of a moment, her eyes landed on the famous man's face.

He was staring back at her as if…as if…what?

She looked away. That was bizarre. The guy definitely possessed some unusual qualities.

4

Haunted

∞

The reporters who tracked Garritt back to Michigan concluded their segments by saying something like, "He can't remember much of what happened, but the passengers whose lives he saved are calling it a miracle."

Not a miracle, he knew, because what saved others had pretty much ripped his life to shreds—again. He couldn't sleep for wondering if he were going mad, or if he would pay for his sins in eternal torment later on. His parents would certainly say so. If they knew what he'd seen, what he'd done, they'd be clamoring that he had come under the influence of the Devil, and that his eternal soul was in more serious jeopardy than ever.

That is, if they cared at all what happened to this recalcitrant sinner they'd cast out, which is how they saw it. Technically, he was the one who rejected the religion of his ancestors and walked away on his own two feet, enduring the curses of his parents, his church family, his school friends, his *dominee*. Outcast, yes, but by his own choice.

That was twenty years ago, yet leaving generations of belief wasn't so simple, he'd discovered. Deep inside, the patterns of thinking beaten into him kept surfacing, haunting him, especially now, after he'd come so close to dying. They say your birth religion surfaces under stress, no matter how long ago you've cast it off. He hated that.

Still, he couldn't stop wondering if he would be consigned to hell now, despite his supposed position among God's "elect" by virtue of his ancestral Dutch heritage. Had he succumbed to demons, back in that jungle?

No. Couldn't be. Whatever it was had kept him alive, and saved the lives of so many others.

Yet he'd heard sermons argue that some "miracles" were indeed the work of the Devil, an attempt to deceive good people. The folks he'd saved on that flight from Ecuador, they were mostly brown-skinned. His father would say it was a fool's errand; that they were already doomed by the sins of their ancestors, clearly visible from the color of their skin, so why risk his life for them? But his heart had said otherwise when he heard their cries. He simply defied the pilot's command to stay with the plane and ran for help, knowing they'd never be found if he didn't.

But had he also defied God's will?

The back-flipping doubts tormented him day and night.

In fact that was nothing new. Garritt's spirit had floundered like this since high school, decades of adulthood trying to find Truth, but more importantly, trying to figure out where he fit in. So far? Nowhere.

First question people in his hometown of Holland, Michigan, would ask a newcomer: "What church do you attend?" Without a firm answer, you were no one. He'd been someone when he (did he have a choice?) attended his parents' Dutch Reformed church. He'd become a nobody the minute he left it. So he sampled everywhere, looking for his real tribe, his soul mates, people who understood him. Surely they must exist?

Locally, the most popular alternative was neo-paganism. So he tried that first.

"If you're not a believer, then you must be a witch," resistant thinkers were told—and treated with scorn and cruelty. Some of his parents' congregation would be perfectly capable of lighting fires beneath the pagans' feet, if they thought they could get away with it in the twenty-first century. Garritt viewed these faithful adherents as miserable fanatics, terrified of their own shadows. They'd glare with hatred at any hapless soul who ignorantly wore a bit of glittering jewelry, or a patriotic star on the Fourth of July. In their minds, *Five points = pentagram = witch symbol.*

He once watched an attractive, kind-faced young woman in the Holland Public Library, clearly not from the area. She wore a tight little white t-shirt with the word *Angel* emblazoned across her lovely chest in pink rhinestones. When she asked for help from a buzz-cut reference clerk, all of eighteen if a day, Garritt thought the boy was going to leap out of his chair and strangle the unsuspecting Outsider on the spot, he gave her such a hateful look and dismissive word. He wanted to go to the woman's rescue, explain the local customs to her. Instead he stood glued to the spot, unable to figure out how to justify his cultural brethren's rude hostility.

In his hometown, you weren't allowed to mow your lawn or go bowling on a Sunday—by local ordinance—let alone wear sparkly accessories, or make blasphemous claims such as that spread across the poor girl's frivolous t-shirt. He'd stood there like an idiot, feeling humiliated by his Dutch heritage, helpless to combat a vast, suffocating community of believers that stretched across the western half of his state.

He wasn't entirely alone in this frustration. Plenty of local offspring threw up their hands at such treatment from their own parents and simply started calling themselves *Wiccan*. By proclaiming to actually *be* witches, they found companionship in their rebellion, and as a bonus, got to dance naked in the woods during the full moon. He imagined there were more proclaimed pagans in Michigan than anyplace else in the country. When he was nineteen, he met a girl who'd taken a variation of this path, with long, strawberry hair and a wild gleam in her eyes, full of fun and seductive ideas. He fell hard, which made it easy to pursue his first religious adventure outside the Dutch community. But while he found her nature-loving philosophy quite appealing (except for the mosquitoes), he soon balked at a too-familiar structure lurking beneath the supposed freedoms. It turned out that neo-paganism asked for yet another form of obeisance to gods who ruled mortal lives, giving the mortals no choices—or more specifically, giving them brief periods of belief that they *had* liberties and choices, such as running *sky-clad* or having sex in the woods, but which could be yanked away by the whims of all-powerful Beings of questionable mental stability. Too much like the Christianity he'd witnessed. No self-responsibility; all about God's whims. Or the gods' whims. And who knew if any of it proved to be more than a weak fairytale to placate our fears of the unknown? More specifically, our fear of death itself? Paganism wasn't for him, he decided, and sadly the girl went with it.

Next, his ex-wife Elizabeth had encouraged him to try out the claims of self-empowerment coming from the New Age movement. After a few exciting months of hopeful involvement, he witnessed so much ego-stroking and platitude spouting, he felt as if he'd been simmered in a pot of half-boiled toffee. Ideas bubbled up all around him, some made of nothing more than fanciful imagination—which is a fine thing, but a sugary bubble felt like nothing to rest the heavy burden of his soul upon. And for some, their New Age quest seemed to be more about the competition over who could be first to adopt the latest trend, and less about creating a "deep inner connection to the Divine." What a few claimed to experience while they toned, chanted, and meditated didn't always jibe with how he saw them treat others, either—whether of their own ilk or not.

Maybe that was his old religious training rising from the deep, seeking Godly behavior in mortal beings. But that's how he came to see the New Age movement: fostering as much prejudice and hypocrisy as any religion, only with different dogma and insider lingo.

Plus, he witnessed a lot of the same charismatic greed he found in some liberal churches he explored. It seemed any ego-inflating ploy to lure the masses was justified, if it filled the coffers of the latest guru. He concluded that these New Agers didn't threaten damnation before they passed the plate; they promised eternal health, wealth, and joy while they reached into your pocket. After Elizabeth left him, it was easy to move on. He was terrible at faking enthusiasm for things that didn't sit right with him.

He tried dating a proclaimed Buddhist after the divorce, but that fell apart when he went online and found modern interpreters meandering through complex rationales and arguments, exactly like Christian theologians. Besides, he loved a good steak. And he didn't believe for an instant that a fully-developed human being could reincarnate as an animal. Haunt maybe, but not embodied within. Whether Buddha really meant that or not, they fought over it, she threw some things at his head (very un-Buddhist-like), and moved out in a huff. He'd been mostly celibate ever since. (Thanks a lot, Buddha.)

Hinduism? By now, far too complex for a newbie. Islam—same tendency to breed violent fanaticism as Christianity, although he'd met this gorgeous Persian woman in college but back then, he hadn't yet shed his Christian prejudice. And Elizabeth had stepped in.

Judaism—he couldn't get past the outwardly cruel manifestations of Israeli politics; plus, where he lived it was nearly impossible to find exponents of that faith to re-educate his perceptions. Maybe he'd meet a hot Jewish girl one day and she could tell him all about it, he laughed to himself (not without a little hope).

He could probably find interesting friends in some other Holland church. "One on every corner," stunned visitors would observe. It was a Calvinist's dream town, so steeped in "Godliness," it choked out any form of independent thinking. Which was why he hated it. Back into that web? No thanks!

True enough, Juan had recently introduced him to some female Catholic relatives who sent his pulse racing. But now that he was approaching forty he'd mellowed, and learned to separate his lust for spiritual advancement from the feelings in his loins. It wouldn't be fair to any of those women to get involved when he knew he could never share their beliefs. Far too important, love and spirit, to let one cancel out the other.

Which led him right back to his parents' insistence on Dutch Reformed purity, a concept he despised. Took years, but eventually he admitted to himself that his marriage to Elizabeth was mostly defiance against that rule. She wasn't Dutch, she wasn't Reformed, and she wasn't exactly pure when he met her, thank goodness.

Science? Possible last resort. If only his freshman chemistry teacher hadn't ruined it for him. She wouldn't (or couldn't) define *mass* or *matter*, other than to say that one was a quantity of the other. When he pointed out how nonsensical that sounded, she told him to re-read the textbook. She couldn't admit, *No one knows yet, least of all me.*

Hubris. Again.

So far, the closest he'd come to feeling God and community had been on his knees in the dirt on the organic farm he and Elizabeth had tried to turn into a thriving business. (They hit the market too soon.) Watching green and growing things sprout into life, when so many forces of death threatened to exterminate them, he'd thought, *God must be a force of life.* He liked that: *The Force is with us.* No wonder so many kids in the seventies secretly worshiped *Star Wars* while dutifully following their families to church on Sunday!

Nevertheless, his quest for spiritual companionship had forced him to think things through, instead of swallowing them whole at his parents' insistence. Even among the Dutch he'd met good people, sincere, dedicated souls looking for answers just like he was. He simply couldn't stop in the same eddies where they'd found happiness. He hadn't found his yet, which left him feeling painfully alone and completely misunderstood.

And none of this exploration left him with any insight into what happened to him in that rainforest.

At the time, it all felt so natural. Now the memory of it terrified him, although no demons had come to collect his soul. So far. But he still couldn't sleep. When he did drift off, his nightmares often began with a plane crash and ended with some monster slurping him off the edge of a cliff. He'd wake up falling. Like this morning.

By the time he got to work, he plunged gratefully into the distraction of Avery's morning chaos, where Juan and Agnes were arguing the merits of last month's Goose Festival, Veenlanden's annual tribute to the migrating geese filling its fields and swamps, versus Holland's gaudy, week-long Tulip Time.

Agnes complained that the local bands and goose-calling competitions gave her a headache.

"All those screaming kids hyped up on cotton candy, and their cranky parents expecting us to run our feet off." She shook her head and picked up a dish of Pamela the baker's popular rugelach. "You can keep it. I'd rather go look at tulips blooming on every street."

"And put up with those phony smiles?" Juan countered as he faced down a stack of greasy bread pans. "Here in Swampland, we're starved for company. We welcome outsiders with open arms!"

Fresh out of high school, their dishwasher bore a sharp view of the world that Garritt especially appreciated. Juan got the translation of the town's name right but Garritt wasn't sure about the welcoming "open arms" part.

"Holland hosts a million visitors a year during Tulip Time," Agnes protested.

"Yeah, but it's like, 'Hey, welcome! Spend some money! Look at our tulips! We will happily take your *dinero* for one week only,' and then it's, *Adios pendejos, and don't come back till next year!* The dominees must think it's God's will. Remember, it's 'God in all things,' including business." Juan laughed bitterly, "That's why they won't hire Catholic heathens like me except to clean *los baños*."

Garritt felt too ashamed of his background to tell them the truth about Tulip Time. The famous Five Points of Calvinism form the acronym TULIP. To many Hollanders, it wasn't just a pretty flower to attract tourists, it represented their core beliefs: *Total depravity, Unconditional election, Limited atonement, Irresistible grace,* and *Preservation of saints.* To elaborate on these phrases involved ideas Garritt found horrific, even as a child. (His blood might have been Dutch, but his mind never was.) They boiled down to: *If you're not among God's elect, nothing you do can save your soul; you're toast. You can't even* find *God unless he's chosen for you to do so. Conversely, if you are among the Chosen, nothing you do will keep you from God eventually.* And for one week every year, Holland, Michigan, lured the damned from around the world to worship all things TULIP.

Hollanders loved to play that kind of inside joke on Outsiders. After their founding father, Albertus van Raalte, urged his pioneer community not to do business with "Americans"—his name for settlers of any nationality who were not Dutch—the community had carried out his wishes for more than a hundred and seventy-five years. Another reason Garritt hated the place.

When Juan and Agnes's argument reached a high pitch, Corbyn burst from his office in his crisp designer suit. He owned the restaurant with his partner Avery but had long ago handed the cooking over to Garritt.

"That weekend put us in the black for the rest of the month," he announced, waving a pointed finger. "Paid both your salaries. So God save the geese! Now get back to work—and Agnes, tell your dad I need to discuss our Thanksgiving order." He headed for the back door of the kitchen which led out to a parking lot behind the old building. "I'll be back before lunch if anyone needs me."

Agnes's family supplied the restaurant's poultry. She could tell you how to gut a chicken without contaminating the meat with offal, or exactly which months to pick blueberries or raspberries, but she'd probably never left this rural county. Like many other non-Dutch, her family's church nevertheless forbade dancing, or the wearing of bling. Gentle and plain, everyone liked Agnes. But Garritt often caught her gazing with envy at Samantha, the hostess, a shimmering bauble from a Detroit suburb who stood out against the local preference for bland conformity. Both women were at least a decade too young for him, although Sam offered a nice break in the visual routine. He tried not to stare at her tattoo sleeve, though. He couldn't decide if he liked it or not. In the wrong light, it made her arm look dirty.

In fact it was Sam's description of rainbows over Machu Picchu, her treks to experience shamanic rituals, and her completely illogical infatuation with ayahuasca ("You threw up how many times? And you want to do it again?!"), interwoven with anecdotes about tribal people she'd met, that made Garritt's stomach quiver, and set off something else that rumbled deep in his innards. Guilt? Fear? The stories triggered a feeling that he needed to finish something he couldn't remember.

He liked to confront things, liked to figure them out as he went along. That's why he'd enjoyed the endless challenges of farming, and how he learned to cook after he sold the farm, and ultimately what drove him to book a flight for Peru to find out what caused this bizarre reaction to Sam's tales.

He never found out. But this morning he needed to talk about it. When they closed briefly before lunch, he sought her out.

He found Sam glued to her phone behind the new glassed-in display counter. Avery's had grown very popular among locals for their regional cheeses and homemade baked goods, so Corbyn added the take-out items to boost their bottom line. That certainly kept the local goat farmers happy, and gave Pamela full-time baking hours trying to keep up with demand.

"I still don't understand why the rainforest felt like home to me," he picked up a conversation they'd left lying days before. "In all your travels, have you ever gone somewhere you've never been before and felt like that?"

"You should read more about the Incas," she suggested mildly as she flicked along, not looking up.

"Why? Didn't they kill themselves off in some mysterious way?"

"No, you're thinking of the Maya." She shook her head at something she saw on her phone, which made her earrings jangle. "Didn't you read anything before you left?" She still hadn't looked up.

Agnes, quietly refreshing tables in the back, lingered over a salt shaker.

He didn't mind. Eavesdropping might broaden her world—although he found her innocence one of Agnes's most appealing qualities.

Sam finally glanced up for a few seconds, then talked as she fingered through a dazzling array of sites, looking for whatever nugget she was after. At one point, she burst out laughing and he realized that whatever amused her had nothing to do with him. It was an amazing feat of multi-tasking, actually, because what she said to him next struck a note of familiarity. Again.

"The Incas built roads through the Andes and they had runners—like you—who carried messages and delivered things. They ran miles and miles, through terrain so dangerous and high in elevation, it killed a lot of the Spaniards who came to steal their gold."

She looked directly at him. That was so rare, he found it unsettling.

"They think the Incas had bigger lungs. That's why their descendants can live in the high places today, and why they can play pan flutes. Oh my god," she set down her phone, interested now. "Have you ever tried one? I practically fainted!"

"So that's why they could run?"

"Actually, no one knows how they ran so far, so fast, in terrain like that. It's as much of a mystery as the pyramids. Or you."

He wanted to divert the questions that almost always followed such a lead-in, the how-did-you-do-it questions. He thought of telling her that he used to scare girlfriends in high school by holding his breath underwater for long periods of time. Or how that skill saved him the year he took up the lunatic Michigan surf craze and wiped out near the Grand Haven pier. He would have drowned for real if he didn't have this strange ability.

Of course, that wasn't at all what helped him get through the rainforest but she couldn't know about that.

"If you'd ever made it to Cusco instead of coming back to the States with the others—" she stopped and her freckles disappeared in a flush. It must have finally dawned on her what a trauma the whole experience had been for him. "Well, you would have learned all about it from the tour guides, the ones I told you to hire, the Irish people who run those cool Peru Hop buses." She suddenly stared into his eyes so penetratingly, he thought she might be pretty if she weren't so self-absorbed.

"Did you ever think you might have been one of those runners?"

"What?"

"You know—in a past life."

She looked as if she expected him to laugh, so he did. "Yeah, right. Come on, we'd better get this show on the road."

He moved toward the kitchen, then turned and winked at her. "You never know when I might just *run off*—and then you'd have to do all the cooking!"

He lobbed an apple he'd grabbed from the counter at her before he ducked through the kitchen doorway and out of her reach. He didn't want her to know he half-believed her.

"Garritt!" he heard her holler as she caught the apple in self-defense.

"Ugh."

He found Juan idling at the work station, poking at his phone instead of handling the squashes he'd been asked to sort.

"If you like this job, stop texting your girlfriend. Corbyn will be back any minute."

"Dude! Have you seen this new crop circle?" Juan's passion for quirky Internet sites took up almost as much time as his passion for Luciana. "Check this out, *güey.*"

That was Juan's favorite slang for him. Sounded like "way," and meant something like *dude,* though probably more vulgar if he knew the boy at all.

"Avebury. You know, near Stonehenge." He shoved the phone under Garritt's nose.

The image displayed precise, intricate patterns cut into a sprawling field of golden wheat. No tracks led to or from, according to the helicopter shot.

"I wonder when they're going to start making them in Michigan," Juan said, his voice full of longing. "We've got plenty of big fields."

Garritt had to admit, crop circles baffled him. Who made these things? Why? He handed back the phone. "Impressive. Now wash those squashes please. We're open in five."

As happened every day now while his hands moved over plates and stirred sauces, Garritt's thoughts drifted back to the rainforest. He let himself get lost in the sensation of swirling along in joyous harmony with the natural world. *Don't know how those Inca runners did it, huh? Well, I do.*

Past lives? He couldn't rule them out. Elizabeth believed in them. According to his parents, he would go to hell simply for listening to her.

Or not.

What if Sam and Elizabeth were right? No hells—only a series of lifetimes to suffer through?

Maybe that's sufficient perpetual torment, he decided.

Elizabeth used to tell him, "Everything we do stays with us, shaping our future lives. It's the blueprint we live from, so it matters what you say and what you think. It's energy; like software you write. You can't destroy it. You can only own what you've written, or do something to rewrite it." That was her idea of karma.

He liked it, because it meant that human beings had choices. Bad choices come back to haunt you. Good ones support your life. And as you learn better ways, you can rewrite your software. So much more appealing than a life spent worshiping a God who sounded less like a benevolent force of life than an egotistical dictator, all-powerful, who demanded obeisance or else.

He reached to dip a potato out of a boiling pot to test it, Avery's solution for the gluten-free. Suddenly the kettle disappeared, and in his memory he saw a long, spear-shaped, water-holding curl of leaf—exactly as it looked when it saved his life in the rainforest (after he'd picked out the wiggling insects). He could feel again the cool liquid, soothing his parched throat as he opened his mouth and poured. Gratitude for the way he'd been led to it engulfed him, just as it had in the forest.

He judged the potato undone and put it back.

Again, he felt himself floating above the river gorge, although his feet were grounded to the rubber mat that covered Avery's cement floor. That didn't prevent him from sensing once more the sudden uplift that had saved him from a grisly death at the bottom of the river.

The flashbacks came often. Every time, they left him with the same question: *How evil could that have been?* He was still pondering the unanswerable when he called out an order. He glanced up and happened to see the reporter Agnes had warned him about earlier.

For a startled moment, the woman stared back at him.

Whoa. Flashing, twinkling, golden sparks blinked on and off like fireflies all around her dark wavy hair.

Just like in Peru.

The lights he could never tell another soul about.

Had the demon finally come for him?

5

Vanished

Min didn't wait until dark. She needed to resolve this as soon as possible. Anyway, the park was deserted. Tourists gone; locals already snugging in for winter. She paid the self-serve entrance fee with cash. Hah! That was one benefit of working for Blackthorn; sneaking around in the middle of the night, no one pays a fee.

She pulled the rented Ford as close to the trailhead as possible and traded her high-heeled boots for an old pair of sneakers she'd shoved under the clothes in her suitcase. She climbed out onto the barren parking lot, now strewn with islands of wind-blown sand.

The place looked so different in daylight. The only thing familiar was the sand. She couldn't tell an aspen from an oak even if they had leaves, but all the hardwoods were stripped bare now. Only the wind-warped pines colored the gray woods with swaths of dark green. Picnic tables and grills sat deserted. No lines for the restroom, no trash spilling out of cans. Boardwalk trails lay buried in places from the shifting dunes. Not a soul in sight, nothing but a chill wind that pierced her chic little jacket and made her curse her failure to pack a heavier winter coat. She'd forgotten how frigid the brink of these dunes had been.

Last time she was here she nearly died. She remembered the nightmare she'd had after the blow to her head, the dancing trees and the disappearing lights that tricked her forward—until she'd sat down in defiance and called on Jesus, an old reflex from her grandmother's training.

She smiled at that now. She didn't know about Jesus, but the thought had certainly taken her straight to Gramma Julene and her mysterious pastor in some celestial church. Maybe it wasn't such a bad technique after all.

She felt warmed by the idea that her grandmother was being cared for by whoever that man really was. He seemed, well, *angelic,* for lack of a better term. She only wished she'd had time to ask him at least one question before they yanked her back to life. That was like releasing the genie from the bottle and then, right before you made your wish, accidentally splashing a little wine on him and discovering that made him disappear—forever.

She stepped onto the boarded trail. Immediately, an electric tremor shot through her and she had to grab at the marker sign to steady her balance. *Don't be silly, Minda,* she chided herself. *You've done this sort of thing a million times.*

She straightened up and took a deep breath, centering, focusing her mind. Inwardly, she clearly saw the dip between the dunes where she first located the artifact. A thin autumn daylight bathed the area; she was viewing it in the now. She willed herself to move her inner vision to the top of the sandy cliff where she'd taken it, where Wade, creep that he was, had shoved her over the edge. Once fixed in her mind, she started to walk that direction, ignoring the marked trails. This time the vision remained clear, leading her forward.

She reached the spot, certain of her accuracy. A steady wind coming up off the lake pushed at her, shoved her back from the edge. She should thank it for that, she thought dryly. Far down below, the waves still lashed at the beach in angry disorder. She shivered. Eager to get back to her car, she knelt quickly and dug into the sand.

Nothing.

She dug nearby. Nothing.

She dug up a foot and a half of stupid sand all around the area and found nothing at all!

Wade. Her mind raced. Had he seen her bury it, then? If so, why hadn't she been questioned? She'd broken protocol when she didn't radio the team immediately, she wasn't wearing gloves—another violation—so what if he watched her try to hide it? Maybe he thought—what? How could he rationalize what she'd done? But the artifact was missing. Had to be Blackthorn. So maybe Wade saw the disturbed ground and dug to see what was there, found it, reasoned maybe she'd hit on it while she was supposedly off peeing in the woods, and then…that she planned to retrieve it and tell the team (but that would also be a violation) but he pushed her before she could. Yes, that could explain the lack of disciplinary action.

And she didn't believe that explanation for a minute.

He should have studied the remote viewing team's maps in advance, also protocol, which would have shown him that her artifact wasn't on their map. Though he was new. So—maybe he skipped that step, then pretended he knew about this target in advance. Right. *Lied to cover us both.*

Or— could be they brought in another viewer to finish the job while she was in the hospital. Then they might have discovered it right where she'd stood before her fall, obviously buried by human hands hours before they dug it out.

Why hadn't Blackthorn reprimanded her? At the very least.

She shuddered and stared out over the blustery lake. Unless—no, not possible. It had to be Blackthorn. Who else would stumble on to this thing? But if Blackthorn had it, nothing about this made sense to her.

A few yards to the south of where she stood, a large bird swooped off a branch and soared out into the air currents glancing off the dunes. It glided serenely past her, the lengthy wingspan and blinding-white head instantly identifying it as a bald eagle. The magnificent predator settled with a *whoomp* on a long, bare branch, a few feet away from her. She caught her breath and froze.

He was huge! She'd never seen the national emblem in living reality before. She would have thought the symbolic creature a figment of her guilty imagination if she hadn't spotted a faded photo of bald eagles on an interpretive sign in the parking lot. It warned visitors not to disturb nesting pairs common to the area.

Slowly, the impressive raptor turned his wind-ruffled head and focused one fierce yellow eye directly on hers.

She felt his predator energy pass down her spine, sizing her up. He let her know immediately that his hooked golden beak could rip her heart out with no problem.

Okay, okay! So I've been ready to betray my patriotic duty. I get that, she spoke to the creature in her mind, not the first time she'd practiced animal communication (another of her many secrets).

He turned away, unimpressed.

Well, who's to say which duty, which path, is more patriotic, if patriotism means actually serving *the people in this country?*

The eagle took another look at her, blinked mildly, and went back to his survey of the endless expanse before them, as if she moved him not at all.

Talk to me, Eagle. Did you see an ugly White man come here? Take my golden artifact away? My very own piece of history?

Suddenly the magnificent bird gathered his energy and pushed off the tree with a great sweep of wings. He soared all the way down toward the beach, then veered out of sight beyond a treeless dune to the north. He left no answers behind.

Min kicked at the sand with a foot and some of it poured over the edge of her sneaker. It slid inside her low socks, grating against her skin. Why had she chosen sneakers? This was no warm summer's day at Cardiff-by-the-Sea.

Stupid, Minda. Stupid, stupid, stupid.

The wind picked up, strong enough to ripple her stiff jacket.

Well, what did you think? That you could just waltz on up here, pick up, oh, just a little debris fragment of a blazing interstellar spacecraft? *Keep it as a personal talisman?*

Or were you seriously thinking about going public? Did you even consider what that would do to your life—if you lived, that is?

Sometimes that voice in her head took on a tone she really hated.

She honestly didn't know what to do next. The ship sightings, Sourav's death, the sleepless nights…she couldn't keep the lie anymore. People need to know what's behind those stupid government documents that do nothing but pull another veil over the truth by dribbling out more vague nonsense every time citizens demand to know what their own supposed leaders know.

But who would believe her now, without proof?

All her doubts rushed back in. Even with proof, the company would make sure that no one took her seriously. Best scenario, they'd have her locked up as a mental case. Worst, they'd silence her once and for all.

Wade might have already been following those orders. So why was she standing here, free to wonder? This made no sense at all.

Disgusted with herself and the whole subject, she turned and headed back to the car. The trees minded their own business this time and kept their branches leaning away from the shoreline winds in the usual manner. No lights appeared to guide her, although at this point she might have welcomed their assistance. No cops, no park attendants, no tourists, and no blooping artifact.

Soon she'd have to go back to work, and then what? Keep up with the lie. Keep her job. Don't sucking rock the boat. Be like the 'possum; play dead. And if she were already "dead"...

A flash in her head and she saw it again, the fragment glowing golden, yet full of circulating colors if you knew how to look.

Why didn't I think of that?

If she could locate it buried in a sand dune, then she could sure as sugar locate it anywhere in the world. She hurried to the dusty Ford and opened the door, grateful for the warmth built up inside as she ducked out of the wind. The afternoon was darkening early. Maybe a storm blowing in off the lake? *But think, Minda—no, don't think. Tune in. Focus on that colorful slab of who-knows-what.*

She breathed, in, out, trying to calm her suddenly racing heart. She was afraid she'd see the fragment at Blackthorn headquarters, or on a truck on the way to some warehouse.

The fear blocked her. She couldn't see it. She knew it was out there, though, that it hadn't stayed where she buried it. Of that she was now certain. But where?

She tried for a long time to remote-view the object, yet her fears kept her blind. Instead, after nearly an hour of effort, her stomach sent a clear message and all she could see was that restaurant with the overpowering aromas and the excellent wine list.

Oh, that'll clear your head, the voice in her head chided.

She ignored it, although she was beginning to think it sounded an awful lot like Gramma Julene. But she needed food to see.

∞

Now that it was the end of the workday, a few more people clustered here and there along Veenlanden's main street. As she stepped out of the rental car in front of Avery's Cafe, a few of them turned to stare at the stranger.

She was about to wave and smile when a clear vision of the golden fragment pressed into her mind—as if to torment her now that she'd given up on finding it. The gleaming slab lay among a clutter of dirty dishes and papers on a rough-hewn, wooden table. She couldn't see much more in the dingy space but she could almost smell the foulness of it.

Before she could probe the room further, a siren erupted down the street from where she stood and screamed straight toward her.

She threw her hands over her ears as a blue-and-white police cruiser screeched to a halt behind her car, lights flashing in hypnotic beats.

Her heart stopped. They'd found her.

6

Misperception

∞

Two uniformed officers leapt out of the squad car and headed her way. She knew it; they'd sent the local "friendly to our mission" officials to round her up. One of the cops—short, stocky, balding—sized her up rudely as he drew closer.

And then he breezed right by!

They barged into the restaurant, that one and a taller cop with dark-slicked hair. Both loped in with distinct purpose and hands on their guns. It took her a few beats to believe they weren't after her.

Min gulped a grateful breath and collapsed back inside the Ford, quickly pulling the door closed. She squeezed her eyes shut and tried to ignore her shaky hands and the scene outside the car in order to bring back the vision of the missing artifact, the rustic table. People were streaming by, craning to see what was going on inside the cafe. They distracted her completely from the flash vision she needed to pull back into focus.

Small town life. Not much excitement. In the city they'd all be ducking for cover, expecting a shootout.

A few stared through her window for a moment, as if she had something to do with it all, before the cops burst out dragging a kid by his elbow, hands cuffed behind him. She wondered if this teenager had actually done anything wrong other than living in their white-bread community. She waited until they'd screamed away before going in. (Did they really need sirens for that?)

The pierced girl body-blocked her path. "Sorry, we're not open for dinner yet."

"It's okay, Sam." A slightly sweaty guy in an apron stepped in front of the girl.

Garritt. The one who stared at her earlier. The weird one the reporters were after.

"Sorry about that. Samantha's a little freaked out." He gave the girl a look. "So am I, in fact."

With one hand, he brushed away a wavy strand of hair that had slipped out of its messy ponytail. That left a trace of flour across his pale, stubbled face. He held his other hand out to her.

"I'm Chef Vanderhoeven. Weren't you here earlier?"

Michigan Dutch, she confirmed Agnes's proclamation as she reluctantly accepted the handshake. He loomed over her, taller than her six-foot brother.

Before she could answer, Agnes came out of the back, wiping tears off her rounded cheeks. She lit up when she spotted Min. "Yes, she was! I'll take her to a table."

"Um, this is Agnes." The chef seemed embarrassed by the girl's enthusiasm.

Min found it endearing. She'd encountered a lot worse greetings. And he couldn't know they'd already had quite the conversation.

"Actually, I was wondering if I could sit right here at the window?" It hadn't been Blackthorn after all, but her hands were still shaking.

"Of course you may," Agnes assumed authority.

Sam, meanwhile, shook her over-styled head and went back to her stand to gaze into her phone while Min settled in gratefully. She wanted to keep an eye on the street for any other unexpected arrivals.

There must be a back door out of here. She looked around and decided it was probably through that arch, the one that led into the kitchen. Good to know. Beyond that, she had no clue where she might run if she had to.

I am really not the right person for this job. But who else could—or would—do it?

∞

Garritt lingered for a moment. Exactly as Agnes had described, a recent-looking scar slashed across the woman's smooth forehead, although it looked like she'd tried to hide it beneath a sweep of black-olive bangs.

Normally, this wouldn't distract him from the sudden arrest of his dishwasher and prep cook—and closest friend, if truth be told. Except that the woman kept vanishing in a swirl of twinkling glitter, dazzling lights that flickered on and off like they had in Peru. And they brought him the same torment: Was he seeing angels? Or the Devil's trickery? Had she come for his soul?

The religion hammered into his brain as a child told him she was to be feared simply for the light bronze of her skin "because it represents the sins of her ancestors." Was that the clue he'd been seeking? By that measure, she must be demon and therefore, the lights as well.

But he couldn't deny that she seemed to be lit from the inside. Her face reminded him of sculpture, neatly-boned and even, with pleasing contours and confident lines, easy to look at—in fact, beautiful to contemplate, the more he stared directly at her instead of at the consort of lights surrounding and guarding this queenly being…

The clash in his mind, evil vs. alluring, jerked him back to social awareness. He'd been staring rudely.

He stepped closer. "Sorry—I'm, um, a little distracted. I just lost my co-worker, Juan. But, uh, you look familiar. I mean, not just from earlier…"

Lame. Pitiful lame.

"Are you the one who makes the pizza?" she deflected.

Grateful for the save, he answered, "Yep, that's me."

"And the ciabatta I had earlier?"

"Uh, no." He glanced out the window. Four or five people lingered outside, probably gossiping about Juan and the stranger in the cafe, if he knew them at all. "That would be Pamela, our resident baker. Good stuff, huh?"

She smiled at him. "And that's why I'm back."

The glitter intensified, making it hard for Garritt to maintain eye contact. "Well, um, just let me know if you need anything special. I'd better get back to work." He turned to go.

"Hey—what did they bust that kid for?"

"I'm not sure they did," he turned back, glad for the excuse. "They said they just needed him to answer some questions."

"In handcuffs??"

"Well, they don't get much to do around here. I suppose they were being extra cautious."

Immediately, he realized that was a bald lie. If Juan were White—better yet, Dutch like Garritt—they wouldn't have handcuffed him.

"Hm," she nodded knowingly. "He's Mexican-American?"

"Yeah. You're right," he sighed with the admission of what they both understood. Then added bluntly, "We're not all assholes, you know."

Oh shit, what had he said? He spun quickly and headed toward the kitchen, narrowly missing the empty child chair boosters piled near the arch.

If she *was* a demon, he might well lose his soul, because his eyes and his instincts told him otherwise. She'd have to grow horns and replace those liquid green eyes before he'd believe this woman to be a thing he should avoid. Far from it.

Min smiled as she slipped out of her jacket. *Well, that's refreshing. A guy who gets it.*

She glanced over at Sam, who finally regarded her with some curiosity from behind the display of breads, pastries, and "locally sourced cheese."

Right, and if the kid were Black, he'd be lucky to be alive.

She sank back in her chair, tried to shove away the bitterness. What happened every day on the streets should have swayed her convictions about patriotic duty, but she was grateful for all the Navy had done for her. She once believed that forces for good also work within every government. For years, aligning herself with that seemed wise. Now all she wanted was to spill the government's biggest secret, and so far, she'd failed. Possibly at the risk of her own life.

"May I take your order?" Agnes reappeared and the formality didn't last. "I'm glad you came back—and I love your sweater," she gushed.

This girl belongs somewhere better, Min decided, instantly distracted from her own overwhelming sense of inadequacy. She looked down. The black-and-white sweater bore an asymmetric streak of rhinestones from shoulder to waist and it fit her tidy figure perfectly. Totally inappropriate for digging up artifacts.

"Thank you," she managed to smile. "I'll have the *Portobello & Brie Single Pizza* with a glass of house red."

As Agnes moved to scoop up her menu, Min laid an impulsive hand on her arm, which felt surprisingly warm for such a cold day. "Wait a minute. Is that Inn down the road a good place to stay?"

"Oh yes, it's the best bed-and-breakfast in Veenlanden. Well, actually the only one. But it's really good! The Petersons are great people. Will you be here long?"

She looked eager to ask a lot more questions, so Min said simply, "I hope not," and turned to her phone.

∞

Two hours later, after an awkward scene with the proprietors that eventually landed her a room at the B&B—but only after she mentioned Agnes—Min finally looked into a mirror. With a shock, she realized that they all must have been staring at the hideous scar on her forehead, which had worked its way out from under her bangs. She sighed.

No wonder aliens won't land on this stupid planet. We're primitive apes, suspicious of strangers. Kill first, investigate later.

The wind howled through the sash in fierce agreement.

She emptied her overnight case on the four-poster bed's flowered duvet and plopped down next to the small pile, not sure what else to do. She only had this week and next before she had to be back at work. Once on the job, they would track her every move. Unless they already were.

She reached up to be sure the foil was still in place and hoped she'd be able to sleep with it on. The pizza-and-wine fog should help.

She was too tired and buzzed to try to recapture that snatch of a vision she had outside the restaurant. She'd try again in the morning. But it looked like Blackthorn did not have her artifact; someone else did. That opened up a whole new range of possibilities, and a far better chance to get her hands on it again. The artifact itself would be her protection from Blackthorn—if she could get it to the right people as fast as possible.

Something started to ping against the paned window. Min turned out the lamp to peer outside. In the light cast by fixtures under the eaves she could see what looked like sleet driving straight at her. *Whale snot,* one of Blackthorn's pilots would call it. Not good.

7

Devotion

∞

Late in the dinner shift, Garritt heard someone bang on the back service door. Corbyn, who'd donned an apron and taken up Juan's dishwashing chores, reached it first.

Drenched from head to toe and shivering like an aspen, an attractive teenager stood there with sleet lashing at her and a desperate look in her eyes.

"Is Garritt here?" she wheezed.

Corbyn started to protest but Garritt hurried around him to let the poor girl in. "It's okay; I know her."

He took her dripping coat and handed her his own from a rack near the door. Her tiny frame disappeared inside it.

"Corbyn, meet Luciana. Corbyn owns this restaurant," he added for her benefit, hoping she'd take the hint and realize that he was *el jefe*, Juan's boss.

She nodded shyly at the owner.

Corbyn raised an eyebrow at Garritt.

"Luciana is *Juan's* girlfriend," Garritt returned a look as he guided the pretty teen to a bench along the wall. He grabbed a white bar towel and offered it for her soaking-wet hair.

She must have run all the way from her family's house, which wasn't far but the storm outside had grown increasingly wicked. Mascara streaked down both her cheeks as she clutched anxiously at the towel, twisting it in her hands while her hair dripped freely onto the painted concrete floor. She seemed unable to speak, as if suddenly intimidated by her surroundings. Garritt prompted, "What are you doing out on a night like this?"

That brought her around. "It's Juan—he's gone missing!"

"No, not exactly. He's been arrested. What have you two been up to?"

"No, NO! You don't understand! He's not there," she wailed.

"Where?"

"At the jail!"

"What?"

"His dad went there."

"Slow down," he urged. "From the beginning."

"They told his dad that Juan wasn't there, that they'd never heard of a Juan Talamantes. But everyone saw it! They were Holland cops, right? Everybody in town watched them drag Juan away—*in handcuffs!*" Her voice cracked higher. "That's how Luis knew and called me, and now Juan has disappeared," she sobbed.

Garritt's impulse was to put his arm around her shoulders in comfort but he hesitated over whether or not that would be appropriate. He settled for an awkward lie.

"Shhh, shhhh. Everything will be okay."

He wasn't sure about that, but what else could he do? Watching her cry gave him pain. He patted awkwardly at her hand.

She jerked it away. "No it won't! He's not Dutch like you," she spat. "You could never understand!"

"Luciana, try to get hold of yourself. This is America, in the twenty-first century. No one is going to hurt him—except maybe to lose his job." He flicked a look at Corbyn, who'd gone back to work. "That's his own fault for getting himself arrested."

He couldn't let her see his doubts. For instance, why Holland police, not Veenlanden's? And computers—wouldn't they have a record, no matter who arrested him? Most of all, Juan wasn't a kid to break the law if he could help it.

"But he didn't *do* anything!" Luciana wiped at her face, spreading the mascara.

"Then why would they arrest him?"

In fact, as Garritt recalled the scene, they hadn't supplied a reason, other than the curt "ask him a few questions" as they hurried out. They'd all been in shock because the officers didn't announce themselves in any courteous way. They merely barged into the kitchen, grabbed Juan, cuffed him, and dragged him out. Poor Agnes nearly fainted. If it hadn't been for their uniforms…

Luciana looked at him now as if in pity for his ignorance—or deciding whether to tell him something she shouldn't. He glanced at Corbyn and lowered his voice, "Was he involved with something illegal?"

"Not really," the girl hesitated. She flipped wet strands of jet-black hair over the shoulder of Garritt's heavy coat. The smeared face did nothing to mar her youthful beauty. "It's…complicated."

"Talk to me, Luciana. We want to help Juan but we need to know what's going on."

She sighed heavily. "Okay, but you have to promise not to tell him I told you. Okay?"

"I promise," Garritt assured. He remembered what it was like to be seventeen, still in high school, when you still believed that such promises could be kept and that secrets never leaked.

"You know the corn maze, out at the U-pick?"

He nodded. It was their most popular innovation at Ichabod's. They started it every spring with volunteers planting seeds in complicated patterns, which grew by fall into a terrifying maze of twelve-foot corn stalks that he wasn't keen to venture into himself. Kids loved getting lost in it, though. Apparently teenagers did too.

"And you know how Juan likes to talk about UFOs and all that stuff?"

He nodded again.

She took a breath. "We used to sneak out there after the U-pick closed and it got too dark for the farmworkers to be out. Juan knew a way to break in that he learned from his cousin Luis." Her cheeks burned with a rosy glow and Garritt didn't need to ask what they were doing on dark nights among the paths that wove in and out of the tall corn stalks.

Why had he never thought of that? He recalled that time in high school with Sarah, out among the dunes with the razor-sharp beach grass and sand burrs, the gritty sand in all the wrong places…

Immediately he recognized that the discomforts teenagers put up with for sex went far and beyond his current tolerance. He drew his mind back to the present.

"So they arrested Juan for breaking and entering *a corn field?*"

"No—we never got caught. But Juan started meeting friends out there, Diego, Ramon, and some new friends. They just sat around, drinking beer, looking at the stars, smoking, and talking about stuff. Weird stuff like he likes to talk about, you know? I got bored. So I stopped going on those nights." She blushed again, probably thinking of the other nights. "That's where he heard about a guy who had actually seen one—a UFO."

Garritt had stopped listening to her at the mention of teenagers smoking in a dead corn field. He imagined the eerie rasp of dry cornstalks in a night breeze, their stiff leaves scratching together—perfectly primed for a single spark to set them ablaze. The fire would quickly engulf Ichabod's outbuildings, then spread to the retail store where they gave out the apple and pear samples and sold pies to the tourists. *Stupid kid deserved to be arrested—*

"Well they found him—and he had a piece of one."

"A piece of what?" Fruit pie came to mind.

"A UFO."

"Luciana…"

"I'm serious! This old guy, Bobby Lee, he lives in a cabin near Swan Creek Marsh where he fixes lawn mowers and stuff."

Garritt knew of him. Heard he could repair anything, a real tinkerer.

"They went to see him and he told them wild stories about lights over the swamp, how he sees them all the time, UFOs. They went back a few times because he told such good stories. They almost believed him. But then, Juan said one night he pulled out this piece of metal—it looked like gold, about the size of that." She pointed to a dinner plate. "All jagged, like it broke off a bigger piece, and he wouldn't let them touch it. The old man swore it was a fragment he found from an alien ship."

"Just like that? He went out and picked up a piece of a UFO?"

"No. Not exactly. Juan said Bobby invented some kind of metal-detector thing he used to search with. He wouldn't tell them where he found it. Said it wasn't safe to know too much. The next time they went back—he was gone."

"You mean he wasn't home? He was out looking for UFOs?" Maybe he should talk to this Bobby Lee about his Peru experience, since he didn't dare tell anyone *sane* what happened…

"No. I mean they found the door open and the place was a mess, like someone came in and smashed everything. They were scared and ran away. They planned to go back tomorrow. I heard them daring each other and calling insults, *no huevos, maricón—*" She stopped and stared in horror at Corbyn, who politely pretended not to hear, or at least not to understand the insult—a fighting word on every continent.

So she did know about Juan's boss.

"Go on," Garritt urged her past the awkwardness. The more volatile the word, the more Juan and his friends would find it fun to hurl at each other.

"That's it. And now they've arrested Juan and taken him away. He could be in one of those horrible ICE prisons, like where they took the stolen babies! But he's *legal!* He was *born* here! They can't deport him," she pleaded. "He says you're his friend. I need you to find out where he is. Please!" She dropped the too-huge coat from her shoulders and tugged at him with fingers way too cold. "You can do things we can't."

So that was it. Because of his Dutch surname, she figured he could get information neither she nor Juan's family ever would. Much as he hated the fact, she might be right. No matter what kind of person he was or how badly he failed in life, his name would always place him among the privileged here.

"But I don't understand how any of what you've told me relates to Juan's arrest."

"Don't you see? If it's not ICE, if they're just cops, they might think he's the one who broke into Bobby Lee's place! Because he's been there before and because…"

She hesitated to spell it out but Garritt knew what she was going to say next.

"Because he's *Mexican.*"

In Holland, Michigan, that was an insult second only to *queer.* As he often did, Garritt cursed his lineage and wished he'd been born somewhere kinder. The truth was that Juan was the fortunate one, to have a girl like this who would run through a freezing storm for him. Garritt felt more than a touch of envy. He didn't like to wonder who'd go begging for his own well-being. The list was non-existent. Only one person he knew had ever treated him like that: Juan Talamantes.

8

Marooned

∞

Almost the minute her head hit the down pillow, Min passed into a deep sleep. Outside, the sleet had turned to snow but in this cocoon of gentle slumber, she soon drifted into her grandmother's celestial church.

Reverend Ben came to her immediately, holding out both hands to grasp hers.

"Welcome back, my dear," he said, and it seemed the most natural thing to her sleeping mind that he knew her, that he had always known her, and she him.

But now he had hair, jet black and wavy. And his eyes were reflective black marbles. His skin no longer shone deep ebony but tawny brown. She'd remembered him towering over her but this time they stood face to face. Still, she knew he was the same man as her grandmother's Reverend Ben.

"We are happy to see you here again," he added with an East Indian accent. "We had not finished our conversation."

"Reverend Ben?"

He waggled his head sideways in the Indian affirmative, as if to say, *Yes, that will do for now; it's of the least importance.*

She went on anyway, in a hurry for his help because she well remembered what happened last time, how before she could ask a thing, he vanished—or she had.

"I have so many questions but right now I think I'm in serious trouble."

"And why do you think that?"

"Because I've taken something—well, I took it but then I lost it."

"Would this be that golden piece of metal that does not belong to you?"

"Yessir."

"And you feel guilty about this because it belonged to someone else?"

"Yessir."

"And to whom do you think this piece of metal, a fragment really, belonged?"

"Well, sir, it probably belongs to my company, I mean the company I work for, because they are the ones who hired me to find it."

"Are you certain about that?"

"Um, well, no sir. That's why I'm in trouble. I thought I knew what was right but now I am not so sure."

Calling him *sir* was a military reflex. Despite his shorter stature, his bearing told her that this man was a superior, no question about it. She felt a deep respect she couldn't explain since she'd only technically met him once before, and even then he'd been in a different body. Strange, because authority figures usually triggered distrust in her. (The Navy tried to cure her of that, without much success.) Anyway, she guessed that his name probably wasn't still Ben. He didn't offer another.

Instead he led her to an alcove in the church, nestled into a bay window made of stained glass. Beams of colored light danced throughout the space. They settled on a bench she couldn't really feel, while swirls of color circulated around them in patterns that made her a little dizzy.

"Just rest here a moment while you get your bearings. I am going to tell you a story, if you don't mind."

"Please."

"*Haa*," he breathed, swinging his head again in that elegant, side-to-side movement. So *haa* must mean *yes*. Just like before, his voice melted into her ears like chocolate pudding on her tongue; she could listen to him all day.

His congregation is lucky, she thought, although he'd claimed last time that he wasn't actually a preacher, and this wasn't exactly a church. She desperately wanted to ask him why he looked now like he was from Mumbai, not Mombasa, but he'd already begun his story.

"Your planet Earth is very ancient, you know."

She nodded, as one does to be polite when someone begins a long story. All the manners her grandmother drilled into her came to the fore, drawn up from dusty memory to supersede her typical skepticism, doubt, or outright rebellion. Why did he affect her so?

He didn't fall for the polite nod.

"No, you don't really know how ancient. No one now living on your planet comprehends the full antiquity of its history. Nor do you remember the extraterrestrial origins of the peoples who populate your world."

"Extraterrestrial?"

He sighed. "So many beings, from so many parts of your galaxy. It wasn't an ideal situation but the Minds who devised this plan had little choice. Worlds had been destroyed. The damaged ones needed a place to rehabilitate themselves, a world not so different from what they had known. They would also need new bodies to inhabit. These Advanced Leaders called on populations of worlds ready to transform, to go physically extinct, populations who agreed to make a great sacrifice for the benefit of all humanity."

"You mean they supplied the...bodies?"

"You see, those who obliterated entire planets simultaneously exploded their own evolutionary blueprints, as well as those of the destroyed planet's inhabitants. None of these individuals could form physical bodies after this cataclysmic destruction. It was like self-annihilation. Yet their damaged mental bodies, what remained of them, continued to exist, trapped in astral, non-physical states. They had thrown themselves back to a primitive state of being.

"To rectify this, they would need physical form in order to return to the scene of their crimes, so to speak, and rebuild their inner software from the ground up. Literally. Those who pledged themselves to this slow rehabilitation were given help to achieve this opportunity, a gift of life, selflessly supplied by others."

Entire planets destroyed? Like the Death Star?

"Yes, good example," he agreed, though she hadn't said it aloud. "George Lucas apparently held some memory of this ancient era. He and his collaborators got many things wrong—but a few correct."

This was a lot to grasp. He seemed to be saying that the people on Earth were once criminals—or victims. Which was it?

His dark eyes glittered kindly at her. "I know this is difficult to understand at your stage of evolution. Minda, my daughter, you are a facet of a jewel so magnificent, so infinite in its manifestations, that I cannot tell you much more than this. You will learn through your life experience, through your many lifetimes, whether on Earth or elsewhere."

She entirely missed the "elsewhere," she was so eager to ask: "What about the ships, the ones that hang in our atmosphere but never seem to land? Who are they? Why don't they set down, open up, walk out, and introduce themselves—maybe like in *Close Encounters* if they don't look like us, so no one freaks out."

He smiled broadly. "Would you believe it? That we were coming as friendly, peaceful neighbors?"

"Yes! I would!" And she might be one of the few, she realized. Her face fell. "Why are we like that—kill first, question later?"

"Minda, you will learn all that I can tell you one day. For now, you must realize that your planet has reached a critical stage. Worse than your pandemics and pollution, your wars and your overpopulation, worse even than your invention of technologies with dangers that you do not yet recognize, the people on your world remain ignorant of the fact that they are like radio transmitters and receivers. Their thoughts—whether beautiful or ugly—radiate collectively out into the infinite universes. Your bodies are little more than electronic communication modules. You are connected to the Infinite Source, yes, but also to one another, and to every living thing on your planet: human, fish, or fowl; plants, rocks, and bodies of water—*everything*."

She couldn't think of words to question this, let alone comprehend the enormity of its implications.

"That means also that your individual and collective actions create much more than the ugly, smoggy atmosphere that surrounds your little world. This smoggy thinking creates ripples in the galaxy and far beyond, ripples that also travel into other dimensions."

He hung his head, very unhappily. "We have to protect you from calling in the monsters from the deep through your ignorance. And we have to protect ourselves, as well, from you. It is like keeping the cupboards locked until the toddler grows up. Except the toddler also has very sharp teeth."

"You mean like the Galactic Zoo hypothesis? It's true?"

"Dr. John A. Ball. Yes, he was very close to the truth."

"But who are you to do this to us?"

"Listen carefully; you will leave in a moment."

She heard a new urgency in his voice.

"You need to know that the artifact you touched, without your protective gloves, it is very dangerous. It can—"

Her eyes popped open. Someone was hammering on her door, which knocked the dream right out of her memory.

"Miss? You asked for a wake-up call? Breakfast will be served in the dining room in fifteen minutes but no hurry," Mrs. Peterson called through her door. "We'll keep it warm for you. It looks like you won't be going anywhere soon."

Min rolled over to look out the window. A crust of wet snow clung to the bottom half and blocked her view.

She quickly showered, dressed in a pale blue sweater and jeans, and walked into the antique-filled dining room twenty minutes later. That's when she saw Agnes tumble in the back door of the open kitchen. A pile of snow came with her.

"It's freezing out there," she heard the girl exclaim to Mr. Peterson as he rushed over to relieve her of a burden of boxes. "Lake effect," he nodded. "Early this year. Climate change. Not even Thanksgiving and we got ten inches overnight."

He brought the fragrant boxes through the open dining room door. "You're lucky to be here this morning, Miss." He opened the lid of one box to reveal fresh bread, and another, filled with sweets from Avery's talented baker. He lifted them out and laid them reverently on a magnificent, cut-glass platter.

She couldn't agree more. The mirrored sideboard already featured warming trays of scrambled eggs, bacon, sausage, and waffles. Alongside them on a lacy doily: three kinds of jam, honey, maple syrup, coffee, tea, cream, butter. So much food, and as far as she could tell, she was the only lodger this morning. Her mouth watered from the aroma of the baked goods and she sat herself down and dug in. Dessert first, she believed.

Before Min could get back up for the coffee she'd forgotten, Agnes, ever the perfect waitress, set a steaming cup before her. She hadn't bothered to take off her wet boots or snowy parka first. "How did you sleep? Isn't this place beautiful," she plied eagerly.

Mrs. Peterson bustled in, stared at Agnes's snowy boots on the antique Persian carpet, hesitated, then said gently, "Agnes, dear, maybe you'd like to take off your coat—and your boots?"

"Oh no, I'm fine, Mrs. Peterson," she answered innocently. Apparently she missed the subtle inflection, which Min did catch. "I brought the pastries myself this morning so I could check on your guest. She's snowed in now, so we need to take good care of her."

"Snowed in?" Min coughed on a cranberry in her mini muffin. "What are you saying?"

"She's right," Mr. Peterson called out from the kitchen. "No one's going anywhere today. They're predicting another foot of snow by tomorrow, and probably more on the way."

Lake effect, she'd overheard him say. *That's not a myth?*

She thought her cousin's family was simply bragging about why they got more snow than the wimps in Chicago. That wind last night—blowing from west to east. She visualized it picking up water from the Lake and dropping it frozen, all over the western half of Michigan.

"Don't worry," Agnes chirped. "You can come over to the restaurant—it's close enough to walk. We'll keep you company if you get bored here. Did you bring some boots?" She was staring at Min's sneakers, now free of the sand they'd acquired at Rosy Dunes so their bright pink-and-blue butterfly print was easy to see.

Mr. Peterson cleared his throat. "Are you sure your boss won't mind, Agnes?"

"Oh, he won't care. Corbyn isn't there today anyway. They went off to see about Juan." She stopped suddenly and blushed. "Well, I'd better get back now. Enjoy your breakfast!" She waved cheerily to Min as she hurried out the back door.

"How long do you think this storm will last?" Min asked quietly, between sips of perfectly brewed coffee and bites of her second mini muffin. This one tasted like pumpkin spice.

"Oh, not long, dear," Mrs. Peterson encouraged. "Just enjoy a little rest and we'll be sure to set out some lunch for you. Unless you want to go back to Avery's. I think Agnes would like the company. Poor girl doesn't get out much. I think her imagination takes her over sometimes." She gave her husband a worried look. "What was that she said about Juan, dear? You know, the boy who works in the back?"

"Don't know. Didn't hear her. I'd better start shoveling. Never know when someone else might roll in."

Min could swear he changed the subject on purpose.

As he retrieved his coat from a hook just inside the kitchen, he added, "City folk, tourists who come up from Chicago, don't know enough to stay off the roads in weather like this. They get stranded out on the highway when their cars slide into a ditch because they drive too fast. Of course they don't think of keeping warm clothes and blankets in the car this time of year." He looked at her pointedly and she wondered if he'd raised teenagers.

"If they're *lucky*," he emphasized, "someone will come by before they freeze to death. We're the best place to stay between South Haven and Saugatuck." He thought for a tick. "Lucky you came in when you did." He zipped up his jacket and went out the back without another word.

Mrs. Peterson seemed suddenly uncomfortable alone with her guest. She rose from the table and made some excuse to leave the room. As she disappeared up the stairs, she called back, "Just make yourself at home!"

As if.

Now what?

Min pulled out the pay-as-you-go phone and texted Amrita, explaining the new number with a lame excuse about losing her iPhone. Am was probably still on Do Not Disturb anyway; it was early there. But after last night's wine and pizza, Min had forgotten her promise to check in with her roommate.

Snowed in. Nice B&B. Call you later.

Amrita would love the idea that she had nothing to do but rest. But Min couldn't shake her unsettled feeling. Once she sipped some coffee, fragments of her dream came back. She'd forgotten most of it but certainly remembered that Reverend Ben, or whoever he was, was talking about the artifact when Mrs. Peterson's knock shocked her back into this world.

Dangerous, he was saying—but how?

She gobbled a mound of eggs from her plate, stood up, hesitated, then decided it would be okay to take the flowered porcelain cup to her room. As she headed for the stairs, she glanced out the sitting-room windows.

Her white rental car blended into a drift she hoped would blow away soon. No way would she walk over to some fricking restaurant in this weather! More snow was blowing sideways and she could hear the wind whistle through the window sash. On second thought, she ducked back into the dining room, stuffed a raisin scone and two pieces of bacon into a napkin, then hurried up to her room. This trip might cost her a few pounds but she had serious remote viewing to accomplish and an empty stomach would not help.

She set her food carefully on the antique desk, grateful that Mrs. Peterson had started up the gas fireplace in the quaint room. Pricey place, though she fully understood her good fortune not to be stranded out on the highway. She kicked off her shoes.

Boots. Out in the snow-buried car, of course. City boots, fit for a hot and dry San Diego autumn. And no, unless one came with the rental, no emergency blanket.

After a few more minutes of her coffee-stimulated mind jumping from minutia to minutia, Min realized she was stalling.

Truthfully, she feared what she might see when she tuned in to the golden fragment. She gave herself a pep-talk, forced her body to sit and do her heart-breathing, centering exercises.

It took only moments before the golden slab appeared in her mind. It lay on the same rugged table, surrounded by trashy heaps of paperwork and food debris. Clear as day, the teenager she'd watched the cops drag out of the restaurant stood on the far side of that table.

Startled, her eyes popped open and the vision dissolved.

She assumed she could only see the teenager now because that's how her skill worked: she could remote-view just about any item, if she'd seen at least a photograph or a sketch of it beforehand. The food, for instance. She could find restaurants serving her favorite dishes, such as the pulled pork that drew her to Avery's. Often the surroundings would then come slowly into focus—sometimes vividly, sometimes not so much. It varied. Avery's had been surprisingly easy to see in full detail, though, which was strange…

Time, on the other hand, that was trickier. In the not-so-physical environment of her visions, time rarely stabilized. This might have been a scene from this morning, last week, or even the future. And the future was wacky. Constantly changing.

Her mind churned up a dozen scenarios. Most likely the kid stole the fragment from the site, or from someone else who found it. He'd taken it somewhere to sell because it looked like Earth gold—

The people who dragged him out in handcuffs! She knew that trick; she'd heard co-workers brag about it. Violating their secrecy oaths, of course, but when did *macho* respect rules? That's why she believed they would come for her.

This was not good. That young man was in serious danger, if not from the artifact itself—after all, it hadn't hurt her, had it?—then from Blackthorn. Or, she shuddered to think, from any one of a dozen bad players in the world who would love to get their hands on such an item, if they knew it existed. Chances were, they did.

And this was her fault. She was the one who dug up the artifact and left it thinly buried up on that dune, maybe one of the park's most popular overlooks. She was the one who didn't come back for it until weeks later. To risk her own life for truth was one thing, but this young man's?

She groaned at her ineptitude. She only wanted to do the right thing! And now, what a mess—with an innocent kid's life at stake.

She threw on as many layers as she could, stuffed bacon in her mouth, and cursed herself again for leaving her boots in the car. That would mean long, icy minutes to dig open the door…and those boots had *heels*.

9

Compassion

∞

Min leaned into the driving snow, blue silk scarf wrapped over her face. It did nothing to stop the icy wind as she plunged through knee-high drifts where she hoped a sidewalk might be. Finally she gave up and climbed over the snow-plow mound and into the street.

"Get out of the street, lady! Plow drivers will never see you in this blizzard!"

Rude as he was, the man in the car creeping by had a point. She moved cautiously to the side just as another car pulled out from a corner and came straight at her, going way too fast. She had to leap into the snow mound when the car skidded on a patch of slushy salt-melt, spraying her jeans with dirty crud. She let out a choice word and turned to see that it was Samantha from the restaurant, eyes front, oblivious to Min's presence, caught up in her own world.

Young women drivers, Min sighed, worse than the vapers back in San Diego. She brushed herself off, put her head down, and forged on. No time for anger. She might actually be able to help the young man at risk but this Sam person would have to learn the hard way—if she didn't kill someone first.

Despite a cold that froze bones she didn't know she had, she pushed on past buildings, benches, and parked cars draped in white blankets. Relentless crystal arrows shot straight at her nose and cheeks where they stung and burned until she finally went numb. She might have admired the pristine Christmas-card beauty of it all, if her task weren't so urgent. The dizzy spells didn't help.

At last she reached Avery's glass door. A sign read, "Closed. Reopening at 11:30." She pounded anyway, hoping Agnes would hear.

Her frost-ravaged mind spun out on conjecture about that girl, so different from Sam. Did she ever go home? But who could blame her; living out on a farm, maybe only chickens for company. Here, the world would come to her. Sort of. And certainly not today. In a dizzy haze that Min hoped was brought on by her elevated blood pressure, she wondered vaguely if chickens laid eggs in winter in this part of the world. Maybe that was another thing shipped in from Arizona, or California…

Beneath her jacket and two sweaters, she felt the piece of foil she readjusted on her back that morning stab at her. Her frozen body failed to warm the metallic square. She pounded again, squinting against the driving snow.

Finally she heard the door unlatch.

"Oh, it's you again," Sam greeted her as she slipped out of a thick, warm coat that filled Min with envy. "We *are* closed, you know." But she stepped aside.

Min barged through and stamped her feet, leaving patterns of white on the clean floor. "Where is your boss? Where is Chef Vanderhoeven?" Somewhere in the universe, she won a whole booklet of gold stars for not strangling the girl on the spot.

"Garritt is not my boss. He's out with Corbyn, who is my boss."

"When will they be back?"

"How should I know?"

Min swallowed hard for control, while still trying to catch her breath. "This is urgent! It's about your dishwasher—"

Agnes hurried out from the back. "Sam, it's okay. I invited her."

"You did what?"

"She's snowed in at the Petersons' and I told her she could come here if she got bored."

"I am not bored! And even if I was, I sure as sugar wouldn't relieve it with a mile-long hike in that." She jabbed toward the white maelstrom outside the windows. "I need to talk to Chef … to Garritt. Now. It is extremely important. Your co-worker is in trouble."

"Yeah, we know. Stupid Juan, getting caught," Sam agreed. "Whatever he was doing, he probably deserved it."

"Listen to me—" Min began.

She wanted desperately to shake this young woman but at that moment she heard the back kitchen doors burst open. Two male voices piped across the empty tables, carrying an argument in from the storm. Without waiting for an invitation, Min pushed past Sam and Agnes and headed straight for their raised voices.

"I don't know what more you want me to do," the older man was saying. "If you've got any brilliant ideas, I'll be glad to listen. But meanwhile, I've got a restaurant to run! I can't rush off after every fucking kid who gets himself in trouble. Bad enough I had to call on favors to get a dishwasher in here. I won't hold his job much longer, I can tell you that!"

Clearly the boss. She saw him set his galoshes neatly by the back door while Garritt kicked off massive, snow-caked blocks of rubber with the words "Ice Dragon" emblazoned across the back. They both turned to stare at her.

"Excuse me but your employee is…in more trouble than you think." Her heart was still pounding from anxiety and the frozen hike, so the words came out ragged. She didn't care. "You've got to do something… before it's too late!"

"Look, lady," Corbyn stared, still fuming, "I don't know who you are, but we've just spent two hours trying to do something for that kid. I'm not his father—"

"She's a customer," Garritt interrupted quietly. He looked as if he might take her seriously, thank the heavens above.

∞

When Garritt turned to see the woman from yesterday hurry toward them in her flimsy jacket, he was once again struck by the sight of glittery lights pouring from the ceiling, encasing her in a brilliant golden column. Whatever she wanted, he'd better pay attention. Angel or demon, the lights said she mattered. A lot.

"I'm sorry, Miss—um, I don't think you told us your name?"

"Minda. But that's not important now."

"Minda, why don't you come out here with me." He led her toward a back table in the empty dining room, away from Corbyn's irritation.

Had she come for his soul, or his heart? He tried to seem cool but his hands shook visibly. He shoved them in pockets. Those lights carried life and death significance in Peru. Why would now be different?

She wouldn't sit. She stood like someone ready to flee because they expected the ceiling to collapse at any moment. That didn't help his own heart's beat slow down.

"This kid who works for you, he's gotten himself into trouble with some—well, they aren't good people. If we don't find him soon, they might hurt him. Bad."

She seemed genuinely concerned, which caught him by surprise. Not very demonic of her. A single light twinkled above her head, urging him to trust. He had trouble with that.

"How do you know these things?"

Her intensity wavered. She braced a hand against the table.

"I, well, I just sometimes…you know…"

On a hunch, he replied, "It's okay. Sometimes I do too."

She's psychic.

It came to him in a flash. He could understand her reluctance to say so. Around her head, gold sparks glinted sporadically. *She's like the leaf filled with water, or the right path through the jungle.* Devil or no, whoever she was, whatever she knew—or however—she was a path he needed to take.

"This young man—Juan is his name?"

Garritt nodded.

She lowered her voice, speaking rapidly as if someone might stop her before she could get all the words out. "He went to a cabin where he shouldn't have been, and he had something he shouldn't have stolen, sort of like an antique. Those people who took him off in handcuffs, they might not be who you thought they were."

"First of all, Juan is no thief," Garritt snapped. "But you are right about one thing. We've just been to the police station where they've never heard of him. He's not in their computer system, so as far as they're concerned, he was never arrested. Except that we all saw them do it."

"You've got to find him. He's in serious danger. They—they want what he stole, and they might do anything to get it. Please trust me—for his sake. I think I can help you find him."

Dangerous people. Bad enough to impersonate police officers. But why would she know this, or think she could help? He took in the vicious scar on her forehead. Stranger. Recent fight? If it weren't for the golden sparks telling him otherwise…even Agnes had sensed that she was hiding something, and Agnes's intuition was known to be very accurate.

What if she was one of the people who wanted what she claimed Juan had stolen?

But he had to trust the lights. With his life. They'd taught him that in the rainforest and now they said, *Trust her.* He glanced around, spotted Sam and Agnes behind the cheese counter, whispering between themselves. He was grateful they were distracted because anyone would think he'd lost his mind for what he was about to do.

"Stay here a minute."

He strode back to the kitchen and poked his head into Corbyn's office. "I need the rest of the day off. Before you explode, listen. Juan is in real trouble and I can't let it go. This woman claims she can help me find him. I hate to ask, I know he's retired, but can Avery take my shift?"

Corbyn's partner hadn't actually retired. As Garritt's cooking skills developed, Avery spent more time at their sprawling lakefront home in nearby Saugatuck nursing Glinda, their Pekingese who'd had dental surgery. Avery insisted on blending special foods for her and soon he'd need to do the same for her sister, Elphie. He convinced Corbyn that he could do the books from home, that Garritt was ready to take over as head chef, *blah, blah, blah.* To make Avery happy, Corbyn agreed. That made Garritt happy, too, because he no longer had to listen to them bicker the way happy couples sometimes do. Bottom line: the kitchen grew a lot more peaceful after Avery left. So Garritt knew he was making an audacious request, especially with the blizzard raging outside.

This Minda had reminded him of Luciana's fear, that Juan might be trapped in a migrant deportation prison. Some people didn't survive those places. If he didn't follow every lead, if something happened to Juan, he would never forgive himself.

Corbyn stared in astonishment.

"You know me, Corbyn. You know I have to do this. I owe it to Juan."

His boss looked him up and down, considering.

Finally, he threw up his hands, "Go. If a death-defying leap and lurking pumas couldn't do it, I'm sure I'm not the one to stop anything you put your mind to. So go. Bring Juan back here, or tell him his ass is grass! I'll do the cooking myself. Better than risking Avery on these roads. And don't take the van this time; take your truck."

"Right. I put snow tires on last week." Which was odd. Before this freak blizzard was even on the radar, a strong inner prompting urged Garritt to do it early, a task he normally procrastinated.

"Wait." Corbyn pulled open a drawer. "You might need this, although I don't know how it can help you."

He held up Juan's phone, the treasured possession that inspired the teenager to scrub dishes, floors, and restrooms all through his summer after high school in order to pay for it.

"Found it stashed among the soap tubes under the dishwasher. That kid is in a pile of trouble."

Garritt hurried back to Minda with Juan's phone held high. "We've got something to go on."

The woman stared at the phone.

He answered her thought, "I know someone who might be able to break into this. If we can get to her. Come with me."

"Where? In this blizzard?"

"What else can we do from here?"

"Hold on," Sam called out.

So! Those two *had* been eavesdropping.

Sam reached under the hostess stand and pulled out a fuchsia wool cap. She walked over and held it out. "You're going to need this."

The woman looked stunned.

"Take it," Sam shoved it into her hand. "And when you find him, tell that little prick to get his butt back here!"

"And this!"

Not to be outdone, Agnes hurried over from the kitchen where she'd retrieved a long, red-wool scarf. She wrapped it around the woman's bare neck. "My grandmother knitted it."

The stranger managed an astonished thank-you, as if she'd never experienced such generosity. And then, after an awkward pause, she said, "Agnes, could you ask the Petersons to charge my card for another night?"

"Of course!" Agnes sang, probably thrilled that this fascinating stranger remembered her name. The poor girl was starved for excitement. She'd lived her entire youth in the stultifying sameness of farmyard routine. Garritt knew it well.

Then Agnes added, "And if some man comes looking for you, we'll tell him you were never here."

That struck them all silent.

Except for Agnes. "There's a shelter in Holland, you know."

"Oh!" Minda reddened at first, then burst out laughing. "You think I'm on the run from some wife beater?" She touched at her forehead, feeling for the scar. "I guess I do look a little beat up," she chuckled awkwardly, clearly embarrassed.

Garritt was every bit as curious about what she might say next, despite the part of him that cringed on Agnes's behalf.

"This? Work injury. Accident on the job."

Agnes's eyes grew bigger. "What kind of work do you do?"

"That's enough now," Garritt cut her off before she could blurt anything worse. "We have to get going."

Minda seemed grateful to escape through the kitchen with Garritt, where he opened the door to let the storm swallow them in billows of blinding snow.

No turning back now. If finding Juan cost him his soul, then so be it. He swallowed his uneasiness and climbed into his truck beside the bronzed beauty, breaking all the rules of Michigan Dutch society, passed down for generations. But not without a flash of memory: A visit to Muskegon as a toddler, a place where "others" lived, where he first heard the sound of his mother's fear. "Don't touch that; it's dirty." And, "Those people aren't like us." And, "Don't stare. Stay close to me."

More determined than ever, Garritt pressed the gas gently and they slipped and slid out of the parking lot.

10

Whiteout

∾

They found Luciana at the **high school in a** chaos of fleeing teenagers set loose before lunch because of the snowstorm. She broke into Juan's phone with no problem. ("What kind of girlfriend would I be if I couldn't?") But what caught Min's attention was the fact that the girl was pregnant. She wasn't sure if she could tell by the vibrancy of the girl's skin, or a baby bump—or her own visionary powers—but it was clear as day to her.

Of course, Garritt didn't notice. He was too busy mulling over a text they found from a *Viejo Gordito,* Juan's nickname for some old guy Garritt and Luciana seemed to think important. All it said was, *Plan E. Stay clear.* She hadn't paid much attention. She was just eager for a quiet place to do more remote viewing. Then she heard them say this guy lived by a swamp, in a cabin.

"Could you draw a picture of him?" she interrupted.

"No, I never met him. They told me it was no place for a *chica.* They wanted to be all macho, make it sound scary. He must be kind of, you know, gray-haired and chubby—*viejo gordito,* you know?" She blushed a little as she translated, "Chubby old man."

A cabin in the woods—exactly the place to find the kind of rustic table Min saw in her vision. This man might have her golden ticket! When she told Garritt she could help him find Juan, she meant through remote viewing. He never gave her a chance to explain that. Good thing, because now she could remain incognito while he drove her straight to the man who might have her alien artifact.

Luciana refused their offer of a ride home. "The walk will help me stop worrying," she said, then threw her arms around Garritt. "Thank you so much for helping us! You saved those people in Peru—I know you can find Juan! Tell him…tell him his family waits for him—*all* of us."

Yep, she's pregnant. And she just gave me an opening.

Min had been dying to ask about the things Agnes told her over lunch yesterday. The minute Garritt climbed into the freezing cab beside her, she blurted, "You're that guy, aren't you? The one who ran through the rainforest and leaped over a river."

He groaned, but before he could respond they hit a patch of ice and slid sideways, narrowly missing a rusty parked Honda, even uglier than his battered truck. Her fingers gripped the armrest and she braced her feet, hissing through gritted teeth, "I hope you can drive in snow as well as you run through jungles."

"Doesn't matter. You're not going with me."

"What?"

"I'm dropping you off at the B&B. Unless you'd rather go back to the restaurant? But then you'd have to walk in this again and you're not dressed for it, despite that very adorable hat you're wearing," he chuckled.

She reached up and touched the fuchsia hat, flipped down the visor to stare at herself in the mirror. *A pussy hat!* She hadn't noticed the cat ears. Garritt laughed at her, a nice laugh—the kind you share with friends.

She'd been so astounded by Sam's offer. That girl had cast shade right up until the moment of her freakishly compassionate generosity. She laughed at herself for not noticing the details. Nice one, Sam.

"It's her favorite hat, you know."

"I'll bet."

"Seriously—she lent it to you in all kindness. You're not prepared for this weather."

No joke.

This Samantha was a contradiction, she couldn't argue that. Apparently she'd gone out to march for women's rights, while her personal, one-on-one, social objectivity needed an upgrade. Min shook her head. Sam was young; maybe she'd learn.

And then Agnes and her red scarf! Knitted by her grandmother, no less. Primping in the mirror, Min decided she liked the bright red and fuchsia side by side. These treasures would certainly keep her warmer, although her toes had already gone numb inside her thin leather boots.

"I'm going with you," she insisted, flipping the visor back up.

"Why should you? You don't even know Juan."

She needed a good lie. "It's a lot less boring than sitting in that quilted bedroom."

"I don't believe you."

"You think the fat old man, the *viejo gordito,* might know where Juan is, don't you? So why are we going there instead of contacting the FBI?" She already knew why she wanted to find Juan. She wondered what was on Garritt's mind.

"Two reasons," Garritt said as he turned east on Main Street, opposite direction from the B&B.

She smiled. He trusted her.

"One, you described Juan in a cabin—before you remembered that you would have no ordinary way of knowing that, and shouldn't be telling me."

He glanced at her significantly and she tried to keep a straight face. This is why she knew she could never do an Ed Snowden. No guile at all.

"Bobby Lee lives in a such a place," he continued. "And two, Luciana came to see me last night. She convinced me that the man knows what trouble Juan might have gotten into."

Even if the filthy table belonged to this Bobby Lee, Min wouldn't have seen him in the vision. She'd never laid eyes on the man like she had with Juan.

That's why she asked Luciana if she could draw a picture, so she could remote-view his location.

"What else did his girlfriend tell you?"

"That Juan and his friends visited Bobby Lee because they liked his stories about UFOs, which happens to be Juan's second favorite subject—Luciana being the first. He convinced them he had a piece of one, and that it was real."

So he did have it! How would she get it out of his hands?

"I don't know what he really had," Garritt was saying, "but my gut tells me he's connected to Juan's arrest. Someone broke into the guy's place and Luciana thinks they might accuse Juan because he's Mexican-American.

If we find the old man, maybe he can help us prove Juan's innocence."

"If it *was* the law who took him," she said.

"What do you mean?"

"I mean there are worse things in the world." She worked for people who committed worse things, from what she knew of them.

There it was. Her loyalty turning. Crossing the fence. Traitor to her company and possibly her country. Could she live with that? No, better question: Could she *die* for it? Because she'd have the artifact in hand very soon now.

"There's too much you don't know, Garritt Vanderhoeven, Dutch hero." A hint of compassion bled into her words. He was one of those who'd been deprived of the truth.

"About that—I believe you. Why don't you tell me some of it? For instance, you know an awful lot about Juan's situation. Why are you here, Minda Whatever-your-name is?"

"Blake. Minda Blake. But most people call me Min. And I am not your enemy—or Juan's. At least, not anymore."

"What do you mean?"

"I mean, I know the people who are after what old Bobby Lee thinks he's found."

"And what is that?"

"A piece of the future. And the past. Invisible in the present except to those who are among the privileged."

"Could you be more cryptic?" he asked sarcastically. "Who are you? Who do you really work for, Min Blake?"

He kept glancing at her forehead. Couldn't blame him. To him, she was just a beat-up stranger talking total nonsense, who claimed to know things she shouldn't be able to know.

"Last week, I worked for *them*, the privileged ones."

"And this week?"

"I'm not sure."

And she'd never said anything more true.

Thankfully, he let it drop as he concentrated on maneuvering through the blizzard, the likes of which she'd never experienced before. She'd seen snowfall in cities around the world, of course, but that was more about what happened in the streets afterward. Here, this force of nature unleashed its power unhampered by the human structures that create an illusion of safety. The rawness of it frightened her.

After three miles of silent anxiety, pulling clenched fists up into the sleeves of her flimsy jacket in a futile attempt to warm her fingers, the wind finally stopped buffeting the pickup. Soft, fat flakes filled the sky, piling up faster now that they had stopped blowing. Despite the heater, the cab felt refrigerated. She wrapped her arms tightly around her torso and tried to stop shivering from the combination of fear, excitement, and bitter cold.

Garritt slowed nearly to a stop and eased into a forty-five degree turn on to a wide, unbroken plain, like a white duvet spread across the land until it met a frame of dense woods on either side. The open break in the forest gave away the fact that pavement should lie beneath their snow-packed tires. Out her window, she could see an open ditch channeling water in shallow glints beneath the invisible road.

They must be on a little culvert, and apparently the water running in the ditch had no time to freeze before this freak storm blanketed the landscape.

An unpleasant shiver of memory passed through her as she stared at the culvert's concrete edges. She felt dizzy again.

"How did you know where to turn?" she asked to distract herself from it. "I couldn't see any road here at all." And no trace of a GPS in the derelict pickup. His phone sat untouched on the dash.

She glanced at her burner phone. *No service.* Great. But she'd missed a text from Amrita—a row of rude gestures. Oops. She'd forgotten her roommate was sleeping three hours behind Michigan time. No wonder it took her so long to reply. The gestures were followed by another text:

> Snowed in at least you can't get in trouble.

Hah. If she had service she would answer, *In truck with strange man driving in blizzard to remote cabin.* A snappy comeback to make her friend sympathetic—but instead it made Min think of things she hadn't considered, she was so focused on the artifact and Blackthorn. But what if the real threat to her life was right here, right now?

At the high school she overheard that the lake-effect snow now swaddled half the state of Michigan. Foot-and-a-half so far and still falling. She shouldn't be out in this storm at all but especially not with a lunatic stranger. Didn't it take a crazy person to leap off a cliff to certain death? Whatever scam he pulled in that rainforest, he hadn't told the world the truth, that was for sure. And now she was trapped out here with him, no other way to get back to her room, her car, her life in sunny San Diego. Not another soul in sight, nothing visible for miles on this solid white plain they'd plunged into, truck spurting along in fits and slides.

Stupid, Min. Stupid, stupid, stupid.

∞

After a few grim moments of trying to keep his wheels connected to the ground, Garritt finally answered her question.

"I know the neighborhood."

Not a total lie. He did know the area well. But outside, golden lights twinkled in profusion over the road ahead—so vividly, Garritt marveled that the woman next to him couldn't see them. She seemed awed instead by the famous Allegan woods. He had to admit the scene was pretty, with the snow piling heavily on the green pines and clinging to the black trunks of bare hardwoods—white piping over dark chocolate ganache. Not another soul or creature in sight.

"I know exactly where this man lives."

He slowed the truck to a halt and turned toward her. "Now tell me everything, since you say I know so little. Before we go another foot."

She twisted quickly to look behind them.

"Don't worry. Only fools are out driving in this. No one is going to sneak up behind us."

"You don't know that. And you don't know what your friend is dealing with. These are not nice people. They are not Dutch. They are mixed and confused, is what they are," she mumbled, more to herself than him.

He heard some sadness in her voice, and more than a little fear.

"They are patriots, most of them. They are doing what they think is good and true and right. So we can't afford to stop like this! We have to find your friend as soon as possible." She swiveled again to look behind them, as if she expected an army to arrive at any moment.

"Is that you? Are you doing what is good and right *for* them?"

"I am just a woman who had a skill they wanted. And yeah, I believed in them. I've done what they asked and I thought it was for the good of all."

Garritt lost patience with this banter. He hardened his voice.

"Believe it or not, we are out here risking our lives on this road, and you've told me only enough to believe that we might risk Juan's life as well in the next few miles. That is, if we find anyone at all. Luciana said the cabin was deserted when Juan and his friends went back, wrecked like there'd been a robbery. It wasn't them, she insists. They got scared and ran off.

"There, now I've told you something you didn't know. Your turn."

"Wait—you already know that no one is out here? And you've brought us anyway? Friggin' idiot! I'm freezing my toes off just so you can be a hero again!"

That stung. Garritt couldn't tell her that the flickering lights had led him to do this. And they were still leading, dancing off the front of the truck. *Don't linger,* they seemed to agree with her.

He ignored them. This woman needed to come clean. He wouldn't explain his history with Juan until he knew more about her. "Tell me, are you just using me to get to Juan yourself? Maybe you're the one who wants whatever he's supposed to have stolen. Why should I take you to him?"

He knew exactly why, of course. He'd made the choice to follow the glitter's directions, whether demonic or divine, and she was part of that. But he hoped she might tell him more if he sounded tough or intimidating.

And then it struck him. *People do not open up unless they feel safe.* What makes us feel safe? When the other person exposes their own vulnerability. He wasn't going to do that.

For a long, silent moment, he stared off toward the cotton-wrapped woods, taking time to quell his simmering irritation before he spoke again. "You're not going to tell me, are you?"

"Not a thing. So maybe you want to turn this truck around and go on this hero mission by yourself."

The glitter grew brighter in Garritt's sight, its glow intensified by the dimming sky.

The storm had picked up again, probably another system coming off the lake. He refused to react to her dig, bait he knew better than to swallow. He put his foot on the accelerator, lightly.

The tires spun for an instant on the slick surface beneath the snow, then caught hold. From the looks of things, reaching the cabin by the swamp wasn't going to get any easier but he needed to see with his own eyes that it was empty before he'd give up on the idea that it might hold some clue to Juan's disappearance.

He heard Min breathe a soft sigh as the truck plunged ahead again, plowing through drifts.

"Let's just get there first, before we get stuck here till spring," she said. "Then we can talk."

It sounded like she was trying to placate him.

"Anyway, it might be warmer than this," she added.

He noticed her reach down to massage her toes through the soaked leather. If nothing else, her face told him that this quest meant a lot to her. But why? She hadn't given him any sensible reason. What a fool he was, thinking she could help him find Juan, this perfect stranger with suspect motives and demon-sexy eyes.

So why did he feel a terrible, secret, warm pleasure to have her here beside him, even as he feared for his best friend's life and his own soul?

"By the way, did you know your friend's girlfriend is pregnant? She practically said as much."

11

Blue Light

∞

They stayed silent for long moments after she told him her assumptions about Luciana, while Garritt navigated the nearly impassable back road. He was working over how this development would upend Juan's relatively easy, youthful lifestyle. That is, if he survived whatever mess he was already in. These mere children were both Catholic. Abortion would not be an option. He'd always felt a protective, almost parental concern for Juan but he had no idea what counsel to offer in this circumstance. He'd never actually been a parent. The responsibility of raising a child freaked him out, almost as much as the woman beside him seemed freaked about this relentless blizzard.

As he pushed his old green truck through growing mounds of white, he could feel her alternately clench her teeth or hold her breath. He didn't say anything to comfort her, though he wished she would stop doing that because he could sense her every gasp and grimace. She made *him* nervous. But he didn't feel like talking. He needed to focus on the road.

A bright sphere of blue light suddenly flared up inside the cab. It startled him and he slowed to a near stop—just in time. At that moment his tires hit buried ice and lost traction. The truck made a graceful, almost balletic slide sideways and they drifted in slow motion to a gentle stop, nose-first in a roadside ditch.

No skidding in a one-eighty. No nipping into the tree on the left. No flipping over as they plunged into the deeper gully on the other side of the road.

No one hurt.

He let out a held breath and said a silent thank-you to the light that had warned him to slow down. Once again, he felt that this couldn't be a demonic connection. So what was it? *Life-saving.* That's all he knew. Every time it happened, he grew a little more trust. "By their fruits," his father's Bible said.

Although the woman spat out some very strange words during the slow-motion skid—silly things that made him laugh, like "Holy fuddleduck!"—she didn't utter a hint of blame or protest when he yanked open his door, commanded her to "Stay put," and jumped out to pull a shovel from beneath his covered truck bed. The snow was streaming sideways again. He'd been right; only a fool would be out on these roads in this weather.

Or walking toward them through the blizzard?

Working to clear the tires, at first Garritt didn't see the figure. He thought he heard a shout, then decided it was wind howling through trees. Then he heard it again.

The man who emerged from the woods wasn't traveling fast. His legs sank up to his knees with each demanding step.

Garritt's grip tensed on the shovel. He moved toward the front of the truck, ready to jump into the cab if necessary. It was a strange thing to think in these parts, where crime wasn't usually on the minds of strangers. But Min's dire hints had gotten to him. What if the blue light wasn't warning about the ice, but about something far more sinister? He prepared himself for anything.

"Can you help me?" This time Garritt heard the shout clearly.

Reassured, he relinquished his hold on the shovel and set out to meet the figure. As he got closer, he thought he recognized Bobby Lee from Luciana's description, although the man wore an elaborate hat with rabbit fur sticking out of flaps that nearly covered his bearded face. He couldn't be sure. He hollered back cautiously, "What do you need?"

Garritt's own head was bare and freezing. Long strands of his hair blew in the icy wind; his ears stung with cold as he caught up to the man near the edge of the woods.

The guy looked exhausted. Frost coated the tips of his beard. Sweat poured off his ruddy forehead despite the freezing air. A trickle of snot ran into his mustache.

"I need a ride," he wheezed, bending to brace hands on knees. "Jeep broke down. Need a part."

"Are you Bobby Lee?"

He didn't answer but the look on his face said yes.

Garritt stuck out a bare hand. "I'm Garritt Vanderhoeven. We were looking for you, in fact."

"Why?" A fresh sheen of sweat spread over what Garritt could see of Bobby's face. "What for? You can't be needing a lawn mower in this." He said it with a sarcastic smile.

"Do you know a kid named Juan?"

A flicker of surprise, then his pale eyes grew flinty. "Depends."

"He's been arrested, only he's disappeared."

The eyes went dead, a blanket of cover. "I thought you said he was arrested."

"It's a long story. Let's get you into the cab where you can sit and catch your breath and I'll tell it to you."

Garritt led the way back toward the truck, where he hoped to find out why Bobby acted wary when he brought up Juan's name. Luciana said they were friends of a sort, and the text they'd found certainly confirmed that. Was there more she hadn't told him? In any case, the man looked like he might keel over at any moment if he didn't take a rest.

"Can you give me a ride into Hamilton?" he called over the wind as they fought through the drifts.

"If I can get this truck out of the ditch," Garritt shouted back. "I was ready to walk to your place if I couldn't. All we know is that the kid's in trouble."

"You won't find anything there except a broken Jeep," Bobby grunted. He drew up suddenly when he spotted Min, who stared back at them through the snow-streaked windshield.

"Who is she?"

"Her name is…Minda."

"Is she a friend of Juan's?"

"Not exactly. But she's worried about him and I think she knows something."

"Yeah, so do I. I'm not going with you," Bobby announced, and turned his back quickly.

"What? Why not?"

He started to move off. "She's not who you think she is. Don't let her near Juan," he threw back over his retreating shoulder. He had to yell it over the gale-force winds that had kicked up again, streaking new snow and catapulting what lay on the ground up into the air, adding density to the whiteout. For a big man, and considering his fatigue and the depth of the snow cover, he moved with surprising speed into the brush at the edge of the woods.

"Wait," Garritt hollered. "The police don't have him in custody! No one does! What's he caught up in?"

He heard a voice through the wind, "Ask *her,*" though he could no longer see a body attached to it.

He knew it! She'd been holding back.

At least she wasn't some linebacker kind of dude. A woman her size couldn't be much of a threat. They were stuck together for now but he'd sort this out as soon as the storm let up. Find out what she knew, then send the she-devil on her way.

Angry at himself for being so vulnerable to a pretty face, he grabbed up the shovel and attacked the freezing clumps that blocked the tires. He kept his head low and cursed the hair that blew into his eyes. He wrenched out the bag of sand he'd thrown into the truck bed when he changed the tires and threw some down. Then he yanked opened the driver's door.

"Get out! I need your help."

Min immediately complied, although she looked startled. She sunk her city boots into the snow and worked her way to the front of the truck as if to push.

"No," he shook his head at the idea of this five-foot-two, small-boned woman thinking she could push the heavy pickup. "Over here. I need you to steer."

As she picked her way toward him in her ridiculous boots, she called out, "Who was that guy?"

Gold flickers sparked around her.

What!? What are you telling me? Is she a dangerous liar? Or is she the answer? Why can't you just talk to me!

He brushed past her to the front and shoved at the truck, as much in frustration as an effort to get it moving again. *Because you aren't listening,* came the next thought.

He dismissed it as a product of his eroding physical and emotional energy.

Despite his exasperation, he couldn't help but notice the way Min had dipped her dumb pointed boots in and out of the drifts with ease, like dipping a delicate finger in to taste a morsel of vanilla ice cream. She moved like a dancer. It took her only a few tries before she adjusted to the clutch's idiosyncrasies and timed her efforts with Garritt's rocking pushes—a vaguely sexual cooperation that his forced resistance to her charms would never allow him to admit. He busied his mind thinking about how to chase down Bobby Lee.

Min might not be telling him much but Bobby's attitude gave him the creeps. If he had to choose whom to believe, he'd go with the woman encased in her entourage of golden lights.

By the time he worked the truck back to the main road a plow had come through, although fresh snow was piling up quickly on the polished surface. Min went back to gripping the armrest or letting out little gasps of alarm as he crept along, alert for deer, ice, and the unexpected.

They passed dense forest and swampy marshes, most of which he could no longer see but knew to be there from a lifetime of living in the area. He was grateful she didn't tell him how to drive like some women would, if they were as panicked by the road as she seemed to be.

"Who was that man?" she asked him again.

"Bobby Lee."

"What!? Wait! Turn around! We have to talk to him!!"

"He said you already have all the answers."

"Me?" She looked down at her wet boots. "I don't, honestly." A pause. "But I know a way I could find out more."

"And you didn't mention this before?"

"You already had us on this track, remember? The phone? Luciana?"

He yelled a word he rarely used and slammed his hand on the steering wheel hard enough to hurt himself. At least it saved him from the sudden impulse to hurt her.

"I need a quiet place," she practically whispered. She seemed frightened by his outburst.

She should be. He hated when he lost his temper like that—exactly like his father, a trait he'd tried to overcome for decades. He didn't say another word as he worked to quell the sudden eruption, which always left him feeling sick to his stomach.

12

Evidence

∞

No woman had crossed Garritt's threshold since he got back from Peru, and certainly none like Min ever would, if his Dutch Reformed upbringing had remained intact.

While she made a beeline for the bathroom off the kitchen, between two tiny guest rooms he never used and thank goodness he'd kept those doors closed, he dashed around, shoved dirty laundry out of sight, pushed some dishes into the sink, realizing too late that he needed to hire a housekeeper. He slipped into his bedroom—nothing a woman should see in its present state—to find something to replace Min's ruined boots.

When he came out with an old pair of Uggs, size 12, plus huge wool socks, he found her staring in wonder at his living room. He followed her gaze. Strewn across his coffee table, spread onto the floor, covering half of the old maroon couch Elizabeth had left him, lay a dozen DVDs, pamphlets, and books. Mostly books.

She picked up a thick brown volume, ragged from age and use. "*The Infinite Concept of Cosmic Creation?* I thought Agnes said you were Dutch Reformed."

"I am Dutch."

"And your church approves of this stuff?" She picked up another, *Proof of Heaven: A Neurosurgeon's Near-Death Experience and Journey into the Afterlife.* She flipped through it, read the back cover. She looked interested.

"My *parents'* church would excommunicate me, or at least ostracize me. But they already have. I am now completely unreformed," he smiled.

"*Avatar!*" She pounced on the DVD. "I loved that movie! Zoë Saldaña, she's so gorgeous. And," she spotted another, "*Close Encounters?*" She laughed heartily, as if at a private joke.

He felt a little exposed and defensive. "Those are Juan's. He's trying to educate me about subjects my childhood did not allow."

"Right. Okay," she composed herself, clearing her throat. "Let's see if we can find your dishwasher friend."

"And how do you plan to do that? Besides, even if we knew where he is, there's not much we can do about it." He thumbed toward the windows. "Have you forgotten what we just drove through? We're stuck here for a while."

∞

She hadn't forgotten a minute of that terrifying drive. Or the look on that old man's face when he saw her. She sensed something truly wrong about the guy. Hard to explain. As if he were, not one, but several people in one package. If that was Bobby Lee, then this situation had just gotten a lot more complicated.

Not to mention that she was now stranded in a strange man's house without trekking gear or pepper spray. (Routine issue, currently back in San Diego.) About three frozen miles back down the road, they'd passed an aging trailer park but that was it for neighbors. Just fighting their way on foot through the drifts clogging Garritt's driveway took all her strength. If she had to flee in this blizzard without snowshoes, she'd be easy prey for predators of any kind, animal or human.

She took in the surroundings, sizing them up for safety. The house itself seemed little more than a flimsy, rectangular pre-fab plopped over a basement in the midst of a cleared spot in the woods, larger than a double-wide mobile home but not by much. The yard was surrounded by dense trees, with remnants from the clear-cutting visible along the perimeter: old stumps, piles of debris sticking out of white mounds. She tried not to think what vicious animals might lurk behind or in those wood piles, things bigger than the chipmunk that scurried away after taking their measure and chirping his warnings.

Born and raised in arid Southern California meant that densely wooded areas made her uneasy. Worse, though, was the fright caused by Garritt's angry outburst in the truck. The shock of his language, the physical violence when he slammed his hand...men who lost control that way threw her off balance. Time hadn't mended that reflex. So when she saw his copy of *Close Encounters,* the irony of it made her laugh out loud, which shaved away some of the rigidity that had settled over her during their drive.

Of course he was right. She'd lied to him by omission and he could sense that. She tried not to think about what would happen if he got angry again while she was stranded alone with him in this house. She had promised to come clean. How clean? How much would satisfy him, and how much could she withhold and still feel safe here?

When she first spotted Garritt's secrets lying all over his untidy living room, she was grateful it wasn't porn. Yet this spirit-nerd material didn't fit the perception she'd formed of him and that creeped her out all over again. What else was he hiding? From the looks of things, he didn't have a wife or girlfriend.

He did have good taste in literature, though. She'd have to look up that neurosurgeon book—and the other one, the *Infinite* one, that one gave her chills when she held it. Old and mysterious, exactly the kind of book she loved to find on her quest for arcane tomes about subjects that frightened most people. She wondered if Tippi at Short Stacks could find her a copy. She'd have to snap a photo when he wasn't looking. At least her stupid *no service* phone should work for that.

So. Dutch boy. Couldn't be that familiar with much beyond his religion, despite the reading material. She'd have to figure out how to do her remote viewing without revealing everything. He only wanted to know about Juan. She didn't have to tell him about the artifact even if she saw it—and she hoped she would.

Take it slow, she decided. Maybe don't hit him right off with the history of the government's Stargate program, which gave birth to Blackthorn's current status.

They'd had to go underground in the mid-nineties, after Jimmy Carter let it slip to the media that during his Presidency a Stargate remote viewer located a downed Russian spy plane for the CIA. That set off a huge conflagration of ridicule in the media over what was supposed to be top-secret research, which hugely embarrassed the top brass who'd supported it. And to those who hadn't, remote viewing was either "horseshit" or "demonic," depending on the man. (And they were all men back then.) The powers in charge quickly agreed to denounce, de-fund, and dismiss the project. Never mind that they'd instigated the program because their intel confirmed that both Russians and Chinese were far ahead of us in their applications of extended human mental skills. That left entire teams of trained researchers and remote viewers with nothing to do but write books or sell "psychic training" classes.

Min met some of those pioneers during her own training. Most blamed Carter for the shut-down but she privately believed that the real reason was because a *woman* viewer found that plane back in the Cold War seventies. A mere woman—a psychic, no less—who out-performed all their expensive war toys. She loved the story:

Program developer Dale Graff at the Air Force's Foreign Technology Division was approached by a low-ranking service member from a secretarial pool who'd heard rumors about his psi research. She felt she had the right qualifications to train as a remote viewer. (In books he wrote about it later, he gave her a code name but another colleague blew Rosemary Smith's cover.) He invited her to join the group that conducted some of the earliest government experiments in remote viewing. But then one day, desperate, the brass handed her a photo of a Russian-designed bomber and told her to locate it "somewhere in Africa." Typical! *Oh, and hurry,* they said, because other countries were also looking, eager for its juicy contents. Two weeks with planes and satellites had yielded nothing, so it was all on Rosemary Smith.

Within moments of quieting her mind, Rosemary drew a map-sketch. Within hours, they'd given her a real map and she circled a location, and then, at their request, she placed an X where they would find the spy plane crashed in the jungle. They were searching in the wrong area. (Other viewers were brought in for support but only Rosemary's data reached the distant search team.)

Two days later, they found the spy plane within *three miles* of Rosemary's coordinates. That was extraordinary success for a remote viewer back in the early days of the program, and it was her first official operation. How humiliating for the old men! A *secretary*. Using only her mind.

To appease skeptics at the top ("a low-ranking female *psychic?*") the Air Force, CIA, and NSA security conducted investigations but the facts showed that Rosmary's data was definitely received by the search team before the airplane was located.

Min laughed hysterically when she first heard this tale. The military-industrial contractors who build fancy search technology must have soiled their trousers when they heard it.

Behind the velvet curtain today—that was another story. One that would surely blow this insulated Dutch dude's mind. She'd better take it easy on him.

"Listen, since you're reading all this," she gestured at the books, "you probably know that some people are psychic, right? I mean, I don't know what your family's church thinks of it—most fundamentalists consider it the Devil's work—but I was born this way. That's how I knew your friend was in trouble."

She hoped that would satisfy him. No need to go into the sophisticated corporate or military applications of formal remote viewing. Nothing about the extensive training she'd been through. Just your neighborhood psychic, an everyday fortune teller. She needed a more appropriate outfit to play the role convincingly, maybe some hoop earrings, a bright scarf around her head…

"His name is Juan. And I knew that about you. You gave it away at the beginning," he shrugged. "What do you need, then? Incense? Candles? You asked for a quiet place and the snow has certainly given us that." He indicated the muffled beauty outside.

She laughed at herself. *Why was I even worried?*

Big puffs of white were coming down so fast that when she looked out through the matching sets of windows, front and back of the room, the forbidding woods weren't visible. On another day, the place would have been filled with bright sunlight, surely a strategy of the prefab designers to make the house seem larger to potential buyers. She found the snowfall mesmerizing and beautiful, so rare in her experience. She could stand and stare for hours…

"Wait, I forgot to give you these."

Garritt stepped toward her awkwardly and held out some gray socks and a massive pair of Ugg boots. Once again she felt tongue-tied by a stranger's kindness. She quietly reached to accept his offering, pushing aside a slight squeamishness she hoped he didn't detect.

Since she hadn't responded to his question about candles and incense, he made his own decisions. He brushed past her to drag an aging recliner, covered in faded, navy-blue corduroy, closer to the empty fireplace. He gestured for her to sit.

That's when she realized that, oddly, there was no television in the room to play those DVDs. Must be in his bedroom, behind that closed door. Or maybe down the wooden stairs she'd passed in the kitchen that led down to another closed door, which probably opened into a basement room. A tremor of *Psycho* reaction shivered down her spine. Like every serial killer movie she'd refused to watch…

"Let me get some wood for a fire. You put those boots on and I'll be right back."

He disappeared out the kitchen door and reappeared in the back yard. She watched him through the window as he scraped snow off a bright blue tarp with his arm, then pulled it back to reveal a tall pile of neatly stacked firewood. He certainly was prepared.

If only he'd conjure up another pizza, she couldn't help thinking while she slipped out of her wet anklets and tucked her frozen feet gratefully into the SmartWool, ignoring her skittishness about wearing a strange man's socks. They seemed clean enough. Or her toes were frozen enough not to care.

But remote viewing on an empty stomach, that was not a joke. If skewed by hunger, her visions could come out scrambled, if at all. Balanced blood sugar—sometimes she thought that was the whole secret to her skill, except she was the only viewer she knew who had this need.

She tugged on the boots and despite her reluctance, luxuriated in the warm sheep's wool as it cushioned her abused toes. *Ahhhh…*

This might in fact be her best chance, while he was out. She settled back into the old chair, cast off her uneasiness, and focused.

Nothing. Useless as the phone that lost service when they left Veenlanden.

She tried again.

Pizza, at Avery's Café. That's all she could see.

Stop with the stomach, Minda!

Food had always been so important to her. Gramma Julene used to tease her, "If you were a jelly bean, you wouldn't be happy until you had mashed potatoes and fried chicken for friends!"

At the thought of her grandmother, she suddenly felt her presence in the room.

Honey, don't you let that boy hurt you, she could hear her saying. *Not again. You keep your wits about you. You know what to do.*

The thoughts came so naturally, it was as if they were her own. But she knew better. She felt her grandmother's love pour into her at the same time, filling her with comfort as it often did.

Only Gramma Julene knew what happened when Min was ten. They agreed never to tell her mother; it would break her heart. Instead, her grandmother spirited her off to a place where she knew the man who managed it: a training gym for would-be boxers. That's where she first learned how to defend herself, after school before her mother got off work. Cale, her protective older brother, was busy with his high-school friends and never suspected or he might have done something stupid.

The old guy who taught her—wiry, tall, gray-speckled hair—he wasn't tough with her at all. When Gramma Julene told him the story (she left out a few parts for Min's sake), he quickly agreed to show the fourth-grader how to poke an eye, deliver a knee or foot to the groin, twist her wrist out of a grip, and most importantly, run like the wind the minute she got free.

Later on, the Navy filled in a few more tactics and Blackthorn gave her, not only more training, but state-of-the-art military equipment to back her up. And pepper spray. If only she had it with her.

She wondered again how dangerous this Dutch boy could be, with his unusual interests so close to her own, not to mention his skills in the kitchen…

Focus, Min, focus.

Before she could scold herself again for her food obsession, or the distraction of this man, Garritt came back in a blast of cold with an armful of snowy logs. In no time, he had a fire going and Min propped her feet gratefully near the flames.

"I'm starving," he announced. "I'm going to fix us something to eat. You hungry?"

"Ravenous."

"Good. You enjoy the fire. I'm pretty sure a full stomach makes the psychic chores easier, right? I'll be in the kitchen."

How did he know that?

Confession

The thing Garritt learned, searching through those books and videos, was that his golden glitter lights weren't exactly impersonal. He'd found it in the last book he read, the first one Min picked up.

The book described how "Advanced Minds" from other dimensions could flash a concentrated beam from the center of their energy bodies to provide support to people on a certain kind of evolutionary-growth quest. They wouldn't interfere, these spirit mentors, but they might shine their light in a spectrum humans could perceive. They did this to provide moral support during one's earth journey. For people who'd studied with them in between or in past lifetimes, they might flash their lights to confirm a thought, inspire, encourage—or warn. The book said different colors signified different specialties of the Beings behind the light. That part confused him. And what if the person failed to notice them?

If a tree falls in the woods and you're not there to see it, does it make a sound? Science says no; a pair of ears are needed to perceive the air's vibration. But he wasn't sure he perceived these light-energies with his physical eyes. Vision is a complicated process. Could it be that his eyes registered inter-dimensional signals, a perception that began in his mind?

And did that matter? Fact was, he perceived them and they guided him. All of this indicated that they were not, in fact, demons tempting him to save brown-skinned, non-elect people in defiance of his father's interpretation of "God's will."

Another chapter in the book hinted that these mentors might do this light-flashing to alert their charge to imminent, life-threatening danger.

Since it was up to the individual whether or not they noticed and heeded the warning, that wasn't considered interference; only warning.

The blue flash out on the road—it had definitely warned him! Which is what brought the chapter back to his mind while his hands were busy in the kitchen.

But was the blue light warning about the ice, or Bobby Lee? At this point, he couldn't know. He needed to get to Bobby Lee as soon as the storm let up. He'd seen the man's face. He knew more about Juan than he'd let on.

He really should finish reading that book. It was the most helpful so far, starting with words that told him he wasn't going crazy. *Maybe it can help me over this fear of demons,* he thought, as the she-devil herself clomped into his kitchen wearing his sheepskin boots.

"Let me help."

He laughed and pointed with the knife in his hand. "In those?" The Uggs had to be at least twice the size of her dainty feet.

"Well, at least they're bringing life back to my toes! Thank you," she smiled. "Now stop pointing that weapon at me," she added seriously, and firmly moved his wrist away.

A thrill ran up his arm from where she touched him.

"How do you feel about eating more pizza?" he asked to distract himself. "It's not very original, but I've got some ingredients that might make it work. And a frozen crust from Avery's."

She smiled—no, she glowed—and the smile was more like a grin. "Perfect. What can I do?"

"Here. Wash this parsley." He shoved the dripping, dirt-covered bundle at her and couldn't help but notice the smoothness of the skin that stretched up her wrist and disappeared under her powder-blue sweater, although the flicker of surprise on her face told him that she hadn't really wanted to get her pretty hands dirty. He laughed at her again and this time she joined in, gamely rinsing the greens under his faucet.

So, she's not much of a cook.

An hour later, they were seated on the floor by his fireplace at a low table made from a brass serving tray he found at a garage sale. They toasted their feet as they toasted the storm with matching jelly glasses of Chianti. It was only three o'clock in the afternoon but the darkened skies outside made it feel later—and awkwardly cozy for two strangers as the fluffy white crystals now floated elegantly beyond the windows, all sweetness and charm.

"How does it work?" Garritt asked to break the stillness.

"What?"

"Your psychic powers? I've always wondered. It's not like I could ask the dominee."

"Dominee?"

"Pastor in our church."

"Oh. Right. Um, I don't know, really. I've just always known how."

She seemed reluctant to pursue it, she was focused so intently on her pizza, which really wasn't his best work. He'd found some mystery-meat leftovers in the freezer that he threw on over the garlic oil and dried thyme, and some dried mushrooms he reconstituted and added to the seasoned, sun-dried tomatoes from a jar. Only the parsley she washed was fresh. Mostly he buried everything in goat cheese mozzarella made at a nearby farm and that seemed to do the trick.

He suddenly, desperately wanted to know this woman better, the one hiding behind the cool façade. The only way to do that, he knew, was to make himself more vulnerable.

He took a deep breath and said, "Not me."

"What do you mean?" She paused with a hearty slice halfway to her mouth.

Garritt weighed carefully. He would probably never see this woman again. She was so far out of his tiny circle of community—so very far, even from the few people who still spoke to him after his renouncement. In fact, if his neighbors could see through this blizzard, tongues would wag so fast, the sound would reach his parents in Holland and his phone would be vibrating by now, his mother demanding to know if he had lost his mind. Most thought he lost it long ago. But this…having this woman in particular in his own house…it violated all their prejudiced concepts of what was good and proper.

So why not?

"You know that story about me, the one you probably read about?"

"Running through the jungle—that one?"

"Yeah." He sipped some wine. "No one really knows what happened."

"Right. They said what you did was impossible."

He could see that she was trying to be dainty with the pizza, which oozed over her fingers from too much cheese.

"It *was* impossible. I couldn't have done it without help."

"Help?"

"Yeah."

"What kind of help?"

She set down the slice, finally as interested in him as she'd been in the pizza, although it seemed to him that she was being extra thorough as she licked the cheese off her fingers.

"The kind that only appears when it feels like it."

"So are you going to tell me, or are we going to play guessing games?"

"It's just—I've never told anyone. In fact, I've never spoken it aloud. It's too bizarre."

"But you can tell me, because I can see a kid I don't know in a cabin I've never been to, and that's about as bizarre as it gets?" She picked up the slice again.

"Um, yeah."

"So?"

"So something surreal happened to me in that rainforest." He had a thought. "You know those scenes in *Avatar*, on the planet—what's it called?"

"Pandora?"

"Right—you know when they're running through the forest, how the ground lights up beneath their feet when they run over it?"

"Yeah, and everything glows?"

"Exactly. That's close to it. I saw lights."

There, he'd said it.

"I still do."

And that.

"What kind of lights?"

"Little flashes of gold. Like, well, like it was glitter poured from a bottle—only from the sky."

He could tell she couldn't grasp it but she asked, "And then what happened?"

"The glitter showed me the way."

Min shoved more pizza in her mouth to give herself time to think about how to respond, forgetting to be ladylike. This guy definitely wasn't what she'd thought. At all. Sitting across from her in the firelight, hair gleaming, he looked like a schoolboy waiting for her to strike him for blasphemy.

A pang of compassion rang through her. He must feel like an alien in his own culture—like she felt, until the Navy and Blackthorn, Amrita, the others. (And now she was thinking to ostracize herself from them as well.)

"I believe you," was all she could manage. Not very supportive but she had so much to conceal herself.

He looked relieved.

"But how did you leap across that river gorge they talked about? Agnes said it was not humanly possible. Until you, apparently."

"Honestly? I have no idea. I was insane to try it. Or desperate enough. I think now the lights had something to do with it."

His eyes turned inward, as if they'd gone back to the scene, and she went with him.

"I ran…my feet left the cliff…I could feel my momentum slow and gravity pull at me—and then something lifted me up from below."

She felt it, too, heart pounding in her chest.

"I kind of floated up over the edge of the cliff on the other side of the gorge before I fell. On my face. In the mud," he laughed.

Min's vision faded as he came back to her in the present. She took a breath to clear the scene from her own head—but not before she understood, viscerally, the terror of that leap. The certainty of his failure.

"How did you ever get the courage…" she whispered in awe.

He shifted uneasily.

"That was very strange. I reasoned that I was going to die anyway, from jungle rot or starvation or hungry jaguars. This way, at least I would have tried, you know, to get help for the others. On the slim chance that I might make it. I mean, I saw vines hanging off the opposite cliff that maybe I could grab. But mostly I thought of the little girl and her mother who'd been sitting next to me on the plane.

"She was so excited to visit her *abuela,* her grandmother's village. I speak a little Spanish I learned from Juan; the mother and daughter knew some English. We used hand signs," he gestured. "They were South American, like most of the people on the plane because we flew out of Ecuador. They were the kind of people—"

He stopped suddenly and the stricken look on his face told her everything.

"Brown-skinned?"

He reddened, which his pale skin did so thoroughly. "Yeah." He took a deep breath and went on grimly, "I was going to say, the kind my parents believe are not among God's elect. His Chosen…because—this is the sick part—because their skin color means God is punishing them for their ancestors' sins. That's what we were told as kids."

He paused to gauge her reaction and she could see how ashamed he felt over his parents' beliefs.

"Please forgive me; I don't believe that shit. And not one of them will admit to this racism outside their church walls. That's one of many reasons I left that place as soon as I was old enough."

She wiped her fingers on her napkin, took a sip of wine. She wasn't offended. In fact, she admired him for having the guts to admit what many churches never would: that their very interpretation of their scriptures was clotted with racism.

She also admired his courage for walking away from what must have been his entire family and social circle. Poor guy seemed mortified to have brought it up. He tried to cover it by going on with his story.

"Anyway, when the wind sheer dropped the plane out of the sky, I don't know, I just threw myself over the mother and daughter to protect them—which was stupid, really, because how could I? The plane around us was going to shatter.

"But the girl reminded me of Juan's little sister. Coquis, they call her. I've known her since she was seven and this little girl looked so much like her. After the crash, she and her mother were lying beside me in the jungle. People were screaming, crying, praying—the ones who lived, anyway."

She saw him go back to it—and the scene unfolded in her own mind again. She tried to resist it—the sounds, the smells, sights—horrible.

And so vivid! Why was she seeing this? This level of psychic connection did not happen to her! At least it never had before.

"The pilot," he went on, lost in his memory, "his co-pilot was dead. Decapitated, actually," he grimaced. "You couldn't blame the pilot for his reaction but he'd lost his mind. I didn't trust him. He ordered everyone to stay with the plane but I knew he was wrong. I could smell leaking fuel and there was no way any rescue planes would see us from the air. The canopy closed up over us as soon as we hit the jungle floor and the jet split in half. Before he realized what he was saying, the pilot told me that it all happened so fast, they hadn't sent a distress signal. Then he pointed to a little pile of rubble. 'That's the transmitter,' he said."

"The emergency locator?"

"Yes." Garritt sipped, eyes glazed, barely aware of the wine in his hand. "It's the standard advice, you know: stay with the wreckage, wait for rescue."

She nodded, the scene heartbreakingly vivid in her mind. Mangled airplane parts, a fuselage split in two, scattered filthy clothes and a few bloody but dazed people digging through broken luggage. She tried to mentally turn away from the rest, the smells of fire and death, the still bodies—hollow abandoned shells—and the scattered scraps of human flesh…

"I felt so strongly that we would find help if we walked east. With the impassably steep Andes behind us to the west, it was the only way. But we had to go soon, before more people died." He shook his head, back in that moment. "Nobody would listen to me. One guy who spoke English told me all the reasons I was wrong, all the ways to die if we left the plane…but I couldn't shake the sense of urgency. I had to go. Alone, as it turned out."

The visions piled up as if she'd set out to remote view the whole incident: the suffocating humidity, the wailing. She hadn't asked to see this. She did everything she knew to block it, in fact. Nothing worked.

Her hands began to shake. The panic and fear were…primal. Garritt's frustration penetrated her liver. As he described reaching the pongo, the deep gorge that blocked his progress, then fighting his way up and down the length of the cliff looking for a shorter way across, she could feel him yank at vines, wrestle with the tangle of vegetation clutching and scratching at him. She felt the sting of a million tiny cuts in his flesh. Where the river carved that deep canyon through the rainforest, sunlight poured in uninhibited by any tree canopy. Plants grew in riotous response to this life-giving force, turning the sparse, shady rainforest floor he ran so easily across into dense jungle along the steep sides of the canyon. She could hear and smell the water far down a dizzying drop, where the river rushed over massive boulders the size of small sheds.

She also felt Garritt's inner turmoil, the drive to live versus the drive to serve, all his confusion about whether what he was about to do would be "what's right." That feeling was so familiar, it twisted in her belly.

"From the sun's position, I could see that the river flowed north. There was no other way to go east but to cross it. Still, to answer your question, when it came right down to it, no, I did not have the courage. My feet refused to move toward that gorge, to certain death on the rocks below." His eyes filled with shame.

The pain of his injuries, the sorrow over his cowardice, and the relentless heat made the air in his living room almost too heavy to breathe. Sweat ran off his/her forehead. She'd never experienced this form of psychic entanglement before.

Hurry, she wanted to say. *Bring us back to the present.* But her tongue wouldn't move any more than his/her feet would. She couldn't help but think of her own recent lapse of courage.

Don't feel bad, she wanted to say, *it's a survival instinct, the most powerful instinct we have!* But she couldn't speak. Her heart pounded with his. Why couldn't she stop this?

"I'd even cleared the brush with my bare hands so I could get a good run-up to the ledge. It was all ready. But I couldn't do it. And then I heard—no, I felt something like an inner voice, strong. It said with infinite calm, *You can make it.*"

She held her breath with him, felt something pass through her, something bright and sure.

"I think if I'd been paying attention, I might have seen the lights then. But I was too scared. And too fixated."

He shrugged. "Maybe that same force had guided me all along. Maybe that's what got me to run off on my own in the first place. I don't know. But I did it. I backed up and ran. I jumped. And halfway across, I felt that bizarre lifting sensation, and something else—the golden lights just ahead of me."

She couldn't see them—the first thing he'd described that she didn't see or sense.

"After I landed, I got tangled in vines. Lianas, they call them. I fought them, ripped my clothes half off trying, but I couldn't budge. Then I heard something rustling behind me."

He paused, took another sip of wine.

She flashed first on the opossum at the dune, then dread cascaded through her as Garritt's fears flooded her mind again, one after another: black jaguar, tawny puma, patterned viper wrapped around a vine, slithering, deadly. She shuddered violently and the sweat trickled down her back. Amazing that he didn't notice her visible reactions to all this.

"I thought, *this is it*. The monkeys were screaming everywhere. I turned, expecting a fight for my life, and there it was again: golden glitter, pouring down from the sky like someone had taken a God-sized tube of it and tipped it over. Big, fat flakes like the kind they let you use in elementary school. They were so vivid, so real, I reached out to catch some. Nothing. I moved forward, because the vines somehow suddenly fell away from me—and I reached for the glitter again. Still nothing there. By the time I realized it was only light, I was already traveling along a clear path and I just kept going."

Wonder. Awe. Gratitude.

"After that, I ran. Every time I needed direction, the lights would appear. *This way*, they said. The monkey calls started to sound like directions. Magnificent birds in fabulous colors—they flew where I needed to go. Branches swept out of my way and the ground before me cleared.

"I left the dense jungle along the river bank and entered the cooler rainforest, where shade kept the undergrowth in check, which made the running easier. I slid down hills and fought up rises, and all the while I felt safe, guided, and definitely not alone. Once, I caught my foot in a draping liana and went flying, but time slowed down and I was able to right myself, regain my balance, and land on my feet. They just kept running."

"Wow," she breathed, overcome by the exhilaration he'd felt. She'd seen everything except the lights. "No wonder they called it a miracle."

"It wasn't," he turned to her for emphasis. "And it wasn't me. I had a lot of help. And everything I'd ever been taught about the world told me that such things were not possible. That only demons would do this, to trick people. That my soul was on the brink of destruction, soon to be claimed by dark forces who would come for what I owed them. That I was losing my mind."

"Do you believe that?"

"Not anymore. Oh, I won't say it hasn't scared the shit out of me for weeks on end. I still have nightmares. When I got back, I couldn't tell anyone the whole truth. They'd say I'd gone mad, or I was doomed to Hell, or both. So I started reading." He indicated the books lying everywhere. "That helped some."

She wanted to comfort him, to tell him everything she knew about such matters. But she didn't know where to begin.

"One more thing," he said. "I didn't see those lights again until you came into the restaurant. You must have wondered why this guy was staring at you. They completely surrounded you. Why?"

His blue eyes lanced her with sudden accusation.

Taken aback by his intensity, already unsettled by her new psychic acuity, she mumbled, "I have no idea. I don't see lights like that."

Why not? Why could I feel everything, see everything, but not the lights?

"But I'm certain they aren't here to escort you to Hell," she laughed nervously.

He kept staring at her like he wanted to separate the fibers of her DNA with his eyes alone.

"What?" she flinched. "You think I've come for your soul?" At that, she laughed uproariously.

He didn't join in.

They lapsed into staring at the crackling fire, whose flames licked up around the logs like the silence that rose to envelop them.

She thought of the deep ignorance they shared about things that affected them every day, and for which no one had prepared them. Not Gramma Julene's Baptists, nor Garritt's Dutch dominees. Neither films nor books nor social chatter, nor any of the crazy things they could find on YouTube or Instagram.

Reverend Ben. She wanted to tell him about Reverend Ben.

Instead she said, "You know, when I was little they didn't believe me. They thought I'd gotten inside information somehow, or that I was making things up. Until one day, when my brother Cale set off to school, I saw trouble up ahead for him. I tried to tell my mother. She ignored me. Later on, when he came home with a broken arm, she came to me and hugged me and said she'd never doubt me again. That changed my life. Because if she believed in me, then I could believe in me. From then on, I learned how to use my skill.

"And it is a skill, by the way. You used those lights to guide you. How did you know to do that?"

"I…hmm. I never thought of that." His face softened a little.

"Exactly. Because this is a skill no one teaches us! Because it scares them to even think of it."

She took another bite of the now-cold pizza. With a greasy thumb, she pointed toward the books on the couch and talked around it, forgetting about Gramma Julene's rules of decorum. "Those people—they are trying to think of it, and to tell others. But they don't really know the answers either."

"So who does?"

"We do."

"How do you figure?"

"*We* are the ones experiencing it, right? And we *use* it—yes, that's right. I use my skills all the time, for lots of things," she admitted when he looked at her in surprise.

If he only knew.

"By using it, we learn."

"You could be right. I experienced much more than these books describe."

"Exactly. Don't you think that's enough?"

"So is this how you can help us find Juan?"

"Yes, and now that my stomach is full, I am ready to try again."

She was too embarrassed to explain that he'd been correct, that without his pizza, she would not succeed. Every one of her arcane books suggested fasting, or vegetarianism at the very least, for "enhanced psychic powers." Not true for her. The other viewers always teased her about this glitch in her abilities. "Experts" all over the internet insisted that fasting was key to releasing one's psychic skills. More BS to fool the masses, she decided. Or to keep them down. "Thank you for that delicious pizza, by the way." Somehow better than the one she'd eaten at Avery's.

He blushed and started to clear away the mess, leaving the emptied jelly glasses and the traw-covered Chianti bottle, still half full. Tasty as it was, more drink would not help her viewing at all. She resisted the temptation.

"I'm only sorry it wasn't up to my usual standards." He turned toward the front windows, fist full of dirty paper napkins. Outside it was still snowing, and growing rapidly darker. "I don't think we're going anywhere tonight."

She'd been afraid of that.

"I'll call the B&B for you to let them know you won't be back. At least my phone has service here."

"I wish I could reach my roommate in San Diego. She's probably worried about me," she said suddenly. Truthfully, she was the worried one. Where would she sleep?

"Do you want to use my phone to call her?"

"Oh, that will reassure her, calling from some strange man's phone."

They laughed, and it had a cleansing effect, washing away the unexpected intimacy of Garritt's confession, lightening the mood. After the psychic communion of his jungle experience, she was feeling even more vulnerable than when they first arrived, Too bizarre. She could never tell him about that. She wondered if her head injury did something the doctors' tests couldn't detect. "Let me see what I can see before we call anyone, okay? Even if we're stuck here, I'll feel better if we can locate your poor dishwasher." *And my alien artifact.*

She got up from the floor to settle herself on the couch and he went back to gathering paper plates.

"Would you mind? Just sit still for a minute," she commanded. "If you move around too much, it distracts me."

Really, Minda? Is that what's distracting you? His movements?

"Sure." He set the debris on the table again, dropped into an easy lotus despite his extraordinarily long legs, and watched with great interest while she straightened her spine, measured her breath, and tried to calm her emotional state. She closed her eyes. She gasped.

14

A Broken Oath

∞

Garritt jumped up from the floor. "What is it?"

She didn't know what to say. Wade. She'd seen Wade, not Juan. Face down at the edge of an icy lake, dark blood staining the snow beneath him. The last time she remote-viewed a dead body it was her baby cousin.

"What did you see? Juan—is he okay? Are you okay?"

"I saw…someone else. Lying beside some water. Blood in the snow."

A waterfall of cold plummeted through her stomach and out her toes, leaving her weak. Was Wade dead? Who killed him? Why? Where was the rest of their team?

"Wait," she put up a hand as Garritt started toward her. "Let me see more."

She sat up straight again, closed her eyes, tuned in to other members of the team, Alex, Ripper, Susan, Wren, Luther. She'd never seen faces so clearly before: distress, confusion. They were sitting at a conference table in a familiar space, Blackthorn's San Diego headquarters. She opened her eyes as a wave of dizziness passed over her.

"What? What is it?" Garritt towered over the couch.

She stared up at him. Stared through him.

"Is it Juan? Is he … "

"He's in dire trouble but no, I didn't see Juan. Not yet."

"Then what, dammit. Say something!"

He knocked books from the couch to sit beside her, which jolted her uncomfortably. She hadn't fully come back from the vision yet, and she didn't have the physical or mental coordination to explain that to him right now. She was surprised to see that he looked protective, not pissed, which is what she'd expected since she hadn't answered his rapid-fire interrogation.

She took a deep breath, let it out.

"The people I work for ..."

"What about them?"

She sank back against the maroon fabric to move away from Garritt's clamoring energy. "The dead man—he was one of my co-workers."

"You never did explain what you do for a living." He stood up again, this time definitely irritated, waving his arms around. "I'm sorry for your loss but I've brought you here, to my home. I've told you things I vowed never to tell another soul. I think it's high time you told me who you really are."

"Or what?"

"I'm not sure yet."

He strode toward the fireplace, toyed with an old Christmas candle on the mantel shelf that looked like something his mother—or wife—would have given him. He bent to grab the iron poker and stab at the logs, which blazed up anew. A waft of acrid smoke filled Min's nostrils.

Is he threatening me? She sat up straight again. She didn't feel that. She felt hollow inside.

Who would kill Wade? The vision certainly looked like Michigan, not San Diego. Right here, right now, in this snowstorm. So why was the team out west and not with Wade, or out looking for him? She cursed the fact that she couldn't tell if it had already happened, would happen, or was happening now.

"Luciana said Bobby Lee lives near a swamp."

"Yeah, why?"

"What else do you know about him?" She should let the team know that Bobby Lee might harm Wade—if he hadn't already. And how did Wade know to go after Bobby, if that's what happened?

"I don't know any more than I've already told you. But I'm the one asking questions." He strode back to loom over her. "What's your part in all this?"

I have to tell him.

She was completely in his power right now. In his home, reliant on his transportation—if the storm ever let up. She couldn't even get a call out on her own phone. From his perspective, she could be just some random woman with a scar, a runaway abuse victim of a probably-lunatic husband who might show up any minute to kill her and maybe a lot of others in the crossfire. Such things happened all too often. And yet Garritt brought her on this quest for a kid he must really care about, based only on her psychic vision. He'd accepted that without question. Trusted her.

He was right. He'd brought her into his home, fed her, worried about her freezing feet so much, he lent her his own socks. With his long hair and his nurturing pizza—this was no ordinary white guy.

And his golden lights! He'd shared his most important secret with her, the one that made him believe he was losing his mind. *Sometimes you have to trust,* echoed the voice in her head. She sighed deeply. "I work for a company called Blackthorn."

"That's a start. Who are they? What do they do?" He was pacing now.

"We are government contractors. We find things and we move them."

"Things?"

"You know, pieces of things that nobody wants to cause trouble in the world."

"Wait a minute—are you telling me…"

"Yes. We scavenge bits of extraterrestrial craft that have crashed anywhere in the world, and we—dispose of them." She kept her voice gentle; held him in a steady gaze. He collapsed into the dark blue armchair and stared blankly at her. "It's true," she said, now eager to convince him.

She had never broken her oaths of silence before, never told a soul. Buoyant peaks began to bubble up in her brain. Liberation called to her.

"It's as true as your golden glitter—or my ability to pinpoint with eighty percent accuracy where we might find these troubling artifacts. I'm even more accurate when we're on site."

He sputtered a word she couldn't understand, sucked in a breath, gripped the chair, leaned toward her, and spat, "Why would you *do* such a thing? More than anything, people want to know if we're alone in the universe! Can you imagine what it would mean if they could believe what you're telling me? Holy *shit*, woman!"

"Yes, I can," she answered smoothly. "Which is why I'm here."

"Wait—I don't get it. Why *are* you here? Did Bobby Lee really have a piece of an alien spaceship?" He laughed derisively. "You've got to be kidding me! Come on, this is not a joke. Where is Juan? Who *are* you?"

"I am exactly who I've told you I am. My name is Minda Blake, I work for a government contractor called Blackthorn, and we do clean-up work all over the world. We keep this big secret and you, Garritt Vanderhoeven, must swear to keep it as well. I have never, not ever, told a single other soul what I've just told you—not even my own mother," she added quietly, "and it could cost me more than my job."

She watched her meaning sink in, the light going on in his eyes as he connected the dots between her vision of a dead body and what she'd just said.

"They would kill you for telling me this?" His voice had dropped a few levels.

"Such things have been known to happen." She turned to stare out the front windows.

"Did they kill your coworker, then," he asked the back of her head.

She didn't turn around.

"I don't know. I don't think so. Wade—that was his name—he wasn't the type to spill secrets."

Or was he? He was new, after all.

More likely he'd come for the artifact and tangled with Bobby Lee and that's why Bobby was running through the blizzard…because he'd shot Wade and left him to bleed to death in the snow.

"You mean they kill people for telling the world what it deserves to know?"

"Not exactly. Sometimes people who know too much simply disappear." She turned back to him and shrugged, "Maybe they commit suicide because the pressure of keeping the secret is too much."

It was the same explanation they'd given her when she asked, a story she highly doubted. Most of her coworkers bought it, because it soothed their conscience. After that, she asked no more questions about sources who couldn't be found when their families and the media went looking, like the man who reported the UAP that led them to Rosy Dunes.

Which gave her an idea about how to convey the seriousness.

She stood up. "Did you hear about anyone in this area who's gone missing recently? Besides Juan, I mean."

He thought for a minute. She could see wheels turning, then his face flickered with surprise. Then doubt.

"An old guy down in Allegan who lived alone—why?"

"That old guy, do you suppose he was ever out in the woods in the dark? Likely to see something other people didn't?"

"Maybe," he said slowly. "Franklin Visser was a relative of the super-wealthy Grand Rapids Vissers, second only to the Richard DeVos family. Those families run everything in the Dutch Triangle so the story made the local news. What does this have to do—"

"What did the news say about his death?"

"It was an accident. The guy liked to fish before dawn on the river. They said he probably went over the Allegan dam in the dark because they never found his body. Are you saying…" He stopped.

She moved toward the fireplace to warm fingers that had gone cold when she saw Wade bleeding in the snow. "That he might have made a phone call, to report a UAP—an unidentified aerial phenomenon. A UFO. Over the dunes. Which of course was relayed to our offices in San Diego and a team was sent out." She turned to look at him. "Mine."

He seemed dazed.

"That's okay, you don't have to believe me. But maybe now you understand what your dishwasher friend might be involved in. He's in serious danger. I will try again to see if I can find him—"

"Wait a minute. What do you get out of this? Why did Bobby Lee tell me not to trust you?"

"Did he?"

"You're what scared him off."

Why would the old man know anything about her? Did he know about Blackthorn?

"You said you know where to find this man?"

"Yeah, Burt's Crossing—in Hamilton. It's the only logical place."

"Can we get to it?"

She started to kick off Garritt's Uggs—reluctantly.

"Are you crazy? We barely made it here! And put those boots back on," he ordered.

She ignored his command. "Life and death, Mr. Vanderhoeven. Other peoples' lives might be at stake." *Or mine,* she thought.

Or Garritt's, she realized with alarm.

"I'm not taking you anywhere until you explain why you're here. You haven't yet."

"True," she conceded.

She sat down again, reluctant to take off his socks. She perched on the edge of the cushions, sized him up again. He'd not only shared his own secrets with her, but now she saw how she might have put his life in danger. Especially if the alternate scenario taking shape in her mind were true.

If Wade was already dead, Blackthorn might think she had something to do with his murder. Meaning, if they knew Wade was the one who pushed her down that dune, they might think that gave her motivation for revenge. In truth, she had been thinking of how to get even with the creep but nothing even close to killing the man!

It struck her now as strange that none of her hospital visitors asked how she came to plunge down that dune; they only talked about her recovery. Maybe they already knew about Wade's prank (if that's what it was). If they also knew that a few hours ago, she and Garritt drove close to where she believed Wade's body lay in the snow, near Bobby Lee's swamp…

She'd been out of contact with Blackthorn since she left her iPhone in San Diego and disabled her tracking chip. She'd already gone rogue. And technically, she was the thief who'd first stolen the artifact. The other teams, the ones no one talked about, might be looking for her at this very moment for that reason alone.

She made up her mind.

"I suppose you deserve to know, since your life is tangled up with mine at the moment."

He nodded, settling down to listen.

Her feet, still freezing, slipped easily back into his massive boots as she spoke. "I used to believe everything they told me. The Navy, Blackthorn. It was our duty to serve. And serving my country, even though that country hasn't served all of its people very well, gave me a sense of knowing what was right."

She gazed at his honest face, his trusting eyes, deep blue in their lightly fringed sockets, his straight, well-bred nose, firm jawline, a man so clearly foreign to her experience, raised in white privilege but in a community whose very laws were shaped by its uniformity of religion, perhaps the closest thing to *sharia*—religious law—that you could find in modern America. Maybe she could make him understand after all.

"Did you ever question yourself? Wonder which side of the fence was the right side?"

"Yeah. Leaving the church at eighteen. My heart said go. Their arguments said no."

"And your parents?"

He shrugged. "They can only see one side of the fence and I'm not standing on it."

"So you left anyway. Made your own way. You listened to your heart."

"I guess so."

"Well, for years my heart went along with my intellect. My brain said, these people are good to me. We are serving a noble cause. It is the right thing to do. I am developing my skill—which they valued highly, by the way, unlike anyone else who encountered it. They paid me a fine wage to learn more, refine my abilities, and use them for the good of all people. What could be wrong with that?"

"I could think of a few things …"

"Right, you can at this moment. But think about it, take it to its ultimate conclusion. If people in this world, screwed up like it is now, learned that there were others who clearly have a better technology, who could maybe provide the first people they contacted with advanced weapons, or technological superiority—what would that mean for the ordinary citizen who would be caught in the ensuing wars over this advanced technology, which almost always means weapons first, civilian applications second. How many would die fighting to own it? How much collateral damage in lives and property, while we fought wars on the ground and possibly in space?

"And that's only if the aliens, whoever they might be, offered to hand their technology over peacefully. And what if they didn't? What kind of devastation might unfold if they decided we aren't to be trusted, if they decided that we need taming? Or maybe colonizing?

"And don't even get me started on the collapse of civilization as we know it when the church leaders and scientists are proven wrong, all of a sudden without warning, on so many of their theories about life and death on Earth. What leaders would people look up to? We are like children here, always bickering among ourselves, fearful of new and strange and different. We look to leaders to tell us what to do. And you know what happens when those leaders fail to lead."

He grimaced his reply.

"Meanwhile, the world's oil-based economy would collapse. People would starve. The ideologies and cultures that keep us sane would crumble. The whole blasted planet would lapse into chaos!" She stopped to gulp a breath. "That was the argument that kept my heart in line with company policies."

"But you're here, snowed in at a stranger's house. What happened?" Then he asked the burning question. "What—or who—gave you that scar?"

For some reason she suddenly, passionately desired to shock him, to knock him out of his insular world like she had been knocked. She wanted to shake up his perception of reality, even though, like hers, his perceptions were already far beyond the ordinary person's. Still, she wanted him to feel the horrible conflict of conscience that she suffered, trying to understand what was truly the right path.

"Wade gave me this."

She waited to see his face change.

"The guy you saw lying dead in the snow?"

"That guy."

"You had a fight with him?" His already pale face lost some color. "You mean, you killed him? But your scar is old..."

"No, he almost killed me. Put me in a coma. That's why I'm not at work with my team. I'm still on recuperation leave."

"Jeezus..." He sank back into the chair.

"He didn't intend to hurt me, just teach me a lesson. He pushed me down a sand dune, a stupid white man prank, and as usual for stupid white men, it didn't turn out like he thought it would. I hit my head on a piece of cement and wound up in a hospital, dead to the world."

Garritt stared at her.

"That's why, a few weeks later, I got on a plane, rented a car, and drove here to find what I'd left buried at the top of a dune the night he pushed me. Wade didn't know about it. No one did." Or at least that's what she thought at the time.

She remembered the sensation of the artifact lying in her hands and suddenly she could see it again—but not in any context, maddeningly. This was a new vision, yet all she could see around the fragment was its own golden glow. In a box? Under ground? No clue. And no idea who had it or where it might be.

One thing she knew: it wasn't lying in the snow by Wade's freezing body.

"Why did he push you? Where were you?"

"Rosy Dunes Natural Area. Do you know it?"

"Yeah, of course. It's only a few miles from here."

"Dead of night." She might as well tell him everything. "I'd found what we came for, a fragment of a crashed ship, using my skills to locate it while the others were looking elsewhere, using their fancy equipment."

"What, you mean they have UFO-detecting devices?" he smirked, thinking he was joking.

"Sort of. They detect metals we're familiar enough with to build field detectors using SQUID, superconducting quantum interference devices." She paused. "You know, your knowledge just passed a very high security level. I only hope you stay in your kitchen in Veenlanden and keep your mouth shut. As you might now realize, your life could depend on that."

"Go on," he urged grimly.

"So I was standing there weighing my options. See, the arguments for keeping the world in the dark had paled for me. I saw things …" How far should she go? "Let's just say, my heart started to disagree with my head."

"You wanted people to know."

"I wanted at least my family to know. But without proof, who would believe me? I know that's crazy, which is why I was trying to decide which side of the fence I was on. I realized that—"

She paused, embarrassed to admit that unlike him, when *she* stood on the cliff of decision that night, she'd chosen the coward's path and no glitter-lights had shown up to change her mind.

"Well, I couldn't do this by myself. Who was I to go against all those organizations and experts and get away with it? So I was weighing whether to radio the team about my find when I heard a sound. It scared me, so I quickly buried the artifact and pretended it didn't exist. But the rustling turned out to be a 'possum looking for food. I relaxed. That's when Wade hit me from behind and sent me flying."

"He'd seen you bury it?"

"I don't know. I thought it was hazing. He would say it was 'training,' testing his stealth and my security precautions. But he never had the chance to say anything. I hit a cement block, they tell me. Next I knew, I woke up from a medically-induced coma in the hospital with a cracked skull." She left out the vivid dreams with her grandmother and Reverend Ben. "I haven't seen or spoken to Wade since."

"So what happened to the artifact, then?"

"That's the problem. I came back here yesterday to retrieve it but it wasn't there." She didn't tell him about her renewed commitment to go public with it. She had enough humiliation already over how deeply she'd failed at this. "I panicked, thinking that Wade saw me bury it, that Blackthorn recovered it, and now my life is in danger. But then this morning I saw your Juan in a vision. He was standing near the fragment."

"So he *is* involved in this high-stakes game."

"I'm afraid so. That's why I came to find you at the restaurant. I felt responsible. If I'd done what I'd been trained to do—"

"No, it's not your fault."

"There's more. Bobby Lee was right to warn you about me. First I put Juan in danger by not doing my job correctly—and now you. If Wade went after the artifact that Bobby claims to have, and Bobby… we were out there near his shack. Blackthorn might think…they could be looking for us right now."

She would not cry. She did not want to cry in front of this man.

∞

She'd told him the truth now, he was sure of it when she explained the threat to their lives. She probably said more than she intended.

Golden lights and a few lingering blue ones flickered in and out of sight over and around her head, confirming her words, warning him that the danger was real. That might be the only reason he believed her wild story. If he wasn't crazy, then she wasn't either.

He leaned back into the armchair's dark embrace, stared into the fire, as if it could help him absorb this new reality she'd unveiled for him. She wasn't after Juan; she wanted her alien artifact. Maybe she even wanted the same thing he did—to save Juan's life—because she looked genuinely devastated over the life-threatening situation she believed she put them in.

He didn't blame her. He'd spent his own moments of uncertainty trying to parse out what the right move would be, whether he was using his life to save others, or whether he had only made a series of terrible mistakes that would end in disaster. She couldn't have known.

And that man who pushed her down the dune—that wasn't her fault. Everything she'd said, the trust she'd put in him this afternoon, told him she was not a bad person. Hadn't she just risked her life with him to go in search of a kid she didn't know? Wasn't that some kind of atonement for any misjudgments she made earlier in her life, working for these mercenary bastards?

His heart broke loose another measure of compassion and the thread they'd woven between them took on a stronger tension. Oddly and unexpectedly, they had reached a moment of shared risk, of tangled mutual goals.

"That's it? You've got nothing to say?" She shifted uneasily.

"Can you see Juan?" was all he managed. The rest was too complicated.

"I will try."

She sighed and closed her eyes.

When she opened them again, he could see her fighting back tears.

"It's my fault! All I wanted was to help the world, and now there's a dead man and a teenager who—" She stopped.

"Who what?"

"It's bad," she whispered. "Very bad."

"How so?"

"Someone has him locked up and I don't know where. He's been hurt." A rivulet flowed down one cheek and she hurried to brush it away.

"But he's alive?"

"Yes—for now."

"Thank the Infinite! Can you see anything at all about where he is?" She shook her head.

"I need to call my friend," she said abruptly, wiping again at her face. "May I use your phone?"

He got up and retrieved it, handed it to her. "Does she know about your work?"

"Somewhat. She knows I'm here, anyway."

He looked down at the petite, exquisitely formed head of a woman he'd never seen before yesterday and felt more awe than he'd ever felt in church. He felt an irresistible urge to touch her, an overpowering impulse to comfort. She hadn't done wrong. Her choices were unfair, whether to carry this heavy burden of secrecy no one should be asked to carry, or to risk her life to bring the truth out into the open.

He reached out a tentative hand to stroke away her tears and confusion.

Within seconds his thumb was in her grip, twisted in excruciating pain.

As he dropped like a stone to his knees, she jumped up from the couch and swiftly looped a leg around his neck, forced him to the floor, and planted an Ugg on his neck and face.

His own boot.

Wrenching his arm to the screaming point, she shouted, "What the *fuck* are you trying to do?" Her eyes glowed with a black heat so vastly different from the weeping he'd witnessed seconds before.

He couldn't speak. He could only utter exclamations of pain.

"You fucking keep your *fucking hands off me,* you hear that? Never fucking touch me again!" she boomed, loud enough for distant neighbors to hear. She twisted harder to emphasize her point.

No way. He hadn't even touched her the first time! Never. No. *Dang, that hurts!*

Finally she let up on the boot at his throat but didn't let go of her grip on his thumb. The heat in her eyes cooled, though not entirely. She had him completely incapacitated.

"What kind of move was that?" she demanded.

"Sorry," he whimpered. "It was a mistake. I was only trying to comfort you. Sorry!"

"Well, don't fricking try it again." She threw his pained arm down in disgust, turned her back, and walked to stare out the front window, where darkness now enveloped his white lawn and the outdoor lights that had blinked on at dusk illuminated the relentless snowfall. He could hear her trying to calm her breath. In a quiet hiss she added, "Never touch *any* woman without her permission."

He sat up and rubbed his thumb, flexed his twisted arm. "You can count on that," he muttered.

"Damn right!" she agreed.

Suddenly the refrigerator hum in the next room went silent. Outside, the safety lights blinked out. In the hallway, a nightlight in the wall outlet went black. The only remaining illumination came from the dying fire, which he'd forgotten to stoke while she filled his head with the fact that everything he had thought to be true was wrong.

Everything, his aching thumb agreed.

15

Breakout

∞

Min stood at the dark window with her back to Garritt so he wouldn't see her tears, or notice the rapid rise and fall of her chest.

Too late, she realized he hadn't meant to hurt her. This man—he couldn't hurt anyone. But his touch triggered a volcano that must have hidden inside her ever since Wade pushed her down the dune, ever since that male teacher after the field trip in fourth grade, ever since the boy down the street, ever since…

For one blinding moment she had meant to hurt Garritt—hurt him bad. And that scared her far more than his fingertips on the side of her face. It wasn't Garritt she swore at, in words that shocked her as they poured straight from some deep crater she thought she'd healed. No conscious choice intervened, and her loss of control left every nerve in her body shivering. She was only grateful she stopped when she did, and the lava began to cool before she could wreak more harm. How would she ever explain?

She heard him at the fireplace and shifted so she could watch him stab out the flames with a poker until nothing remained but angry little embers. The room darkened and chilled. With no power, the furnace had stopped blowing heat. She knew the thin, prefab walls would do little to protect them from temperatures that plummeted when the sun went down. So why put out the fire?

She wiped her face quickly while he was distracted. Already, she felt frigid air seeping in through the cheap window frames. She imagined it creeping up from the basement.

That reminded her of where she'd seen Juan. She lied when she let Garritt believe she had no clues. Juan lay in a small, makeshift cage, about five by ten, bare of any furniture. He looked like he'd been beaten. Blood streamed down his face and bloody contusions showed on his torso where his t-shirt was torn. His kitchen apron long gone, his jeans showed dark wet spots—blood or urine. He lay crumpled on what looked like a dirt floor, as if thrown against the cement-block wall behind him. No clue where he was in the world, no indication who caged him. This wasn't Blackthorn's style, at least not in the U.S. This looked like an overseas operation. If that were true, he'd never come home.

Garritt struck a match and lit the candle he'd fiddled with earlier. He walked over to the window where she stood and handed her the red wax replica of a wooden snare drum. Little Drummer Boy. Of course.

"Take this and do whatever you need to do. We're leaving," he announced grimly.

While she obeyed without question—one last pit stop before they escaped from this frozen tent of a house—she heard him flip on what must have been a battery-powered weather radio in the kitchen. She overheard them say the storm was a record-breaker. Another foot had landed while they were inside; more on the way. Garritt shut off the radio and she heard him go out the door to the garage.

With deep regret, she slipped out of his boots, neatly folded his wool socks, and left them with a pat by the door. She let out an involuntary squeal as she tugged on her wet socks and cold boots. *Useless city boots.* She briefly weighed that trick women do in movies, snapping off the heels, but instantly realized that was the work of male directors who didn't know any better. She wrapped up in Agnes's beautiful scarf and pulled on Sam's pussy hat, both of which cheered her up for a minute, until she recalled why she was doing this insane thing. She blew out the candle and left it on the kitchen counter. Rummaging through her purse, she pulled out a pen-sized flashlight. At least she wasn't totally unprepared, she thought wryly, thinking of what her old instructors back in San Diego would say about all her personal safety violations in the last twenty-four hours.

When she reached the truck, Garritt handed her a second shovel. Without a word, the two of them worked in the dark with only Garritt's lantern-sized flashlight to check their progress. They soon freed the truck from its white tomb and set off down a road that was surprisingly passable.

"Neighbor," he said gruffly. "He keeps us mobile before the county rigs can get to us."

The single slick lane felt like luxury after what they'd gone through on the way in.

As she watched her breath fog the passenger window, she realized she'd grown up like pampered royalty. Her grandmother's stuccoed house south of San Diego proper, where they'd moved after her father's death, was a flower-strewn castle fortress by comparison to the way these Michigan people were forced to live. No prefab; it was built by fine craftsmen long dead, not far from a glorious ocean. No forced hibernation, no icy death roads. At least not so far. Although as the climate warmed, the threat of hurricanes coming farther north from the tropics than ever before did give pause.

Garritt's voice erupted over the noisy truck, slicing through the shield that had risen between them.

"Like I said before, we're not all assholes." He shifted his gaze from the thin headlight beam to catch her eye.

She looked away again, staring into the dark woods beyond her window. She knew what he meant but didn't know how to apologize for her violent reaction. Then she would have to explain, and that was a story she wasn't ready to tell, no matter how compassionate this man seemed to be.

She felt bad. In the hours before she attacked him, they'd shared their sacred secrets. Undeniably, despite their outward differences, in that flickering firelight they had built a fragile and rare intimacy, a *soulic* intimacy. It happened without either of them willing it, falling easily into place as if they'd always had it. And then—she shattered the delicate connection. Now she didn't know what to say.

"You scared the crap out of me back there, you know."

He laughed when he said it, a sound that filled a little gap in her heart she hadn't realized was there. When did that develop?

"I could pick you up and toss you across the yard without breaking a sweat, and you had me down for the count in an instant. How the heck did you do that?"

"Training. And I am sorry for it. I—"

"No, I'm just grateful you didn't crush my windpipe with my own boot! Now that would be a heck of a thing to explain. Although I suppose I wouldn't be explaining anything; I'd be trying to figure which kind of heaven I fit into. The Dutch wouldn't have me, and I'm afraid I haven't been wicked enough for the other place. Maybe I should do something about that, secure my future," he chuckled as he braked carefully before turning slowly on to the main road. "Now I feel like I'll be safe, no matter what villains we meet. I know you can defend me."

She struck at his arm playfully with the back of her hand, unconsciously breaking her own "no touch" rules. "You just mind your p's and q's, guy, and you'll be fine."

"Don't hit me," he pretended to whine.

She laughed with him this time and it felt good. He was talking silliness, trying to ease the mood. But she knew something about those alternate heavens.

"It's not what you think," she couldn't help saying.

"What?"

"Heaven. I've been there. At least for a visit."

"You mean when you were in a coma?"

"You've been reading, I see. Yes."

"Minda Blake, you are one extraordinary woman. Either you are an imaginative liar, or you travel the world, collecting debris from interplanetary spacecraft; you've visited Heaven; you can see through time and space; and you can kill a man nearly twice your size with one flick of your wrist."

"You are not twice my size!" she protested, laughing in spite of herself.

"Even with all this snow, I feel like I'm back in that jungle, flying through the air in defiance of all reason. Who knows? Maybe I *am* in a kind of heaven."

∞

With a very unique angel, he added to himself.

She might have humiliated his male ego, but that didn't diminish his growing belief that the lights weren't wrong about her. Extraordinary.

Special. As treasured as the curled leaf in the rainforest that bore water when he would have collapsed from thirst, if the lights hadn't led him to it.

By now the county had plowed and salted the main road, creating two lanes relatively free of snow for the moment. Slush from the salt sprayed up under his truck's thick tires with a steady slapping sound as it hit the undercarriage. He picked up speed and the thick white flakes whipped into a tunnel that mimicked warp drive, which added to the out-of-body sensation he'd felt ever since he told her about the lights.

"Where are we going?" she finally asked.

"To find Bobby Lee. He's our only connection to Juan now. If your vision is true, we can't leave my friend where you saw him. You say you're eighty percent accurate? I hope you're wrong about Juan—and about your co-worker."

"So do I."

Reluctantly, she told him more of what she'd seen about Juan's confinement and...torture.

He felt sick. Juan didn't deserve that; no one does. He was sure the kid hadn't done anything that wrong. It wasn't in his nature. He knew exactly what lay at the roots of that boy's being.

Suddenly a palm-sized, cobalt-blue light glowed into view on his windshield, hung suspended for a long moment, then faded slowly.

Immediately he slowed down, sat up, made himself alert to every nuance in the truck's movement.

Within moments, a solid beam of light enveloped them from above. He craned his neck to look up through the windshield. "What is that?"

"Frigging fappleburgers..."

"What?"

She didn't answer as she was busy tearing off her jacket, then started to pull off two layers of sweater to reveal a lacy blue bra that showed off the smooth curves along the tops of her breasts.

He cleared his throat and like a gentleman, pretended to avert his gaze.

"Um, this isn't exactly the time and place ..."

He looked up again but the overhead light was too bright to see what caused it.

She spat out more strange words, one at a time with heat, as if counting a rhythm to her motions as she tugged at the last bits of sweater. Was she swearing? She certainly hadn't hesitated to shoot him with f-bombs back at his house.

"Am I the only one seeing this?" He pointed up, then glanced down from the windshield long enough to see her rip at a mangled piece of aluminum foil taped to her back. "What on earth is that?"

"A stupid idea that clearly didn't work," she fumed. "Pull over."

"I can't do that. If you'll notice, there is no 'over.' That's a five foot wall of hardpack from the plows on both sides of us."

He'd already slowed the truck to a crawl but the overhead beam kept pace with them, growing brighter until Garritt finally heard the chopper engine.

"No, wait," she changed her mind. "Don't stop yet." She turned toward him as she crumpled the foil and pulled one sweater back on, which actually relieved him from distraction so he could think again. "Listen, they tracked me here."

"Who? How?"

"Blackthorn. I want you to stop this truck, get out, and run for your life."

Despite the silly words she'd uttered moments before, she seemed dead serious now.

"If Wade is where I saw him, they tracked me there, too. We were close to Bobby Lee's swamp, remember?"

"Swan Creek Marsh, yeah—so?"

"They must think I've got something to do with Wade's murder. He nearly killed *me*. That's motivation enough." She slipped back into her jacket. "Run. And don't look back. I'll tell them I stole this heap."

He tried to compute the logic of what she was saying.

"The minute you stop," she commanded breathlessly, "open the door, keep low, and slide along the side of the truck. Then disappear into the storm as fast as you can."

The helicopter drifted down, trying to block their path. Heavy flakes stirred around the rotors, which kicked up billows from the ground. Garritt had no choice but to brake in order to avoid a deadly collision.

Instantly, Min shoved her body into him and pushed him out the door that his hand had opened before he could tell it no.

"I'll leave the keys for you," she shouted through the din from the helicopter. "Run for your life, Dutch boy!" This time he felt the care in her words.

He stumbled back along the driver's side as she floored the accelerator. The truck swerved, nearly knocking him over before he dove out of the way. She dodged the chopper and took off fishtailing down the highway, leaving him standing alone in the dark snow.

They hadn't seen another car since they left his house, and no wonder. He reached for his phone—dang! Should have grabbed it from the dash. He rarely kept it on his body. (Too much RF energy, Elizabeth insisted. Not safe for sperm or other precious body parts.)

He didn't run as Minda commanded. He stood there, staring down the straight-line road as the massive black helicopter chased his truck, dipping and weaving. He was trying to figure out how to save her from Blackthorn's henchmen. He watched as they rose up to position themselves in front of the truck again.

Only when the chopper set down smack in front of Min did he run—and not away, but toward them. He had no idea what he could do but he wasn't about to abandon this crazy woman who'd touched his heart like no other since Elizabeth.

He made it only a few yards before he slipped on the slick road and slammed into its unforgiving hardness. His right leg slid out into a split while the left curled behind him at an unnatural angle. He yelled in pain and frustration, unable to get up. Long moments passed as he cursed the world, helpless to stop the helicopter that soon rose again and disappeared into the dark snowy sky, leaving behind only a muffled silence that pressed on his despair.

What would they do to her? Where would they take her? He had no way to contact her. He might never see her again. His mind filled with horrific imaginings as he struggled again to stand. His injured leg wouldn't hold his weight. Thankfully, Elizabeth's yoga classes had left him unusually limber or he would be dealing with a groin injury as well. Far as he could tell, man parts survived the splits but his left ankle and shin hurt like fire.

Finally he managed to cast himself up on one leg to peer around through the blizzard. He calculated that he was roughly two miles from Burt's Crossing and ten miles from his house. His pants were wet from where he'd landed. His hands were bare and cut from the ice, and his head was uncovered except by the rapidly falling snow. Now that the chopper lights were gone, he couldn't see his truck at all. He hoped like hell she remembered to leave the keys as he forced himself to hop painfully toward where it should be.

Bitterly, he wondered why he hadn't managed that other-worldly, midair maneuvering skill he'd discovered in Peru.

An inkling in his head responded: *Panic.*

16

Blackthorn

∞

"Well, you've been a busy girl, m'lass," Alex shouted over the thump of chopper blades. He seemed to believe his Irishness gave him license for any kind of foul innuendo, so he always exaggerated the accent beyond believability.

Min braced for the punchline as he ducked under the rotors of the jet-black craft, a decommissioned gift from clients in Iraq. She had shut down Garritt's truck and leaped out when they landed in front of her. Her muscles tensed now, ready to drop him and run if she could.

"If your mother could see who you're keepin' comp'ny with these days. Why'd you shuttle him off into the storm? Dint 'e measure up?" He chortled at his own rude gestures.

"What are you doing here?" she demanded as he strode closer.

"Boss wants to see you." He was glorying in this dramatic entrance, playing it to the max. It wasn't often Alex got to be in charge.

Where were the others? Why wasn't he talking about Wade? She didn't move; kept her reflexes ready. She'd never been able to take Alex during training but there was a first time for everything.

"If you'd care to step into my office?" He stopped a few feet away and indicated the waiting helicopter.

She relaxed a tick. "Which boss?"

"The big boss, my pretty."

She hesitated. "What about the truck?"

"I'm sure yer boyfriend can find 'is way to it. Unless he's run back home. Failed to protect you from an aerial attack, didn't he now?"

He didn't seem intent on arresting her or cuffing her or whatever Blackthornians did to their prisoners. Thankfully, she'd never been present for such dealings. To resist him now would only make her look guiltier, she decided.

She straightened up a little and tossed Garritt's keys into his truck, which sat square in the right lane of the plowed but deserted highway. She lingered over the hot-pink pussy hat and precious red grandmother scarf. Garritt would return them, she was sure, and she might never see this part of the world again. She stroked the precious items for a second in silent thanks to Agnes and even Sam for their kindness, then laid them gently on the seat near the keys, grabbed her purse, and slammed the door.

Before she followed Alex to the waiting helicopter, she turned for a quick glance back down the road. Black night, heavy snow. Nobody in sight.

Reluctantly she climbed up into the helicopter. She hated these contraptions. Such an unnatural way to fly, lifting off with the nose down, and the bone-rattling shudder that never stopped.

"Seriously, where are we going?" she yelled over the *thwack* of rotors.

No one had threatened her or accused her of anything. The strictly functional seats were empty except for her, Alex, and the pilot.

"Midway," the pilot shouted back and handed her a headset.

She didn't recognize him. New recruit? As soon as she put it on, he added over the intercom, "Strap in. We had to wait for the storm to subside before we could get to you. Might be a bumpy ride across the lake. Another squall's headed this way."

Great.

"What were you saying about the boss?" she asked Alex once she'd mastered the intercom. She hated the way he'd talked to her but she refused to match the challenge in it, contenting herself with the thought that this was why Alex lived alone.

"Commander wants a chat so it's off to San Diego with you."

"Not in this thing," she protested.

"Uber," the pilot cracked over the intercom.

She could only see the back of his flight helmet but he was clearly joking. That meant a commercial flight. Meaning she was considered a low flight-risk, i.e., not their prisoner after all. Right? "What about my rental car?"

"Yeah, almost forgot." Grinning, Alex held out his hand. "Give me your key. We'll take care of it for you."

"Over my dead body!"

"By the way, you going to explain to the Commander that you were too busy playing blanket hornpipe to answer his calls?"

Lucky for him, he wasn't looking at her face—and he was strapped in out of her reach.

"Yeah, we've been tracking you for a while now but couldn't get here. Bloody storm."

The Commander could have been calling since Wednesday, when she left her phone in San Diego. But if Blackthorn hadn't started tracking her until this morning, that meant they didn't know about her trip to Rosy Dunes but they might know about Bobby Lee's marsh. She was convinced that was where she saw Wade's body, lying next to a half-frozen waterline. She wasn't exactly a prisoner at this moment, but what did the Commander have planned for her?

"This is quite the vacation spot you've chosen for recovery," Alex said as he gazed out at the near-solid whiteness below them.

"And what about that? I don't belong to Blackthorn until next week."

He ignored the question. "Actually, don't bother with the car keys, darlin'. Luther doesn't need 'em. We dropped him off fifteen minutes ago. Scared the crap out of those nice folks. He's halfway to Chicago by now."

She felt the heat spread across her shoulders.

"What did you tell them?"

"That yer mum had an accident and we had to get you home."

"But she didn't, did she?"

"Now the whole Dutch swampland believes you're CIA," he cackled. "Or a feckin' terrorist. If they only knew, right? Veenlanden—*Bog Land*—sounds like an Irishman named it."

Alex spoke several languages, some of the tools he brought to the team. Apparently that included Dutch. Maybe he picked it up in Amsterdam during brief sober stretches?

And Luther, he'd probably joined the military straight out of prison, before Blackthorn recruited him. Six feet whatever, a wall of a man covered in tattoos, and he could break into anything. Not exactly the guy she'd choose to drive a rental car around the lake in a blizzard with her name and license on the paperwork.

Thankfully, the storm fell behind them as soon as they swooped southwest across the bottom of Lake Michigan. Min's paranoia relaxed somewhat. She should probably be grateful for Luther's help. Team members watched each other's backs like that. Sharing a vital secret—one you couldn't tell your own family—tended to bring the most unlikely people together.

Which drew her thoughts back to Garritt. She'd last seen him in the truck's rearview mirror, standing in the snow, staring after her.

Stupid man; why didn't he run when I told him to?

It wouldn't have mattered, though. Apparently Alex and the others thought they knew all about Garritt. At least they hadn't picked him up and accused him of being an accessory to murder.

They hadn't breathed a word about Wade and she wasn't about to bring him up until she knew what the Commander wanted that was so important, he would fly her cross-country—but not on a Blackthorn jet. Sooner or later she would have to report the dead body in her remote-viewing. If Wade went missing while on duty, Blackthorn would be all over it. Yet these guys seemed oblivious. Unless she really was a suspect?

But if Wade were still alive, her warning might prevent his murder.

17

Church

∞

Garritt lurched toward the entrance of Burt's Crossing, helped by the gale that raged across the nearly empty parking lot. A whisk of snow blew in with him before the heavy door slammed behind him.

The lacquered hostess in the bust-revealing blouse and heavy blue eye shadow jerked up from where she'd been reading a paperback behind a counter cluttered with peppermint patties and chewing gum for sale, and a faded, stand-up flyer from last summer's Little League benefit. One look at Garritt and she rushed out to grab his snowy arm, offering her curvy body as support.

"Are you okay, honey?"

"Not really," he grimaced, suddenly suffocated by the overheated room and the perfumed woman clutching at him. Then he felt a flash of guilt; she'd known him since he was a kid. By sight, anyway.

"Is Bruce in the kitchen today?"

"Yes, but don't you need me to call someone?"

"No, I'm fine for now."

Ignoring her protests, he hobbled through to the dining room where a lone couple sat dining on sandy mounds of fried fish and potatoes. His restaurant savvy registered surprise to see any diners at all in this weather. He could already smell the kitchen: the acrid stench of food frying in rancid oil.

Despite the deep-fried entrées and canned fruits and vegetables on the menu, his parents always raved about the "homestyle" cooking here. He figured that's because his mother rarely ventured into a kitchen, and the stuff his grandparents ate—well, maybe it was healthy once upon a time, but that was before genetic engineering dramatically altered potatoes, tomatoes, squash, apples, sugar beets—bananas coming soon. (The ancestral wheat and corn his parents grew up with were already a rare, nostalgic figment of history.) As a kid, he particularly despised Burt's so-called salads: iceberg lettuce buried in shreds of cheap cheddar that quickly devolved into a watery orange slime.

Maybe that wasn't so bad, he thought now. *Today's fake cheese barely melts at all. Probably half-plastic Frankenfood* —exactly what he and Corbyn and Avery were fighting against, with the help of a lot of passionate, small-farm owners in the area.

He looked up at the toy train making slow, hypnotic circles around the dining room ceiling. His parents always pointed it out when he was young. They must have hoped the novelty would distract him from the rough miseries of an oversensitive childhood.

No argument: their world was too harsh for him. Their foods made him ill, their scratchy bedsheets kept him awake at night, and worst of all, he questioned their beliefs. Teachers didn't like him because he got bored easily and had to find other ways to amuse himself, while the other kids simply found him strange. His parents tried more harsh discipline, which failed, of course. By the time he was a teenager, their mandatory Friday night lake perch dinners at Burt's Crossing were a torture of family arguments that didn't let up until he left their church and its stifling community and escaped to college to study bio-dynamic agriculture, against his father's wishes.

The train theme was overdone anyway. No passenger trains stopped in Hamilton, although freight trains occasionally rattled over a wooden trestle across the Rabbit River. Civil War veterans had built the old bridge out of bare tree trunks. It was now the historic pride of tiny Hamilton. In truth, the village was merely another outpost of Dutch Calvinism: friendly for a moment, but don't expect the neighbors to invite you for tea unless you know them from church. Garritt chose to live here only because that's where he found the cheap prefab in a foreclosure sale.

He burst through the swinging doors into the kitchen, startling the crew. He singled out his old buddy from high school—one of the few who would still speak to him.

"Bruce—have you seen Bobby Lee here today?"

Bruce looked up from the burn-crusted grill top, wiped his hands on a grimy apron.

"Well, if it isn't Mr. Sophisticated Dining." He pulled off his dirty chef's hat to reveal a nearly bare head of sandy red spikes. He used it to wipe sweat from his freckled forehead. "Hey, what's wrong with your leg?"

"Nothing—have you seen him?" He didn't have time for the usual banter.

"Sure. He's in the back with the others."

"Others?"

"Yeah, the rest of the church members. You thinking of joining them? I thought you weren't into that sort of thing."

"I'm not," Garritt assured him, and ducked back out the swinging door, headed for the banquet room.

"Hey!" Bruce called after him. "Nice to see you, too!"

Church of Refined Sensibilities proclaimed a purple cloth banner draped above the closed double doors. He'd never heard of it. Through the thick wood came sounds of a heated argument; not what he'd expect from a local congregation. He pushed one door open a crack.

"You can't do that!" someone shouted.

"Why not?"

"Because it's not who we are!"

"Then who are we? A bunch of old men who think they can change the world before they die? Sorry, Dean, but most of us aren't getting any younger, and that includes you, Harley. You can bet that if we don't get some new members, the Church of Refined Sensibilities will be meeting out there in the cemetery soon enough."

Just as Garritt recognized Bobby Lee's voice, the room went quiet and someone yanked the door all the way open.

He was stunned to see the gathering—men of all ages—jump up almost as one from their banquet tables and reach to the holsters at their sides or tucked inside their suit jackets. It took him a full minute before he realized they must be among the advocates promoting the preservation of Michigan's liberal gun laws in the face of so much public tragedy.

Gun lovers had hosted a picnic in Holland recently, "to help the public feel more comfortable about open carry"—or so he read in the

Holland Sentinel. The accompanying pictures featured men holding toddlers while flaunting their holsters. They claimed that the right of self-defense is a basic human right. He couldn't argue with that, but he found it disorienting and more than a little frightening to see the men in this banquet room wearing guns with their church attire. He'd lay odds that half of them helped storm the U.S. Capitol building back in '21.

The burly, red-faced man at the door moved to block Garritt's view of the room. "Can I help you?"

He could hear them sit down again, chairs scraping, hopefully taking their hands off their pistols.

"Uh, yeah, I'm Garritt," he stuck out his own empty hand. "Vanderhoeven. I'm looking for Bobby Lee."

The man didn't shake his hand. Instead he called back over his shoulder, while keeping his eyes on Garritt and his hand on his sidearm, "Bobby—you've got company."

"Well send him in, then. We're not some secret society," he heard Bobby answer, although Garritt thought that's exactly what they looked like as he stepped cautiously into the room.

It reminded him of a story a fellow student told him at Michigan State, about her adventures as a banquet waitress in a Detroit suburb where the Mafia held its confabs. She described scenes just like this, how the men jumped up and reached inside their jacket panels when she pushed open the door to bring in the coffee. He calculated about forty visibly well-armed men seated around long tables shoved together to form an elongated U. Before them lay a shambles of dirty plates, water, coffee cups. How refined could this Church of Refined Sensibilities be, to choose this place for their church hall? But here they were, yet another splinter of Holland's fierce commitment to religious devotion, which by now had spawned a church for every taste.

Garritt cleared his throat, though not to get attention. Their eyes had never left him. He felt the hostile spears of wariness clog his windpipe and pierce his mid-section as they waited for him to speak. What could he say? Maybe nothing. He had an idea, though, after what he'd overheard.

"Are you open to new members? Sorry I'm late, Bobby," he lied as he slipped out of his coat.

He ran a hand roughly through his wet locks to free them from where they'd stuck to the back of his neck and squinted in the glare of the overhead fluorescents. Steady pain from his ankle and shin spiked his eagerness to get this over with. He would have to feign interest for a while.

He watched the churchgoers exchange looks. Clearly, they had been in a fight they didn't want to share with a stranger—although now that he had a better view, Garritt recognized some of the faces in the room, some he would least expect. A few probably recognized him as well, from his old Reformed days. If they were here, that meant they were renegades like him. Garritt took the name to mean that they considered themselves above the rest, more capable of discerning Truth with their "refined sensibilities."

Bobby Lee held court at the front of the room, directly across from where Garritt stood. He eyed Garritt doubtfully. He knew Garritt was looking for Juan; he wouldn't be fooled by Garritt's "membership" ploy. Would he play along for the sake of the others? Finally, in a hearty voice, he made his decision clear.

"Welcome, Brother. I think there's a seat for you over there."

Garritt nodded a thank-you and wove into the tangle of chair legs in the crowded room, trying to hide his limp. The seat Bobby indicated was on a far corner of the farthest side table, a message from Bobby that he didn't appreciate Garritt's subterfuge. Garritt's ankle screamed at the effort. It was swollen nearly out of his boot by now.

He fell at last into a flimsy folding chair and reached under the table to loosen his laces. As his face neared the next man's cup, the smell of rancid coffee pierced his senses, the first smell in this temple of food to remind him that he'd hardly eaten earlier. Too nervous. It only made him more eager to be done here and free of this claustrophobic gathering.

"As we were saying, and it just so happens you've arrived on cue—Garritt, did you say?"

He nodded, noting Bobby's exaggerated effort to feign ignorance of Garritt's real intentions. The man also looked hardier than the last time they'd met.

The church leader pointed his next words at a man with a chest-long white beard who sat across the room from Garritt. "What our church needs is new members." And to Garritt, "Are you familiar with our creed?"

"Um, no. Although Juan might have mentioned something about it." He dropped the name intentionally and thought he saw some expressions flicker around him. "Can you refresh my memory?"

"Of course," Bobby replied smoothly, clearly accustomed to leadership. He stood up and moved to stand behind the table-top lectern positioned at the center of the table. The front of it bore an emblem that looked like a heart superimposed over a classic, saucer-shaped UFO. Without the rabbit-fur and the biting cold that made him look older and ruddier, Garritt surmised that Bobby must be in his mid-sixties, with a neatly-trimmed beard and an ingratiating smile. A fringe of white circled his otherwise bare head. In this setting, it was hard to imagine him wielding the handgun strapped to his wide waist. When he spoke, his pale eyes softened.

"We gather here every Thursday evening to worship at the feet of the Masters, to pledge ourselves to the Universal Truths that each man holds in his heart of hearts, that we are *not* created equal—not in the sight of the Universe, which is nothing if not infinitely diverse—and that we each hold our destiny in our own hands. It is ours to choose, to shape, and to commit to, without restraint." Though gentle, Bobby's voice rang with sincerity.

Garritt could agree, as long as that "not equal" didn't lead to inferior vs. superior. Nothing in our lives or personalities or physical appearance ever reaches "equal." Even identical twins boast delightful inequalities. So far, he could easily nod as if in solemn support.

"Moreover, we recognize that Earth dwellers are fallen ones, fallen from the planets of the Interplanetary Congress long ago in our extraterrestrial history. That we each live upon this prison planet as a result of misdeeds we committed in the distant past, and that, with personal responsibility, we can atone for those crimes against humanity and rise again to take our place among the stars."

Okay, that went a little too far. He had to try harder to look as if he were soaking this up. Personal responsibility, check. Interplanetary Congress?

"To do that, we must help the world recognize that we are not alone in the Universe. We must defeat the forces that would withhold this information from us, be it man, woman, child, or religious doctrine! Or government agency." He looked directly at Garritt, as if he alone were the devil of government secrecy.

Garritt tried to look innocent, which wasn't difficult because he wasn't the devil of anything. In truth, his thoughts flew immediately back to the sight of Min being chased by that military-looking helicopter.

"For we know that many on this planet profit from our ignorance! They keep us downtrodden! We suffer the ills of overpopulation, corporate greed, and the destruction of our natural resources. Our Extraterrestrial Brethren have promised to come to our rescue, if we but recognize that they exist. That is our first step."

Okay, wait right there. *Rescue* means *interference*. What kind of ETs would interfere in a people's need to learn and grow in their own time? What about *Star Trek's* Prime Directive, Gene Roddenberry's brilliant contribution of humanist philosophy to the collective consciousness? If some alien beings were willing to interfere, to save us, then who knows what else they might do. Anyone who watched TV knew as much.

He couldn't help but think of Min and her Blackthorn rationale. Maybe they were right. Maybe we don't need to know who's out there until we can learn to love one another on this planet, despite our differences. Maybe we don't deserve to know. But he held his tongue, hopeful he might learn what drew Juan to this bizarre "church," with its mix of New Age humanism, old style religion, and adherence to tenets of the National Rifle Association.

"It is our godly duty," Bobby was saying, "and we are each a facet of that Infinite God, to spread knowledge far and wide about the reality of space travel, other-planetary civilizations, and the global conspiracy to prevent the people from knowing the truth."

Garritt's restraint failed. "And how can we do that!? I mean, most people scoff at the mere idea that UFOs are alien-occupied." He hoped to spark something connected to Juan.

Several members turned to stare at his rudeness.

Bobby's face blazed and his eyes grew sharp. "Because we have proof!" he slammed a fist on the lectern.

A rumble of affirmation passed through the gathering.

"And that proof must see the light of day soon—very soon! Before the forces that would stop us descend."

The room grew quiet, expectant. Garritt shivered at some new undertone he heard in Bobby's voice.

"Gentlemen, I leave it to you. To pursue the course we have set for ourselves? Or to run back to our homes and hide with our ham radios and our conspiracy sites. How long can the world go on like this? I say, not long—no, not long indeed! We are on the brink of collapse, economically, environmentally, and above all, spiritually. The churches have sucked up the mental manna of humanity for far too long!"

Bobby's discourse was no longer sweet or subtle, but Garritt had to agree about that last bit. He nodded along with the others.

"The banks have taken our wealth!"

"Hear, hear," the congregation concurred. Even Garritt had to admit the truth of that.

"And the government is waging secret wars and making alliances with aliens without telling us a single truthful thing about them!"

But how could that be? Garritt's rational mind popped back to life, never mind that Bobby's oratory stirred his blood with the same pace and rhythm that lulled congregations everywhere into harmonies of belief. And why weren't there any women in this room? The imbalance added to his uneasiness. Something very wrong here.

A blue light appeared over Bobby's head—gleaming in, then out.

Garritt hadn't seen any lights since the one that warned him about the helicopter. He responded automatically out on the road, didn't even realize he'd seen it until he remembered it later. This time he sat up. *Be alert. You are still in danger.*

The danger wasn't physical, he realized. Bobby's speech had taken on a familiar rhythm, common to preachers and pitchmen. It captured the heart, this hypnotic sound. It began with statements with which anyone could agree. Soon you'd hum along in alignment with the melodious highs and lows, your blood keeping pace with the orator's words, your mind bending to concur with this appealing, soothing, exciting, rhythmic, pulsating ideology.

To contradict? That would mean to fall out of rhythm! To disrupt the lullaby! To destroy the glorious sensation of community! *You would become the dread Outsider.*

So you hum along, and by the time the speaker reaches his thrilling conclusion—no matter how ludicrous—your spirit and your brain nod in harmonious concurrence.

Unless you take the painful steps to break free.

Garritt knew that sting from long experience. He could never fully commit to such oratory. Always, always, the speaker would reach a point where Garritt's logic interrupted and he became the harsh crack of Spock's intellect against everyone else's smooth dance of allegiance to Captain Kirk's charisma.

Bobby dropped his voice to a near whisper, hissing, "And it is up to us, gentleman, to stop them. *Using whatever means we have.*"

Gooseflesh rippled down Garritt's arms as he thought of the firepower seated around him. Had they shot Min's co-worker, what was his name? Wade?

What about Minda? Would she be next if they got their hands on her? And Juan?

He couldn't stop himself. He leaped out of his chair. "What have you done?"

"What do you mean, Brother Garritt?" Bobby answered smoothly.

"Where is Juan?" he demanded.

"Juan is on a mission," Bobby replied.

"What kind of mission?"

"A mission to find himself."

The room shuffled nervously. One man cleared his throat, the white-bearded fellow across from Garritt.

Garritt zeroed in on him. "You! What do you know about Juan? He's just a teenager! And Bobby has lured him into serious trouble with this slick talk, hasn't he? I watched the kid get arrested for no good reason, and now he's not in a jail, he's not at work, and he's not at home. Where is he?" Garritt's pulse pounded. As the words poured out, he realized how important they had become.

The bearded man looked incredibly uncomfortable but said nothing.

Garritt turned back to face Bobby and his voice rose considerably, his sense of indignation with it. The dam of anger he'd been holding back for decades threatened to burst, to release years of accumulated frustration from knowing that what he'd heard espoused in pulpits was so *deeply wrong!* Yet he could never divert people from their wild course of insane ideology, even when that ideology caused pain to others. He'd hit his head on that brick wall so many times before … people who wouldn't listen to him, who couldn't see reason. He wouldn't stop this time until they heard him!

"Where is Juan?" he fumed.

He started toward Bobby.

Feelings churned, washed, spilled over that dam of silence he'd adopted. The man knew something. He needed to share it, *now*.

"Tell me, what have you done with him?"

He was mere inches away, eyes focused on Bobby's throat…

The room rose in a clatter and guns were accessed and Garritt's progress was halted by hands on him and shouts and an arm cocked around his neck. Soon his own limbs were twisted behind his back. A further scrambling of chairs and bodies and he was on the floor, face down, a heavy knee in his back.

"Gentlemen!" Bobby called for calm. "It's all right. Sit back down. Please."

Reluctantly, the man with the knee and the cocked elbow finally let go of Garritt, whose fever had cooled considerably when his face met the foul-smelling carpet.

Second time in one day, Garritt thought bitterly. Pain laced his leg as he clambered up and brushed himself off. This time it was his own temper to blame.

Still, he couldn't resist a sardonic, "Nice church you've got here."

"We are sorry about that, Garritt. You must realize that we are in a crisis point of danger. Government forces have already invaded our local sovereignty. In fact, you have been trafficking with one of them!"

Garritt's face burned.

"I tried to warn you about her but apparently you didn't listen," Bobby continued in a voice no longer saccharine. "I've seen what they do. But that won't last for much longer." A strange look came into his eyes. A terrifying look.

"Where is Juan," Garritt insisted, more convinced than ever of Min's warnings. "What have you done to him?"

"Juan is right where he needs to be. Don't worry. He's being well taken care of."

Right. Collapsed in a tiny cell, bruised and bloodied, she'd said. "So you know where he is?"

"We do. He is safe. We are protecting him," Bobby added brightly, as if he'd just thought of it. "He saw things that might have gotten him killed by these government agents. We staged his arrest to put them off the track, especially since their agent was about to reach him when we arrived on the scene."

Min! He meant Minda. "Who arrested him, then? Holland Police said they'd never even heard his name."

"Well, that's not entirely true," Bobby smiled. "Some of them did." He indicated the man who'd just had his knee in Garritt's back. "Garritt, let me introduce you to Zacharia. Sorry you didn't meet under better circumstances.

"Zach here has sworn an oath to uphold the laws. But he has also sworn an allegiance to C.R.S. to uphold the rightful truths to which all men are entitled. He is committed to keeping the peace, but also to elevating the consciousness of humanity. He probably saved Juan's life."

Bobby smiled a smile that made Garritt's stomach turn.

Meanwhile, sleek, dark-haired Zacharia held out a hand to Garritt, which he was loathe to take.

"That's all right, Zach," Bobby oozed. "You can understand why Garritt might be reluctant."

"Sorry," the cop shrugged. His eyes glittered slightly, as if he weren't sorry at all. "We can never be too shore," he drawled, adding extra syllables here and there. "You know the government sends agents to infiltrate UFO groups, raht? They try really hard to make us sound crazy, from the inside. We have learnt that they are willin' ta go further then thay-et."

A grumbling of agreement around the room.

"You heard about Frank Visser?" Zach asked Garritt.

He grunted assent. He wanted to get the hell out of this room full of fanatics with guns. His ankle throbbed incessantly, wrenched again during his tussle with this Zacharia. Clearly they weren't going to tell him where they were holding Juan—that is, unless he could convince them that he was sympathetic to their cause.

"We think Frank was murdered by these agents," Zach said. "He'd been fishin' that area fer years, and that story 'bout him goin' over the dam in the dark is pure *bull-ull-shee-it.*" More nods and epithets from the other members.

"And whut was his crime? He saw a god-damn UFO and made a phone call like the good citizen he wuz. Fortunately, he called Bobby first."

"So how are you going to tell the world?" Garritt managed, though further put off by Zach's strange twang, so rare in the Dutch Triangle. "About aliens, I mean?"

Had he actually said those words? He put all his weight on his good right foot, held on to a chair back for support. The others began to settle back down, tucking their guns away.

"We have a plan," Bobby assured him. "We thought Juan might be a part of that plan but he seemed reluctant to go further, so we have taken him out of harm's way for now."

"Can I see him? Talk to him? He's about to lose his job, his family is near hysterical, and his girlfriend is worried beyond her years. Why hasn't he called them?"

The white-bearded man spoke up. "I think it's safe for Juan to go home now, don't you agree?" He narrowed his eyes at Bobby. He must be the "Harley" Bobby argued with earlier.

"One more day," Bobby replied coolly. "I need to talk to him, explain the dangers he faces, before he goes home and says things to the wrong people." He turned to Garritt. "You will need to help him keep this secret, now that you've stumbled into it. And you will do that, won't you?" He darted his eyes around the room at his armed followers to emphasize his point.

Garritt got it. "Of course," he quickly agreed. "Just let him call his family. If what you say is true, I would be interested to learn more about your, um, missionary work."

So I can call the FBI to report a kidnapping as soon as I get the hell out of this room.

But second thoughts erupted: How involved was Juan? Had he committed any crimes? Or, worse, would calling the FBI bring Blackthorn down on Juan's head? Because Min's theory that Blackthorn had taken him appeared to be wrong, and they might still want him. Garritt's phone call could draw the wrong kind of attention.

Who was telling the truth—Min? Bobby Lee? Zach, the two-faced cop, willing to carry out a fake arrest? The government? Blackthorn? Were they one and the same? And, *holy hell*, did they all believe in aliens? Garritt realized he was in no shape to determine *up* from *down* right now. But if he could gain the confidence of this group, he might be able to extricate his friend from their grasp and that's all that mattered to him.

"Your philosophy interests me," he said, dredging up sincerity. "You meet here every Thursday night?"

"You are most welcome to join us," Bobby answered in oily tones, and the others nodded, although he heard a few mutter in doubt. "The initiation to become a member is fairly simple, should you choose to do so." He smiled benignly.

Garritt's stomach quivered. He wondered if that was what they were doing to Juan, "initiating" him. They carried some bizarre beliefs… but were these churchgoers capable of the kind of torture Min saw? He needed to get out of here and think.

"I'll be back next week, then. Right now, I'd best go see someone about this ankle."

He threaded his way toward the door, shaking a few extended hands on his way out, hoping they believed his false sincerity.

As soon as the door closed behind him, he heard White-beard's voice rise. "And that's exactly what I've been warning you about!" Followed by a lot of hissing and shushing.

As he staggered back to his truck in the dark blizzard, excruciating pains shot up his left leg. Could it be true that Min had come to Avery's to seize Juan for Blackthorn—except these guys got there first? She'd certainly been eager to find him, which was almost as strange as her sudden appearance in Veenlanden. She was so out of place here, with her martial arts, her voodoo psychic skills, and her designer clothes. Not to mention the warm color of her skin.

But when he pictured that beautiful, smooth arm, those delicate hands with their hot pink nails, the swell of her breasts peeking from the lacy bra, and most of all, her patient empathy as he reeled off his story—her instant comprehension and sincere encouragement—a comforting feeling spread through him.

Forget her combat skills; he could not visualize her as the villain these C.R.S. lunatics assumed her to be. *Not possible.* She had shared her own secrets with him! His instincts told him she meant it when she said he was the first to hear them.

The "proof" of aliens that Bobby preached about must be Minda's lost fragment. That was undoubtedly this church's most prized relic—until they made it public, if he understood their intentions correctly.

So, what if Bobby had trusted it to Juan to—what? Take it somewhere? And then Juan got scared, didn't do what they said, and they nabbed him and beat him up.

Or was Bobby telling the truth, that they swept him off to protect him, and their artifact, from government agents, aka Blackthorn? Then why throw him in a cage?

What if Min was not who he'd thought she was and she had wormed her way into his affections, almost killed him, told him dire things to frighten him and make him even more eager to find Juan, and then got herself rescued by helicopter, leaving him in the snow to fend for himself. What did that make her?

The pain in his leg was clouding his thinking. Had she used him for her own purposes? He shuddered to think how she might make sure he never shared her secrets with anyone, so why not tell him things just to make him feel at ease.

As he struggled into the frigid cab it filled with brilliant, piercing, golden pinpoints, each of which gleamed at him for a nanosecond, then disappeared.

"Thanks a lot—that really makes it all clear," he said aloud.

If only he could hear what they would say to him right now, because he was totally confused and his leg hurt like the devil. Sure, the lights were nice. But what did they mean? Why could he see them? Why had he *ever* seen them? *What kind of screwed-up world is this, anyway?* Right now what he really needed was a Min word.

"Flubbergusser!" he yelled for everything and nothing and shoved the truck into reverse.

Oddly, it did make him feel better. Until he almost hit the coat-less restaurant hostess scrambling across the slick parking lot to catch up with him.

"Here," she shoved a folded piece of paper at him through the window he cracked open. "I was told to give you this."

"By whom?" he called to her back as she slipped and skidded her way back through the restaurant door. He opened it.

An address. And one word:

Hurry.

18

Soonika

~~

Garritt stared at the slip of paper. *Hurry?* At this moment, going anywhere but for painkillers seemed sheer lunacy.

He squinted out the driver's side at the unremitting snowfall. He'd be lucky to make it the few miles home to ice his throbbing ankle. He looked at the note again. No way to determine if it was sent by friend or foe. But he recognized the road name.

Apple Drive passed through Soonika, a straight shot now with the new bypass but way the heck out in an unincorporated area where they mined zinc back at the turn of the nineteenth century. Not even a post office remained after the mining panned out in the 1920s, and every farmer knew that Soonika's sour, acidic soil was good for blueberries but not much else. He could stick to the main highways and get there in an hour or so, if the county had their plows out of storage by now. (Nobody expected a storm this heavy before Thanksgiving, though by now the phrase "climate change" justified all kinds of precautionary measures, budgets be damned.)

Even if Juan's parents filed a missing person's report as the police told them to do, how long before they developed a lead like this one? In fact, now that he'd seen Zach's face, he knew Zach wasn't one of the two who pretended to arrest Juan. So how many of his fellow cops were in on it? He guessed Zach said nothing to them about alien invaders or black-ops agents infiltrating the Triangle. More like, "Let's go teach this Beaner kid a lesson"—such as not to break into Ichabod's at night.

Garritt recalled the look on the desk sergeant's face when the woman suggested that Juan was probably blowing off work and they should just wait for him to show up. Not only was that unlike Juan, it seemed a very un-cop-like attempt to dissuade Garritt from pursuing the issue. Shouldn't the Holland Police Department appear concerned that someone was out there impersonating them, fake-arresting people?

Of course they were part of it. The kidnappers didn't fake that squad car.

Maybe Zach slipped him this note; maybe his conscience bothered him. Maybe things hadn't gone the way he imagined and now he wanted out of the scheme.

Garritt twiddled the paper nervously, flipping it between his fingers. Soonika wasn't a place from which Juan could escape and make it home on foot, especially in this storm. Juan didn't have his phone, either. Garritt might be the kid's only hope. He knew what that felt like, and he would never stop being grateful for the day Juan rescued him when he was in trouble.

Not as familiar with the area as he was with Veenlanden or Hamilton, he plugged the address into a phone app, shoved the truck into gear, and slid carefully out of the parking lot. One thing he knew for certain: this wasn't Bobby Lee's address, and despite the man's charismatic platitudes and proclamations, Garritt knew the moment he heard it that Bobby Lee was lying when he said Juan was in safe hands.

A grueling hour and a half later, the app proclaimed, "Your destination is on the right."

He strained to make out the address on a plaque attached to the top of a mailbox nearly buried by passing plows. Beyond an open gate that looked non-functional, a single-story house loomed in the darkness, set far back from the road and mostly hidden behind a thick line of trees that edged along Apple Drive.

Directly across the street, a much nicer house he'd rather visit basked in the warm glow of windows and safety lights that lit up the snow, which was pelting sideways again. By contrast his "destination" was pitch black. He could only see it because the snow on the ground reflected enough ambient light to cast the building in silhouette. The place gave him the creeps. If Juan was here…he didn't want to finish that thought.

He drove past the driveway and parked off the road, hoping the trees would obscure the sight of his truck from anyone inside the house. He gambled that he'd be back with Juan before another snowplow came by. Bundling himself into stocking cap and gloves, he took a deep breath to steady his pounding heart and reached to retrieve his big flashlight. His leg screamed at him as he limped back down the snow-packed road. Icicles froze inside his nostrils and the snow blew his eyes into a squint. A steady burn tunneled through his sinuses and he cursed the whole situation.

In the driveway, his light picked up recent vehicle tracks. They'd plowed right through the heavy drifts. From their size, he surmised it was something big, passing both to and from—or from and to, he couldn't be sure which. This was not a good sign.

"Juan, you bastard, you'd better be here," he muttered as he stepped along the ruts, grateful at least for the broken path.

The tracks led to a ramshackle garage attached to a house badly in need of new paint. It might have been sky blue once. Beneath the soles of his snow-covered boots, Garritt felt long breaks in the concrete slab supporting the garage, and the shabby, lift-style door had warped so it no longer fit against the outer wall. The house must have settled, more proof of Soonika's swampy soil.

As he fought his way to the front steps, Garritt wondered if plunging his legs in deep snow counted as icing. He grabbed an iron railing and pulled himself up the icy levels to read a neon-orange notice tacked behind a rusty screen, half torn and flapping in the wind:

CONDEMNED
DANGER—KEEP OUT
This property has been deemed unfit
for human occupancy or use by the

Crockery Township Building Safety Department
Reason: *well water contamination*
Dated: *March 15, 2018*

It is unlawful for any person to use or occupy this building. Any unauthorized person removing this sign will be prosecuted.
DO NOT REMOVE

Beneath dark picture windows, heavy snow crushed the overgrown junipers into the same white blanket that covered the entire yard. Garritt played his flashlight around the surrounding property, parts of which were black as Hell itself. Neither vehicle nor human in sight. Nothing moving down the road, either. The place looked and felt completely deserted. Which was both good and bad. Where was Juan?

He climbed carefully off the icy steps to fight his way through thigh-deep drifts to the back of the house, despite the sharp sensations that seared up his leg. The only tracks marring the unbroken white were small rodent, bobcat, and a family of deer, very recent, which meant that the vehicle probably left the driveway hours ago, leaving an eerie silence that invited the wild creatures to venture closer. No gold or blue light sparkles appeared to give Garritt encouragement—or warning. Still, he wouldn't leave until he made certain Juan wasn't here.

The deer tracks led to an old fruit orchard at the side of the back yard, every tree different, the way a family might plant for their own use. His light played over a few soggy, twisted leaves fringed with ice, clinging to wet black branches that offered bits of rotting apples and bird-ruined cherries, blackened by the cold. Out along the front driveway, he'd seen a row of bunched red branches rising out of the snow: blueberries, stripped clean of foliage. Someone had put a lot of work into this little property.

Too bad about the well, the farmer in him sympathized. They could make a tidy little sum selling extra fruit, if only from the two trees near the house that still bore a few brown Bosc hanging from their branches, tempting the deer and the climbing woodchucks. (Nobody believed him but he'd watched the greedy monsters methodically steal pears from one of his own trees.) He cast his light around the back yard and quickly discovered the source of the water contamination. It filled him with disgust.

Yards from the back of the house stood a decrepit cinder-block shed, half-hidden behind the autumn ravaged remains of blackberry vines and a grape arbor tangled together. Beyond the shed, an animal pen—probably pigs, from the looks of the broken-down troughs. Beyond that lay a tangle of brambles, weeds, and scrawny saplings that, in summer, would hide the property's shame: a trash-filled, sickly-yellow creek that ran around a discarded washer and dryer lying on their sides in the boggy waters, leaching foul chemicals that would seep down into the groundwater. He cast the beam farther and it picked up old farm implements and small hills of white that likely hid heaps of refuse, along with an old iron laundry sink. Unfrozen fetid rivulets of contaminated creek water splashed against it in steady slaps. Even the snow couldn't survive in this museum of human disrespect.

Near where he stood, an old clothesline tied to rusty poles drooped to the ground, and a warped table bore a white drift where a summer picnic might have lain. On the far side of the house, an ancient propane tank failed to evoke any promise of warmth or comfort. From the looks of things, the place was abandoned long ago, though as he struggled closer to the back door, he found a trail of boot tracks that led out to the shed and back again. Many tracks, some old, some new. His throat closed off.

He stopped moving and quickly flipped off the flashlight. Flakes gathered on his eyebrows and tried to linger on his nose which was almost too cold to melt them now. Beneath the parka, his muscles tensed. Except for the wind, the night was silent, all reasonable humans tucked in like the family across the street. No distant truck or car sounds superseded the steady stream of air muffled by his insufficient wool cap. He didn't dare call out for Juan. Feeling suddenly exposed, he recognized the need to find cover as quickly as possible.

When he moved again, two eerie red lights appeared side by side through a small window at the back of the house, like a glaring creature. He caught a breath and held it as an electric current passed through him. He was a dead man if anyone had the intention. A long, frozen moment of dread passed by. He still stood. Cautiously, quietly, he moved closer and peered inside.

Shadows scuttled across a kitchen floor. Mice. Or maybe rats from the size of them. The red lights seemed to come from the living room, which lay beyond the kitchen through an archway. Beyond that, he could see all the way through the house, through the big windows that had looked so black from the front steps. Some trick of reflection through prisms on an old lamp picked up the neighbor's lights across the street and sent sparks into the back yard, like tiny red warnings.

He laughed at himself and his grip on the flashlight relaxed. It reminded him of Juan's tales of *El Chupacabra*, the red-eyed, goat-sucking monster of South American folklore, so called because it drained the blood from its favorite victims. Still, he realized the huge mistake he'd made coming here alone. If anyone had been hiding inside…

He flinched as he recalled Min's, *I'm freezing my toes off just so you can be a hero again!* Was she right? Did he suffer from a savior complex?

He couldn't flee with any speed; his ankle wouldn't allow it. And he had to check that shed. Anyone trapped there in this cold—his stomach clenched. He had to be certain.

The chupacabra lights gave him an idea. He flipped the flashlight into emergency mode and covered all but a tiny spot of the red light with his hand, letting just enough bloody glow between his fingers to see the next step in front of him as he worked his way across, limping silently as possible, trying not to wonder how those footprints—and tire tracks—came to be in this deserted place.

As he feared, the boot tracks led to the wooden shed door, which hung crookedly on its hinges. Nearby, a bucket cast aside in the snow told him someone had used it as a toilet and he hitched his collar up, not to block the cold but the smell. He took a deep breath and put a shoulder to the door, wishing he'd thought of a weapon.

He had to shove hard before the door scraped loudly across dirt-strewn cement until it struck old tools propped behind it. Nobody. He let out a breath and opened the red beam wider.

A floor-to-ceiling cage stretched across the stinking shed, exactly as Min described it. Only it was empty.

Next to it, a shiny new space heater, cold as death.

Convinced he was alone, he reached for a pull string attached to a solitary bulb hanging overhead. He pulled. Nothing. He bent down and flipped a switch on the heater. Dead. From where it sat, aimed toward the cage, the place must have had power earlier, now killed by the storm. Not uncommon out here in the boondocks for one side of the road to have power while the other does not. Separate power grids.

The cage was vacant, yes, but someone had clearly used this place for he didn't want to think what, and it was important enough to them that they'd been paying the utility bills. Until the power went out. The footprints, the bucket, the new space heater…if Juan were held here, someone moved him when the electricity failed. They didn't want to commit murder—because clearly anyone in this tomb would die of hypothermia in no time at all.

So why had the note sent him here? Was it a trap? Didn't seem likely. They would have sprung it already. Maybe his secret adviser didn't know that Juan had been moved. Garritt felt confident that if he were set free and sent home, Luciana would have called him.

He patted his pocket for his phone. *Shit.* He'd left it in the truck again. He hated carrying that thing on his body but it was never handy when he needed it. He'd better go check for missed calls. He took one last look around the fetid shed, eschewed the opportunity to examine the inside of the cage, which seemed irrelevant and distasteful anyway, and turned to go.

A barn owl screeched over the swamp, which sent shivers up his spine and distracted him from the ridge of rotting wood at the base of the door frame. Seconds before his boot caught, he saw a flash of blue light, too late to stop him from catapulting sideways into the muddy snow outside the door. His elbow jammed against the used bucket and sharp ice crystals slashed his cheek as his face hit the ground. His ankle wrenched again and he howled like he'd broken the bone. He nearly passed out from the pain.

For a long time he lay stunned where he was. When he finally tried to stand, he couldn't put any weight on his foot at all. He fell back on the dirty snow. The flashlight had flown out of his hand when he went down. In the darkness, he couldn't see it anywhere within reach. No telltale red beam.

He spat a foul word, then hollered a stream of them at the top of his lungs, this time hopeful someone would hear him. After all his fleet-footedness in the jungle, what the hell was going on with him? He would have to get to his feet or he'd freeze to death in this pigsty.

He dragged his body painfully toward the shed, black as sin inside. He'd remembered how the door stuck earlier. Praying that all black widows hibernate in the cold, he fumbled behind it with his good arm until his hand hit a hard object and he was able to wrap fingers around it. When he yanked, a stack of long-handled tools clattered down on top of him but he had it: a wide-toothed garden rake. He used it to pull himself upright and leaned heavily against the handle. The house would provide better shelter than the useless shed, but to reach it would require a long scrabble through deep snow. He might make it if he kept to the boot tracks.

An eternity of pain and struggle later, he reached the back porch. The chupacabra lights mocked him from the kitchen but the porch windows were cheap, probably replaced by screens in summer. He pried at a flimsy frame. The cold made his fingers useless. His patience evaporated with the pain and the numbness and the steady burn in his nostrils from the wind. With a grunt of fury, he raised the rake and smashed at the glass. It shattered dutifully, scattering large, jagged pieces all over the interior floor.

Not safety glass. Not in this hovel, he noted foully.

He hadn't considered the challenge of climbing through the empty frame with one foot that couldn't hold his weight. One side or the other, he'd have to put weight on it anyway, unless he dove head first. With the floor covered in broken glass, he decided a boot-clad foot was preferable to an unprotected face. He knocked the remaining window shards from the frame and launched his hurt leg through.

Any neighbors within range should have heard his scream. The fact that no one came running as he lay there panting did not reassure him, except to confirm that the place housed only the fat rodents that scrambled off when he fell. He would love to remain where he landed but the porch wasn't much warmer than outside, and getting colder from the missing window. That's when he realized he'd left his rake-crutch lying outside, beyond reach.

With one good foot and his good right arm, he pushed and dragged himself to the kitchen door. Sitting up, he reached the doorknob, which twisted open easily. Despite the chill, the place smelled of mold and rot and piss. He boosted himself up along the door frame to balance on his right foot. A biting pain in his left palm drew his attention to a piece of glass embedded in his glove. He pulled it free and peeled back the material to stare at the fresh blood gushing out. His left ankle, leg, elbow, and now hand all throbbed like the fires of Hell.

"What's good about this?" he prompted himself aloud, almost unwillingly. It was a trick he'd learned from Elizabeth.

She insisted that whenever a "thought-train of negativity" threatened to push you over the precipice, you should stop yourself and ask, "But what's good about it?" She generally brought this up after he unleashed a tirade about ugly politics, especially Michigan Dutch politics. He never admitted to her that it actually did help him feel better.

He came up with: *Juan isn't out there in that cage, freezing to death.*

He thrust himself toward an old kitchen table and managed to catch the edge of it with his right hand. From here, he could see into the living room beyond.

Thank the Lord above, he thought, and immediately hated the fact that he'd dragged up the old phrase. Nevertheless in the dim light reflected from the neighbor's house, he'd seen his potential salvation: a pot-bellied iron stove dominated one end of the long, narrow room.

Funny how we revert when we get in trouble, he mused as he hobbled toward it, supporting himself against the walls. *We call on the gods above as if we believe they would never leave us here to suffer alone, even after we've left them.*

A golden light flickered in and out of his awareness.

"And you!" he called aloud. "Where were you when I needed you?"

This time, the light that responded was not gold, but a large, silvery-edged, diamond shape, with a dazzling center that seemed to open into Infinity. He'd never seen anything like it before.

Here all along, it seemed to say, *had you but turned your thoughts our way.*

That broke him. He slumped down to the floor in a tsunami of self-pity. Defeated. Helpless. In need of rescue. In over his head.

And no one to care about him anymore—not his ex-wife, not his parents, no old friends from school. Juan, who might have cared, lost and hurt, and he wasn't capable of doing a damn thing to help the kid. And the woman he'd just met who might have been a match, maybe the real partner he longed for, someone who drew secrets out of him he never intended to share? She was wrong in so, so many ways. And she had also vanished. He hadn't even had the sense to get her number. To top it off, now this light said he screwed up because he didn't think to ask for help?

Nonsense. Had he asked for that bright blue light of warning back in the shed? No, and it showed up anyway. In fact, maybe that flash had alerted his subconscious, mitigating the fall. It could have been so much worse. He could be lying unconscious in the snow, dead before he knew what happened.

If he couldn't get to that stove and light it, there was a serious chance he could still die. He already felt groggy, an early symptom of hypothermia. With or without help, golden lights or silver, pain like hellfire or not, he realized he had to make it.

Except that he couldn't get off the floor.

Shit.

He'd had no right to set off on a rescue mission when he could barely walk. And now look at him, sitting in the dark like an idiot.

And what an idiot he'd been. Trying to play hero.

Loser!

Maybe Elizabeth was right. He'd not only inherited his father's temper, but also his conceit. He couldn't escape it—or the Calvinist work ethic that meant he could never let things be. He had to push himself to interfere where he wasn't meant to.

The flood of recriminations crushed down on his soul so hard, they twirled him into a sewer of self-disgust. He felt like hurling, as the cold seeped up from the dingy floor, penetrating his wet jeans, freezing his senses and his balls.

Frosted balls.

He snorted.

Snowballs.

He started to chuckle. He had become the proverbial snowball in Hell!

His sense of the ridiculous came spiraling back to him and he laughed a little. The more he thought about how screwed he was, the harder he laughed, until tears came pouring out of his eyes and the dark cloud pulled back down the hallway that led, presumably, into filthy, rodent-hosting bedrooms of frigid horror. He laughed hysterically at the image because it probably wasn't even exaggerated.

I'm every movie hero who plunges ahead while the audience yells, "Don't go in there!"

What ever made him think he could rescue Juan from people bold enough to steal him out from under their noses? In broad daylight?

The laughter shook his sides until they added to his list of hurts—and shattered his self-pity trance. He struggled up from the floor against a cascade of hurt that caught in his throat and sobered him back down. Panting, he leaned against the wall to catch his breath.

Juan is probably safe at home now, making out with his girlfriend. He's telling her exaggerated tales of his kidnapping at the hands of evil government agents, while I'm here freezing my balls off. He thought of his close escape in Peru, of the crazy chances he took there. *This time I probably will die—and it will be my own damn fault.*

Steeling himself against the pain, he hopped slowly along the wall to the pot-bellied stove that suddenly looked like something out of a Disney cartoon, fantastical and too perfect. He wasn't even surprised to find a basket of neatly trimmed wood and kindling by its side. He hooted hysterically when he fumbled around in the dark and found a box of long matches waiting for him.

First his budding hypothermia made everything seem hilarious; now the cold dulled his brain but he tried to reason, *The tire-track people would have needed these things. There are rats in the kitchen because they left food. Maybe they left some in the refrigerator that hasn't rotted yet.*

That motivated him to move faster as he strained to lay the newspaper and kindling. He had enough brain-power left to realize that he couldn't drink water from the sink because of the contaminated well. His parched throat began to ache. He fantasized about melting snow atop the wood stove, if only he had a container full of it, and he both cursed and laughed at the fact that he'd worked so hard to get out of the snow and now all he wanted was a kettle full of the stuff.

Before long, the stove flamed up to consume the dry logs in its belly. Light cast about the dreary room to reveal worn and dirty, pea-soup colored carpet and an old beach chair someone had set up beneath the window. Empty beer cans stuffed with cigarette butts lay near it on the stained rug. Garritt managed to pull the chair closer and fall into it. He reached to warm his hands as the stove's iron sides began to throw off gales of heat. Then he dragged the wood basket nearer and propped up his injured ankle. That made it hurt worse but at least he'd finally elevated it, as grandmother wisdom commanded.

By then he was so exhausted, he contemplated leaving the snow-packed boots on his feet, following a cloudy idea that the stove would melt the snow and maybe he could drink it somehow. But after a moment he thought better of that plan and laboriously unlaced both boots.

Pulling them off required a fight but at last he saw the horrible purple swelling in his left ankle, which made him instantly nauseous. When he pulled up his pants leg, he saw the reason for the pain in his shin: a long scrape and bruising, and a welt the size of a tangerine in the middle of the mess. *Bone bruise.* He'd heard of them. Painful and long-lasting. Was it the pavement or the door frame, he wondered groggily. He decided to leave his wet woolen socks on, hoping they'd dry in the heat, and endured sharp stabs as he adjusted more firewood under his foot for better support. He collapsed back against the beach chair, breathless.

He felt his last bits of energy flood down his arms and out the tips of his fingers, trail away from his hips and down legs that had been frozen inside wet jeans for too long. He couldn't stay in this place. He didn't know when someone might come back and he'd done nothing to find Juan. He had to get to his truck, as soon as he brought himself back from the brink of hypothermia and regained enough strength to undertake the journey.

After a few minutes, his head grew heavier and fell to the side. He shook himself awake.

I can't fall asleep. He readjusted his posture.

A minute later his head fell to the other side and he reasoned sleepily that maybe a minute or two wouldn't hurt.

As he lost consciousness, he heard himself emit a deep, troubled snore but he didn't care any more and let himself release into sweet oblivion.

∞

Min couldn't stop seeing that mental image of Garritt in the rear-view mirror, worry creasing his face until he dissolved in a storm of white and stupid Alex ordered the helicopter to block her path down the road. Couldn't the guy follow simple directions? She told him to run. What if they'd wanted him, too?

She fussed with the seat belt on the passenger jet, trying to get comfortable.

Amrita had sounded happy on the phone to pick her up in Min's Tesla. Her meeting with the Commander wasn't scheduled until tomorrow morning San Diego time; she might be able to catch some sleep first.

To distract Amrita from asking awkward questions during the call, Min asked how her training was going.

"For a long time, I thought neck meant peninsula but last week it was neck and the quake happened somewhere in the middle of Morocco," her roommate sighed over the phone.

To Min's way of thinking, merely sensing an earthquake before it happened was astonishing enough but Amrita was that kind of perfectionist.

"I know I can master this," she said. "There has to be a pattern, a language to it—else why can I feel it? What use is this weird ability? And by the way, it is *not* pleasant to feel that kind of pain. There must be a purpose!"

Min managed to end their call before Amrita brought up questions about her love life. That was precisely not the territory she wanted to explore right now.

She plugged in her earphones and tried to take a nap that didn't have her dreaming about muscled farmer/chefs. She hoped to see the mercurial Reverend Ben and ask all the questions he hadn't answered.

Instead, she dreamt of tanks and troops emerging from the swirling snow in black stealth gear.

19

Trackers

∞

Agnes had been checking on Garritt's location almost hourly since he and Minda disappeared out the back door of Avery's that morning. She knew she shouldn't. He'd only given her his passcode one day when he couldn't find his phone and she was probably supposed to forget it. But she couldn't help herself. The blizzard was breaking all records; no one should be driving in it. He hadn't called or texted. Not even to Corbyn.

From the tracking app, she could see that they'd gotten close to Swan Creek Marsh, but then they turned around for some reason without ever reaching it and went to Garritt's house outside of Hamilton.

The hours they spent there—Agnes didn't want to think what she was thinking. But the woman was very pretty, after all. And he was a handsome man, still in his prime as far as Agnes could see (never mind that he was more than ten years older than her). It's what men do, she told herself. Like the roosters in the barnyard, sometimes it didn't mean anything. Especially a man like Garritt who'd had his heart so badly broken by Elizabeth and who probably needed comfort…

She managed to put the thought out of her mind until Doris arrived to take her lunch shift. (She'd traded for Doris's dinner shift—long story but it had a lot to do with Doris's date with the widower Ed, which was pretty amazing for two people that old.) Once she went home to rest, the idea of Garritt and Minda together drove her crazy and she started checking the location of Garritt's phone every half hour. Still at his house.

Then, right in the middle of the blizzard, which was piling snow up all around her family's two-story farmhouse, Garritt's phone moved.

Insane to go out again in a freak storm like this one! They were moving down the road to Hamilton, she could see. Maybe to dinner together?

No, Agnes. Forget that. You have to go back in to work now.

And that's where she learned about the helicopter (!) that had landed in the middle of Veenlanden while she was at home. She'd missed it! The most exciting thing EVER to happen in tiny Veenlanden!

Every customer who braved the storm came in babbling about the three men in the black chopper who had terrified the Petersons.

"Dropped smack down in the front yard and made off with that tourist woman's old Ford…"

"Said they had her permission."

"Nobody believes that—but who's gonna argue with the CIA?"

"I heard Frank Peterson came out the front door with his shotgun."

"Hah! Old Frank couldn't take out a helicopter with a cannon. Hell, he can't hit the side of a barn. Eyesight ain't what it used to be…"

And so on, through the dinner shift.

Of course, Agnes herself had half expected an angry husband to show up looking for the woman, with that scar and all, but not the CIA—or whoever they were. She suspected most of her customers came in that night only to gossip and speculate, given the fearsome amount of snow still blowing down the street. She didn't live far at all and she'd had a heck of a time getting back to work.

Then around nine, Juan's girlfriend Luciana showed up begging to know if Corbyn or she or Sam (who was also working the dinner shift—another long story) had heard anything yet. They exchanged numbers and Agnes promised to let her know about any news.

Everyone Agnes spoke to seemed to be in a state of curiosity or agitation, or like Luciana, pure anxiety. Agnes wasn't convinced that Minda was some kind of agent whose partners came to relocate her Ford, like most were saying. On the other hand, some speculated that with her sleek little jacket, junky car, and that terrible scar on her forehead, she might be some criminal they were after. An *international* criminal, maybe a drug runner or a terrorist. Or like in *Ozark*, some kind of money launderer.

That made Agnes fear for Garritt all over again.

But what if they had it backwards? What if the helicopter men were the bad guys, and what if *Minda* were the good agent?

Wouldn't that be a switch, thought Agnes, and she liked the thought because she had instinctively liked the woman. People had stupid fixed ideas, she decided. *Bigots, all of them, always thinking the stranger's face is the guilty face.* Her new friend wasn't the one stealing a car and terrifying the poor Petersons, now, was she?

But why here? Why now? And where were Juan and Garritt?

Soonika, she soon discovered. Of all places!

She had a cousin who bought a farm there once. Crazy desolate place, nothing to do out there. Only the blueberries liked that sour dirt, so her cousin soon sold the farm and moved his family to a house in Spring Lake, which was a bold thing for anyone in Agnes's family to do, to give up on farming like that. That's how bleak Soonika was. She couldn't understand why Garritt would make that dangerous trip in the blizzard—unless he thought Juan might be there. That must be why. So what did that have to do with the helicopter?

She kept checking through the evening. His phone didn't move. He was still in Soonika.

What if they got stuck in a ditch and no one was out in the storm to find them? Because who would be in that place, where there was nothing? As far as she could tell, Garritt's phone never moved again.

She couldn't shake the premonition that something went wrong, that his life was in danger. She could feel it deep in her heart and she was trying not to panic. What if they weren't in a ditch but the people who took Juan had now captured Garritt and Minda, too?

All her life she'd had these little premonitions. "Women's intuition," her mother called it. Supposedly it ran in the family but skipped her mother's generation. "You're just like your grandmother," she told Agnes.

It was true that she could sense things, and she was more often right than wrong. She frequently knew what people needed before they asked for it (if they ever did). She knew better than they did, which is one of the things that made her so good at waitressing.

Finally, desperately, just before they locked up, she whispered to Sam, "We have to save them."

She wasn't friends with Samantha. She'd actually been very jealous every time Garritt came out from the kitchen to flirt with her. But Agnes had cooked up a plan and she wasn't willing to execute it by herself, and sometimes Sam was okay. Besides, who else would be crazy enough to go with her in this blizzard? Certainly not the other hostess, Courtney, who complained about the smallest inconveniences. Lucky that Sam was on duty that night, plucky Sam who loved to talk about her wild exploits around the world.

Right now the hostess was busy gathering up her things, barely paying attention to Agnes.

"What? Save who?"

"Garritt and Minda—*Min*," she corrected, deciding that they would be friends from here on out.

"Garritt? Why? Didn't you say he was at home?"

Agnes blushed. "He was. But then he left—or they left. Then the helicopter—don't you find that very strange? And then—" she blushed again.

"You've been tracking him!" Sam smiled at her for some reason, as if she'd just done something amazingly wonderful. "You little stalker!"

Agnes didn't know what to say. If she weren't so terrified for him now, freezing to death in a snowbank, or something worse—if not already dead because he hadn't called to say otherwise—she would never admit she'd been tracking Garritt all day. She just nodded.

"Well? Where is he now, little creeper?"

"Probably stuck in the snow. Or held prisoner in Soonika!" she blurted. Tears streaked a white line through the last of the blush that had nearly rubbed off her round cheeks during a long, sweaty night shift.

"Soonika!? Isn't that way the hell out in the boonies, a long way north of here?"

"Yes," her voice cracked, "and he hasn't moved for hours."

Sam sighed, plopped her rucksack back down. "I'll probably never see my pussy hat again."

"Sam! Garritt could be dead—or dying! We have to go find him. And what about Juan? And that woman?"

"Did you tell Corbyn?"

Corbyn would never let her hear the end of it, her tracking Garritt with a phone app. *He* would immediately understand why she did it, so of course she hadn't told Corbyn.

"No."

"Yeah, I don't blame you. He's too worried about Avery and his little doggies. And the restaurant, what with the storm keeping people home—not to mention having to play chef all day. Okay, so how do you propose we get to him?"

Agnes felt a wave of relief. Thankfully Sam hadn't teased her about her feelings for Garritt, which must be so obvious by now. But then, Sam was often so caught up in her own concerns, she failed to notice the people around her.

"We're going to take my brother's truck. He's got snow tires."

"And how do we convince him?"

"I know where he keeps his keys."

"Agnes!" A twinkle of respect flickered in Sam's eyes. "You are just full of surprises, aren't you?" She elbowed her.

Agnes giggled a little and pushed Sam's arm away. She did feel a thrill at the audaciousness of her plan.

"Lead the way, then. I wasn't eager to drive myself back to a cold studio in Saugatuck anyway. Wait—" She reached back behind the retail counter for some water bottles and a few fistfuls of provisions, throwing deli meats, cheeses, and leftover rolls in a paper bag. "He probably hasn't eaten in a while, and maybe we might need to eat something, too," she explained and grabbed a few more things. "Emergency rations. Don't tell Corbyn."

"Of course not," Agnes whispered conspiratorially.

By the time they reached Soonika, it was near midnight.

Agnes had driven them into a shallow ditch almost immediately, trying to get her brother Stewart's Dodge Ram out of the farm's long driveway, which was incredibly slippery because her oldest brother, Nathan, had cleared it earlier, leaving a slick layer of ice beneath the new snow, so really, it wasn't her fault. But Sam had to get out and push/rock until Agnes got the old truck back onto the drive. Thankfully, her family was well asleep by then. Most of them got up by five every morning, and they were far enough from the farmhouse, none were likely to hear her rev the engine, especially with the muffling snowfall. But after that, Sam insisted that she should drive, that Agnes was far too worried.

"You can't fool me. Every time you talk, your voice goes up another notch."

Agnes couldn't argue. It was true. She panicked to think of all the ways Garritt could be in trouble. She'd seen and heard a lot of things—tractor accidents, people falling down old wells, getting trampled by cows, or dropping dead while trying to work in cold that was so shocking, it stopped their hearts.

Of course, that last was a story Stewart told her when she was little and she wasn't sure whether it was true or not. Stewart loved to torment her with scary stories, right up to the present day, long after she'd become an adult, purely because they both lived at home and he could. She was an easy target, always gullible, and she couldn't seem to stop being that way. He got her every time. But she hadn't given up. One day, she'd be quicker.

At last, many scary miles later, they crept along Apple Drive, no other cars in sight. That's where the app showed Garritt's phone to be.

"Look! Over there!"

Sam slowed to a stop. "Where? I don't see anything."

"On the right, just ahead. Keep going—slowly."

Sam eased the silver Dodge forward until Agnes yelled at her to stop. Agnes tapped her phone light on, jumped out the passenger door, and ran down the icy road toward the green panel that stuck out from a bank of plowed snow. Tears froze on her cheeks, which she could no longer feel in the bitter-cold night.

He's dead.

Her heart pounded with dread and anxiety and a host of other feelings she'd never in her life felt before, one of which was a slim hope that they'd arrived in time. If not dead, he surely must be unconscious, or he would have fled from this smashed wreck that was once Garritt's beloved truck.

From the looks of it, the snowplow had clipped the back corner, hooked on it, and twisted the truck deep into the ditch. The county driver must not have seen the green pickup, between the spew of the rig and the wind scuttling more snow across the landscape. Agnes played her light across the thick white blanket that obscured the cab and covered the truck bed, adding to their invisibility. As she drew closer, it looked as if a second plow came through and buried the truck deeper.

Breathlessly, she scraped frozen layers from the window with her mittened fingers while she tried the door. Locked. She shined her light through. The cab was mostly intact—but no Garritt, no Min. She could see his phone still attached to a holder on the dash—and another—Juan's—wedged into the seat crease at the back of the passenger side. Garritt's phone had been here for hours, she knew. So where were they?

Sam shut off the Dodge and trudged slowly toward her, as if she didn't want to see what was inside.

"It's okay, he's not in it," Agnes shouted back to her.

"So where do you think he is?"

Agnes mulled this for a moment. She stared down the deserted road one direction, then the other.

Behind them, on the same side, a mailbox poked through a drift. Beyond the bare trees that lined the road, she made out the silhouette of a darkened house. Across the road from where they stood, amber night lights blazed from a house that looked almost festive in its snowy drapery. He wasn't there, intuition told her, and she felt a deep plunge in her gut when she realized they needed to focus on the dark house down the long driveway.

"Come with me," she called as she plunged straight into the ditch, then climbed up to the tree line where empty branches whipped and whistled in the strong wind.

"Are you crazy? I'm freezing my ass off out here!"

"Come on!" Agnes insisted, plowing through deep snow. "But keep quiet now."

Sam muttered something but gamely followed Agnes's tracks as they broke through the top layers of icy white. Cold flakes skittered across the frozen surface. They were yards from the driveway, plunging straight toward the house through the edges of the snow-bound property.

Agnes wore winter stockings beneath her midi-skirt but she would have gladly traded for some of Sam's woolly leggings. She sank up to her thighs in the deepest spots, soaking her thin work clothes. Fortunately they'd both worn boots and heavy coats that day. She pulled her stocking cap low over her ears and inched up the collar of her Army-green jacket. She could hear bare-headed Sam mutter what Agnes suspected to be curse words and she was glad she couldn't hear more in this wind. She didn't like it when people took the Lord's name in vain, and this wasn't a time to offend Him, in her opinion. They needed all the help they could get to rescue Garritt and Juan and Min. (She ticked them off in that specific order.)

As they came out of the trees, Agnes stopped abruptly and Sam, probably busy looking down, bumped into her from behind. A shiny black SUV sat in the driveway. No snow lay piled on its top, meaning it hadn't been there long.

"Shh," Agnes put her hand up to stop Sam's grumbling. She caught a blur of motion inside the house, followed by the distinct sound of men's raised voices, loud enough to hear through the wind and the wool that covered her ears.

20

Rescue

∽

Garritt was enjoying a nice, dreaming sleep next to that wonderfully warm stove. In fact, he dreamed about how he and Juan first met.

He was lying in a snow bank at the edge of a parking square. A fringe of black dirt crusted the tops and sides of the icy, half-melted pile, where recent lot scrapings churned up as much slushy dirt as snow. It was early March, some time after one a.m., and he'd been drinking—heavily. Elizabeth had recently left him, saying that she couldn't tolerate another summer on the farm, that he was too much like his father, believing life was about work and never play.

She said that her way of thinking could not acclimate to his lifestyle of toil and more toil, from morning till night. That she'd made a terrible mistake marrying him. That their dreams for the farm had not come true, and that he was childish to think they ever would. His parents' curse on their marriage was like a foulness that seeped in, she told him, and their influence could not be removed unless he came away with her to Arizona, but she wasn't even sure she wanted that. In fact, she knew she didn't. She needed to be free again, to breathe-in nature without any need to control it. She must flee from him, or she would be trapped forever in this suffocating marriage that had sucked all the joy from her...

In the dream, she loomed over him like some kind of dark angel as her words echoed the curses his parents had uttered. In life, those words repeated inside his head but in this dream, they danced above it like typewritten text.

For weeks, in life and in this dream replay, he drank and he drank and he drank. He started in the mornings and stopped only when he passed out. But the words kept circling. Finally, he decided that drinking at home wasn't enough. That only made him more depressed. So he took himself to a bar all the way over in Veenlanden where no one knew him, one he'd never entered before, a dark little place down the street from where Avery's Café would one day come into existence.

A local Mexican-American family owned the place. Piñatas hung over the bar and mariachi hats decorated the walls. He drank margaritas with an extra shot of tequila on the side, ordering one after another. Eventually he switched to straight tequila, until at last he passed out on the bar and the proprietor threw him out, bodily pushed him out the door and slammed it behind him.

He'd staggered for a while, then landed on what looked like it might be a white featherbed. It was hard as stone, the packed ice, and in fact real stones from the parking lot stabbed at various parts of his foul-smelling body. He was beyond caring. He hoped to die there, frozen into white oblivion, and that would show her. Then she would care. She would be so sorry for the words she said, which pierced his heart and carved the life-giving portions away as surely as if she used the kitchen cleaver. She would see how he suffered.

Then Juan, just a youngster. Garritt's dream displayed the colors more vividly than the original event and this time he could see things from Juan's perspective, looking down at the disgusting, vomit-covered hulk lying in the snow.

Why he'd stirred the boy's compassion, he would never know. That was Juan's secret and he had never explained. But without him that night, Garritt was certain he would have gotten his wish. He would have died in that parking lot.

The boy dragged him by a boot back toward the building—no easy task, as Garritt wasn't helping. Juan pounded on the back alley door, yelling in Spanish, until the man who'd thrown Garritt out appeared.

"*¿Que chingados quieres?* What are you doing?"

"This man will die if we leave him there, *Tio*."

"*Ay, Dios mio!*" And far more foul words poured from the uncle's mouth.

"*Por favor,*" Juan begged on Garritt's behalf.

The uncle muttered again under his breath, *"Poquito pito."* Grudgingly he opened the door wider and shoved Juan aside to drag Garritt by himself toward the men's room.

"Clean him up and when he's awake, keep him out of my sight," the uncle ordered. "And don't ever do this again if you want to keep working for me!"

The dream shifted and Garritt saw Juan standing beside the river holding a fishing pole, months later, after their friendship evolved.

Juan's uncle had called the police immediately that night. But before they could take him off to sober up in a cell, Juan managed to sneak him out the back door and down the street to the place where his family lived. It wasn't a fancy house by any means, but it was warm and lighted and so much more comfortable than the snowdrift as a place to die.

Instead of cursing like her brother, Juan's mother simply shook her head, patted Juan's shoulder, and called him her sweet son—*Mijo*—in a tone that even Garritt's groggy awareness could appreciate. She kept the secret from Juan's father somehow, and after Garritt got to know her better, he realized she must have bought her brother's silence as well with some kind of sisterly blackmail. Now when he thought of the abstract concept of mother, he thought of Juanita—not his cold, repressed, biological mother who had stopped speaking to him years ago.

Garritt spent many evenings eating the enchiladas Juanita made while he listened to Juan gripe about his teenage woes. He learned countless vulgarities in Spanish, which liberally seasoned the language of the men in Juan's family. The Talamantes saved his life in so many ways: their closeness, their jokes, their laughter, even their religion—which was supposed to be among the most repressive. Compared to the frigid Calvinism of his upbringing, it seemed liberal and life-affirming to Garritt. Color, warmth, effusive emotion, dancing, feasting, and happiness in the midst of what his own parents would consider extreme poverty—this made Garritt happy. Juan and his family were gracious enough to welcome him into that life, time after time, as he regained his sobriety and his willingness to live again.

Then the dream turned and Minda Blake's radiant face came before him. She was bringing him a gift. What was it? He couldn't see. A box—but what was in it? She wasn't smiling. She looked so serious, as if his life might depend on what it contained. He reached for it but she turned and set it down on a table he didn't recognize. He tried to walk toward it but the box had gone. He turned and she was gone as well. But he heard a voice, distantly, calling his name.

He opened his eyes to see a bright blue light flash before him and hear the front door rattle as someone inserted a key. The pot-bellied stove had gone cold and his skin colder. His leg throbbed like hell. He reached down instinctively to grab a fire log just as the door flew open and two men surged into the room. He couldn't stand so he swung wildly at the first guy who came near. The log smashed into the arm the man threw up to block the blow.

The second man grabbed Garritt's arm on the backswing and twisted it painfully until he dropped the piece of wood.

"You're coming with us," he yanked Garritt to his feet.

Garritt yelled as the pain gripped his leg.

"Serves you right, asswipe."

The man whose arm he'd struck forced a black bag over Garritt's head. He heard one of them pick up his boots. The other flex-cuffed his hands in front of him.

"Boss wants him unharmed," he ordered, and Garritt figured that saved his life.

∞

Agnes swallowed hard to keep the lump in her throat from emerging into a sob or a shout as they watched two men drag Garritt out of the house. Juan and Min were nowhere in sight.

By now she'd gripped fingernails so hard into Sam's mittened palm that she had to catch herself and let up the pressure before Sam started to protest. In this blizzard, with her light off, at the edge of clustered trees, frozen in horror, she hoped they were nearly invisible. She didn't dare move her head to catch Sam's eye or wave at her to be quiet.

Despite the cold seeping down into her bones, despite the scene before her, Agnes's mind spun out plans. The minute she felt it was safe, she yanked on Sam's arm and dragged her helter-skelter back through the trees toward her brother's Dodge pickup.

The black SUV had started to move but she calculated that the deepening drifts would slow its pace. To avoid them, the driver wouldn't risk a turn-around. They'd have to back out. That gave Agnes and Sam a few extra minutes.

"You drive!" she shouted when they reached the cab.

Sam obediently climbed behind the steering wheel and fired up the engine, which thankfully started on the first try. "We're following them, right?"

Agnes felt a wave a gratitude that Sam understood. She'd chosen the right partner.

"Exactly." She pulled out her phone to start a series of rapid texts to Luciana.

Found Garritt.

Where?

Men in SUV have him

OMG

We are following. Hope it leads to Juan

R U crazy?

Gather friends and brothers. Text address when we get there

Si – I understand.

"Who are you texting?"

"Luciana. Told her to bring friends."

Sam nodded knowingly.

Agnes didn't have to tell Sam to wait until the SUV disappeared down the road and into the white-out before she pulled the pickup out to make a careful U-turn. In this weather, it wouldn't be difficult to catch up, and the heavy snowfall offered perfect cover for tailing them like some random vehicle that was forced to creep down the icy road behind the slow-moving SUV. Stewart's Dodge truck probably had better traction but they would pretend it didn't.

Thankfully, Sam seemed to be all-in on this expedition and kept her distance like a pro.

Agnes went back to work on her phone, calling a number, hanging up, calling again, hanging up ...

"What are you doing now?"

Sam followed the SUV down a road that passed through Spring Lake on its way to Grand Haven, a Lake Michigan resort town near the north point of the Dutch Triangle, just south of Muskegon.

"Calling my brother."

"The one whose truck we've stolen?"

"It's okay. I left him a note. I know he's getting up early for work tomorrow so he's got his phone on Do Not Disturb. Two rings will break through in an emergency, and this is definitely an emergency."

Finally they heard Stewart groan over the phone's speaker.

"Stew! I need your help!"

"Agnes?" came a sleep-clouded voice. "What? Where are you?"

"I'm in your truck on the way to Grand Haven, I think."

"You what!??" Wide-awake yell now.

"I'll explain everything later but they've taken Garritt and we're following them into Grand Haven and we need you and your friends."

Then she thought of her oldest brother who lived down the road from her parents' farm. Why not? His truck had the plow on the front.

"And wake up Nathan and ask him to bring his shotgun and his hunting friends—you'll need his truck anyway," she added a little sheepishly. Then realized, "And don't wake up Mom and Dad, whatever you do! Not yet, anyway."

Her brother tried to interrupt with all sorts of groggy, shouting, angry protests and threats about when he got his hands on her again, along with a few questions, but she just kept repeating herself and making herself perfectly clear as often as necessary to get through to him. This was a once-in-a-lifetime necessity to be brave and bold, she insisted.

"Your little sister's life might be in danger, and Juan's!"

Stew knew Juan. Everyone liked Juan.

"And Garritt! And the scar-woman with the helicopter." That did it. Everyone knew about the helicopter. She knew her brother couldn't resist an inside scoop. Not to mention his sister's rare state of agitation, and maybe a slight respect for her past expressions of "woman's intuition" that had bailed him out of uncertain situations more than once.

Reluctantly, he agreed to come to whatever address she texted him. But she had to work hard to convince him to wake up his older brother and all their friends. She gave him as many dramatic, intriguing possibilities as she could.

They would all be as bored as anyone who lived out in the country. Rural people would leave their couches to stream out in the middle of the night if some barn or house caught fire, just to be the first to post photos of the smoke or the flames lighting up the sky. Probably a hereditary instinct from the days when they'd be first on the scene to help put the fire out. Sometimes that still happened, filling a dull night with unexpected heroism. Most would also go boldly out with their shotguns to investigate any loud explosion echoing through the woods that didn't sound like a gunshot. Usually it was nothing more than a falling tree, but one could never be too sure. Whatever happened next, she knew these guys would compete to be first on social with the news—their own form of contemporary heroics.

She won the argument, hung up satisfied, and went back to texting updates on their location to both Luciana and Stewart, as promised.

Heading south toward Grand Haven

"Agnes," Sam said quietly.

"Yes?"

"Why aren't we calling the police?"

"Because they're the ones who took Juan and lost him. You think they're going to help us now? I don't trust them."

Sam just nodded thoughtfully, as if that made sense to her. She wasn't exactly a God-fearing, law-abiding citizen, Agnes knew, although she wondered how deep that posturing went for Sam, whether it wasn't simply a part of her tough-girl act and not an inbred distrust of government authority like Agnes was raised with.

They followed the speeding SUV at a safe distance through the little town of Spring Lake, mostly asleep now, and then across the Grand River near where it flowed into Lake Michigan, then turned south on old Highway 31, passing a Taco Bell, KFC, and Great Lakes Greek Chili Dogs.

"Hey, hand me some of that deli cheese, will you? I'm starving!"

"How can you be hungry at a time like this?" Agnes's own stomach churned so rabidly she wouldn't dare eat a bite. She handed Sam a chunk of Midnight Moon from the restaurant bag.

"Stress makes me hungry," she explained through the expensive cheese in her mouth. "How about some bread?"

Agnes tore off some of the sunflower bread Pamela had baked that morning, taking a small chunk for herself, thinking maybe she should try to eat something, keep up her strength. It balled up in her mouth and wouldn't go down so she rolled down the window and spit it into the wind, which was still blowing intermittent squalls across Lake Michigan.

At the moment, they had good visibility and the SUV stuck to primary roads, all plowed and sanded now.

"They're still going straight," Sam announced unnecessarily, because Agnes had her eyes glued to either her phone or the tail lights of the SUV carrying Garritt to some horrible place, she was certain of it.

When she'd seen them drag him out of that deserted house with a black hood over his head, she'd flashed on scenes from her late-night TV binges up in her room, on the little used flat-screen she'd bought with money from waitressing. Endless violence, always someone hurting someone else. In addition to her woman's intuition she also had a vivid imagination to churn up terrifying scenarios.

She blamed the mundane quality of life on the farm for her tendency to imagine things. Not that nature wasn't ever-changing, so that no two days of feeding or plucking or weeding were ever the same, because something different always showed up in nature to keep humans on their toes, but that the steady, day-in and day-out routine demanded by plant, animal, and human created mind-numbing monotony over the years. At least now at the restaurant she had the potential to meet new faces—such as Garritt, who'd gone off to South America and come back a hero. Or this Minda woman, who posed the biggest mystery Agnes had ever encountered.

Where had the scar-woman disappeared to? She wasn't with those men…unless…

Just as her thoughts swung to another ugly scenario, the SUV made a turn. They were headed straight for the lake shore, south of Grand Haven now but north of Rosy Dunes. Agnes grabbed up her phone to text both Luciana and Stewart. She had to reverse directions in her mind; they'd be coming up from the south:

Take 31N to Robbins and turn left

And a minute later:

Left again on Lakeshore Dr

Far up ahead, the SUV made another turn. Agnes couldn't read the sign until Sam reached the spot.

Right on Brucker St

Luciana replied: On our way

Stewart: You are so dead we're a few miles south

Their confirmations made her sit back with a nervous smile. She'd read once in a self-help book to "act first without permission and ask forgiveness later." This might have been her first opportunity to live a real life. The blood coursing through her veins settled into a steady fire of commitment. She liked this feeling.

The SUV turned again, this time down one of those winding lanes, not so well plowed, that led to a network of private dirt driveways, most unmarked. Those would lead inevitably to the edge of the dunes, where rich people built their sprawling summer houses.

"Stop here," she commanded Sam.

"Why?" Sam squinted at the narrowly-plowed path down which the SUV disappeared.

"They'll never find us if we keep going."

"Who? And we'll lose *them* if we don't!" She pointed at the SUV's brake lights as they turned out of sight.

"Luciana and my brother—they're bringing friends."

"I heard that but I didn't think Stewart would listen to you."

"He did," and Agnes had to pause to allow herself a small triumphant smile. That must be a first. Then she brought herself back to the situation at hand.

"We should be able to follow their tracks from here, since no other idiots are out in this weather. But what would we do if we followed right up to their door? What then, when they saw us?"

"I was trying not to think about that," Sam admitted.

"So we just wait here for now. They can't go much farther anyway. The lake is right there"—she pointed—"a couple blocks west of here." But she had another idea. She opened a different app.

Sam turned on her, incredulous. "You're going on Facebook now?"

"No, I'm going to find my friend Denise. I know she's up and she's always on Facebook. She's got skills."

Sam shook her head. "Redneck tribe."

"Exactly," Agnes agreed, completely unoffended.

It was true. This is what rednecks did when they weren't mucking out horse stalls. They dreamed about moving out of state to find a different life than the one their parents were born into. The internet made the alternatives more real than before, although just as difficult to attain. The hardest part was to break free of the status quo. That meant leaving family, and family was sometimes one's most important social group, much as Agnes and her friends hated to admit it. Whom did they rely on for advice, support—monetary and spiritual—and sometimes sheer rescue? Family. Moving away risked the loss of one's support system. She knew she wasn't ready for that. Not yet.

And then there were friends like Denise.

A few frenzied exchanges later and Denise was on standby, ready to plug in an address to see if she could find out who owned it.

Agnes sat still for a moment, breathing, watching the flakes fall slowly from the sky. She fervently hoped the wind would stay calm just a little longer until the whole posse arrived. She said a little prayer for Garritt, Juan, and yes, Min, so no harm would come to them in the meantime. Then she turned admiringly to Sam, for whom she suddenly felt immense gratitude.

"You sure drive good for a city girl," she grinned.

Sam actually blushed at the compliment. "Thank you. That's what we city girls are good for. But Dude, trade places with me before your brothers show up with their shotguns!"

"I'd be glad to but we're not waiting for them." Agnes scribbled something on a scrap of paper, the back of a church flyer she'd found stashed in Stewart's glove compartment.

"We're not?"

Agnes was already out of the truck with her phone light on.

"Shit! Wait for me," Sam called as she scrambled out after her. "How will your people find us?"

"I left a note," Agnes assured her. "Told them to follow our tracks."

"What about your friend with skills, Denise?"

Agnes texted as she walked down the road. "She's going to track my phone now and look up whatever address we arrive at."

Then she sent another text to her brother, telling him not to be concerned if "a bunch of Mexicans" converged on the site at the same time. They'd be friends, not foes. She knew her brothers would be fine but she wasn't sure how their friends might react. They weren't exactly palsy-walsy with "Mexicans," even though Juan and his friends were all born in the U.S., technically Mexican-American, but both groups stuck to their own communities. Most of her brothers' friends were brought up by parents who didn't know any better, so they perpetuated the local standard prejudices (to Agnes, totally exasperating) which they'd been taught as youngsters. Some of those boys in their twenties still hadn't grown up.

She texted Luciana:

White boys coming too. My brothers and friends. Keep them from fighting ok

How? you know how men are

Juan and their sister in danger. Common enemy

I get it

"You sure are clever for a country girl," Sam called out as she tried to keep up with Agnes's determined pace.

"Thank you," she called back. "It's what we country girls are always underestimated for."

21

The Basement

∞

What's good about this? Garritt forced himself to consider. What's good? He'd found Juan at last. In fact, his friend lay nearby, bruised and battered exactly as Minda described, but alive and reasonably well, considering. Not so good? Now they were both captives.

Moments before, he'd been half-carried down into an unfinished basement, tossed onto a cold cement floor and the bag ripped off his head, his boots thrown down beside him.

This wasn't at all like the place he'd been captured. The lights were off but the room smelled of new lumber. From faint light reflected through ground-level windows, he could make out sturdy beams, copper piping. Solid construction. The basement wasn't exactly warm but it wasn't at frost level either. If not for his thirst and hunger, he might have been grateful for his "rescue" from the rat-infested death-trap. That is, until he heard the door open above the wooden stairs and saw Juan scoot warily back against the wall.

"Dude, it's okay. If they'd wanted us dead, we would be."

"You don't know these *pendejos* like I do," Juan said, his own hands bound by rope. They were the first words he'd spoken since Garritt's arrival.

Before Garritt could answer, one of the goons who'd brought him in rumbled down the stairs in a hurry, severed the tight plastic cuffs cutting into Garritt's wrists, and half-dragged, half-helped him re-mount the open wooden steps, although he managed to bash Garritt into the unfinished railing.

"Sorry," the man with the earpiece offered, no sincerity whatsoever. Same guy whose arm Garritt had bashed with the fire log.

"Hang in there, *amigo*," Garritt called back to Juan, in case he'd never see him again. Feeble, but he couldn't think what else to say.

Juan's silence frightened Garritt more than anything. Juan was never a man without words. He was barely even a man at all, except that in so many ways he was more mature than any teenage boy Garritt had met.

That made him feel worse; he hadn't been able to rescue the kid who'd rescued him. He clutched at his boots, which he thought to grab before this rough trip up the stairs, and made a silent vow to get them both out of this situation.

As soon as he did, a bright golden pinpoint flashed, reminding him that they weren't alone. Never fully alone. *No one is.*

It struck him suddenly that he saw the gold lights when his intentions were good, like in the rainforest, thinking of others. Or while making commitments to his own self-betterment. Was that coincidence? Their language of light, maybe he was beginning to comprehend it?

Anger, fear, panic, frustration, guilt—the lights never appeared. Maybe negativity blocked his perception of them.

Calm, selflessness, positive thinking—no, he wasn't calm in the rainforest, and all his actions were based on an assumption of the worst outcomes if he didn't act, but still he saw the lights. Why?

Constructive intention, maybe that was it?

He'd seen the lights when he had a need, but also when nothing at all was happening other than his upbeat attitude, which they seemed to intensify. They showed him spectacular pinpricks of color and twinkle that made him feel that a more liberated life must exist, somewhere in the universe. If nothing else, if they weren't leading him to save lives, their presence gave him hope. Size and color varied, but the lights were always strikingly beautiful. By now, he'd even seen a few white, red-gold, violet, rainbow, and indescribably multi-layered lights. Some flashed, others lingered, like the large blue spheres. In every case, he could feel a sentient presence behind the light.

Somewhere he'd lost his fear that they were demonic. Maybe it was after the blue light at the shed. If it hadn't triggered a subconscious reflex, he might have fallen differently, twisted badly, hit his head. He could still be out there, rigid as the iron sink lying in the swamp. If these were demons, then they were the most helpful demons he could imagine. So why not ask for their help now?

Struggling up the stairs with his captor, he tried it. He fumbled to find words less like a prayer and more like, *Um, hey, Lights, if you're out there...*

No reply that he could detect. He felt silly, yet the effort instantly made him feel lighter, to believe that someone out there might care, believe it enough to ask for their help. Maybe they'd answer in the way they had in Peru: opportunities would become evident; paths would show themselves. If they weren't allowed to interfere, these Beings, whoever they were, then he shouldn't expect a giant angel to appear and disintegrate this jerk dragging him up the stairs. It would be subtle. It could be anything. He vowed to pay attention.

The basement stairs opened into a very modern kitchen. The illumination that poured in from outside lights blinded him for a moment, but as his vision cleared, he found himself looking out over Lake Michigan from a cliff high above, staring at miles of darkness totally unbroken by human incursions. He could almost hear and feel the pulse of waves resonating through the sandy earth.

Clearly, this was a private home—a lavishly expensive estate with a view that would cost high seven or eight figures to own, depending on how many bathrooms and acres. Despite the snow and the darkness, he counted a lighted tennis court, a covered hot tub, and a deck that clung across the front of the house. He could guess exactly where to find the long wooden staircase that would lead many flights down the dune to reach a private beach below.

As a teenager, he'd marveled over the catamarans and jet skis people like this left lying all summer on their "private" strip of lake shore, though it was surrounded at both ends by public beaches. Maybe if someone stole these items, it was nothing more to these folks than what a child's toy lost in a dirty back yard was to the rest of us. And like every other beachwalker, he crossed the *Private: No Trespassing* signs to continue splashing along the waterline on hot August days. But he always wondered if anyone was ever arrested for the violation. As a ten-year-old, ignoring the signs made him feel invincible. When he got older, it struck him as sheer arrogance to believe that any human could own part of a lake so big that you could not see across it to Wisconsin or Illinois.

And now? Well, he'd finally been captured by the super-wealthy.

The chef in him noted that the kitchen boasted the sleekest appliances, a visibly well-stocked wine refrigerator (probably matched by a hidden basement alcove where the pricier choices were kept), and a gleaming, black-granite island that matched the ample countertops. Copper pans hung from a circle of steel overhead, looking as if they'd never been used, and a gas stove, shiny-new and huge, could easily feed a house full of guests if it were ever tuned on. Any private chef would drool over this setup.

"Come on," the man yanked roughly, "Boss is waiting."

They limped through an archway into an exquisitely appointed dining room with floor-to-ceiling windows that took advantage of the view. From there, they passed into an enormous, split-level room with a massive stone fireplace at the far end of the lower level. It stood cold and empty. Vast black windows wrapped around the room, looking both west and north. Nothing conveyed a sense of warmth or family despite the tastefully selected, though austere, furnishings. Garritt caught a glimpse of a formal entry foyer as they passed it. Cloaked in darkness, it offered no light to welcome visitors privileged enough to enter through the front door.

What stopped his gaze cold was a row of paintings on the windowless east wall. They depicted religious scenes too painfully familiar. Beside them, a series of silver-framed photographs brought bile up into his mouth.

"So, the prodigal son returns," boomed an unusually tall man who emerged from a dark hallway at the north end of the room. He wore a long, burgundy-silk robe and expensive lambs-wool slippers. Garritt heard someone close a door softly, down the hall where he presumed the bedrooms were situated.

The largest framed photograph captured his father taking the oath of office. And another, with his perfectly coiffed mother on the steps of the Capitol in Washington, D.C. And one more, shaking the hand of the President.

22

Common Enemies

∞

Senator Volkert Vanderhoeven, new member of Congress, stood before Garritt looking as threatening as ever. As a child, Garritt feared this man with good reason. Now, after so many years of nearly complete silence between them, he felt a tight ball of hot tar come to life and roll around in his gut.

"I don't think it counts if the son is hooded and kidnapped and roughed up by your goon squad."

At a nod from his boss, the black-suited man with the com device deposited Garritt in one of the designer chairs—the least comfortable one. Sadly, Garritt recognized the thing. It was a classic model, black leather Eames lounge, the chair that put its Dutch manufacturer on the map in the 1950s and still sold for around seven thousand dollars. It came with a matching-leather ottoman that cost another absurd amount of money.

The man rolled that over and, without asking, jerked Garritt's leg up on it—tit for tat, apparently, as a volcano of pain erupted through his leg. When it subsided, Garritt reached with a grimace to peel off his day-old sock. Beneath the halogen overheads someone had switched on, the ankle showed an absurd amount of dark purple swelling, surrounded by skin withered from hours of dampness.

Through all this, his father remained standing and wordless, a tactic he used to add to his powers of intimidation. Garritt knew it well. Friends called him Kert and that suited the man perfectly. His reddish-blond hair gleamed with strands of gray now but he'd kept his figure trim for a man in his late fifties. Everything about his features conveyed the image of a no-nonsense disciplinarian, a man who meant business and who would not "suffer fools gladly," to quote his beloved Bible.

When Garritt was younger, he couldn't figure out what his mother saw in his father beyond his imposing stature. As he grew older, he experienced her own version of chilliness and gradually understood that she was capable of marrying a man purely for her personal advancement. She had taken a step up in society and wealth by attaching herself to the Vanderhoeven family.

His Dutch grandfather built the family's name and fortune by selling used versions of the chair Garritt was sitting in, along with other discarded office furniture, out of an old warehouse on the outskirts of Holland. Until he rebelled in fury, Garritt was forced to work there without pay after school and on weekends to "build character." The day he walked out was his first step toward full emancipation from his parents, their religion, and the tightly-bound Michigan Dutch community as a whole.

After his father took over the business, as his fortunes rose and business expanded, Volkert Vanderhoeven made his voice heard in local government—mostly by greasing the right wheels with cash contributions. Soon he rose to a position of influence throughout the state, and eventually gained favor with the most powerful politicians in the country by funding their political ambitions—or rather, by fueling their party and their political action groups with "soft money." Kert Vanderhoeven was blatantly open about his millions buying influence. He once told reporters that he did, indeed, expect a return on his generosity. Apparently his conservative constituency ate that up, never mind if it was legal or ethical. He was that confident that his agenda was the right agenda—aka, "God's agenda," to hear him tell it.

Garritt meanwhile, working as a cook for Corbyn and Avery in Veenlanden, pretended not to know the man who had once been his father and who now cultivated a public image that rang false to his son in every way. From what Garritt read (or what others told him, because he avoided this news whenever possible), his father quickly became a favorite of the multi-billion dollar arms manufacturers who build everything from state-of-the-art aircraft and missiles to battle-ready communications equipment. To keep the money rolling in, these companies also sell their military tools around the world to anyone willing to pay, whether friend or foe to the U.S. at any given moment. (Since that was always shifting, who could tell which a weapons buyer might be, friend or foe?) Every political campaign that led his father up the ladder was backed by money pouring out of the hands of these global merchants of death. Not that he needed much. By then, he was a very rich man himself, eager to protect his personal investments in these corporate war-mongers.

Knowing it was expected of him, Garritt sighed and broke the silence. "What do you want with me? I see you've gotten everything else you ever wanted."

"Oh, you like the new house? We bought it last year. We haven't quite finished it. Our duties keep your mother and me in Washington most of the time. All this could have been yours one day, you know," he said, twisting his tone for impact more vicious than generous.

Garritt didn't take the bait.

"Where is Mother?"

"Not that you care, but her dog died last year, Kookoo, the poodle she loved so much, remember?"

Garritt recalled a sickly puppy that soon became insufferably spoiled.

"She had him cloned. Cutting edge science. She's gone to South Korea to retrieve the puppies. Then she'll fly back here to work for our charitable foundation. Doing God's work." He narrowed his eyes to convey what remained unspoken: *Unlike you, you heathen restaurant cook—you, who are no longer a son of mine.*

One of the great ironies of his parents' religion was that they're renowned for charitable giving—as long as those charities actively promote their Christian agenda.

"To serve the poor? Or to serve your public image by making a good show of it?" He'd never learned to keep his mouth shut.

Swiftly his father advanced on his adult son and raised a hand, a reflex born of long habit. He stopped himself an instant from rendering the expected blow, which Garritt remembered all too clearly. Instead he growled, "I am still your father. You will not speak to me like that!"

Unlike what his campaign ads would have you believe, his father was a volatile man prone to sudden outbursts of violent temper. Garritt never knew when the next blow would come flying out of nowhere. He'd always felt sorry for the people who worked for the man. "I thought the prodigal son was swaddled in riches and treated to feasting and kindness," he spat now, more bitter than angry. "I see that your new status hasn't changed you at all. May I go now? I have a friend who is tied up in your basement and he needs urgent medical attention."

"You are going nowhere," his father shouted, striding back toward the fireplace where he spun and fixed a look on Garritt that could pierce iron.

Even as a toddler, Garritt possessed this knack for arousing his parent's ire.

"You are here for one last chance to prove your worthiness to God! Although I think you are not as grateful as you should be for this unprecedented opportunity." He waved the suited thug out of the room.

Garritt watched the goon slink back to the kitchen and thought he caught a smirk on the man's face.

"I thought the Secret Service only protected the President and the Vice President outside of D.C."

"These are private security, local company. You know, the one started by Betsy DeVos's little brother."

"You mean the ones who screwed up in Iraq and got caught? Are you fearing for your safety?"

"Hold your false tongue and listen to me. It's your safety I'm protecting, the Lord only knows why. You've got yourself mixed up in something well beyond your comprehension."

"You sure about that? Is that why you've *kidnapped me?* Why you're torturing an innocent teenager in your basement?"

His father turned an angry shade of vermilion. "I am not torturing anyone. Like your mother, I'm also doing God's work, trying to help you, your little migrant friend, and the world. But you'd know nothing about that. You're too busy with your fame-seeking heroics and your fancy restaurant, working for a man who is—" he sputtered for a moment, sincerely lost for words, and finally landed on, "an abomination to God!"

His father had never forgiven him for those media stories, for doing something that brought him public admiration, although Garritt had never sought it. Moreover, the man probably couldn't fathom any effort to save the lives of God's "non-elect." God hated entire races, according Calvinist doctrine (which practically invented the false concept of "race")—so why bother? At least, that was the only explanation Garritt could find for the way Reformed Christians called their behavior "God's work."

Oh yeah, charity was their big thing—especially after disasters when it was good PR—but not respect or kind treatment in ordinary, everyday circumstances. They believed that the downtrodden were down on the bottom of the heap because God wanted them to be there, so why should they treat them any differently? Pity allowed, but not actual support in ways that might transform "their lot in life."

Corbyn, a gay man who knew all about abusive disregard, kept telling Garritt that wasn't it; that his father was simply jealous. "Ever since you outgrew him by two inches, he's envied you. And now, not only have you stolen the front pages, but you've humiliated him by being called out as—not just any hero—but, *'Senator Vanderhoeven's estranged son, who saved a hundred people from certain death.'* What a deflation!" Corbyn had laughed with vicious delight. He'd been tormented all his life by people like Garritt's father.

Now Garritt glared back at the senator. "Juan doesn't look like you've been doing a very good job of 'helping' him."

"That wasn't my doing. Your new friend Bobby Lee—he started this mess. We only stepped in to keep the boy alive when Bobby's clumsy fanatics nearly killed him with their primitive methods. The migrant's lucky we arrived at that pig pen when we did. And for that matter, so are you."

"How did you know I was there?"

"I have my sources."

"Wait—did your 'sources' send me to that place?" He remembered Zach saying something about government infiltrators.

"You didn't think I'd pull you out of a church meeting in handcuffs, did you? If you can call that a church."

"So what is it that you want of me, your heathen son? Or Juan for that matter?"

"Convince the boy to tell us where he's taken the artifact."

"The artifact?"

"You know what I'm talking about. I know you went to Bobby Lee's church meeting to find the migrant boy."

"He is not a migrant, and his name is Juan," Garritt fumed, finally taking the bait—as he always, inevitably did, which then gave his father the upper hand. He tried to stand but realized his ankle wouldn't have it, so he rose up as far as he could in the chair and formed his words like knives that would slice wherever they could, taking off bits of this horrible, arrogant man who could not possibly be his real father. "He's a fucking *American,* born on fucking *American* soil, one whose interests you are supposed to represent. Or does he not deserve your Senatorial protection because his family is Mexican-American? Or because he's not one of God's Elect, because he's not *Dutch?*"

"Your mouth only proves you've fallen in with the worst elements, you, who were among the Chosen, who could be at the top of the shining mountain! You break my heart," he added with bitter melodrama.

"If only you had one."

"Whatever you think of me or your mother, we are doing our best to bring peace and quality of life to the people who deserve it. We don't pander to the underclass as you've done, and we don't shirk our duty to stand up and be counted for what's right and just.

"Listen to me," he continued, "you are way over your head here. You've been seen by my associates with the proponents of deception, with the dark forces trying to keep this world in their control.

"That dark woman," he hissed (further proving to Garritt that his father was the snake, not she), "that woman works for people who would keep the truth from the public and put us all in peril, including your migrants and your Mexicans, your Americans and we Dutch. Their game is to keep people ignorant, so they can make back room deals with the invaders who want to take over this world and steal our resources. Sooner or later, these people will hand them the keys, and no one will be the wiser because they've made sure the public believes that UFOs are a fantasy of the lunatic fringe, not what they really are: the super-high technology of a civilization that is actively scouting this world for investment opportunities, making whatever alliances they can before they attack us full force."

"Are you telling me that you believe in aliens and UFOs?" Garritt laughed at the lunacy of the idea—not of aliens, but of his Christian father buying into it.

"Of course," he snapped back. "They are in the Bible—if you'd ever read it. Only, in terms people could comprehend back then. God doesn't rule just one planet, you know. We can see that, for Heaven's sake, now that technology has given us a clear view of what surrounds us. He still rules over us all. And these are not God-fearing people, Garritt, no matter what you think, no matter what twisted ideas that Elizabeth woman planted in your brain."

He bristled. She might be his ex, but his father's attitude toward her had always pissed him off.

"Or this woman you've taken up with. That's why my man sent you out where he knew we could easily take you out of the picture."

"Your man?"

The senator smiled as if he'd just outsmarted his opponent at chess. He spread his long fingers in delight. "One of my employees has recently become a member of Bobby Lee's church. Bob-by Lee," he drew out the name. "He's not one of us. But when he came to my local office claiming to have proof of these invaders, my associates alerted me in D.C. They knew that after my first year in office, I went on a search for the black money that had disappeared into the coffers of some underhanded, invisible government operation. For one thing, you can't just *lose* $3.3 trillion from the Defense Department's budget!"

Garritt could hear the politician's fake indignation in his voice, warming up for the stump speech. His father paced, throwing his hands around for emphasis.

"Maybe they've got lousy accounting systems and they've made mistakes. Maybe they've funded projects that Congress did not authorize by transferring funds from one account to another, as they testified when their feet were put to the fire. But that still doesn't account for *trillions* in missing funds!"

Garritt recognized that his father was more interested in this political bombshell he'd discovered than in convincing his estranged son about aliens. The man would try to use this precious, juicy secret to pull off some kind of political coup, which he could lead, thus making himself more important than he already felt he was.

Suddenly the whole scene felt surreal, and Garritt wondered how much effect the lack of food and water and the constant pain in his leg were having on him. No longer cloudy-headed now that he was warm, he nevertheless felt like he'd been eating psychedelic mushrooms.

"If you'd been a member of this family for the past few years," the senator was saying, "you'd know that was one of my first campaign promises: to clean up and expose the culprits who've stolen these funds from Americans."

"If I'm not a part of this family, it's because you disowned me," he replied calmly. He was preoccupied, trying to reshape his ideas about who this man really was, stalking back and forth in his elegant tomb of a house.

Losing funds due to an accounting error—no, his father would never tolerate such a thing. But government insiders funding a conspiracy to join forces with aliens? Not at all the man he grew up with. He'd felt more comfortable when his father wanted to hit him. At least that, he could comprehend.

Government skulduggery. That went so far beyond the life Garritt had chosen for himself, a life that celebrated small, basic necessities, such as growing and eating healthy food. Not until a few hours ago, when Minda Blake explained her job to him, had he ever considered that such things as alien invaders might be real factors in this world, let alone his own small sphere of it.

"So what does this high-level larceny have to do with Bobby Lee and Juan?"

"If what Bobby Lee has is really a piece of an alien craft, one that can be tested and proven to have come from off this world, then we will achieve a long hoped-for solution to any and all alien invasions. With public support, Congress will be able to fund the development of real weapons that can defend this planet."

"Weapons in space?" He seemed to recall the phrase from prior years.

"Weapons in space. The U.S. will preserve its pole position in the new weapons race. We will build up our Space Force, and when push comes to shove, we will be prepared to defend our world."

And you'll be at the head of that army. So that was his scheme!

Whatever project arose, his father always put himself at the forefront. This one would have global implications, exactly the kind of venture a man like Volkert Vanderhoeven felt he was born to lead.

"You realize they are already way ahead of us, technologically speaking? If their ships do what I've heard they can do." He thought of Min again. Was she really working for the bad guys? Bobby Lee had wanted him to believe that.

"All the more reason we need that artifact to gain public support for our efforts. Catching up on our technology will be expensive—but so will losing our freedom to alien invaders."

Garritt found it difficult to argue with this reasoning. Maybe too many movies, too many depictions of space-based warfare had filled him with a vague sense of inevitability about this. He'd never had a motivation to consider that before. Could it be that his father, the Bible-quoting, Calvinist politician, for once in his life had reason on his side?

"What do you want me to do?" he ventured.

"Help us solve a minor setback. Bobby Lee had that artifact only because Juan recovered it before the mercenaries sent to destroy it could return to the site. It's a long story, trust me. But shortly after Juan delivered it to Bobby's shack in the woods, someone broke in and stole it. Thinking it was Juan, Bobby had his own man, a Holland officer, gather up some fellow cops to scare him, ostensibly to stop some small mischief the kid foolishly bragged about to Bobby. As far as the public would see, he was just another wetback getting arrested. You know how cops jump at any opportunity to put the fear of God and country into some delinquent, especially a migrant worker's son."

"That went well, didn't it? Juan not only has a family who dotes on him, his co-workers are also friends who care about him. And his father is NOT a migrant worker."

"You could never mind your own business, even as a child. I don't condone the way Bobby and his gang treated your 'friend,' but he hasn't told them or us anything, except that he doesn't know where the artifact is, and that he didn't take it. At least they got to him before your twisted girlfriend did."

"She is not evil," he blurted before he realized his mistake. "Or my girlfriend."

"Oh? Short-term relationship?" His eyebrows lifted. "I understand she spent some time at that hillbilly house you call home these days."

Garritt ignored the dig and went straight for the core of the issue.

"I don't think her intentions are to do harm. In fact, I think she shares your objectives. I think she wanted to betray the people she works for and expose that artifact to the public."

"Good. Because her company works for people who want to sell out the entire population of this world. Look, Bobby's church is not my church; his beliefs don't measure up to my own, but we share a common enemy. For now, we must join forces. We must do as Bobby's church intends: we must get that artifact into the hands of the scientists who can validate its authenticity, and then let the media bring the American public up to date on this global threat. Then they will eagerly support the development of space-based weapons."

"We still think Juan knows something he's not saying that he'll take a lot of abuse to protect. Since you've put yourself right in the middle of this business, we think you can convince him to talk."

"Me?"

"He trusts you."

And how did I earn that trust? By caring about Juan's welfare, and his family's.

But what if his father was right about all this?

Maybe if he explained things without the fanatical overtones of either his father and his hired thugs, or Bobby Lee and his crazy, gun-toting churchgoers, Juan might volunteer something helpful. Especially if Garritt could make him understand the importance. Torture and pain never produced anything worthwhile; kindness could work wonders.

Did he want to help his father? Not so much. But he had an inkling that Min might be pleased about the going public part, and that made him more pliable to his father's objectives than he ordinarily would be.

"First thing we have to do is get him out of that basement and let him call his family," Garritt insisted. "And his girlfriend. They're worried to death about him and you can't blame them. Your new partner Bobby's tactics—dragging Juan out of Avery's—that was pretty stupid. Didn't they think we'd immediately head to the police station to bail him out?"

"Bobby didn't consult me first. I would never have approved of it. But before you take another step, we need to do something for that ankle of yours. Your mother would not forgive me—"

"Never mind about me. Juan needs more medical attention than

I do. Get him out of that frickin' basement first of all. And he needs immediate food and water. We both do."

His father paled a bit, probably at the thought of inviting Juan to share his table, if Garritt knew anything at all about this man.

"I'll, um, call for some delivery. Better yet, I'll have my assistant look for something still open at this hour." The senator pulled a phone from his robe pocket to text.

"A phone call for Juan, remember? It's a basic right for the incarcerated. And my phone is back in my truck, along with Juan's."

"We'll bring you a new one."

Easy to see that his father basked in his new role, commanding a larger pack of underlings. Garritt's stomach quivered at the thought. From what he knew of the man's beliefs, any humanitarian impulses he professed now would soon be supplanted by his "us" and "them" philosophy.

Of course! Other-planetary civilizations. They epitomized the full meaning of "Outsider" to a man like his father. They could never be welcomed. Exactly like the tribes of old who, when they encountered strangers, would first determine if these "others" shared any commonality with them. If not, the only response was to kill the newcomers. Or to be killed by them. No further questions asked.

Just then a well-groomed young man in expensive, neatly ironed yet casual work clothes emerged from the dark hallway with a phone in his hand.

"Kert," he began in a familiar tone, but when he saw Garritt he blanched and corrected himself, "Er, *Senator,* I got your text but how many meals are you ordering? It's late, uh, sir ..."

His father whisked the young man back through a pair of French doors leading directly off the far north side of the living room. Through the wide opening, Garritt caught a glimpse of an expensive glass desk, an Aeron chair, and a leather couch before his father swiftly shut the doors.

Odd, that the handsome assistant was barefoot on such a frosty night, though he wore nice slacks and an expensive shirt that was casually-on-purpose inserted only into the very front of his waistline—a perfect "French tuck," as Avery once demonstrated. Which would mean nothing at all, except that the dark-haired young man hadn't emerged from the office, but from a room further down the dim hallway where the bedrooms must be. If this were anyone other than his father, he'd think—

"Take your hands off me, you stupid jerk! I'm here to see Garritt!" The feminine shout came from the kitchen.

"Agnes?" Garritt twisted in the chair in disbelief. "Sam?"

23

The Posse

∽

"Garritt, what did they do to you?!!?"

Agnes turned and leveled a fierce knee-kick at the man who held both her and Sam by the arms. When the bodyguard doubled over in pain, she broke free and dashed to crouch at Garritt's side. She babbled and fussed over his black-and-blue ankle and his cut wrists.

"What's all this?" his father emerged from his office.

"I caught them trying to peer into the kitchen windows, sir." The goon, upright again, had managed to keep his grip on Sam.

"Where is Juan?" Samantha demanded of the senator.

Garritt had never been so happy to see Agnes's caring eyes or to hear Sam's plaintive indignation, but he was especially gratified to witness the unfolding horror on his father's face. He wasn't sure if that was about Agnes besting his trained guard, or Sam's tattoos—or the revelation of something much more disturbing.

But it couldn't be. Hadn't the man just called Corbyn's lifestyle "an abomination to God"? Maybe his father was so caught up in his own self-interest that he didn't see the way this aide looked at him. When the young man re-emerged from the senator's office, protective concern was written all over his face. Garritt's own mother displayed less affection for her husband.

Hero worship? Employee loyalty?

Lights suddenly flashed through the glass windows on either side of the double front doors, illuminating the dark foyer. Garritt heard multiple vehicles pull up, car doors slamming.

The security agent dropped Sam's elbow. She hurried over to Garritt while both goons drew weapons and rushed to the entranceway.

Opportunity, the one he'd been waiting for.

Garritt grasped Sam's arm and whispered, "Juan's in the basement. Down the stairs from the kitchen."

"Got it," she whispered back and slipped out. Neither his distracted father nor his young aide noticed her absence, and both guards were glued to the foyer windows.

Meanwhile, Agnes clambered to her feet, smiling happily.

He gave her a puzzled look.

"They're here," she said.

"Who?"

"Everyone."

He couldn't fathom how these two women found him but oddly, Agnes's fuss over his leg had given him strength. He climbed up out of the Eames lounge and let her help him toward the foyer, while his father lingered behind, spouting words they all ignored.

"Sir, we have a situation," the first man to the glass reported. "How would you like us to handle this?"

"What situation?"

"There appear to be approximately a dozen people outside. Some are carrying weapons—rifles, shotguns, clubs, possibly a few handguns. I recommend we call for immediate backup."

Just then a shot took out one of the bright motion detector lights and a section of the yard went dark. Garritt thought it sounded like a .22 rifle.

"Do it," the senator commanded.

"Where is my sister?" someone shouted outside.

"And Juan!" another echoed.

Garritt peered over the guard's shoulder at the lavish entry plaza, a wide circle centered by a naked tree that probably bloomed in spring. A crowd stood in the falling snow, guns in hand but not aimed. He recognized Agnes's brother Stewart in the lead, shotgun at the ready. Behind him, young men with hunting rifles whom he didn't know, except for her oldest brother Nathan. Beside them, Juan's father (was that a baseball bat?) and uncle (a pistol he'd once seen the man brandish at his bar), Juan's friends Ramon and Diego, and his cousin Luis, all armed with what looked like the .22 pistols they'd use for target practice or shooting at snakes. Garritt feared for their safety more than anyone else's. Someone had already fired a shot, causing material damage. Firing back could be justified. *What the hell are they thinking??*

"Agnes?"

She beamed with what looked like utter satisfaction.

He glanced over at the two trained killers who'd just called for backup. He looked again at the farmers' sons and his adopted Mexican-American family. As far as he knew, none were combat trained like these two but they were visibly nervous and upset. A bright blue light glared in his sight and lingered for a moment before disappearing. He wasn't surprised to see it. The potential for bloodshed was palpable.

"Move aside," the senator commanded.

Garritt waited for his father's outburst. It didn't come.

"Let me talk to them."

His aide had been hanging back, trying to stay inconspicuous, but now he rushed forward. "Are you sure that's wise? You're not even dressed!"

Garritt heard the deeper undertones and marveled that no one else seemed to notice.

"What do they expect, Evan? Tuxedos? Give me my coat," his father ordered one of the agents.

The man grabbed the senator's cashmere dress coat from a nearby rack. "Do you want us to call in the local authorities as well?"

"Definitely not," his father barked as he threw the coat over his robe. Then he yanked a door open—and stepped out into a deep pile of snow in his lambs-wool slippers, oblivious to the fact that this might ruin them, something that Agnes would make much of later.

Garritt was relieved to see his father go ahead of his mercenaries. At least the senator wasn't pointing a gun at these people, who looked ready to do anything to get their loved ones back.

Shouts about Agnes and Juan erupted immediately, along with a lot of swearing and gun-brandishing, fist-waving threats. The group advanced toward the senator until Stewart—thank goodness—stepped to the front of the little mob and waved them to a halt so he could speak. The move probably prevented immediate violence.

Garritt knew these Michigan farmers' sons wouldn't normally comport with Mexican-Americans, and vice versa. Some might say they'd found a common enemy—Garritt's father. Watching the way they moved, hearing their voices, Garritt realized it was more than that. Corny as it sounded, what they shared was familial love—the kind he'd never felt.

"What have you done with my sister? We know you have her!" Stewart shouted. "We have proof!"

What proof could that possibly be? The senator had only hosted Agnes and Sam for about fifteen minutes now. Garritt turned to Agnes in time to see her grin expand.

"And Juan!" echoed Juan's father, Alonso. "We heard you know something about my son!"

This was followed by a smattering of Spanish epithets Garritt translated in his mind. Most were accurate assessments of their senator.

As the threats escalated, both mercenaries ignored the senator's orders and stepped out into the light, their guns drawn and pointed.

"Back off!" the talkative one ordered.

The mob shuffled nervously. A moment of uncertainty stopped its steady press forward.

"You are addressing a member of the United States Senate and you will display the appropriate respect. Attacking or threatening a senator violates Federal law." He gestured with his gun. "Who wants to go to prison? Huh? Just say another word," he dared the crowd.

The senator opened his mouth to speak but stalled as a news van pulled up behind the trucks and cars blocking the driveway. The mob must have destroyed the security gates on their way in, Garritt realized. A woman in a bright orange parka jumped out, with her camera operator close behind. They started to film immediately.

Agnes, peeking out from behind him, clapped her hands together in joy. "Denise! You are a genius!" she called out to the heavens.

"Who is Denise?"

"My friend. I got her to track my phone so she could look up who owned this place."

"But how did you know—"

"It's a long story. Sam drove. I texted. We got everyone together. And now they're here! Aren't they beautiful?"

"And what proof—"

"I texted a photo of the guy grabbing Sam outside the house."

"Agnes, do you realize what could happen here? For one thing, they're all on security cameras. They're just lucky it's cold and snowing so hard you can barely see who they are under those hoods and stocking caps."

"Look," she pointed at three young women who stood behind the men, holding up their cell phones. "Luciana and her friends are recording everything. That's their protection. You know," she thought for a moment, "it might have been Luciana who called the media, but not the cops. She's not happy with them right now, as you can imagine. I wonder if that's the same reporter who's been doing a series on discrimination against Mexican workers around Michigan's fruit belt." She sounded like a proud mother.

He took a long look at her, this mousy waitress who rarely raised her voice. She'd instigated an army, a modern Joan of Arc, and yet she didn't seem to realize how close they were to tragedy.

"Why are you standing here? Why aren't you going out to calm down your brothers before someone gets hurt?"

"I'm not moving until I find out where Juan is and who hurt you and why your own father kidnapped you." She stepped backward a few steps, away from the door.

"Who told you that?"

She rolled her eyes at him. "We saw them drag you out in a black hood."

"Friends," his father's shout interrupted. "What brings you to my door on this blustery night?" Pretending he hadn't heard their demands, he called into the blizzard, "Can I offer you some shelter from the storm?"

His voice hit that sweet pitch mastered by every politician who wants to impress a news crew. The bodyguards exchanged a look of alert that frightened Garritt. He knew they were calculating how to protect his father from this angry posse with guns, if he insisted on inviting them in.

A flurry of profanity in two languages flew back at the senator.

Nathan stepped up beside Stewart and shouted through the wind, "What have you done with my sister?"

The cameraman whirled to catch a close-up of the brothers, while the reporter leaned forward with a mic to capture every word. Luciana and her two friends turned their cells on the reporters, then the senator.

"You must be mistaken, young man. I've never met your sister. You should go to the police if she's missing."

"I'll go to the police all right!" Nathan yelled back. The crowd around him nodded and agreed, gripping their rifles.

From the hunting guns, Garritt understood these guys didn't mind taking a life, but would they shoot a human being standing peacefully on his own doorstep?

The golden flickers that appeared told him no, not likely. But the powder in this keg was dry enough, it would only take a single spark. What if one of the guards decided to wound someone to make a point? They looked eager to do it. He fumbled for a way to defuse the situation before someone fired so much as a warning, which would start a shooting match that couldn't end well. Already, these men and women had risked a trespassing conviction to save their loved ones. At this moment, they didn't seem to care about consequences. They might risk much more.

He pushed Agnes farther out of sight, then hobbled forward and supported himself against the frame. He cleared his throat to get his father's attention.

The senator turned.

"Agnes is here," he said quietly, so only his father could hear him through the muffling snowstorm.

"What?" he hissed back. "Who is Agnes?"

"Their sister." Garritt nodded toward Stewart and Nathan. "You seem to have kidnapped her, as well."

One of the guards moved to grab Garritt but a sharp look from the senator stopped him. The reporter and cameraman—and Luciana's cell phone—focused intently on this action but they were too far to hear.

"What are you saying? This girl who broke into my home?"

"She didn't break in; she only looked in. It was your man who pulled her in. And the girls only came to rescue me. God only knows how they knew that you'd cuffed me and dragged me here against my will. They didn't realize that you have Juan tied up in your basement as well."

His father hushed him angrily.

Garritt glared back, relishing the fact that the senator's control over everyone and everything was rapidly eroding. What Garritt didn't understand was why he'd just moved to protect his father, who didn't deserve it.

That's when two identical, unmarked SUVs pulled up behind the news van. Eight men in heavy black vests with devices in their ears and automatic weapons in their hands jumped out, combat ready. They were not police officers. They ignored the cameras and circled around the crowd of vigilantes. They didn't hesitate to aim their weapons.

"Call off your men," the senator commanded the two at his side. One spoke rapid orders into his device.

The mercenaries lowered their guns but held their positions, while the crowd of white and brown men and women stared back at them defiantly, albeit with a dangerous show of nerves.

"Senator," the reporter came forward, darting an anxious glance at the impending bloodbath behind her. She shoved a microphone his way. "Can you explain for us who these people are and why they've come to your home tonight?"

The senator was beginning to lose his composure. Garritt could see the tell-tale color creep across his bare head beneath the white flakes accumulating there. For the first time in his life, Garritt understood that his father was a very weak man, indeed.

"No, young woman, I cannot," he finally spoke. "I know nothing about this man's sister. But I do know that these people are trespassing."

Luciana rushed out from behind the others now. "What about Juan? Where is Juan?"

The reporter hurried back to her, the cameraman following closely. "Who is Juan?" she probed.

"Juan is my boyfriend. He was dragged off from his job by the Holland Police two days ago and when we went to bail him out of jail, they said they'd never heard of him. Where is Juan, *pendejo?*" she shouted again at the senator, striding angrily toward him. Her two friends grabbed her and tried to pull her back.

"Luciana," one hissed. "Remember the little one! *El niño!*"

"I am remembering his father!" she snarled back.

"Why would the senator know about your boyfriend?" the reporter interjected eagerly.

"I am sorry but I don't know what you're talking about," Garritt's father lied to Luciana. "Go home, all of you, before someone gets hurt! Before I call the police!"

He spun back toward the house, all his intentions to woo this crowd with fine words defeated.

Garritt recognized the additional lie. His father wouldn't dream of calling in law enforcement at this moment—not with so much damning evidence piled up behind him, hidden inside his opulent estate. Some protections, money couldn't buy. At least, Garritt wanted to believe that was still true.

A rival media van pulled up, and now Garritt could make out the rotating red and blue of a police cruiser, traveling through the blowing snow down the road that would lead to his father's long driveway. Outdoor lights flicked on at the closest neighbor's house. They had probably called the cops when they heard someone shoot out the senator's light. *Finally!*

But the cruiser passed the senator's driveway and headed south to the neighbors' house.

That's when Sam brought Juan outside into the light. All his injuries and his bound hands were in full view of the cameras, the crowd, and Luciana. She ran to him in tears and embraced him as if he'd come back from the dead. And from the looks of him, he had.

Both camera operators dashed in for nice, clear images of this bittersweet reunion, while the two reporters now on the scene practically chased the senator back into his own house. They rattled off a dozen questions he refused to answer as he slammed the doors, taking his security guards with him.

Garritt had ducked back in just in time, but this left Sam and Juan out in the snow, where Juan clearly displayed evidence of beatings and deprivation. Through the window, Garritt saw him collapse into the arms of the family and friends who converged on him, cut him free, smothered him in embraces.

Too bad Garritt's father missed the cue to protect himself. He should have claimed that he saved the teenager from the hands of worse enemies. Although that wouldn't explain the still-bound hands.

I could never be a politician. I'm too eager to answer questions, preferably with some truth.

Stewart and Nathan and their friends pushed past the reporters and rushed the door fearlessly despite the lingering mercenaries.

Stewart pounded the expensive carved wood. "Where is my sister, you bastard!"

"Agnes, you'd better get out there now before someone gets hurt. I don't know how you found me but I will never forget it." As the feelings welled up, the ones that told Garritt his real family wasn't blood-related, he saw colored lights twinkling all around her lovely sweet head.

"But you need medical attention!"

"I'll be okay, I promise. Go back home with your brothers, and make sure Sam gets home safely." She'd been the only kidnap victim who didn't have friends or family here to plead for her release.

Agnes looked doubtfully at the senator. He'd retreated across the room and mumbled something to his aide, then barked at the security agents to do something about Stewart and Nathan. They were still shouting threats.

"This is not a time to hesitate," Garritt warned Agnes.

"What happened to Minda? Was it the helicopter men?"

"How did you know about that?"

"Everyone knows about them. They landed in the middle of Veenlanden and one of them drove off with her car. They all think she's CIA, or the men were, or both. What happened?"

He wished he knew. But for all she'd done, he owed Agnes some explanation.

"I don't think she's CIA. But yes, they took her away."

It didn't satisfy her. "Why did he do that to you?" she whispered urgently. "Your own father? Why did he let them drag you off in a black hood all bound up like that? And why were you at that creepy house? Garritt, there's so much I don't know." Her eyes darted around the room. "Are you really sure you're safe here?"

He smiled. "Yes, Agnes, I'm safe now. Truly. And in no small part, thanks to you." He gave her a peck on the cheek, which left a blazing blush behind and made him realize that might have been a mistake. "Now let's go calm down your brothers before they shoot something—or someone."

She sighed reluctantly. He stepped around a guard to pull open the door. "Guys, she's okay, I promise."

Agnes went out and Stewart threw his arms around her, then stopped and pulled back, confused. "I don't know whether to shoot you or hug you!"

The cameras loomed.

She grinned. "Just hug me, you big hero! Both of you heroes!"

Nathan looked from one to the other of them. "I'm not sure what we did here, but can we go home and get some sleep now?"

"Of course," Agnes said. "And you may never know how much you've helped to save a little piece of the world tonight! We're not done yet… but this was a really good start. Now we just have to get Sam back to Saugatuck," she ordered. When they groaned, probably eager for warm beds, she added, "She's the one who saved Juan, remember?"

Garritt followed Nathan's gaze across the plaza, where Sam was jumping from foot to foot and looked as if she were about to turn into a colorful Popsicle.

"I'll make sure she gets home," Nathan offered. He seemed pleased at the prospect.

Garritt watched Agnes thank her brothers and their friends. "This has been the best night of my life," he heard her say.

And he thought he'd known this girl!

"You've got a lot of explaining to do," Stewart swatted at Agnes as they headed for his truck. Behind them, the two reporters were filing stand-up reports. The mercenary vans had driven off. Excitement over, no one hurt.

He turned back to see his father slumped on the couch and his aide sitting stiffly on a nearby chair. Both held glasses that Garritt knew didn't contain the water he was suddenly desperate to drink.

Twenty minutes later he heard the doorbell ring from where he stood braced against a kitchen counter. So civil, after all the commotion. He hopped to where he could watch his father answer it himself.

"Good evening, sir," he heard one of the two officers say. "Is everything all right here?"

Garritt laughed. *Cops don't follow social media? It must be boiling with video by now.*

Which is how he remembered his missing phone. And his truck. His poor truck.

24

The Cabin

∞

Bobby Lee scratched angrily at a bump on his back, tossed and turned in his rumpled bed, and finally threw off the tattered blanket to stalk from his sleeping alcove into the dim kitchen area of the claustrophobic cabin. He jumped at every sound.

He shouldn't be here. He would have left yesterday if the damn Jeep hadn't failed him.

After the church meeting, Dean helped him secure the part he needed but it was too cold, and damned if he was going to try fixing the thing in the dark. He decided to wait until daylight. Maybe that wasn't smart.

He paced for a minute, then grabbed a Pop-Tart and shoved it into the old toaster, one of his first repair jobs as a teenager. He'd kept the old thing going for years as a matter of pride. He could fix just about anything, and he did. But he was tired of living hand to mouth. The church had brought him closer to the level he believed he should be, but it wasn't far enough. Now he was close. So close.

Soon he'd be preaching in a magnificent temple better suited to his grand vision of the universe, sermons he would put together from his years of private research. He had studied the great religions, borrowed ideas from crumbling books. He surfed the Internet late into the night to cull secrets from a tangle of obscure sites. Physically, his new church would resemble the Goetheanum in Switzerland because he liked some of Rudolf Steiner's concepts. But his own ideas went far beyond. His new religion would suit the fast pace of the twenty-first century, and history would add his name to the roster of great spiritual leaders.

In youth he'd felt like a loser, born into that god-awful basement. His father never bothered to build a house over it. The old man liked to relate how Bobby's mother had grunted in the corner under the tarped roof "like a wild animal" when she pushed him out into the stink of frying fatback that never left the cramped quarters. It filled Bobby's nose and stank up his hand-me-down clothing. As soon as they were old enough (barely fourteen), his two older sisters escaped by marrying poor unsuspecting fools, which left their little brother to his drunken father's beatings and, later on, after his mother died of exhaustion and abuse, his father's unrelenting bitterness.

But Bobby had a talent. He could fix things. Before he turned seventeen, old Walter Toskin took him in, trained him up, and taught him how to run a fix-it business. Before long, old Walter sat back and let him do all the work, and a few months later, Walter was out fishing while Bobby ran the shop. He moved out of his father's basement shortly after.

Getting free of his father's ugly mindset was tougher. Bobby spent some of his new income on self-help books. They helped him—to a point.

And then, one day, he found himself preaching to the people who brought in their broken tractors and called him out to fix their washing machines. He talked; they listened. He preached what he'd learned from those books and it made him feel good. Especially when customers looked back at him like he knew something. A light would break on their faces and that filled him up with a pride he'd never felt when he fixed a blender or a fridge. Something special passed from them back to him. He basked in it. He wanted more.

Soon, he was holding meetings in old Walter's cabin, which he inherited when his mentor died. They shoved the chairs into a rough oval, pushed the table to the side so they could face him, and they listened. They gave him all their attention for as long as he wanted to talk. He drank it up like his old daddy drank moonshine.

And talk! Oh, he could weave a tale that would have them sucking in a breath and holding it for God only knew how long. Not fire and brimstone, like the preachers in the local churches. He told wild, fantastical tales about aliens and ghosts and weird happenings all around the globe. He found them on the Internet and wove them into his unique blend of Christian New Age Spiritualist Self-Help.

He talked, and they gave him their attention. He fed on it like a hog snuffling in the trough.

Soon, some of the women were even willing to give him their love—which is the last thing he expected to happen, but when it did, he quickly learned to agree, although not as quickly as they might have liked. He was too cagey for that. They would sneak back after the meeting with some basket of baked delicacies and they would sidle up to him, real sweet, and he would lead them on for a while, pretending not to know what they were after. Before long, they were like butter on the waffles he churned out on the maker he'd found at the junk store in Muskegon and brought back to life.

But then there was Maddy, and that was the end of that. He'd had to ban women from the meetings. Best idea he ever had, because once they were gone, the men realized they could talk free and his little congregation grew fast. Carrying guns—that was one of his most brilliant ideas, something he woke up with one morning after a night of the voices chattering in his head. Told the men they needed to protect themselves from alien invaders, if it came to that, or government agents who wanted him to stop teaching them about what was really going on behind the scenes. After that, his congregation swelled beyond the room in the little cabin.

Which is how they wound up in that stinkin' restaurant. He could barely stomach the smells coming out of that fry kitchen; reminded him too much of his daddy's old basement house. He wouldn't be stuck there much longer, he consoled himself. Once again, fortuitous opportunity had found him! He would soon preach to hundreds, maybe thousands, if he built his new temple the way he envisioned it.

Now he wandered restlessly through the tiny cabin in his torn fleece robe, trying to stave off the bitter cold that seeped in the cracks so relentlessly that the old wood stove in the corner couldn't produce heat fast enough. One good thing about the old basement house: the surrounding dirt kept the family insulated while his old man brewed the moonshine he sold down at the factory at night in the dark parking lot. Moonshine for which Bobby and his sisters provided the manual labor, under threat of more whippings.

Bobby wished he hadn't involved Juan in this scheme. He was a good kid, really. Open-minded. Eager. Juan's karma put him in a bad situation, was all. Wrong place, wrong time. But his own mission here was too important to let Juan interfere. He had planned to give the boy a quick and relatively painless but permanent exit, but Zach convinced everyone that they could simply bully the kid into giving up the location of the artifact Bobby told them he stole.

He laughed, a short chortle that sounded more like a burp. Not in a million years. Because Juan didn't have it.

Once they all voted to carry out Zach's plan, what could he do but go along? The cop had orchestrated Juan's capture and started tormenting the kid. That's when Bobby backed out of the picture. He absolved himself of all responsibility for the boy's welfare. They'd taken it out of his hands, he rationalized. Nothing he could do. Nature would decide, and it looked as if Nature had produced this out-of-season blizzard to make sure Juan would never say anything to stop Bobby from the magnificent plan that had unfolded before him. *A sequence of miracles,* he called it, although he was starting to believe that he had new psychic guides nudging him along.

First: he stumbled into the government's black-ops agents and saw the artifact in that woman's hands. That was Miracle One.

Then he hit on the idea to run loudly away so the male agent would follow him instead of finding what she buried. Back in his cabin, when he picked up the phone to call Juan, his ace in the hole, he knew the agent lurking outside saw him do it but by then it was too late. Juan was already on his way—a kid eager to go out in the middle of the night, follow Bobby's directions to the letter, and bring the item straight back to Bobby, a genuine UFO fragment. Miracle Two.

Juan really was a good kid. So enthusiastic. Too bad his karma gave him such a sucky role to play in Bobby's mission to save the world.

Miracle Three was his own senator's political and financial interest. At first, he thought the senator and his friends—and their money—would fulfill his dreams.

But then the inspiration to search the dark web struck. Pure genius, a flash from beyond that led him forward. He might have to give credit to his new mental connections for this one, but still, Miracle Four.

All along, he'd gotten these promptings. They led him, one step after another, these friends of his on the other side. Ever since he laid eyes on that beautiful slab of golden spaceship, they had come more frequently, coached him along, so many helpers and friends to offer their input and advice. He had always believed in spirits, but these—he could sometimes hear their voices audibly. He'd never experienced that before. So fruitful, their directions!

The buyer he found online—he questioned them severely, applying the rigorous standards he used for all his cyberspace endeavors. He insisted that he would not part with the artifact unless he had written assurance that it would be made public, as soon as possible, and that his own name would not be associated (at least not at the beginning). He also demanded a hefty purchase price—in dollars, not bitcoin. He'd learned a lot about financial negotiations during his years as an independent operator. He talked them right up to high-nine figures without breaking his poker face, so to speak.

Not that he ever met them in person, of course. From what little he knew, these people thrived on anonymity. They said their only passion was to reveal any government or public figure's hidden agendas and secret plans to the public—the poor, misled public.

Where they'd get the money to pay the price he asked, Bobby had no clue and he didn't care. As long as they paid. Half in his new offshore account moments before he handed over the artifact, half when he did. They were fools, anyway. If they were who he assumed them to be, these people were always running, hiding, one step from arrest or death. They constantly had to shut down their operations and flee from country to country. Horrible way to live.

In his plan, as soon as the deed was done and they announced the artifact's existence to the world, which would pave the way for public tests and experiments that proved it was genuine, he would make himself known as the discoverer and start to profit from speaking tours and sales of the books he would write. His sudden emergence as the man behind the artifact would create a second surge of publicity, maybe even controversy if the media refused to believe him. Either way, his viral status would rise. More fame, more fortune. His new followers would donate more funds to insure that his mega-church would be, not only built, but endowed for longevity.

Later on, he would reveal more of what he knew (because by then, he would know more, according to his new psychic companions). That would lead to another wave of public interest. And on. And on. And on.

He just needed this first nest egg to put his dreams in motion. So his mental friends helped with a brilliant idea for the hand-over. He couldn't simply get on a plane in Grand Rapids, where anyone could track his movements. No, their plan was perfect.

Bobby heard a noise outside and reached for Walter's old .410-gauge, which he kept loaded in a corner of the cabin. He crept across the tiny room to peer out the glass peephole. The sound had come from the plot where he grew his corn, tomatoes, greens beans, and carrots—a penny-pinching habit he'd learnt from his mother.

The pale light of early dawn revealed a woolly creature snuffling around the old melon vines he'd planted last June. Fat as a pig, low to the ground, son of a bitch.

Bobby whipped open the door and blasted the groundhog into smithereens.

"Serves you right," he shouted at the bloody dead animal. "You shoulda been hibernatin'!"

He slammed the door. He'd clean up the mess later—or better yet, leave it for the stray dogs. He had more important things to do right now. But the woodchuck reminded him to clean his handgun before he left.

Never know what you'll run into, he thought, as he reached for the holster.

25

Ocean Blue

∞

As Alex told her on the helicopter, when the boss calls, no one denies his requests. They didn't call him Commander merely as a courtesy.

So it was that Min found herself standing on a flat beach in Cardiff-by-the-Sea, a surfer's haven north of the Navy-dominated San Diego Harbor and beyond the "jeweled" La Jolla Cove, where the sea lions wage a turf battle with insensitive tourists. A wave lapped over her bare feet and the sand squished up between her toes as suction from the retreating water dropped her heels deeper into the wet, and the ocean exhaled the *whoosh* of surf sound that people program into devices to help them sleep.

Keep me, she thought as her feet sank up to her ankles when the second wave retreated. She inhaled the salty air and let the pull of water drag away some of her stress. If only it could take it all…

She searched for the tiny crabs she remembered here, the ones that burrow beneath the sand when the waves recede. If you were quick, you could catch sight of a fingernail-sized lump or tiny, thrashing legs for a second or two. The sand would bubble with them. Then, as if you'd imagined it, they vanished, leaving only a glassy, polished expanse that belied the teaming life hidden beneath. Sadly, she saw not a single crab. Maybe they were seasonal?

She turned her face up to watch the gulls wheel and cry as the sun broke through the forecaster's "marine layer"— nighttime fog and clouds that pulled back out to sea on a typical morning here, except in late spring when the tourists arrived. Then the beaches stayed overcast for most of the day. Locals called this *May gray* or *June gloom* but you wouldn't catch a hint of it in a travel brochure. And now, even that was no longer assured. Climate change. Buggering up everything we once counted upon.

On this morning, a week before Thanksgiving, the water felt chilly and the beach was nearly deserted except for Min and the Commander, a few locals walking their dogs, and the sanderling flocks playing tag with the surf. After the Michigan snowstorm, she would be in total bliss if it weren't for the man walking beside her, solid tanned muscle and a hard-planed, unsmiling face. He didn't wear a uniform but his bearing made his khaki shorts and Hawaiian shirt look like one.

"Low tide," the Commander observed.

"Right," she replied, falling in line beside him. Her soaked jeans collected rims of scratchy sand. Salt spray coated her face; she ran her tongue nervously over her lips to confirm it.

She still knew nothing about where she stood with Blackthorn. They'd been strolling the beach like this for twenty minutes, single words, grunts, nods, coolness like the air around them. He suggested they "take a walk" the minute she appeared in his office across the street that morning, where he had launched out of his desk chair, ready surfboard propped nearby.

Suddenly too warm, Min slipped out of her lightweight jacket to let the sun penetrate her blizzard-abused bones. Her hands shook a little as she tied the blue arms around her waist. The steady breeze rippled her pale orange blouse as a flock of pelicans skimmed low over the breaking waves, fishing their way south. She dangled her flip-flops from a single, twitchy finger hooked through the straps, wishing her boss would say more soon.

She always thought the location a brilliant choice for Blackthorn's headquarters. The bland office building sat nestled between a notorious biker bar and a popular health-food restaurant, across the street from the beach. Outside its back entrance, Amtrak trains sped by on their way to LA. On the ocean-facing side, the gray building was so nondescript, you'd be hard-pressed to notice it with so much natural beauty drawing your attention toward the ocean. It was hidden in plain sight, tucked in along a strip of the famous Highway 101 that once ran the length of California's coastline. The clutter of public beaches, expensive restaurants, surfers, kite boarders, RV campers, multi-million-dollar cliff-top condos and beach houses kept everyone caught up in their own business, oblivious to the world-defining objectives of Blackthorn's management.

Most of her time in San Diego, though, she'd spent training. That was not so fun. Like the Marines at nearby Camp Pendleton, they drilled in the hot, dry desert out east. They pushed their physical limits—even the remote viewers.

"A healthy body creates a healthy mind," the viewers were told when they complained about the combat-readiness training. The theory traced all the way back to the Stargate program. She wasn't sure it helped her psychic abilities, but it did allow her to eat whatever she wanted by giving her a solid core of muscle to burn off her indulgences. For that, she was grateful. Yet the training proved to be a lot tougher than anything Navy boot camp dished out. And her trainers eventually nagged about her diet. So she learned to sneak. Bad habit.

Now she scanned the waves, searching for the dolphins that often played and fed among the kelp beds in this spot. *If I get out of this alive,* she told herself, *I'm going to convince Amrita to move up here.*

She knew it was a lie. Even if she survived, her luxurious salary would never stretch to the millions it cost to live in this place, not even in one of the sardine-packed dwellings that covered the sandstone cliffs above the salty lagoons that stretched away from the beach.

She sighed, and tried again to calm her mind as she strolled along with her silent boss.

Only moments passed before her thoughts jumped back to the startling news video she caught late last night on social media. Garritt! Same clothes he wore when they shared pizza mere hours before the video was taken!

In her mind, she could still see the firelight glinting off his wild hair, carving out his cheekbones and lighting up the sweet eyes that had gazed back at her, so desperate for affirmation. But in the video, standing in the background, his eyes were full of so much distress, she felt it like a punch in her solar plexus. She'd missed all the hints from Agnes, bless her heart. His father was a senator! Not just any senator but *the* Volkert Vanderhoeven. The name rang a sour note in her memory—a right-wing religious fanatic of the worst kind. But how on earth did he come to hold Juan captive in his house? The news footage showed Sam leading the kid out, as battered and bound as she'd seen in her vision. At least he was alive!

She wasn't the only one with questions. Newscasters said a full investigation was underway. She desperately wanted to ask the Commander what he knew but judged it wiser to keep her mouth shut for now.

Stay focused. You don't know what's coming next. She could be the one in legal jeopardy—or worse. If her vision of Wade was as accurate as the one of Juan—her nerves crackled with anticipation that even the overpowering energy of sky and water couldn't whisk away. And not a clue yet why she'd been summoned.

At last the boss cleared his throat.

"You've been busy," he echoed Alex—only the Commander wasn't joking.

She nodded, not sure what he referred to, she had so many secrets now. If he didn't mention Wade soon, she'd need to report her vision. She kept her gaze on the sand as they splashed through the surf's edge.

"We know what you've been up to."

She nodded again, hoping he'd tip her off about which thing they knew.

"It happens," he added. "You're not the first."

He turned back up the beach toward the highway, toward a peach-colored building on the sand that looked deserted.

Odd. Despite sitting on a super-exclusive strip of real estate, its oceanfront windows were boarded up, as the owners might do if they were expecting the high surf of winter storms. Signs that should have proclaimed its name were stripped down to empty metal frames. A row of protective boulders, so-called *rip-rap,* blockaded the abandoned, sand-level patio. The Commander headed toward those rocks.

A brightly-colored kite sail cut close to shore, distracting her for a moment. The kitesurfer zig-zagged through the line of sitting-duck surf newbies waiting for a wave. Amazingly, he didn't take out a single one. As she watched, another kitesurfer executed a spectacular flip off the back of a wave.

Reluctantly, she turned her eyes from the wave-top antics to rest on a stained glass window on the old building's second story, next to an open balcony that must have offered spectacular ocean-view dining. Why would such a place ever close down?

The Commander slipped behind the boulders and disappeared.

She caught up to find him waiting for her beside an unmarked door painted battleship gray. The door would be invisible to traffic along the highway, as well as to beach strollers who didn't know where to find it. A chill shuddered down her spine and her stomach dropped a few inches. She halted, feet planted firmly in the dry sand.

"Where are we going?"

"You'll see."

She didn't like the sound of that. Especially given Blackthorn's penchant for hazing, initiation, and severe training rituals. Not to mention…

"Don't worry. You're safe with me." He finally smiled at her as he opened the door. That was far worse than his usual grim neutrality.

The surf roared in her ears but she swallowed hard. Sun-blinded from the bright ocean and sky, she stepped into the abrupt darkness. The Commander didn't follow.

"Aren't you coming?"

"This is all yours," he grinned at her. "Enjoy."

Before he slammed the door on her, he added, "Upstairs, to the right. You'll find it."

Still sun-dazzled, she couldn't see anything in the dark hallway, except for a light at the end of it. What a cliché.

Figures.

Eager to get this over with, expecting the worst, she walked quickly toward the light as her eyes began to adjust. Beneath her feet, carpet like you'd find in the finest of dining establishments, so fine she worried for a silly moment about the amount of sand rubbing off her feet and pant-legs onto the tropical flower-and-vine pattern. She padded along the scratchy surface for a minute before self-consciously slipping back into her flip-flops, which grated against the delicate skin on the top of her foot.

The place smelled of seaweed and old cooking oils. It would have been "silent as a tomb," to extend the horror-movie ambiance, if not for the slow, rhythmic reverberation of pounding ocean that shook its walls, reminding her that the world of daylight and safety lay beyond the door she'd just passed through. But this was a test, she suspected. She couldn't take the easy way out.

She was surprised when the hallway led directly into the old dining room. She had expected to find herself in some kind of anteroom, a gloomy, deserted kitchen or a putrid-smelling trash area. She wound her way around half-height, curved barricades that would have separated the now-absent tables into cozy alcoves, each precisely angled for a view of the water. Brightly-painted plaster reliefs of mermaids and sea creatures festooned the walls. The room still felt festive, though woefully empty of what must have been an enthusiastic crowd of diners—until there weren't any more.

Reluctantly, she crossed to the restaurant's formal front entrance. From there, a wide staircase carpeted in aqua and coral shades to match the downstairs dining room wound upward, then stopped at a landing that showed off the stained-glass window she'd seen from the beach. Sunlight passed through it to flood the stairs with vibrant, moving colors. On her way up she paused to catch her breath, but also to admire the window's shimmery mermaid in her undersea bower. In contrast to the sea maiden's peaceful smile, her own heart beat furiously.

The stairs weren't steep. Scary memories had surfaced: pranks her brother played on her, Navy hazings (some not so funny), and Wade's most recent treachery on the dunes of Lake Michigan.

Wade, who might be dead now.

She took a deep breath, thought of her stalwart Gramma Julene, envied the serenity of the mermaid ruling over her watery deep, and pushed herself to climb the last few stairs.

She emerged into an upstairs room with a spectacular wall of glass that provided a panoramic view of sea and sky. To her right, a cozy bar, suffused with red, green, and yellow light shimmering through Art Deco glass embedded above the clear windows. It looked like the kind of place that would draw you in for a long afternoon, maybe not so much for drinking as for sitting and staring out the windows as ever-changing shifts of light and color played across the moving waters.

Far out to sea, she could make out a container ship headed south toward Mexico, like the November gray-whale migration. A big part of her wanted to be on that ship.

"Welcome."

She jumped. The voice came from a dim corner near the mahogany bar that stretched the length of the narrow room. She knew that resonant boom! *How could it be?*

"Reverend Ben?"

26

The Green Drink

∞

"You can call me that if you wish, although I am not a reverend, as I told you before. If you need a name, a favorite of mine from another lifetime might be Benvenuto," he suggested as he stood up—and up. "I would like that." A thick laugh bubbled up from his chest. "He also dealt in gold artifacts."

Whatever the joke, she didn't get it.

"Or you can just call me Ben."

She was stunned to see him standing here, this man of her dreams, in what she believed to be physical, tangible life. At least it had seemed real moments ago, when the ocean caressed her toes with foamy saltwater. Once she stepped into this abandoned building, she wasn't so sure.

She gazed up at him in awe. He was back in his African-American guise, taller even than Garritt. He wore light-colored linen trousers, neatly pressed, and a casual, ocean-lavender shirt open at the neck to reveal a glimpse of his muscular torso.

He strode out from the corner as he swept an elegant arm to indicate a choice between the outdoor terrace, blazing in sunlight beyond the glass door, or the bar which, unlike downstairs, still featured small café tables. "Do you prefer light or dark?" he rumbled gently, and a sly smile made it clear that he understood all the subtleties of that question.

She found it difficult to speak, let alone make a decision.

"Aah, well. Perhaps you've had enough sunlight for the moment. Let us sit here, then."

She fell gratefully into a padded wooden chair at one of the little round tables, and he sat across from her, on a seat much too tiny for his impressive self. Even sitting down he was so tall, he might be standing, hovering like a waiter ready to take her order. She had to look up to see that his shiny bald head gleamed in places like the polished bar. His unusual, honey-colored eyes left her feeling naked. Not her body, but her *spirit* felt exposed.

"You probably need to sip something. Here, let me get it for you."

He stood again so quickly and gracefully, she barely noticed the transition. He came back from a mysterious enclosure behind the bar to hand her a massive goblet filled with green liquid. Ice etched its frosted sides; salt clung to its rim.

"Sip it slowly," he advised.

After her first sip she couldn't help but agree. This was no margarita! Whatever else it contained, the ginger she identified burned her throat and numbed her lips. But with each sip, her brain seemed to clear—exactly the opposite of the alcoholic beverage she'd hoped for. She felt no comforting numbness, only an increased sharpness.

Her fingers trembled as she carefully set the goblet down. Her mind filled with questions.

"That's my special recipe," he smiled at her and she could swear a beam of light emerged from his eyes and pierced right through her. "You are wondering now, how can it be that I am here, and yet you dreamed of me not so very long ago, am I correct?"

She nodded, not sure she wasn't dreaming now. "But you looked different the last time I saw you. You were East Indian," she accused.

He raised an eyebrow. "Then how did you know it was me?"

"I—well, I just did."

"So what difference does it make what body I wear, if you know it is always me?"

Her mouth opened and closed a couple of times, finding nothing intelligent with which to contradict him.

"And how do you know me? I will tell you: by my frequency signature. We each have one. It is our unique, energetic fingerprint in the universe, you might say. We read them from each other all the time."

He sighed. "So many more things are possible than Earth people recognize, possible even now, while they live in their limited, animal bodies. You, for instance. You can locate items in the past, present, and future, through time and space. Your friend and colleague Amrita can sense earth tremors in her energy body before they are felt in the physical environment. She can warn about impending earthquakes all around the world. Your new friend Garritt has established a direct communication with us, which he sees as visible light-flashes projected from the heart of our personal energy anatomies. He doesn't fully understand this yet, but his internal antenna is capable of communication with many levels of beings, living at frequencies from the highest of the high to, unfortunately, their opposites."

She flinched at the mention of Garritt's name but she kept uncharacteristically quiet, awaiting news of her fate, although her mind strained against the questions piling up. Whom did he mean when he said "our" energy anatomies? Was he related to Garritt's lights?

"We know that you were thinking of keeping that artifact you found in the dunes."

A spear of guilt pierced her.

"Minda, you are not in trouble. You can relax now. You have merely moved yourself up a rung on the ladder sooner than we expected. As your Commander said, it happens—but it doesn't happen to everyone." He smiled benignly and indicated her glass. "Drink up."

How did he know what the Commander said? Or what she'd been thinking out on that dune top?

She lifted the goblet, stared at the murky green liquid. Did it contain hallucinogens? *Is this another DARPA.-funded experiment in altered consciousness?* She probably shouldn't trust this man but she did, and so she drank.

It didn't hurt that he was remarkably pleasant company, in a distinguished, older-man sort of way. If the Commander brought her to him, then "Ben" must be a Blackthorn client, the Commander's boss in a sense, and therefore hers. He definitely bore an aura of authority.

"I will answer your questions in a moment," he replied to her thoughts in that disconcerting way of his. "But first, we must speak of you. On that dune, holding that fragment of what you believed to be evidence of an extraterrestrial vehicle, your humanitarian instincts came into play. You felt responsible for the ignorance of your fellow humans."

"Yes," she admitted, and when she did, the righteous indignation she'd carried for months raised its ugly little head. Here was a man who likely had the power to manage things differently, to actually do the right thing. This might be her only chance to speak up, and at that moment she didn't give a flying—what it might cost her personally.

"It's not right that we're hiding the truth from people. They should know!"

"They should. But that is not as simple as you believe."

He acted as if her protest were nothing more than a measly pebble cast against his broad chest! He let it fall away and went on, "Wade knew what you found that night. And by the way, your fall should have been the gentle tumble that children play at every day on those dunes. He didn't expect that cement block, and he is very sorry about it. But your injury prevented you from learning the rest of the story."

So he didn't take her seriously but at least someone finally spoke Wade's name. In the present tense, as if he still lived. That could mean two things: either he was alive, or no one knew about his death yet.

She took another sip of the green drink and it swept away some of her guilt for keeping silent about Wade—yet gave her a keener awareness of her surroundings. She felt as if her physical senses were being upgraded. At the same time, more of her inhibitions fell away as surely as if she *were* imbibing alcohol.

"You haven't explained how it was that I dreamed of you, yet here you are in front of me. Who are you, really?"

"Ah," he laughed at her. "I wondered when you would ask. You know, we really have no separation between our physical selves and our multi-dimensional selves. You and I are more practiced at bridging dimensions, is all. We met in a place bathed in this beautiful colored light, did we not?"

That was true. Sunlight passing through the Art Deco glass faintly resembled Gramma Julene's celestial church.

"We did," she admitted. "Or someone did. The man in my dream told me many things—but I've forgotten most of them." She spat it out as a taunt: *If you're really him, tell me what you said.*

"Not unusual. Those things will come back to you when you need them. As for who I am, what do you think?"

"Angel, demon, alien—or a Blackthorn client who likes drama." She indicated the thick cobwebs on the Tiffany-styled lamps hanging overhead. "Halloween was last month, you know. But you've got your vacant building, your stink of fish, your screaming seagulls and pounding surf. All you need now is either a pitchfork or wings. Or maybe you are some bug-like alien disguised in the flesh? Am I close?" She was tired of this game. She wanted him to get to the point. Why was she here?

He laughed a full-chested rumble that rattled her goblet on the little table. "You are exactly what they've said about you: keen of mind, quick of tongue, fearless in the face of authority. But young lady—or woman, excuse me, I must observe the conventions—we have a situation at hand. For now, think of me as a bit of all four: angel, demon, alien, *and* client."

She laughed uneasily, not sure which were lies and which might be true. "I would never trust you if not for the dream." She thought about it for a moment, then added more softly, "You helped my grandmother, didn't you?"

He nodded only, and gave her no further hint about who he was, or why she'd become his target of interest.

"We have a situation that is much more important than your momentary hesitation on that dune, or anything else bothering you right now. You know why we do what we do, yes?" He caught her eye expectantly.

"Who is *we?*" She stared back, trying to put up her mental guard. It wouldn't go.

"Your Blackthorn team."

"I have heard the rationale and I believed in it for a long time."

"Good. But you have not heard the full story."

"Enlighten me."

"As I was saying, that night Wade knew that you were being watched. He saw the man, down in the gap between the dunes where you found the missing artifact, the one we urged you to find."

"What *we* are you talking about now?"

"Haven't you wondered who gives you direction? Who really shows you, through mentally projected images, where your target lies? Why there are never full ships in these locations around the world, where it seems as if a crash has taken place?"

Yes! she wanted to scream. *A thousand times, yes!* But she nodded mutely, as her limbs began to tremble. She took another sip of the green drink. Her mind cleared again, pushing away her protections, opening her to listen.

"Let me finish this story and you will begin to understand. After he saw the man who saw you, Wade stayed out of sight and followed you both to the edge of the dune. The man positioned himself in the trees where you could not see him, but he was watching you. He's the one who frightened the 'possum, prompting you to bury the artifact.

"Wade wasn't certain how much this stranger had witnessed and he didn't want you to bring the artifact back out, so he took steps to remove you and the artifact from harm. He hoped his calculated display of stealth and strength, pushing you down the dune, would startle the man and give Wade an advantage.

"But the sight of your blood in Wade's headlamp must have terrified the guy. He crashed away and sped off in a Jeep he had hidden among the trees. Before Wade took up the chase, he called for an ambulance and alerted the team to come to your aid."

Min shook her head. Wade always acted like such a prick toward her. She would never guess he'd try to protect her. Guilt for keeping the vision of his death to herself flared back up. She opened her mouth to spill, but Ben didn't take a breath.

"You'll remember it was early October then; no snow. On those country back roads at that hour, the only sound was that of the Jeep. When Wade heard it stop, he pulled over and followed on foot to a cabin in a clearing cluttered with farm tractors, rusty cars, lawn mowers. Broken machines awaiting repair, we learned later. Wade ducked behind one of these relics and watched as the man went inside, turned on lights, talked into a phone."

"Bobby Lee!"

"Precisely. Wade relayed his intel to our recon team and went back to the park to collect the artifact, which your colleagues didn't know about." He gave her a look.

Shame crept up her neck. She should have told them.

"When he discovered the fragment missing, he realized that Bobby Lee's phone call had been to an accomplice. He gave up the search and went straight to the hospital to join the vigil at your bedside."

"Seriously?" She'd thought he hated her, that he was a drawling Southern bigot.

"He was quite distressed, Minda. He never meant to hurt you. Later, under my orders, he began his own investigation of the man you know as Bobby Lee."

He paused while Min gulped the last of the green drink. Some deep instinct guided her hands to her mouth, as if another sip would clear away her astonishment. No one had breathed a word of this, none of the team members who came to visit after she regained consciousness—and Wade wasn't among those.

"Why didn't they tell me?"

"We didn't want to burden you while you recovered. You suffered serious trauma, and we know that you have some lingering effects, am I right?"

She nodded reluctantly. She hadn't told anyone about the dizzy spells, or the strange expansion of her visions—yet another proof that this man Ben knew more about her than she wished he did.

"If it weren't for your recent adventures, I still would not tell you any of this," he added.

So this is why Bobby Lee recognized me. He witnessed parts of our operation. He knows what we were doing out there, what we were gathering.

He knows way too much, she realized with alarm. Had Wade gone back to silence him and something went terribly wrong and Wade was killed instead? Or was he about to be? She had to confess what she'd seen. Again she started to speak but Ben raised a hand to stop her.

"Wade went undercover to infiltrate Bobby Lee's organization. He convinced me that Bobby hadn't seen his face that night. So with his Carolina accent, a feigned belief in conspiracy theories, and a little assistance from our friends in local government, they eagerly accepted Wade as a new member. Turns out they were recruiting anyway. He's been there for about five weeks now."

"What kind of organization?"

He explained the Church of Refined Sensibilities to her as a bizarre blend of New Age religious fanaticism and UFO worship, "but with guns," and told her that Bobby, their leader, had convinced his weapon-carrying believers that they must expose the "truth" about UFOs because secret government agencies were keeping it from the public. (*Every belief system carries some truth,* she mused.)

He added that Bobby Lee stumbled into her by accident while looking for the UFO his friend told him about. The church founder now believed Blackthorn to be the offending black ops arm of the U.S. government, and therefore enemy to everything his church stood for.

"We are, aren't we? A black-ops arm of the U.S. government?"

Ben laughed. "We do promote ourselves that way to new recruits. But no, not exactly. Let's just say, we work toward the best interests of the planet as a whole. We are a kind of consortium. We agreed to protect the world until the time is right for the big reveal."

"You mean—"

"We are keeping the planet isolated only until the people here and the people in other places are guaranteed safety. As I once said to you, we protect you from us, and us from you. This world is fast approaching the time when that revelation will occur, but not yet. You still have too many scientific and social issues to resolve, as you and your family have experienced."

She understood too well what he meant. But who were they to decide what the world should know? At that moment, she was thinking that Bobby Lee's church might be right.

He continued, "One of those psycho-social flaws is a primary motivation for our secret-keeping: the uniform tendency to destroy what is 'foreign' or 'new' to your primitive instincts. Until you learn to live with the diversity on your own planet, you'll not be allowed to experience the infinite diversity of the multiverse. Not if we can keep you from it. And that is where we have run into a current problem."

"We. You keep saying *we*. Who is we, exactly?"

He smiled at her. "We includes you."

"Ugh!" she threw up her hands. "That tells me nothing! Let me ask you this: do *we* kill people to keep our big secret?" She'd been dreading the answer to this question for years now.

This time he laughed so hard he had to wipe at his eyes. She didn't appreciate the ridicule. He must have sensed that because he calmed down and gave her a straight answer.

"Of course not! But we do tend to let our new employees believe that. It keeps things simpler; keeps them out of trouble. For the same reason, we also let them believe that we *are* black-ops subcontractors for the U.S. government."

"Minda, you have earned a new level within Blackthorn. You are being told the truth today. Some among us are not from around here," he smiled. "And we don't kill people. Not if we can help it."

"So you didn't kidnap that Mexican kid and send him off to be tortured, in order to locate the artifact that I lost?"

"No. We did not. But if you let me finish my story, you will understand what has happened here."

"But wait—what about Wade? Is he safe among those fanatics? Because—"

"You can stop worrying about that vision, Minda. You were viewing a potential future. I have seen it too, and Wade has been fully informed. As of this morning, he is alive and well."

She let out the psychic breath she'd been holding ever since she saw Wade's blood in the snow. But once again, Ben proved he'd been creeping through her thoughts. That made her more uncomfortable than the idea that he came from another planet—which is what he implied, wasn't it? She still wasn't certain. Was she actually working for aliens without knowing it?

He glanced at her (probably scoping around in her head again), "After we helicoptered you out of Michigan, your friend Garritt stumbled into Bobby Lee's church meeting last night. He demanded to know what happened to his co-worker, Juan. You should know that it was Wade, posing as Holland Police Officer Zacharia Thompson, who organized Juan Talamantes' kidnapping in order to keep Bobby from doing serious harm to the young man."

"But I watched those officers drag the kid out of the restaurant! I would have recognized Wade."

By now she realized that her every movement, including her efforts to retrieve the fragment, had been an open book to this man. Was he the only one?

"No, because Wade stayed behind the scenes. He recruited others to carry out the staged arrest. We have many official friends in that area. After Bobby told his congregation that Juan stole the artifact—a flat lie—Wade feared for the teenager's life. That's when he realized Juan must be the accomplice who dug up the artifact. Wade proposed that he should interrogate their 'suspect,' Juan, since, as a cop, he had the most experience. Of course, he also thought the young man might give him insight into Bobby's intentions for the fragment. Wade used a location provided by a church member and made a big show of it. He convinced everyone that the torture was real—so real, in fact, that some members with a conscience complained and demanded it stop."

A sick feeling ran through her. She'd seen Juan suffering. She couldn't blame them. And technically, it *was* Blackthorn who kidnapped him.

"Wade's stage play saved the boy from actual harm, Minda. He took some blows, but he will live. As you saw on the news last night, he is back in the arms of his family."

"Yes, but I'm confused. Why did Bobby Lee want to hurt Juan? Did he really plan to kill him? And how did Juan wind up at a senator's house, with Garritt and his co-workers?"

Ben leaned back thoughtfully. "The power of compassion is one of the strongest and most positive forces on this troubled world. It opens doors. It opens minds. It opens one's consciousness to the Forces of Light who would assist in times of trouble, whether the person whose bravery is on the line knows that or not. Your friends are more talented in this area than they realize. Little Agnes has quite a big heart, as it turns out." He shook his head. "Totally unexpected bravery. They nearly incited a riot. They demonstrated why humans are worth all the trouble they cause in the multiverse."

This wasn't telling her much but he didn't give her a chance to ask for more.

"The most important thing for you to understand is that Wade discovered Bobby Lee's dangerous game of deception. He has drawn-in his gun-carrying congregation, the senator and his powerful friends, and now an anonymous buyer he found through the dark web. He believes they are some kind of altruistic organization."

Dark web. She knew the term. It was a hidden part of the World Wide Web, the darknet, where those in the know could buy anything—illegal drugs, prostitutes, assassins, hackers, weapons—using anonymous cryptocurrency payments transferred via blockchain instead of trackable government currencies. Which is why the government had tried to shut it down.

"The artifact Bobby showed off to his congregation was a fake, a poorly made replica. Of course, none but Juan and Wade would know the difference. According to Juan, despite preaching to his followers that making it public was their most sacred duty, Bobby planned to sell the real fragment to his dark web buyer in order to build his mini-empire into a mega-church, like the one in Houston whose pastor he admires and whose lifestyle he would like to emulate."

"Money and power," Min said wryly.

"Power and money," Ben agreed. "Early on, Bobby convinced Senator Vanderhoeven that missing government funds support efforts to conceal information about extraterrestrial contacts with Earth. He offered tangible proof, in exchange for a payoff from the senator's corporate backers, who stand to make trillions building weapons for a war in space, such as they believe this planet has never seen before. They are wrong about that, of course, but that is not the point. To answer your question, that's how the Senator became involved."

"We've had wars in space?"

He ignored her question. "Bobby went back to his congregation and convinced them that working through the senator's office would give their truth-telling campaign more credibility with the media."

"Would the media believe it?"

He nodded, and she thought he looked sad about that.

"But only if they have the real artifact to test."

She cringed inside. "But if our objective is to retrieve these artifacts, why didn't Wade just steal back the real one and disappear it?"

"Because in this situation, we are after a bigger fish, and we hope Bobby Lee will lead us to it. The poor soul does not realize what he stumbled into that night on the dunes."

No shit.

"Neither do you."

"What?"

"Minda, you've been having dizzy spells but it's more than that. Do you recall how it felt in your hands, when you recklessly removed your protective gloves in order to touch the pretty, glowing object?"

She did. Like nothing she had ever experienced, like touching the core of the universe, like every bit of poetry she could conjure to describe it and then more. But what she said was, "What are you getting at?"

"You want to know why you never find entire ships when we send your teams out to collect fragments left over from their destruction? That is because these are drone ships, coming from a civilization that refuses to acquiesce to the agreements regarding Earth's isolation. Our consortium routinely destroys them. They are interdimensional travelers, Minda. Their ships traverse dimensions without harm."

She wondered how that could be possible, yet she'd seen the evidence. And she had also seen a whole ship that must belong to what he was calling a "consortium."

"But if you destroy them, why are there fragments left for us to retrieve? If your ships are that superior, why don't you simply dematerialize all the bits and pieces somehow?"

"We destroy these scouting drones before they reach your frequency, before they materialize in your third-dimensional spectrum. However, because of the interdimensional harmonics involved, some debris materializes on Earth—the fragments you retrieve. You can imagine that if our ships drop down into your frequency spectrum to retrieve these shards of the destroyed drones, we would become visible. That would violate the 'Prime Directive,' as your popular television calls it. So, we have made other arrangements."

He paused to let this sink in.

She realized that Blackthorn was one of those "other arrangements." She really was working for aliens!

"But I *have* seen your ships! Well, one, anyway."

It happened months ago, in the Mojave desert. They'd been collecting fragments from among the prickly pears in the dark when Wade yelled, "Incoming!" and they all threw themselves to the ground. She remembered the dirt, still hot from the scorching day before, and the sharp stone that stabbed at her thigh. And then she'd looked up to see the most glorious Christmas ornament, the size of a skyscraper. It hung motionless in the sky, radiating a golden-orange brilliance that fell over them as if the sun had risen out of turn. It wasn't saucer-shaped; more like a glimmering conch shell that spiraled up to a point at the top, wider in the middle, then twirled down to another point at the bottom. It lingered for long moments, melted into new shapes, then sped off into the night.

No one would talk about it afterward. When they tried, over a pre-dawn breakfast in a Vegas casino, Wade hushed them up fast. (The crowd of all-night gamblers never thinned.) But she could not forget the feelings the ship evoked in her. Fear at first, followed by awe, then a bone-shuddering thrill, and oddly, a pervading sense of calm and homesick longing when it vanished.

"*You* have seen one, and some others have as well. We do follow a calculated program of minimal exposure, though not everyone has the ability to see our ships. It is part of your planet's slow education, although we generally avoid visibility in your spectrum so as not to provide an excuse for your planet to develop weapons to protect yourselves from so-called alien invaders. Occasionally, we make ourselves visible to your military forces for our own purposes. They do provide the best proof to a skeptical world," he winked.

"But these bits of interdimensionally active material, Minda—they pose a larger problem. For an Earth dweller, direct physical contact with one of these artifacts is likely to link them up in ways they are not prepared to experience—or survive. Touching such an artifact can connect you instantly to a polarity-linked chain of Intellects that crosses dimensions. The shock of this sudden opening—it can be too much for younger souls."

"You mean they'd start to download remote visions, although they wouldn't know what they were?"

Was that why she'd experienced Garritt's jungle so clearly?

"Something like that. You might call this a Multiverse-wide Web of Intelligence, or an Inner-net, because you access it mentally. It is activated based on frequency relationship—in other words, harmonics. Just like your internet, what you search for is what you get, only in this case the search terms involve what you hold in your mind, not what you speak or type. What you access will be relative to your own skills, experience, and previous exposure. More vitally, what you receive will vary according to the nature of the thoughts you harbor *at that very moment.*

"Minda, you have been trained to understand this function of mind and energy. You've committed yourself to evolve your skills slowly, carefully, and with due respect for the energy variables that can occur. You've learned discernment. And you have created associations with benevolent forces on the higher levels, those who have your well-being in heart and mind. Am I correct?"

"Yeah. So what's the problem? Wouldn't this stuff just make people more psychic without all that work? How could that be a bad thing?"

"Preparation, and evolutionary wisdom would be lacking. Because the effect happens suddenly, and to a degree most Earth dwellers are unprepared to tolerate or apply.

"For example, suppose a physicist touches this artifact, which opens up this interdimensional access. Their knowledge is likely to explode in the field of physics, as they connect with like minds throughout the infinities of human expression. Or if they're an engineer, the information they tap into will reflect that bias. It may come in a language they can interpret, even if it pushes them well beyond their previous understanding. This principle of frequency relationship goes right down to the finest detail and nuance. So you can imagine what might happen, for example, if the physicist and the engineer encounter knowledge that your planet is not prepared to handle in an intelligent, *life-supporting* manner."

The Manhattan Project—only worse, she realized.

These days, greed propelled much of industry and invention on Earth. Even medical "cures" had gone out of fashion, replaced by medical suppression of symptoms through manufactured drugs, methods, and devices—a better way to fill the coffers of those who managed public health for profit. Men languished in prisons to fuel the greed of corporations looking to cut costs by exploiting their mandatory labor, stealing their freedom. Corporate egos ballooned into mega-sized, monolithic icons that did not care about consequences to the planet or its inhabitants. In her opinion, if unchecked, this obsessive materialism would lead to planetary destruction.

So she did as Ben suggested. She imagined what would happen if these same people could extend their reach into infinite proportions, instantly, while madness still ruled this world. While material gain superseded spiritual wisdom. While greed surpassed compassion.

In a gentle voice, he continued, "In Juan Talamantes' case, his natural ability to read people, to know what makes them tick, his quiet compassion, and his ease of social interaction have all been enhanced into full-blown, telepathic mind-reading. Thankfully, he carries no foul intentions. And his skills are still limited.

"In your case, Minda—your remote viewing abilities have been upgraded. You simply haven't realized how yet. As for Bobby Lee, we don't yet know what effects he has experienced. We fear the worst.

"Without education and discernment, this sudden psychic awakening could be like laying out your cash and your jewels and opening your front door in a bad neighborhood. It could become a Fastpass to the loony bin if an individual allows any astral entity of any character whatsoever to wander—or deliberately plunge—into their mind with unknown intentions. This is why we control and protect exposure to these fragments of interdimensionally active material. Contact with it could go so far as to destroy Earth before your societies have the opportunity to prepare for such awakenings."

"*Jaysus*, as Alex would say."

"Indeed. But one day, this kind of connectivity will be the currency of your lives, as you learn to select constructive mental company on all dimensional levels."

She picked up the empty goblet, holding it to stare through the glass, twirling it between her fingers and thumb.

She noticed that what she'd thought were ice crystals still made patterns on the outer sides, like Jack Frost windows, although the glass felt warm to her now. The goblet itself was crystal, she realized, deliberately etched with elaborate designs.

"Tell me," she asked in a voice that was slowing down, "what was this really?"

"Something to help you process, to lessen the shock so that you could accept things without fear or alarm."

It was true. She wasn't afraid any more. In fact, she felt as if she were sitting on a high mountain top, surveying all that lay below, knowing exactly what it needed, what it was for, why it had always been. More importantly, she had a new vision of her role in it.

"Tell me what I must do to stop Wade's murder, and to retrieve that fricking artifact before all hell breaks loose. I assume that's why you've brought me here? To help somehow? Because I'm the one who started this mess."

He grinned. "Come with me."

27

Suspended

∞

Min tried to stand and failed. "Um, okay but wait. My legs aren't working."

"Take a deep breath and visualize yourself standing up," Ben suggested.

She tried to focus her inner vision as if looking at herself from the outside. She pictured the café table, herself in the chair, and then slowly visualized herself rising. It worked. But that only freaked her out more.

"What's wrong with me?"

"You are slightly more elevated in consciousness, and your body has stepped up to a higher frequency, as well."

He said it so matter-of-factly, she almost replied, *Oh, of course.* But this was weird. She had to *think* her body forward, as if her autonomic nervous system had completely shut down.

"No, it hasn't actually shut down," Ben answered her thought in that irritating way of his, "or you wouldn't be breathing and your heart wouldn't be beating. You simply aren't accustomed to this way of moving yet."

"It was your stupid green drink, wasn't it? What did you give me?"

"As I said, merely something to help you adjust to what I'm going to show you."

She felt divided. She wanted to know what he could reveal, because by now she knew he was a man of deep secrets—if he was a man at all. But she didn't like the fact that her body wasn't doing what it had always done.

"Take a few deep breaths. Relax. You'll adjust. This is how you live in your dreams every night. This is how you live between incarnations. Your higher mind will remember. You can do this, Min, as easily as you have learned to perform your remote viewing."

She'd come this far with Blackthorn, and that was far indeed. She'd seen and learned things that most people can't even conceive as possibilities. She was in too deep to stop trusting now. She did as she was told.

"Good," he observed as she took a few steps. "Let's go outside." He led the way through the glass door to the blazing balcony, which was free of furnishings but abundantly filled with sunshine and the salty, thick air blowing in from the ocean. She gulped in a lot of it—but she still felt strange.

"Now focus your attention there." He pointed out where the dolphins would play, not as close-in as the surfers, nor as far from the coast as the whales liked to travel. "Do you see anything?"

"You mean like dolphins? Pelicans?"

"No—look up higher, above the waves, and try to use your psychic vision more than your physical eyes."

She looked again, elevating her gaze to a few yards above the water. Nothing. She calmed her mind like she did when remote-viewing and suddenly she saw a shimmer. "Wait! I think I see...I can't really make it out. Something like a transparent...conveyor belt? Like those moving walkways they have at the Paris airport, you know? It appears, then disappears. Made of something that looks like Cinderella's glass slipper."

"Excellent. Yes, that's what I hoped you would see. Keep looking."

"Ho-ly fopperdoodles!"

"Well, that's one way to put it," he chuckled.

"Mother of monkeys! Are you kidding me?"

"Not my way of doing things."

"Oh man! It is *so beautiful!*"

"We like to think so."

She never wanted to stop staring, never dreamed she would see again what she saw there, hovering above the waves, the extraordinarily magnificent golden seashell starship she'd seen in the desert. Only larger and more real somehow. A craft from another world. She felt tears stream from her eyes and without thinking, she started to hold her breath, an unconscious reflex. If she breathed, she feared the fragile vision wouldn't hold. Her breath might whisk it away, like the patterns of cream in her coffee cup that disappeared when she stirred.

"Breathe, Minda," the reverend-who-wasn't had to remind her. "It's not going anywhere."

"Can they all see it?"

"Don't worry about them," he urged, "or—"

"Dang! Where did it go??"

"Too late. You switched your focus. The ship is still there, but you've re-attuned to the people walking on the beach. You've lost your connection. Try again."

She was so disappointed in herself, she couldn't bring the sight back, no matter how hard she tried.

"You're working at it. Relax your mind again. Forgive yourself for the mistake; mistakes are how you learn. See if you can let it float into your awareness, because now you *know* it exists. You've seen it twice. You should be able to bring it back to mind more easily."

She struggled to get past the panic that set in as soon as she understood that her own thoughts had betrayed her. She took deep breaths. She focused on her heart area, as she'd been taught to do. She conjured enormous gratitude for the brief moments she'd witnessed this off-world marvel, in the past and now, in the present.

"There!" she exclaimed when a flicker of orange flashed across her vision. "And there again!" It started to take shape.

"You can do it," Ben encouraged.

At last, the whole ship came back into view and stole her breath away again.

"It's the most incredible thing I've ever seen." Wonder and gratitude collided.

"Would you like to go for a ride?"

She heard the wicked twinkle in his voice but she refused to take her eyes off the ship. "Are you serious? It barely exists in my psychic awareness," she breathed out of the corner of her mouth. "How would I ever board such a…a…fairytale ornament?"

Like a deep sea jellyfish, the ship sent coruscations of light up and down its sides, oscillating through shades of lemon, gold, and orange, almost as if it were speaking to her in the language of color.

"No, you have it wrong. Your life here on Earth—that is the illusory one. This ship, which flies between dimensions as easily as you sneeze, this represents the most steady, most coherent expression of energy that you have ever experienced. It has been designed by Minds far in advance of your own—or mine, for that matter. It operates on energy principles that are universally obeyed in all dimensions. This is the most *real* reality you've ever seen."

"But it looks so fragile!"

"That is only because you are not accustomed to using your full, interdimensional sight."

"But it's way out there. How would I even reach it?"

"I thought you said you saw the travelator?"

"Holy fopperdoodles," she breathed out again, at a loss for better words to convey the torrents of emotion rippling through her.

He held out his hand. "Do you trust me?"

Oh boy, what a loaded question. This time she did look into his eyes. Something swirled through her brain and down into the pit of her stomach. She trusted him. Right at that moment, looking into those deep amber pools, she felt as if she could fly to the stars and back.

Oh wait—*shit shit shit*—is that what he was asking her to do?

She hesitated a long moment, and then reached out a slender hand and placed it firmly inside his massive one. She closed her eyes and felt his fingers wrap warmly around her own.

"Min, open your eyes. We need you to stay alert. This is not the *Wizard of Oz*. You don't even have to click your heels together," he laughed.

"No ruby slippers?" She couldn't stop the tremors in her knees.

"Nope. Simply lift your mind with me, lift it right onto that crystal walkway. I want you to learn that you can do this by the power of your own thoughts. What the people of Earth fail to recognize, and have failed for thousands of centuries to remember, is that your bodies are as ephemeral as any atom your quantum physics has attempted to explore. You've never found a solid particle at the roots of your existence, as much as your five senses would like you to believe that you have. You are pure energy. And energy can transform into a higher state of oscillation, or a lower one. For today, we're going for the higher option."

She could feel energy travel up her arm from where their hands were joined. It filled her with possibility, expansion, and belief. She knew that, despite what he was saying, he was also kindling abilities she hadn't known she possessed. Like holding a match to a pile of tinder, he sparked her inner flame with new potential.

Or maybe he'd brought life back to an ember that had died out? Because suddenly this all felt very familiar. She looked down from where she now stood, at the very end of the moving walkway, hovering above the beach. She felt no fear. Only exhilaration.

"Shall we proceed?" he grinned, and led the way onto the fairy gangplank, which glittered more brightly than the sunlight playing on the waves below.

At first, instead of letting the moving walkway carry her, Min tried to step ahead. She quickly lost her balance. If she hadn't been holding Ben's hand, she would have toppled into the waves. Yet how could she hold back? The gargantuan craft looming before them beckoned with all the colors of flickering candlelight, pulsing in and out of her vision. She couldn't wait to touch it, to prove to herself that it was real.

"Breathe, Minda," the tall man at her side reminded her. "You are still flesh and blood. You need to breathe."

"I don't understand how I am doing this at all."

She glanced down at the surf below them, then quickly decided that was a bad idea and refocused on the ship. Ben gripped her hand more firmly. Energy pulsed up her arm.

"As I said, you are a collection of energy systems, right down to your atomic structures, but the systems don't stop there. Your body is the product of an interdimensional pattern of energy—a pattern birthed by an Infinite, Creative Intelligence—or God, as some of your people call this energy force. They've personalized it, which of course would be more familiar to primitive minds. Even so, neither name feels sufficient to encompass the magnitude of that source of life."

She listened so intently, she lost herself in his words and tried to walk ahead again, the way you do on an escalator to reach the top faster. Immediately, she tasted salt and seconds later a wave crashed over her head, pushing and swirling her down deep. She fought to the surface and screamed for help. Too late. All she got was another mouthful of saltwater.

Desperate, she thrashed her arms, kicked her feet, trying to regain equilibrium before the next wave hit. It came. She panicked, and swallowed more saltwater when she cried out.

In a flash, she was back at Ben's side on the crystal walkway, dripping wet. She coughed and gasped. Gently, calmly, Ben patted her back. Suddenly she felt as dry as church on a Sunday morning.

"Your mind, Minda—it is a powerful thing. Only it has trap doors and hidden curses that we each must discover and overcome to realize our full potential. Are you feeling better now? Shall we continue?"

"Are you saying I imagined that?" She noticed that the conveyor had stopped moving.

"You fell through one of your trap doors: impatience."

"It's that easy??"

The wave, the saltwater, the wet clothes—so vivid, so real!

"That was just my mind playing tricks?"

"Yes. But the panic and anxiety were real, of course."

How does he stay so fricking calm?!

"The problem on your planet is the lack of education, mostly," he went on as if nothing had happened, as if she hadn't almost drowned. "You are living from a software that supports your energy body, which in turn creates your physical anatomy. Simple, right?

"Except that these energy systems exist in multiple dimensions, and you shape certain aspects of them yourself, by living. Emotions, experiences—everything is recorded, as you draw down the raw material of the Infinite energy source and make it yours. Added to the Infinite elements, this becomes the program that supports your life. It's unrelenting—but it's not unchangeable. Lifetime after lifetime, you build up your software, tear it down, remake it better, and so on. You shape the raw material of life to create the energetic program that runs your future.

"Trouble is, this is an interdimensional process that's largely unrecognized by current Earth science. You've barely tapped the subject of other-dimensional entanglement, so it's been left up to the spirit nerds and they are…well, *confused,* to say the least."

"Are you talking about parallel worlds?"

"No. Not at all."

The travelator, as he called it, was moving again. Why didn't they provide a guard rail? Her only security was Ben's hand gripping her own—and look how well that worked! No protection at all from the "trap door" in her own thinking.

The moment she thought it, she noticed a sparkling handrail on either side of them. "Hey, why didn't you tell me that was there?"

He laughed. "It wasn't. You've just manifested it."

She halted again, overwhelmed.

"Minda, breathe. You're doing great! To answer your question, not parallel worlds. More like an ice cream cone: a funnel of life that begins at the ice cream—Source—and funnels down through many dimensions of existence. Your present awareness has been focused on only one of those, your so-called third dimension, the bottom tip of the cone. But parts of you—in fact, the greater parts of you exist in dimensions higher on that ice cream cone of life. If you shift your awareness, you can re-center your point of perception. For instance, at this moment you are perceiving life from a higher-dimensional aspect of yourself."

"What happens when the ice cream melts and leaks out from the bottom onto your frigging fingers?"

He laughed at her. "Despite your colorful embellishments, Earth language fails, I'm afraid. Let me try a different metaphor. Your current science has managed to insert a needle into a larger reality, but that probe hasn't yet delivered a large enough sample for complete recognition of what lies beyond particle physics and five-sense-based reality. If they can't duplicate it in a physical, third-dimensional laboratory, traditional scientists believe it cannot exist. They will fight against it.

"A few intrepid souls have tried to break through that resistance to explore the invisible dimensions using your so-called 'scientific method.' You know what happened to the Stargate project. The requirement for duplication could not be met in the ways they expected, because remote viewing relies on other-dimensional realities.

"To put it another way: conventional science loses track of the ball when it disappears beyond your known spectrum, and then re-emerges back in your third-dimension. They're missing a big part of the story. Still, a few visionaries persist. Have you heard of time crystals?"

"No."

"Hm. Well. Let's just say that life on Earth is more of a pulsed-in reality than a solid, steady state. Yet if this were suddenly recognized, it might cause global psychic shock, with all the attendant symptoms. Unpleasant indeed. Not what we want to have happen."

She looked ahead at the ornament awaiting their tedious progress (though she wouldn't dream of trying to speed that up again). "Is that why this ship pulses in and out of my vision?"

"Could be."

At last they reached the side of the craft—and something like a swirling wheel of fire that she hadn't distinguished before, faintly reminiscent of the red spot on Jupiter. Ben let go of her hand. She didn't like that and wished he hadn't but she refused to admit that to him and so stood perfectly still, anxious about losing her balance again. She hoped like heck this flaming spiral wasn't the door.

"Yes, it is. We're going to go through it. But first, I want you to put your hand out and touch it."

"Just a hand?"

"Just a hand."

How bad could that be, the eager part of her argued. *Burns, yes, but only one hand, and how often do you get to explore an alien starship?*

Instantly her smarter self disagreed: *What if it disintegrates my hand?*

What distracted her from these reasonable arguments was the fact that her skin didn't register the amount of heat that much fire should generate.

"Why isn't it hot?"

"Because it is not the fire you are familiar with. It is not fire at all. This spiral vortex echoes the pattern formed when the life force spins into your cells from the Infinite Source. The ice cream at the top of the cone, remember? Look at the cone from above and it would resemble a spiral galaxy, or the swirl you see before you. Do you not trust me? Touch it."

She sighed. Logic told her that he would not have led her this far, and maybe even rescued her from drowning, if he intended to melt her hand off. Cautiously, she extended one long finger toward the glowing spiral.

Still no heat. She reached further. Coolness rippled along her skin. First one finger, and then she quickly thrust in her entire hand.

"Wow! That feels…good!" It reminded her of how the crash fragment had felt in her bare hands, only more soothing and, something she couldn't articulate. Something benevolent.

He smiled at her benignly, eyes full of compassion. "Imagine how that will feel to your entire body."

28

Perception

∞

Well, why not? This was, after all, what she'd been in such a big hurry to experience.

She took a deep, deep breath and let it out as she moved, thrusting herself into the vortex, one foot after another, until she was completely swallowed by the sparking light.

The colors dazzled. They shifted and changed, sliding from one hue to the next. A thrill of joy passed from the top of her head all the way down to her toes.

Love. That was the best she could describe the sensation, like soft flannel pajamas made of pure love.

Seconds later, Ben appeared. He took her by the hand again and led her about two steps forward so that she could see the interior.

It nearly took the top of her head off, literally, because she could not see any upper roof. For that matter, when she looked down, she saw only the ocean beneath them and that's when she started to panic again.

"Relax," Ben cautioned. "Use your heart-breathing technique. I admit, this might be the hardest transition but you can do it. I am confident in you."

She tried to focus on her heart, breathe into it, long exhale out of it—shakily at first. Then more smoothly.

She realized then that her heart was in fact the central electrical component in her bodily system, and that by taking these breaths, she was synchronizing herself with the ship itself.

"That is correct. This ship is the product of the Minds who designed it, and the Minds who operate it, the Minds of all of its crew. You are connecting with them now."

"Crew?"

Inside the ship, she saw no one—and no navigational systems or computers, nothing *Star Trek-y*, or like any other spaceship in her mental image gallery. It was disappointingly empty inside.

"You won't see the crew. They are stationed on worlds that you could not fathom—not yet, anyway. You could say they operate this ship remotely."

"How is it that we are standing in it? Sort of?"

He hesitated.

"We *are* here, aren't we? I mean, you are here; I can feel your hand wrapped around mine." And for that, she remained extremely grateful. But she couldn't really feel the ship; even less than she'd felt the crystal walkway.

"Yes, we are here. Minda, I fear I have deceived you somewhat. In case you hadn't already guessed." He offered an apologetic smile.

She bristled. Of course! She should have known!

The ship began to swirl around her, at least what she could see, which was little more than colored light patterns tracking along what she assumed to be the inner walls. With difficulty, and a tremendous amount of trust in her mentor despite his trickery (justified, she hoped), she managed to calm down. The patterns stopped spinning and fell into a more uniform repetition. She was beginning to understand that whenever she felt an emotion—good or bad—her environment reflected it. She'd fallen earlier only because she'd been afraid she would.

"You are doing extremely well, Min. Better than expected. Some of us weren't sure you would make it this far. But you are an excellent student, one who has been well prepared for this step-up in consciousness."

He looked relieved, frankly. The trickster. Why couldn't he have simply said, *Okay, I'll meet you in your dreams again*?

"I owe you an apology, Minda. I've led you to believe that you have walked onto this ship using your typical body, the one you live in from day to day, the one made of Earth elements. I wanted you to feel how real this level of expression is—truly, so much more real than anything you've known on Earth. And if I'd told you that you would be leaving your earth body behind, you might have resisted or panicked. But now you need to know: your earth body lies at rest, completely safe, with your head on the bar table where you consumed the green drink."

Hah! She knew it!

"So I am dreaming after all?"

"No. This is not a dream. A dream is what happens at random while you are sleeping. Although sometimes what you call dreams are astral journeys like this one, disguised as dreams."

"So when we first met—it wasn't a dream?"

"No, my dear. We met in another dimension, an astral dimension, meaning not physical in the way you understand physical to be. But of course, this is as real as anything else in your life."

She considered for a moment. "I've always thought of those two words, *real* and *physical,* as interchangeable, as in, it's not real if it's not physical."

"And now you see that is incorrect."

If that's true, then…

"Until Earth science discovers the principles guiding dimensional permeability, we will remain committed to protecting citizens of Earth from sudden glimpses of other dimensional realities that could lead to mental disarray, as I've explained."

"But people have mental breakdowns all the time," she protested.

"Unfortunately, many things can trigger them. Psychotropic drugs, for instance, natural or man-made. Emotional events that dredge up past-life traumas. Mental ailments endemic to your world. The rampant ignorance of interdimensional communication causes endless problems on your planet."

"You mean mental illness always relates to cross-dimensional confusion?"

"Even a blood sugar crash can open up one's mental portals into lower frequencies where the psychic company one meets is not, shall we say, of an uplifting nature. Countless murders are committed as a result of low blood sugar, and plenty of marriages fall apart when day to day swings in mental frequency—often caused by poor diets—disrupt the familial harmony as unwanted 'guests' chime in on ugly emotional states.

"So yes, mental illness can often be traced back to shattered dimensional barriers."

"And by psychic company—unwanted guests—you mean what you said earlier, about opening your doors in a bad neighborhood?"

"Imagine you've walked into a room of strangers and don't know anything at all about their intentions and predilections. You've developed your energy-sensing abilities, Minda, so you've learned to discern the nature of the company you keep, in whatever dimension you find yourself. Hence, your work here today. But what of the naïve, or even those who carry misinformed beliefs about their 'protection' devices or techniques? They are easily fooled. Some of the worst entities can show up looking like religious saints. They are masters of disguise.

"People often invite total *astral* strangers into their bedrooms or bank accounts—something they'd never do with a physical human. Or their automobile, kitchen, heart, or mind. Or into their physical body, as trance mediums do. The link is energetic, and the human victim remains ignorant of how their own thoughts and intentions keep the connection active. They can be led to take bizarre actions—such as pulling a trigger, downing a drug, or even surgically altering their body to suit the astral being's preferences. This is tragic but too often true. The hardest part is that the invader's thoughts can feel like one's own, until one learns to identify and dispatch spurious frequencies, as you have learned to do.

"Older cultures on Earth understood this phenomenon right up into the early twentieth century, when even your 'father of modern psychology,' William James, spoke of it."

Min shuddered. "Some of that sounds like relationships I've known."

"Precisely. All human relationships help us learn the interdimensional science of harmonic resonance that determines the nature of the mental company we keep."

"We certainly suffer an abundance of the problems you've described."

"True. And difficult as this is for us to watch, we cannot interfere. Your planetary evolution must unfold at the pace of your willingness. Until the science of interdimensional communication is no longer suppressed by competing factions on Earth, this will be a slow, painstaking process. Like the caterpillar attempting to break out of its cocoon, there will be deadly accidents. This is why you have been so carefully trained to slip the boundaries of the third dimension. Knowledge is the key to your safety."

"What did you mean, suppressed?" She could barely keep her hands from touching the beautiful patterns of energy swirling around them—very distracting. But she'd caught his implication that someone was manipulating her experience on Earth. Who?

"It is better to ask who is attempting to break through that suppression of knowledge. Some of Earth's greatest minds—even political leaders, hard as that is to believe—were trained as visionaries between lifetimes."

They had moved only a few feet from the spiral entrance. Now he led her forward, swept a hand, and holographic images, faces of the famous going far back in history, flashed before her, one after another, too many to identify.

"These individuals used their interdimensional training to help move the planet forward at key moments. Most suffered opposition, sometimes violent oppression, even death. It's important for you, especially, to recognize that their psychic breakthroughs were not unplanned. These were carefully-timed revelations, conducted in concert with countless Advanced Minds along the web of the Inner-net. The *transceiver*—receiver and re-transmitter—of this cosmic insight was always, in every case, a being of tremendous mental development, long trained and practiced in the use of interdimensional consciousness."

"Like Nikola Tesla? I always thought he was lucky to escape the asylum. I have a copy of his autobiography. I've read what he said about his visions."

And by now she realized she was having her own Tesla-like episode. Her visit aboard this alien craft was taking place mentally, though her physical senses still seemed to function. That faint fragrance of roses, for instance, which permeated the ship. But of course this experience was as flimsy as her remote visions. Wasn't it? That's why they were only talking, not going anywhere, and why the interior displayed no real equipment to make the ship fly, she decided. No need for a computer bank. This was an imaginary vessel.

"Nikola Tesla, father of your electrical age. Like Leonardo before him, his visions laid a groundwork for future inventors, well beyond the few breakthroughs he was allowed to bring into fruition during his lifetime. He funneled in information from advanced worlds for future generations on Earth. His insights might not have been heeded at the time, but he expanded the realm of possibility on this planet *energetically*. Even during his short life, other inventors benefited from his work and took credit for it. Although, once he mentioned receiving signals from Mars," Ben chuckled and shook his head. "He might have pushed his colleagues a little too far, too soon. Those of us who know what he was up to trust that he had his reasons."

The holograms faded and Ben drew her deeper into the ship where the clear floor, like the travelator, created the glass-bottomed boat effect. Min quelled her fear with a question.

"This crystal—is it part of the propulsion system?"

"You are wise, my child," was all he said, and she took that to mean, *Yes, and you wouldn't understand how right now, even if I told you.*

So far, he'd answered some things she'd wondered about her entire life. Maybe one day she'd understand those answers.

From where they now stood in the translucent ship, she could take in a panoramic view. Above, sky. Below, ocean. And three hundred and sixty degrees around, north, south, east, west. It felt like being inside a giant soap bubble with its swirls of light and color, so beautiful she never wanted to leave. The last remnants of her earlier anxiety drained away.

Softly, Ben observed, "While you live on Earth, it's as if you're inside a dark cave. You can't see outside it."

"Like Plato's cave?"

She finally let herself touch one of the color-walls and her hand left a radiating imprint, as if she'd stirred a pool of water. The thrill of it made her want to run along, trailing her fingers across the walls. She managed to restrain the impulse. Although she couldn't see any crew, she distinctly felt their presence. She knew she was a guest here. Running around, touching things like a toddler was exactly the kind of rambunctious behavior Gramma Julene used to scold her for. She couldn't bring herself to do more, and her child's heart whimpered in disappointment.

"Yes, exactly. Plato's cave. You can catch glimpses of the light playing on the walls now and then. It inspires you to learn more. Sometimes, that light playing on the wall is our work."

"And who *are* you? The 'our' and 'we' you keep talking about?"

"Well, you are one of us."

"You keep saying that."

"As an older soul you have lived on physical worlds other than Earth. Most of the people who now incarnate on Earth have done the same. This world is always either on the brink of disaster, or astonishing revelation. Your societies vacillate from one to the other, which makes this planet an excellent school for long-term, soulic education. From time to time, certain contingents of extraterrestrials have taken up residence, hoping to improve the status of the natives and themselves. Whether that was wise or not, civilizations have risen and fallen under their influence."

"I knew it!"

She'd always known, though people spent entire careers trying to prove or disprove this lost history.

"Your planet—"

"Stop calling it that! It's not mine!"

He looked surprisingly happy about her pronouncement.

"My apologies," he bowed slightly. "*Earth* has been safe in its chrysalis state for a very long time. Inevitably, that membrane will split. When it does, events might unfold rapidly. Not everyone will be able to adjust. They might die here and be reborn elsewhere, to a planet more like this one's current environment. It's going to be an individual proposition. The universe provides infinite opportunity, of course."

"That reminds me—if I talk about reincarnation, people say, 'But why is the population still growing?' They consider that proof against the idea."

"Yes. Common question. They haven't realized that the universe is vastly populated by human souls. Those here now have come for particular experiences. Right now, the population is rising because Earth offers them a scenario for personal do-overs. Events to come will supply a chance to rewrite the software, to master old phobias or start over with better choices. It should prove quite illuminating, individually and collectively."

"Are you saying our currently screwed-up society might be a good thing?" She could think of a million reasons it wasn't.

"Not exactly. But sometimes we learn faster from pain than pleasure."

"Great. Reminds me of a friend who once said, 'We all have to eat humble pie—and we all don't like it.'"

"Your friend is quite a poet," he laughed. "Wise and true."

She wondered if this meant Earth would never improve, never hook up with an alien society that could show us how to build ships like the one that now felt as if it were hugging her. She imagined the disappointment certain brave scientists like Avi Loeb were going to feel if it didn't happen in their current lifetime. Or—a new thought occurred to her—were they part of Ben's league of advanced humans, paving the way for those who came after?

"If a more evolved society from elsewhere in the cosmos succumbed to an overwhelm of sympathy and sailed in to clean up Earth's problems with their superior knowledge," Ben said softly, "they would destroy your classroom. Hence, our Earth organization, Blackthorn, operated by those of us who have come here via the womb. Without getting further into galactic politics, I hope that helps you understand why we do what we do?"

She sized him up. "If you came through normal birth, then how are you so sure you're not indigenous? Why do you identify as an alien?"

"Good question. Am I standing here on an alien ship with you?"

"Obviously."

"Quickly, name ten people who would believe that."

Her face probably gave her answer away. Among her Blackthorn colleagues, only a bare handful. But she was startled by the first name that came to her: *Garritt*.

"You are correct. Garritt is a special case."

Once again, he'd read her mind. She didn't like it.

"You realize that I only do that when you are about to speak, right? When you've given your thoughts wings, but they haven't yet taken off? I pick them up off the launch pad," he chuckled.

She harrumphed. She'd have to review to see if that were true. Later.

"Garritt's circumstances remain a mystery. Yet we believe he has a role to play in our mission. One of the ways that you will serve us now will be to bring him into our circle. Juan will not be a problem. He has already joined us, although he doesn't realize that yet."

Her eyes widened. "You want me to *recruit* Garritt? How? 'Um, excuse me, but my bug-eyed alien boss wants a word with you?'"

"Something like that," he smiled. "But first let me explain why you are standing on this alien craft with your, I beg to differ, normally-sighted boss."

Yeah, right. Which is why his honey-colored eyes gave her a gleam that just about sent her into the stars without the necessity for any kind of vehicle.

Earlier she'd noticed that the ship was emitting sounds. Now they swelled as if to provide a score for Ben's verbal performance. Elegant and sweeping, or harsh and clashing, depending on what he said. In fact, now she noticed that the color patterns on the walls shifted according to his words.

"What kind of ship is this, anyway?"

"A learning ship. Today, it is programmed for your benefit."

"For me? By whom?" *And why me, when so many others are better suited and more deserving?*

"Today's event is not only the after-effect of touching that fragment on the dunes back in Michigan. My dear, you have worked hard for this opportunity. You have sacrificed much. Haven't you?"

He zeroed in so intently, she looked down at her sandaled feet suspended over the ocean. *Yeah, but so?*

"You set aside relationships that didn't support your work. You have forgone the opportunities to have children. You suffered through rigorous training. And you have given up social events, friends, relatives, all the ordinary attributes of a typical life. Am I right?"

She couldn't deny it.

"You have pledged yourself repeatedly to our cause, set aside the desires of your small-self, and made your choice and commitment clear, again and again."

Hadn't he read her thoughts about breaking her oaths? Stealing an artifact? Taking it public?

His face gentled. "You earned this opportunity many times over, Minda, so stop feeling as if you don't deserve this new level of awareness. You worked for every moment of it."

A little tremor passed through her. Could she believe that?

"Your present life will be a turning point for you. We—you and I—share a past-life history with each other—and with the people of this planet. For our advancement on the ladder of personal development, we needed to return. We must do what we can to rectify our previous mistakes. You have taken all the right turns so far to make that happen."

He was gazing at her in a way she hadn't seen before, something more human than alien. And then his eyes flicked and she got the strange feeling that he meant her desire to spill Blackthorn's big secret wasn't wrong.

"You came in with a goal—and you worked steadily toward it."

"Are you talking about working out karma?" She had to divert the conversation. He had given her that rare sensation of feeling understood, which threatened her with tears. This man recognized what she'd struggled with in life.

"Karma? The term is outdated. It's your energetic blueprint that needs reworking. To do this on Earth, one must return to the scene and make different choices. For us—you, me, and all those who join Blackthorn and its allies—we have an opportunity to redress certain incidents from the past that we have not been able to rectify until the planet reached its current status. Earth has sped forward technologically, but with an imbalanced mental awareness. That gives us an opening.

"This ship will be your new remote-viewing tool. With it, you will help us find Bobby Lee, follow him to his buyers, and secure the lost fragment once and for all. More importantly, you will help us learn more about the real threat to our mission. Bobby believes he will rendezvous with some kind of do-good organization. We know that is not true. But we aren't certain who our nemesis is yet."

"And if I fail?" She squinted off at the earthly beauty surrounding the ship.

He shrugged, "Earth has experienced global resets before. Nothing is lost, theoretically, but a global reset involves a lot of backtracking and slow, painstaking work to climb back to its present state of…opportunity."

"In plain English?"

"In your words? If you fuck this up, the whole place could be destroyed in a flash implosion involving all of dimensional reality, affecting countless life forms in endless places, as the harmonics of this catastrophe ripple out into infinity. Countless souls will be set back in their evolutionary development by millions of years."

"No pressure then."

"You will have ample assistance. And you have passed today's first test. Now, aren't you tired of this view?"

Mischief flickered across his features and she instantly recognized what was coming. "Wait! I'm not ready!" But it was too late. Without any G-force, no sense of movement at all, she found herself staring down at…

No way. That can't be!

"Is that…?"

"Yes. It is. This ship is in fact a vehicle for travel, despite what you assumed. You can take it wherever your imagination allows. Where would you like to go? I've made the first choice to give you the idea."

Oh, isn't he proud! He's positively radiant with self-congratulation! She trembled head to toe as hot lava shot up in fiery spumes all around them, then fell back to spill down over the sides of an erupting volcano. She watched in horror at first, as the black-and-red river of unleashed magma devastated the landscape. It mowed down entire slopes of jungle vegetation, consumed fences, ate up automobiles, set buildings afire and then swallowed them whole. She stared then, mesmerized by the destruction.

Humans and their trinkets—so frail in the face of implacable, natural forces. Something beautiful lay within this power, something that caught her up inside and made her feel whole, made her touch her own inner power, fueled by the same force that drove this monstrous volcano.

"You really go for the dramatic, don't you?"

"I have been told this before. But how better to show you that this vehicle has no limitations? It cannot be harmed by physical danger. The heat from Kilauea has no affect on this craft. Any material ship would have burst into flame, of course. Where would you like to go next?"

"Anywhere?"

"Anywhere."

She went for the cliché. "Paris?"

Instantly, Eiffel Tower and the Seine, crowds of people—and city smog.

"Okay, what about somewhere not so crowded?"

Mount Everest towered majestically before them. She gulped and reached for a hand-hold that suddenly appeared. They sped between the surrounding peaks and then climbed straight up over what was known to be the tallest point above the seas of Earth. And then, no doubt to placate her mentor's penchant for drama, they rose further, and up, and up, until black space surrounded them, high above the planet.

Gradually they gained distance until she, Minda Blake, community college drop-out, stared down at the "Blue Marble" the astronauts of Apollo 17 first captured on film. Seeing it with her own eyes triggered so much more emotion than looking at a mere photograph. Her heart beat faster for a long, long moment of awe.

"Take me back," she whispered.

"You don't want to see the underground cities of—"

"No."

Without so much as a jet trail, she found herself back on Earth, suspended above the Pacific's crashing waves, just beyond the deserted beach restaurant.

"We have to save it," she said simply.

Immediately Ben's face disappeared, his body with it, and everything went black.

29

Orders

∞

Min regained consciousness to find her face smushed into the café table, arms wrapped around her head. Distantly, she heard Ben cajoling her to wake. With great difficulty she made words come out of her mouth.

"Did I pass out?"

"Not exactly."

She managed to lift her head and sit up. "That drink you gave me—was that it?"

"Partly. Minda, you've experienced an out-of-body episode. It was not accidental. Long before you were born, you and I agreed that you would make certain step-ups in consciousness during your present lifetime. You came to San Diego at our request, but truly, your path here was determined by your own commitment and desire, especially your desire to serve humanity. I am speaking, not only of your trip here yesterday, but of your pursuit of remote viewing, and now, your newest skill."

"My new skill?" She was getting used to his long, roundabout way of answering direct questions. If you paid attention, you could actually pick up tidbits of useful information, some of it bone-chilling.

"Think. Remember where you just were."

She sat a little straighter and tried to do as he said. Amazed, she stared at him. "Did that really happen?"

"Yes, it did."

She managed to get up from the table, shakily, and make her way to the glass door. Opening it, she stepped out into the sunlight. She could remember every detail clearly. That didn't make it any easier to accept. "It seems like I've been with you for hours but the sun is still high in the sky. How long were we … um …"

"You've been with me for about half an hour," he answered from behind where she stood at the balcony railing.

That couldn't be right. He'd said so much; she'd changed so much. Half an hour wasn't long enough but the sun's position supported his claim.

Squinting out over the bright waves, she tried to see what she'd seen before: the long, crystalline walkway, the glistening starship. She saw only a pod of dolphins playing in the waves. Ordinarily, that would have been a thrill but today she felt a deep plunge of disappointment. It was only a dream.

"No, not a dream. A visit as real as anything you are experiencing now."

"But how could that be? I can't walk out over the waves and board a frickin' ship to Mars now, can I?"

He smiled broadly. "How do you know you can't?"

"Well, wouldn't I be doing it if I could?"

"No, not likely. Because you can do so many things you don't know you can do. Yet. And you are not doing those, either."

"Gahhh, you and your blasted mysteries! You are driving me crazy!" She twirled away to pace the deck. "Look, I don't know why you've given me this dream but I did enjoy it immensely. Thank you. Trouble is, I'm here, standing in a vacant restaurant with a man who might or might not actually *be* a man in the usual sense, and people are about to be hurt back in Michigan. Or the entire planet is going to go up in a flash at any minute! Or, if all goes well and the planet evolves, *a whole fricking lot of them* are going to die here anyway and live on some other hellhole of a planet until their souls grow up. Did I get that right?"

"Quite," he agreed.

"I still don't know who I'm working for, what your ultimate objective is, and who the good guys really are—if good guys even exist anymore. Are you going to enlighten me now, or torment me with more fancy dreams about impossible feats?"

"Are you finished?"

He looked, maybe not peeved, but extremely serious.

She thought for a moment. Was she?

"No, not really. But I don't know what else to say," she conceded. She felt deeply frustrated over her inability to know all, see all, penetrate the mysteries of the universe.

"Good. Because you are not going to come to the end of the mysteries of the multiverse—*ever*. And that drive, that anger you're feeling, that frustration is what will keep you searching. It will also fuel your work over the next few weeks. You will need to draw on everything you already know, as well as everything I've begun to teach you today."

A certain kind of confident power radiated from him as he towered over her. It wasn't the height; it was the energy he exuded that stopped the questions and complaints she'd had percolating. Stopped them cold.

"Your astral trip today was facilitated—aided, is a better word—by the green drink I produced for you. That is true. But it was only an enhancement to give you the experience. You can take that journey again any time you wish, if you use the capabilities you already had. I merely gave you an opportunity to experience it with my guidance so that you could find your way alone next time."

"You mean I can walk myself onto an astral spaceship any time I want to?" Skeptical didn't begin to describe it.

"Exactly. That ship is now yours to control, using your mind and everything you know about interdimensional physics. That's quite a lot more than your next-door neighbor. This will be your new viewing tool. It will take you far, as I've just demonstrated. It has no limitations."

That wasn't at all what she expected him to say and it took her a beat to recover. With a shade more humility, and a heavy dose of amazement, she asked, "Can anyone do this?"

"Not without assistance. Training. Practice. All of which you have had, both in this world and prior to your birth. You must recognize that all that your experiences, both present and past lives, have taught you, Minda. I hope you realize that your remote viewing limitation, that of seeing only what you've been exposed to previously, is no longer in effect."

"Seriously?"

"You told me you want to save this world? "

She nodded.

"Then let's get on with it."

He opened the glass door and gestured back to the bar, where she was surprised to see the Commander lift a drink of his own. He nodded cordially at her and raised his glass, wearing what her brother would call a shit-eating grin.

Ben continued, "Our primary objective right now is to retrieve the fragment that Bobby Lee acquired, the real one. The relic is dangerous in and of itself, in ways I hope you now understand. We are tracking him using the usual methods but that has limitations. We need your new skills and those Juan will bring to the table."

Juan?

"We've arranged a charter to return you to Michigan posthaste. The Commander is here to drive you to the airport. You should land before dinnertime. While you're traveling, I want you to practice your new skill. See how far and how fast you can move that ship, how clearly you can discern the details of where it takes you. The intelligence you reap using this method will far surpass anything current Earth tech could provide."

"But I'll need the green drink to get on the ship," she protested. "You'll have to tell me what's in it."

"Kale, spinach, parsley, cilantro, apple, lemon, and lots of ginger."

"Wait—what?"

"They sell it across the street at the health food restaurant. I think they call it the Kicker."

The Commander laughed and she shot him a look. "You're kidding me! I thought you said it was your special recipe …"

"Your mind, Minda. I told you it is powerful. Although, you are correct," Ben admitted, "the salt on the rim was my invention. And the glass I served it in." He winked at her. "Brings up the flavor, don't you think?"

30

Truth and Lies

∞

Stranded, in his father's house. A circumstance Garritt believed he escaped two decades ago.

He reached for the stiff jeans he left on the hearth to dry when he banked the fire—the one he built after everyone else disappeared, before he found a throw and crashed on the couch, unwilling to go any deeper into the bowels of this palace in search of a spare room.

This morning he planned to break free as quickly as possible. As soon as someone appeared, he'd beg a phone and call an Uber.

Last night it didn't seem wise to go out in a storm to a house that might not have the power restored, or back to his truck in who-knew-what condition after the plows went through. He remembered that he parked it too close to the road, thought he'd be back in fifteen minutes. Hah. In the light reflected off the snow beyond his father's panoramic windows, his leg looked hideous. Maybe he should go straight to an urgent care?

Then his nose caught the scent of frying bacon, which made him think of his mother, supposedly on a plane somewhere with her Franken-pet. She wasn't much of a cook but her love of bacon meant it often appeared on their morning menu. After he freshened up in a guest bath, he headed for the kitchen.

Too late, he realized he should have aimed for the front door instead.

He reached the dividing archway just in time to see his father—his piously religious father, icon of purity and family stability, Senator and holder of countless humanitarian awards, the man who ranted about

God's will, who beat the Commandments into Garritt's brain quite literally, and who called Corbyn and Avery's lifestyle "an abomination to God"—*that* man. He saw that same man come up behind his cute-boy Congressional aide at the stove and grab him by the ass. Oh no, not in any way other than exactly what it appeared to be: a move only a lover would make. They were laughing and joking with their backs to him, rude jokes of the type lovers share.

Garritt's eyes wanted to fold back inside his head, obliterate the truth before him. Instead, all the subtleties came back to him, all the clues he'd tried to ignore the night before—the looks, the undertones. *Couldn't be*, he'd pushed them aside. *Not my father.*

Sure, the young man clearly had a crush on the powerful old guy, and yeah, he'd caught the aide flaunting his gayness when he thought they were alone.

But Volkert Vanderhoeven? Never in a million years!

In dozens of gatherings over the years, Garritt had heard his father curse the nearby gay resort towns of Saugatuck and Douglas as "Sodom and Gomorrah," sitting at the edge of the Triangle "like a slap in the face" to his holy Dutch community.

Now the truth slapped Garritt's face in the harsh kitchen light.

The homosexuality wasn't what caused his stomach to revolt. What boiled inside him at that moment was how his father's secret lifestyle had rippled through Garritt's own life: the hypocrisy, the self-loathing it must foster in such a man, because as far as Garritt knew, nothing in Dutch Reformed Christianity condoned adultery, let alone bisexuality, so his father had been living a massive lie, pretending to be what he was not only for his personal, material gain.

All those years when Garritt was forced to listen to pious sermons about how he must behave, what he should think, what "God" would expect of him? Total bullshit flowing from the mouth of a man who held power over every tiny life decision in his child's upbringing.

If the man hadn't repeatedly proclaimed himself a paragon, a champion of God's will to any and all who fell under his spell, he could be dismissed as simply another selfish adulterer. But everyone around the Senator had to pay for his self-loathing while he lived out his lies. Especially his own son.

He wanted to vomit but held back the urge. That would be too much respect for a man who deserved none.

Before he could see more, he shrank away, blinded already by a truth that made his own life feel like a monstrous lie. Did they not realize he'd stayed? Did they not care?

His mind raced, eager for logic at the center of its maelstrom. It would have been easy to miss Garritt's sleeping body; the couch faced the picture windows; they'd come down the hallway, quietly enough he didn't hear them pass. Were they so lost in post-coital bliss?

After the police left, Garritt assumed they disappeared into his father's office to monitor the late newscasts, to strategize how the Senator would survive the onslaught of inquiry headed his way. After all, there were—not one, not two—but *four* individuals forcibly detained inside his opulent estate when Agnes's posse arrived. Surely the intense media coverage would not allow the Senator to get away with that?

And now this…

Garritt steamed as he grabbed up his belongings. He wanted to give in to the rage that flooded his thoughts and pound the man's head into a pulp for all the wrongs he'd committed against his family.

Yet in the next moment, Garritt felt pity for him.

Then grief, over his warped childhood, and hatred for the man's abuse.

And finally, as a brilliant pinpoint of gold pierced through his awareness, clarity shot through his entire history with Michigan's Dutch community—where piety meant hypocrisy. Where cruelty hid self-loathing. Where outward beauty concealed the rotten stench of soulic corruption.

No more. He was done now. He felt his ties to the man unravel and fall away. In that moment, he vowed never to rebind to this twisted, contemptuous human. He wanted to strip off his old skin and replace it with something shining, new, and unmarred by the world's depravity.

The starkest realization of all was that it was not his fault. None of it was his fault. It had *never been* his fault. *He* was not the flawed one, as he had so often been told. He was not "a bad child." He'd had a bad father.

Garritt wondered if his mother knew and played out her own charade for prosperity's sake. He shook his head in pity for them both as he snatched his coat and boots and hobbled to the front door. Somehow, he would reach the neighbors and borrow a phone. He would not stay in this psychic hell a single moment longer. He flung open the front door—to meet Agnes's startled eyes.

"I was just about to ring," she apologized.

He threw his arms around her. "You are an angel, Agnes, and you may never know why. Get me out of here!"

She grinned ear to ear, and offered her body to support his as they limped together to her brother's truck.

"Stew won't let me drive my Ford Focus until all the roads are clear."

Garritt laughed, a manic, full-throated cry of liberation. His spirit burst wide, a life-long puzzle solved, the invisible chains fallen away. "Your brother might be an angel, too!"

Agnes cast him a bemused look.

"Let's just say I begin my life anew this morning. No limitations!"

She started the engine. "That's good."

He was flying so high, he didn't notice when she turned toward Hamilton, not Soonika where he'd left his green truck.

31

Friends

∞

Garritt wasn't amazed to see that his neighbor had plowed his driveway; what brought him back to the here-and-now was his beloved green Ford pickup idling there, albeit with a smashed left side.

As Agnes pulled near, Juan hopped out of the truck, grinning. He didn't appear to have more than a black eye—nothing at all like the horrifically bruised and emotionally damaged young man Garritt had last seen rushing into the arms of his family.

Garritt clambered from the silver Ram, painfully reminded of his injuries. "You ripped off my truck?"

Juan slapped him on the back and handed Garritt his phone. "Rescued it for you before the snow plows totally creamed this *carcacha*."

"This was Juan's idea," Agnes said. "He called me at the break of dawn and I dropped him off before I picked you up."

"Thanks, guys. I am in your debt. But what about you, Juan? You looked like hell last night—and now look at you!"

He reached in his pocket and felt his truck key on the same chain as his house keys but refused to consider how Juan got into his truck and started it.

"Sorry." Juan slipped an arm around to help him limp down the slippery drive. "I didn't know whose side you were on until they took you away. Sam told me where they caught you. Thanks, *compa*. I don't know how you knew but you are *muy loco* driving in that storm!"

They glanced up almost in unison to appreciate the light breaking through the departing clouds. Water dripped from the eaves. The record snowfall was already melting in the relative warmth of a more typical November day.

"I don't get it, though. Not that I'm not grateful for my truck—thanks, man—but why aren't you with Luciana?" Had she told him about the baby yet? Couldn't have, or he wouldn't be here.

"It's a long story. You're not going to believe most of it."

"You'd be surprised."

Garritt was relieved to flip on a light and discover that his power was restored. *In more ways than one.*

"Make yourselves comfortable. I need a shower."

He loped into his bedroom before Juan could launch his story. Truthfully, he needed to gather himself before any more startling revelations.

Later, as he pushed a comb through his wet hair, he could only see reflections of his father in the bathroom mirror. Garritt had grown his hair long and kept the stubble on his face because he thought that made him look less Dutch. But his face echoed the senator's own. It was hard not to despise it. Right there, in the mirror, the cruel hypocrite. Mentally freer than he had ever been, yet still bound by blood. Garritt realized he would have to fight, not only the temper, but the habit of self-hatred.

The sound of an argument in the living room made him dress in a hurry. When he pulled open his door, he found Juan and Agnes fighting over a fire log.

"What's going on here?"

"She won't listen to me!"

"It's cold in here, and you need to rest by the fire, Garritt."

"But we can't stay! We have to stop Bobby Lee!"

"Why? You're safe now, Juan."

Agnes was right, of course. Garritt was looking forward to putting his feet up by the fire in his own tiny, messy house where everything you see is what you get.

"No, you don't understand! She can't build a fire—we have to go right now. Before he gets away."

"Slow down, okay? What are you talking about? And Agnes, put that thing down before someone gets hurt."

She grumbled in protest but threw it back in the log basket.

"I'm talking about Bobby Lee. He's crazy! He wanted to kill me just to shut me up. Zach told me, the cop. He's the one who saved me—that is, until Agnes and Sam showed up." He paused long enough to flash her one of the special grins that had made him so popular in high school.

Agnes blushed furiously but with visible satisfaction.

Juan spun back to Garritt, "Zach staged the whole thing, see. The arrest, the interrogation—it was all a show to convince Bobby's church friends that I was being tortured to confess, because Bobby lied and told them I stole his fucking artifact."

He stopped abruptly and glanced at Agnes where she sat perched on a straight-backed chair.

"It's okay," Garritt assured him, "I already know about the UFO, and the artifact. Believe it or not, my father told me some, and Min—you don't know her—she told me the rest. As for Agnes, she's earned the right to know."

He flopped into the blue recliner. At least he could elevate his throbbing leg. He felt neither capable nor interested in going anywhere.

Juan sputtered in foul Spanish, then strode back and forth, agitated, as if his life were still on the line, waving his hands around.

"You don't know what that *pendejo* is up to. He's going to double-cross his church *and* your father and his business pals. See, Bobby promised his church that they'd make the thing public, so the whole world could know once and for all that we are not alone on this planet." He flicked another look at Agnes.

Garritt couldn't think how to soften any of this for her, even if Juan stopped to take a breath.

He didn't. "Bobby convinced his *Church of Refined Sensibilities*"— he said it with particular distaste— "that your father would have more influence with the media, so they agreed. But Bobby lied. He's actually planning to sell the thing to the Russians, or the Chinese, or some corporation that will bury it so they can keep profiting from fossil fuels. Or make some fucking extinction machine…"

This was typical Juan, ranting about fossil-fuel conspiracies. About alternative energy devices snapped up by greedy industrialists who buried them alive to keep their profit centers chugging along.

"Bobby found these people on the dark web. They could be anybody! And there's more you don't know," Juan added.

"Go on."

"It's not just a piece of metal. As soon as I touched it—"

"You touched it?"

"Um, yeah," he shrugged, looking guilty. "Bobby sent me out to retrieve it before the black ops could. He found it, see, and he buried it because they were watching him."

That meant either Min lied to him when she said *she* found the artifact, or Bobby lied to Juan. He'd put his money on Min as the truth-teller.

"I went where Bobby told me to go and there it was. Dude! It's from outer space! And you can tell right away. The minute I touched it… whoa." He shook his head and his eyes went funny. "It…. does things."

"Like what?"

"Like with your mind. I could hear things, I mean, not hear them, but just … know them. Especially Bobby. When I handed it to him, it was like electricity shot between us and I knew what he was thinking, sort of.

"Then he was all over it, and he kept walking around in his cabin, turning it over and over, saying stupid shit, like how he was going to show them all, how he'd build his temple to the universe, and shit like that. About the money he'd make, how he'd use it to become famous … "

By now, Agnes looked like someone had hit her in the face with one of Pamela's blueberry pies. What could he say to her? *It's okay, Agnes; they're only aliens coming to kill or exploit or enlighten us, but no one knows which? And by the way, your Bible predicted it?* No, he didn't think so.

"Bobby wants to kill me off because I'm the only one who's seen the real deal. I know he was passing off a fake. But Zach didn't like the torture idea so he volunteered to be the one, you know? He's a cop. He's got experience. He told me his plan and showed me how to fake getting beat up. How to look like he'd tortured me. We used some stage make-up and all, and I had to let him hit me a couple of times when some of the others were there." He twisted his jaw at the memory. "You saw the cage, right? He put me in there for show, and as soon as the others left, he gave me a key and made sure I had logs for the stove and shit."

So that's how it got there. Cigarettes and beer too?

Juan grinned and puffed into his *macho Latino* strut, "So who's awesome?" Double thumbs jabbed at his chest, "This guy right here. I could be on one of those crime shows, you know? Mexican drug dealer, all beaten down and still he won't talk. I even convinced you," he laughed. "My cousin lives in LA. Luci would love it if we moved to California. She hates the cold."

He got a look on his face then that told Garritt he knew about the baby. Or, if what Juan was saying were true, maybe he read her mind and she had to confess?

Juan—a father. He felt an unexpected twinge of jealousy.

"Bobby would have left me in that shed until I fucking froze to death—sorry Agnes. If Zach hadn't stepped in, I might be dead. I told him everything I knew and the two of us were going to stop Bobby. That's when your father's trained *culos* interrupted."

Agnes finally spoke up. "Is Zach the one who gave you the black eye?"

"Nah, that was the Senator's hired muscle. They screwed everything up. They weren't pretending." He touched the eye gingerly. "Garritt, we have to stop Bobby. It's my fault. I handed him that fragment. I did his bidding and now he's *muy loco*. He could hurt someone. He could hurt the whole world, if he sells that thing to the wrong people. Besides, I know his plan."

"How do you know that?"

"I can hear him."

Agnes scooted forward on her chair. "You can *hear* him, or you think you know what he's thinking?"

"Look, you guys didn't touch that thing. I did. And never mind how I know, I know he's going to hand it over to some assholes who might hide it in a lab until the day they come out blasting fancy new weapons and they're not on our side. That thing is *powerful.* It messed with my head, only I didn't go crazy like Bobby has. We have to go! Now!"

"Why not let Zach take care of him? Leave it to the police department?" Garritt asked.

"Zach doesn't have *you*. Besides, I can't reach Zach. He's disappeared—or at least, he's not answering texts. And you have skills no one else has."

"What do you mean?"

"I told you—I know things now. I know without anyone telling me that a little while ago you wanted to strangle your old man, but you stopped yourself and it scared the shit out of you to be that pissed, until you realized he'd just set you free." He looked significantly at Agnes. "I know that Agnes is just happy right now to be in your house because—"

"Okay!" Garritt interrupted before Juan humiliated her. "We get the idea. You can read minds. So tell me, what skills?"

"The ones that led you through that fucking jungle, *güey!* Oops—sorry again, Agnes. You were trying to save people and you pulled out some special skills. We need those now. This time we need to save the whole planet! Think of what they could make from this thing…" He paused and Garritt wished he hadn't. He didn't want to think of that.

"We gotta hurry. Bobby's still at his house. I checked on my way to Agnes this morning. But he won't be there long. He's trying to fix his Jeep and he's about to find the thing I did to shut him down."

"You did what?"

"Before the cops picked me up. Which was also a scam, by the way. Zach bribed two other cops with Red Wings tickets. Anyway, when I found out what Bobby has planned, I made sure he couldn't go anywhere for a while. Then I was going to get the other church members on my side but Zach's plan kicked in first."

Which explained why Bobby Lee was walking in a blizzard to get to his church meeting.

Garritt shook his head. "You're the *loco pendejo*. When my dad's goons picked you up, why didn't you tell them all this?"

"Fucking assholes. You're joking, right?"

Right. They really did try to beat it out of him. Which is why torture never works. Zach proved that. Juan freely told Zach everything, and his father's hired creeps, nothing.

"So why didn't you tell me any of this when I showed up in that basement?"

"Like I said, I was shocked to see them drag you down there. It didn't make any sense. I never saw your old man. The *culos* did all the dirty work and I wasn't about to tell them anything, so when you showed up—what if he brought you in to trick me into giving up what I knew?"

Garritt felt a twinge of guilt. That was pretty close to the truth. Maybe the kid could read minds.

"That's why I kept my mouth shut. But yeah, by the time they hauled you back upstairs a few minutes later, I knew what was on your mind. Thanks, *compa*."

Before they embarrassed themselves, Garritt offered a high-five and Juan gratefully responded.

∞

Agnes shook her head at the macho display. Men. She didn't mind the profanity—farmers like her father swore worse. But she had trouble with the parts of Juan's story that involved UFOs and alien artifacts and government agents. Did they really believe that? It reminded her of those Netflix series she watched late at night.

When Garritt started to relate what his father said about aliens, she couldn't hold her tongue any longer.

"Are you sure you heard that right? Your father is a very religious man."

Garritt burst out laughing, an ugly, derisive kind of laugh that gave her a pang she didn't like to feel.

"You have no idea, Agnes—and I hope you never do! The man is a sham, a con, and I wish to hell he wasn't my father."

That was all she needed to hear. Her heart overflowed. She left her chair and approached the recliner where Garritt had elevated his legs, his feet covered in thick wool socks. She waved Juan, pacing near, to stand clear.

"Garritt's not going anywhere yet."

To Garritt, she commanded, "Take off your sock and pull up your pants leg."

He looked surprised but did as she ordered.

Gently, she laid her hands on his horribly bruised ankle where the hellish blackness had pooled around his heels. Streaks of dark purple and red and sickly yellow mottled halfway up his leg to a scarlet lump on his shin that turned her stomach. It was big as a Tootsie Pop. Maybe a tangerine. He didn't protest; he only stared at her in wonder.

She'd had this ability since she was a kid, comforting her grandfather at her grandmother's funeral. At first, it was like a calming trick she could do, laying her hands on human or animal. As she got older, though, people started asking her to do it when they had a headache or any kind of pain. Then, for a few of her friends in school, she touched old scabs and bruises, which seemed to disappear within hours.

She made sure only her closest, most trusted girlfriends knew about this. And her family, of course. The laying on of hands was an ancient tradition in her church. By the time she was twenty, members of the congregation were seeking her out for minor aches and pains.

But no one else, at the restaurant or wherever, knew about her special talent, or how powerful it had grown over the years. Even her family didn't realize how much she could do. How many people would descend on her doorstep, if they knew what her hands could achieve? So she'd kept the secret to herself. Until now.

"Whoa," Garritt exclaimed after a few minutes, "your hands are like fire!"

"Shhh," she ordered.

Juan nodded, staring at the process. "You're like my *tia*. She can cure headaches with her hands. Back in Mexico, everybody comes to her for healing."

Agnes didn't respond. She was busy focusing her mind on Garritt's ankle, feeling carefully to see if he'd broken anything. He hadn't. She moved her hands up to his shin, where he'd suffered the bone bruise that broke open so many more veins than the sprain, causing the blood to fall down and blacken his foot. Her father got one of those once, kicked by a cow, which is how she knew what it was.

"The pain is going away," Garritt marveled.

She didn't lift her hands, not for a long time, sliding them from one location to another. By then, Juan had gone off into the kitchen to see if anything edible survived the power outage. That left her alone with Garritt but she didn't budge. She kept the energy flowing through her hands, encircling his ankle, soothing his leg. Occasionally she shifted her hand position, intuitively massaged some places, pressed or simply held others. She had pulled up an ottoman to sit on and was leaning over awkwardly to reach his leg.

"Agnes," Garritt said softly, "you need to sit up. You're going to hurt your back like that."

"I don't care," she answered without thinking.

"Well, you need to care," he insisted and pulled his leg away from her.

They both stared. The bruising had visibly diminished and the swelling was much less.

She nodded knowingly. "Try to stand up," she commanded.

"Seriously?"

"Do it." She felt supremely confident.

He stood. "It doesn't hurt!"

"Do not walk on it more than you have to for the next twenty-four hours. By tomorrow, it will be healed."

"Agnes—you *are* an angel!"

When he said it, she noticed him looking, not at her face, but just beyond her head, which felt kind of weird. But she also felt a little glow inside her light up and radiate through her body. Her face grew hot.

Juan burst back in with a bag of apples and some cheese. "I scraped off the mold, so no worries," he said as he plopped them down on the little brass table. "And I found this in the cupboard." He held up a jar of peanut butter.

She watched Juan's face closely, eager for him to notice Garritt walking toward the front door—without a limp.

"No mames, güey!"

Garritt seemed distracted. "Do you hear that?"

He yanked the door open, letting in a frigid blast.

Agnes saw nothing but melting snow and sunlight filtering through the pines that shielded his house from the street.

"I think you'd better come back and sit for a while," she urged. "Let things connect back up again."

"He can't," Juan insisted. "We have to leave now."

"And then what?" Garritt wanted to know. "How are we going to stop him, even if we find him?"

"We'll figure that out later."

Juan grabbed an apple and the peanut butter jar and headed toward Garritt at the door, thought better of it, and went back for the cheese.

Agnes reached for her jacket. "I'm coming too." She wasn't going to let Garritt out of her sight.

Garritt looked back and forth between the two of them for a moment. "Whose truck has more gas?"

32

Loyalty

∞

Garritt knew he would see Minda again. He felt it. In fact, he'd even heard a helicopter outside his house—or thought he had. She was coming. Every time he thought of her, a golden light flashed in the space before him to confirm it.

It was late afternoon by the time they got to Bobby Lee's cabin. The jeep was gone. No sign of Bobby. Garritt practically ordered Agnes to drive her brother's truck back to Avery's Café. Neither she nor Juan protested. He wondered if they felt the logic of it as surely as he did.

"And when we get there, Agnes," Juan said, "I want you to fix my black eye, okay? Like you fixed Garritt's leg."

"I don't think you could sit still long enough," she laughed.

"Totally! I can totally do that."

"And stay off your phone?"

"Well ..." He was quiet for a minute. "Really, is that necessary?"

She laughed again and Garritt went back to thinking about how he was going to get out of work for the next few days because that's the other thing he knew. Min needed him, and maybe it had to do with Bobby Lee, or maybe with her murdered colleague. So when they walked into the restaurant and he saw Min sitting in the back, devouring the pulled pork ciabatta she'd had the first day he met her, it seemed right.

What completely threw him was the look he caught as she saw them come through the door, before she put down the pork and quickly recomposed her face with the sophisticated haughtiness that belied her strange language and her mystical talent. His insides melted all over again.

Juan must have noticed him hesitate just inside the door because he leaned over and whispered, "Relax, guy. She's only here to offer you a job. I remember her—the reporter. Is this your Min?"

"You really do hear people's thoughts?"

"Crystal. But not everyone's. I couldn't hear Zach, for instance. And it's mostly when they're wrapped up in strong feelings. You'd better turn yours around or even *she* will be able to hear you, *puto.*"

Garritt felt the blood rush to his cheeks as he realized that with Min's skills, it was probably too late to cover the pleasure at seeing her that must radiate like beacons from every part of his body.

Juan's tone suddenly shifted. "Introduce me."

Agnes was already at her side, gushing about how nice she looked and wow, the scar was fading. A minute longer and she might offer to fix it up for her. Or would she? All the time he'd worked with the girl, she never gave a hint about her phenomenal healing ability. He wondered what other talents the people around him might be hiding. Were these skills more common than anyone admitted?

He was grateful when Min spoke first. She stood up from the remains of her meal and reached out a hand to Juan.

"I am so happy to meet you," she said, and the sincerity of that could be picked up by any reasonable human.

"Likewise."

Juan sounded uncharacteristically shy as she shook his hand. Garritt knew he was not the reticent type. What had he heard in her thoughts?

"I hope you and I can talk sometime." She skewered Juan with a stare that went beyond politeness. "I know about your experience. In fact, thanks to Garritt, I had a pretty close-up view of it all."

What did she mean by that? She was withholding something again, even he could tell. But he felt confident she couldn't fool Juan now.

What a wonderful talent to have, he thought—and almost instantly realized how horrible it would be, to always know the truth of what someone felt and didn't say. Especially, as Juan just told him, when the emotions were powerful.

"I am so glad you seem to be as healthy as you are, considering what you've been through," Min elaborated, as if to keep Juan pinned a little longer. Her voice carried a wink; did she know it had all been a ruse?

"Yeah, me too," Juan played along, then quickly escaped with, "I'm going back to plead for my job now."

Agnes, too, scurried off.

Had his co-workers suddenly developed a sense of courtesy? *Am I that obvious?*

Garritt glanced toward where Courtney, their other hostess, chatted with someone at the retail counter. Nope, she hardly noticed him when they came in. Doris swished by with a tray of full water glasses for the only other customers on the scene. She seemed caught up in some kind of daydream; a wistful smile played around the edges of her wrinkled mouth.

"Sit," Min ordered. "You look like yesterday's candy wrapper."

Had her eyes turned navy blue since the last time he saw her? No, maybe not. After a moment they flickered back to the deep, reflective brown he remembered. He must have imagined it.

"Thank you very much. But you look fashionably fabulous as always." He picked up a fancy knitted item from the chair so he could sit, twiddled nervously with the ties and bows. "How do you wear this, exactly?"

She snatched it back. "We don't have to make small talk, you know. And besides, we are all on the clock. You haven't asked me the most important question yet."

"And that is?"

"What that helicopter ride was about, remember? When I left you stranded in the middle of the road in the middle of a blizzard from the bowels of Mother Nature? Stole your truck and almost side-swiped you in the process?"

"Oh. That. You mean when I slipped on the ice and nearly broke my ankle?"

She tried to hide it but he caught the flash of genuine concern before she replaced it with a covering smile. "You look fine to me."

"I have Agnes to thank for that," he told her. "For quite a few things, in fact."

"Right. I saw your television debut last night."

He flinched at the reminder of his father, which diverted him from wondering if this woman was an agent who had used him to get to Juan for her employers.

"Okay, then tell me, why did they scare the hell out of us to pick you up in that helicopter? They terrorized most of Veenlanden, I hear. I can see you haven't been whacked for stealing their ET fragment, or for killing your colleague. Is he okay, then? Was it one of your vision failures? Hopefully?" He sincerely meant this last bit.

"Yes. Thankfully."

Her deep brown eyes flickered navy again as they passed over him a few times, taking his measure. He tried not to squirm under her inspection.

Finally she said, "I have a proposition for you."

Surely she didn't mean what he hoped she meant. Would she ask for that right here, right now? Sadly, he recalled what Juan had told him when they walked in. "What kind of job?"

"How did you know I was going to offer you a job?"

"I have friends in high places. Remember?"

"That's exactly why. We need your skills."

"Who is *we?*"

She burst out laughing.

He couldn't understand what she found so funny about his reasonable question.

Finally she calmed down and leaned closer, speaking quietly. "Listen, the people I work for aren't who I thought they were. We don't kill people, as it turns out. We are actually in the middle of a crisis that will affect the entire world if we don't stop Bobby Lee. Didn't Juan tell you?"

"He did tell me some things." How did she know that?

"To answer the questions you're not asking, I was called back to San Diego for a meeting with my boss—well, for a meeting with the client my boss works for. I can tell you with confidence that I do not actually work for a black ops government contractor."

"You can't know that. Because if they're black ops, they'd never tell you the truth."

She rolled her eyes. "Let's just say I had an experience while I was gone that proved something to me. Getting back to the point: I've been fully briefed. I know that Bobby Lee has taken off with the artifact, the real one, and that he's going to sell it to someone who should never have it. If they get their hands on it, they will put the people on this world in grave danger."

"Yeah, that's what Juan said. He's pretty panicked about it."

"He should be. We are fighting a kind of war and we need your skills—your *communication* skills," she emphasized the word.

He got it. She meant his lights. Exactly what Juan said.

"If you agree to work with us on this mission, later on you will be trained to develop your skills further. You probably don't realize how valuable they are."

"You mean someone might pay me to use them?"

He had to admit, he was intrigued. He hadn't seen her so confident, or so serious, before. When she first told him what she did for a living, she seemed timid and confused. Not now.

"Yes. And we pay better than your restaurant job. Significantly."

Money had never been a pull for him. His life choices had always been about what he didn't want, instead of what he wanted. He *didn't want* to work for his father; he *didn't want* to follow the college track his parents had outlined for him; he *didn't want* to work in a Dutch furniture factory; he *didn't want* to abandon his passion for good food and healthy living after he sold the farm. *Etcetera*.

Only one thing sparked his interest in her proposal. "Train me how?"

"The same way I've been trained." She smiled when she said it, a Mona Lisa smile, as if she had another secret to share—or keep from him. "I had a crash course while I was out west, you could say."

"What would I have to do?"

"Exactly what you've already done. You were out looking for Bobby Lee again, weren't you?"

"How do you know that?"

"We know a lot that you don't. Yet."

"Who is we?" He thought she was going to burst something, the way she laughed.

"Oh, Garritt, my boy, you have to learn not to ask that question. I've tried. Believe me. One day, we will both understand the answer better and when that day arrives, we will know it."

He stared at her. She seemed entirely serious.

"Listen," he decided to answer with the same seriousness because, no matter how bizarre her statements, for deeply felt reasons he respected her. "It doesn't matter. Because I can't do it."

"Why not?"

"I can't just up and leave Corbyn like that. He needs me. Right now he's back there working his ass off, risking his relationship with Avery because of me. When I was down and out years ago, he picked me up and he hasn't let me down. Ever. So I can't do it."

A golden light twinkled over her head when he said it. Did that mean he was making the right choice or the wrong one?

"But Garritt, the world needs people like you and me right now. The danger is—" Her cell vibrated. She grabbed it off the table, stared at the text for a millisecond. Her face revealed nothing of its content but she pulled out a large bill, threw it on the table, and stood up. "I have to go. My ride is waiting. Text me if you change your mind."

And just like that she rushed off.

"Wait!" he called out. "I don't have your number!"

"Yes you do. Look at your phone."

He did as she ordered and was astonished to find a text that said, "This is me. I knew you wouldn't say yes yet. Text me when you realize what is right."

How did she get my number?

As Min reached the front of the nearly empty restaurant, she turned and called back, "Tell Juan: Luciana was here looking for him earlier."

Luciana! Of course!

He watched as she hurried out the door and climbed into a waiting black SUV, which sped off to the west, toward the lake shore.

"What the fuck!?" he said aloud. Then he noticed Agnes at his side, watching her go. "Sorry, Agnes."

"Don't be. She is a strange one, isn't she?"

He thought for a moment. "Maybe. Or maybe she's normal and the rest of us aren't."

Agnes nodded sagely. "You could be right. What did she ask you?"

"If I wanted to serve God and my country," he quipped, not sure what else to say. Then he realized how much that sounded like his father. "Shit. I'm sunk."

Agnes looked at him, got a strange expression on her face, and disappeared into the kitchen.

Loyal, Min thought as she climbed in beside Wade, aka Officer Zach, who was at the wheel of the SUV. Mentally, she added it to her Garritt list, right behind *psychic communicator, ruggedly handsome,* and *gourmet chef,* not necessarily the order in which she prized those traits.

Briefly, she wondered if Amrita was right. What if, like her friend teased after they saw the news story, this crazy Dutch guy...

She quickly shook off the thought. They were too different. What would her family say? What a mess that would be. Right now she had a job to do.

"Where's he headed?" she asked Wade.

"We tracked him to a small airport south of here, a private landing strip at the top of some hills, hidden by woods on all sides. Maps list it as *Hancock Airport.* As far as we can tell, he hasn't filed a flight plan but a short while ago he flew a low-wing Piper from there to the South Bend Municipal, probably to fuel up at the FBO. If he takes off from there, we'll keep track."

"I've got a better idea." *And I've got orders.* "Take me to a place where I can do some remote viewing without interruption of any kind." She'd been told to assume that no one except the Commander and Ben knew of her new abilities.

"How close do you need to be to his location?"

"Not close at all. In fact, the closer to here, the better."

She hoped Garritt would change his mind. If they had to give physical chase, his navigation talents could come in handy. That's the excuse she gave herself anyway.

"Got it."

"And Wade—I don't think I've thanked you for sending the team to pull me off that dune."

His sun-spotted cheeks bloomed with ruddy blotches as he swung north onto the Interstate. "No need. I don't think I've apologized for shoving you down it."

She nodded, silently agreeing to drop the subject, which made both of them uncomfortable.

He handed her a hot cup of take-out coffee from the dash holder, a sort of peace offering she gratefully accepted. Then he proceeded to break every speed limit while she tried not to burn her tongue. He told her they were headed to the house he'd been renting in Grand Haven.

"I know a shortcut," he announced tersely, although it didn't matter. She had no idea where they were. She was busy hoping she'd do better with her new skill than she had during the flight from San Diego.

As Ben commanded, she tried to put herself on that golden shellship mentally, then direct it to take her to various locations. She started with her own apartment, since she didn't have to admit to anyone that a part of her would rather be there, preferably with a good book and a fuzzy blanket and a world that wasn't so crazy around her. She failed.

So far, she had fallen through the ship's transparent floor every time and landed right back in her body with a jolt. She hadn't even come close to making the ship travel.

She did manage to give herself a proper captain's chair with a 360-degree swivel, though, and she chose a color for the floor—lilac—because being able to make it transparent at will was a lot more comfortable than imagining herself flying around in a transparent bubble over freeways and cattle barns. (That was only after she remembered how she had manifested a handrail for the crystal travelator.) Those minor accomplishments made her proud, at least. But her charter jet landed in Holland before she mastered the art of interdimensional travel via psychic starship.

In the end, she gave up and texted Amrita. They tried to keep tabs on each other's whereabouts. Without ever saying it aloud to one another, it was their way of making their make-do living arrangement feel like a home, at least, if not an actual family. But keeping up was near impossible with so many urgent missions they couldn't discuss.

On a new one

Is he tall and Dutch?

Hah nice try

She flicked the texts away and fretted about failing Ben's expectations. It was too soon. She needed more training and more time to practice. She took another sip of the coffee, closed her eyes in Wade's speeding SUV, and sent off a fervent hope that she could do what the situation demanded. She could see the past and the future, find things lost and things unknown, maybe even talk to aliens. How hard could it be to track some redneck preacher across the country by spying on him from the mental construct of an alien starship?

Right. That really calmed her down.

33

Flight

∞

"I'm tellin' you, this is bat-shit crazy," Hancock argued. "After that blizzard we just had? Fuckin' likely you're gonna run into some shit weather this time of year and you're not instrument rated. Hell, you don't even *have* instruments on this old bucket of bolts!"

Bobby's friend had followed him into the hangar after he unlocked it for Bobby. He slapped the fuselage of Bobby's old Piper Cherokee, blue stripes faded almost to white by the beating sun. The small plane sent up a puff of dust. Desiccated grass clippings, blown in the last time Hancock mowed the rugged landing strip, slid off to land in sad little piles on the frigid hangar's dirt floor.

"Look, I'm only going to Joliet, a half-hour flight if that," Bobby lied. He brushed Hancock aside so he could yank out the wheel blocks.

He had to do it this way. The voices gave him the idea, Miracle Five.

He lied some more, "My cousin is sick and needs someone to come and babysit. I promised I'd be there, so get out of my way or help me roll this thing out. Besides," he jerked a thumb outside, "can't you see the sun is shining?"

The homegrown airport, built across rolling, hilltop pickle fields (pickle crops long gone), featured two short runways with enough humps and dips to keep your blood pumping until your wheels finally left the ground, seconds before you crashed into the tall oaks and hickories at the fence line. Bobby had taken off and landed here a few dozen times by now, but it always sucked the life's blood from his extremities to pool in his vital organs for protection against physical catastrophe. He'd never taken off when the runways were packed with snow—*melting* snow, polished clean by Hancock's plow.

In the lower spots, shaded from November's angled sunlight, he hit a few icy spots where melt from the larger bumps had run down and frozen. He managed to keep the wheels moving forward until they hit traction again—until they finally lifted off the ground.

He wasn't about to tell Hancock that he planned to fly under visual flight rules—VFR, the only rating his pilot's license carried—nearly *two thousand miles*. He would cross the towering Rockies, and the Wasatch Range in Utah, then fly over the Sierras to reach Northern California. He'd be flying without instruments, in late autumn, when storms were more likely than not. Hancock was right, of course. Bat-shit crazy. But this was the only way.

Worse, he'd never flown such a distance before—not in a single-engine, private plane. Hell yeah, he was scared. He loved the low-wing Piper, which he bought for a song and reconditioned himself. It was faster than a Cessna so better for a longer trip. But he knew the risks.

Like Hancock argued, the plane wasn't even equipped with the instruments that he wasn't trained to use, and he had never updated his navigation tools to modern GPS standards. He used the ground-based, very-high-frequency, omni-directional range system (VOR) on the brief cross-country trips he'd taken, never more than a hundred miles or so. That was easy. The plane's transponder equipment would detect radio beacons sent out by the short, nipple-shaped white towers that were scattered across the countryside. That gave him directional coordinates to fly toward, and navigating from one white marker to another worked fine for flight practice. But to reach his long-distance destination, he couldn't rely on the aging VOR beacons. Too many had gone dead from neglect as pilots switched to GPS, or the new WAAS system. Once he left the local area, he couldn't trust their accuracy or their existence.

For this journey, he would have to fly low enough to visually scout his way along. He would try to identify highways, train tracks, rivers, lakes, or any other landmark that he could see from the air and match to his map charts. That is, if clouds, fog, snow, or rain didn't block his view. He would cross more than half the continental United States, hopping from one little airstrip to another. To keep his visual line of sight, he would have to fly below any cloud layers, and if the brume and murk dropped unexpectedly to ground level—which could happen at any time without warning—he would be forced down with it, wherever he was, mountain, lake, or plain. Or shopping mall.

His only other option in that case, highly illegal for a VFR pilot, would be to spiral blindly up through the obscuring mists and hope he could break out on top of the clouds before he hit twelve thousand feet, or flew into another plane or mountain. Without supplemental oxygen, which he didn't have aboard, he'd be subject to hypoxia at around twelve thousand and above, with varying levels of opportunity to recover before he lost consciousness. Some pilots lost their senses at even lower elevations. Bobby figured he wasn't one of those. And if he made it above the clouds, he'd have to maintain his western heading and pray for a hole through which he could drop down again before he ran out of fuel.

In other words, flying above the clouds was a risky move he hoped he'd never have to take, although it would be preferable to being smashed down into a forest or a freeway by a dropping cloud ceiling. Best case scenario in that situation would be to find a landing strip quickly and wait out the weather. Without a navigator in the seat beside him, he'd need to find those tiny airfields on his old charts himself. That could be tricky. It wasn't safe to take his eyes off the surrounding space, where air traffic now was so much denser than it had been years ago when he first learned to fly. At low altitudes, even hobby drones posed a threat that had never existed before.

When he stopped to fuel up in South Bend, just south of the Michigan state line, he planned to buy new charts. At the last second, he changed his mind. The flight office looked crowded with the usual amateur pilots who liked to hang around, trade BS tales about near-misses, or fantasy flights to exotic locations they would never take. He didn't want to answer questions. He didn't want to leave a trail. He hurried back into the air instead.

Yes, dammit, Hancock, I know the risks, he thought, as his bones rattled through a patch of air turbulence. But the promises laid out before him had convinced his fevered mind to take them. He had an appointment to keep and this was the plan his guides urged him to follow. They'd been right about everything so far. If he made it? Miracle Six. Bobby wiped the sweat from his mustache and scanned the ground below.

The voices in his head hadn't stopped. If anything, they were more pronounced. As he sweated now in the frigid cockpit, somewhere over Illinois, they persistently reminded him of his goal, his vision, his new temple of righteousness.

And so far, the weather cooperated. Remnants of the record-breaking blizzard fell quickly behind the burring Cherokee 180. Up ahead, toward the plains, he saw blue sky between scuttling high clouds. Current aviation reports promised relatively clear weather all the way across Nebraska.

He slipped on his dark aviator glasses. He couldn't help but believe that he had the influence of Super Beings on his side, clearing a path for this important journey.

The voices kept him from thinking too much about the fact that most of the peaks in the Rockies were around fourteen thousand feet. Even the Wasatch boasted a twelve-thousand-foot mountain. He was gambling that if he did rise above the oxygen requirement, it would be for only a few minutes at a time, no more than the thirty minutes before most people passed out. The worst part, he read, was that the closer you got to losing consciousness, the more euphoric and confident you felt as your brain function failed.

He glanced down at the fuel gauge. He'd been in the air for nearly two hours. He watched the Mississippi pass beneath him, wide and muddy, just like everyone said. His bladder and his fuel tank would both need a stop soon.

He had only calculated allowances for brief landings to fuel up, grab a bite, shake out his legs, and get back underway. He planned one overnight at the halfway point. According to his rough estimates, the second leg of his journey would be longer by a hundred miles but he also noted that sunset would come later as he flew slightly southwest, giving him more daylight hours.

To cross the Rockies—that would be his longest, in-air stretch.

Always keep an emergency landing in sight, no matter where you are, no matter what condition your plane is in, he was trained.

Forested peaks and sharp narrow valleys didn't offer many of those. So he plotted a course that passed north of the highest parts of the range, north of Denver, before he veered south on his way to Salt Lake City. Then, on to Vacaville, California, halfway between Sacramento and San Francisco, close neighbor to Travis Air Force Base.

The engine noise in the cramped cockpit kept him awake despite the monotony but his stomach started to rumble. He reached for his home-brewed airsickness prevention: Mountain Dew and shortbread cookies. An old boat captain once told him that the secret to preventing motion sickness is counter-intuitive; you have to keep a little something in your belly. Without looking down, he took a slug of the caffeine-laden drink and shoved a handful of the stale cookies into his mouth. He kept his eyes roving beyond the plane, watching for traffic, monitoring the landscape below.

That's when the cross-winds hit. Every few seconds, he had to counter a swift upsurge of either his left or right wing. The plane felt like a broken buggy, lurching left and right, up and down, as his reflexes responded with counter-measures to level off again.

After twenty minutes of this, every muscle in his body ached with tension. Veins in his temples throbbed, and a sharp pain soon shot down the back of his neck. He grew terrified the plane would flip over, his childhood phobia of hanging upside-down triggered by the relentless wind.

For a moment he thought he felt something move inside the cockpit, in the passenger seats behind him.

That's where he'd tucked the golden fragment, carefully wrapped in clean red work rags, inside a shave kit lodged between his flight bag and his winter boots. (He superstitiously flew only in the same pair of lucky shoes he'd owned since his first flight lesson, now torn, filthy white, and comfy.) Although his gaze remained fixed ahead, alert for a small airfield in Iowa, he was confused to realize that he was also staring directly at the glimmering artifact, as if his head had suddenly swiveled backwards. He glanced at the altimeter—six thousand feet. Should be safe from hallucinations. What the hell was that?

A gust hit the plane and it lurched again. His mind snapped back to counter the movement. He wrote the vision off to nerves, and the voices in his head sang their encouragement. He was tough, he was confident, he was capable, he would win this race and change the world.

Finally, he spotted it: the distinctive cross-hatch of empty runways surrounded by a vast landscape of snow-dusted, fallow cornfields. No tower controlled the airspace around this rural airport. He needed to safeguard his own landing, make sure no other small planes synced into the landing pattern at the same time, maybe from another direction.

The cross-wind stayed with him as he dropped altitude. He fervently hoped the landing would take him below the wind but in case it didn't, he kept a tight grip as he slipped, first one side of the plane, then the other, to quickly plunge the plane out of the sky to just a few feet above ground, a trick he learned from his flight instructor. As the tires caught the cleared pavement and he felt the G-force of rapid deceleration press against him, he held his breath. The fierce wind screamed against the plane's sides, still threatening to flip the light craft. He skidded down the paved runway with flaps down. Goddamn lucky he wasn't flying a Cessna, with its high wings that beckoned like umbrellas, challenging the wind to take hold and toss him over.

"Hold on, baby," he cooed to the plane. "We're almost there."

The Piper slowed by what seemed like inches and hours, and finally came to a halt, scant yards from the end of the runway and the rusty bunker that served the FBO as a flight office. The place looked deserted.

Stiff, sweaty, his muscles still ringing from the stress and the fear and the plane's steady vibration, Bobby squeezed his ample self out onto the wing and dropped to the ground. He fought off a sudden impulse to drop all the way to his knees and kiss it.

He'd been in the air less than three hours. He had fourteen more hours of air time to go before he reached his destination. Exhaustion already threatened to lead him to the nearest grease-covered couch, which he suspected he'd find inside the bunker. He couldn't give in to the temptation. Fuel-wise, he could have flown further, but the wind, the bladder, and the nerves had worn him down. He had decided to take a quick stop now and make up the time later.

He watched a figure emerge from the office to sell him some fuel and he cursed to himself. Too many people would see him along the way. But what could he do about that? He plastered his best preacher's smile on his face and strode forward, ready to bluff his way with a good story about who he was, why he was here, where he was headed.

He glanced back nervously at the plane, where his treasure awaited the moment he would hand it over and his new life would begin. Then he directed his attention to the man in the heavy-weather gear who swiftly approached.

"Howdy, neighbor," Bobby called out, reaching his hand forward. He completely forgot about the handgun strapped to his torso inside his open coat, now fully exposed by the gesture.

34

Fallen Trout

∞

Garritt, who volunteered to help in Avery's kitchen that afternoon despite Agnes's command to rest his leg, suddenly dropped an entire platter of fresh trout. It made a terrible clatter as raw fish slid across the grimy floor, picking up crumbs and dirt along the way.

"She's in trouble."

Avery and Juan reacted with simultaneous bilingual curses, "What the…"

Garritt stared off beyond the bread ovens. "I gotta go." His voice rose on a panicked, "Now!"

He threw off his kitchen gear and jerked on his jacket and ran out the back door—only to recall that he didn't have his truck. He ducked back through the kitchen and into the dining room.

"Agnes! We have to go!"

After Min left, Agnes had lingered to gossip with Doris. She looked up at him, eyes wide.

"Now!" he shouted and she leapt into action.

"Where are we headed?" she finally asked, as she obediently threw her brother's truck into gear and sped out of the watery parking lot. "You shouldn't be on that leg so much yet."

"Just go west. That's all I know."

He was lost inside his head where he'd felt the powerful thrust of intuition—no, it was stronger than that. It was so loud, it might as well have been a cry for help. The minute he said west, he saw flickers of gold that told him he was correct.

Fully trusting him, Agnes turned left and headed straight toward the sunset and the interstate highway a few miles away, the one that would lead them either north or south.

"I saw her. She's in trouble. I don't see things like that."

Agnes nodded calmly. "Trust it. You have to trust it."

"I know, but ..." He wasn't sure what else to say.

Half an hour ago, he was musing about Min's offer and the fact that he'd said no. Even before Juan picked it up from her thoughts, he'd sensed that Min would ask for his help—but only for a few hours. Maybe a day or two. When it came down to a life-altering choice to maybe do something good for the world? He opted for his old life.

What the hell was I thinking?

When had he taken what was familiar and safe—but dull and soul-sucking—and elevated it to such a high level of importance in his life?

He hadn't lied to Min. He honestly didn't want to let Corbyn down. But he was startled to admit that after all these years he'd become frightened of change. He'd found a comfortable niche that wasn't Dutch. And yet—would he have taken that trip to Peru at all if something weren't missing? After what he saw at his father's house, he had more reason than ever to flee from his old life. So why did he say no?

As far as he could tell, for most of his conscious years—once he was out of diapers, say—he'd been lost. He didn't belong.

His disgust for the past had magnified that afternoon as he fielded texts from his father. They had nothing to do with his well-being, or Juan's, or even his father's jaw-dropping exposure as a bisexual adulterer. So typical of the man! Nothing but politics and commerce.

Where is the artifact? Does he have it? was the first text.

No. Bobby Lee does.

That didn't satisfy. *Where is Bobby Lee then?*

How the hell should I know? And he put his phone in Airplane mode.

He didn't bother to explore the news stories feasting on his father's career suicide, either. But then, because he didn't want to miss any texts from Min that might explain why she dashed off, he had turned the phone back on. Within moments, it vibrated. He picked it up to look.

His mother? She had barely spoken to him since Elizabeth left. He let the call go to voice mail. He didn't want to be blind-sided, caught without an excuse or come-back, whichever the situation required. Yet curiosity pulled at him. Why now?

Finally, unable to let it go, he tapped into voice mail and put the phone to his ear.

"Garritt, your father needs you. They're saying terrible things about him! He needs you to come forward on his behalf. You'll probably get a subpoena; they're investigating the *incident*"—she said it with a particular inflection of disgust—"when those horrible people pointed guns in his face. They actually shot at him! Can you imagine? Well, I guess you can. You were there, I heard. So please return his messages. I'm worried about his state of mind. And his health," she added softly, sounding almost apologetic for the concern. "This is your mother, by the way," she ended the call, as if she finally remembered that she was.

No, "And how are you after your recent ordeal?" Or, "How is your life?" "Are you busy?" "Have you got a minute?" "Did someone tell me you hurt your ankle?" Or, heaven forbid, "I've missed you."

Damned if he'd answer. They could deal with their problems the same way he dealt with his: on his own. For years. If people said bad things about his father, tough. They were probably true. Let *him* suffer for a change. He certainly caused others pain. And if she worried over her husband's health—well, she should probably ask his boyfriend about that.

Garritt set the phone down and tried to calm his reactions by thinking of Min instead.

What doors might she open in his life? Because she was the only person on Earth who knew what he experienced in that jungle, and she had taken it so calmly. She even encouraged him to pursue these bizarre phenomena as "personal skills." How crazy was that? Any job Min offered would live at the fringes of human knowledge, he realized. He would have to leave behind everything he'd been taught about the world, about life itself, take another leap into the unknown. That sounded good right now.

But there were hints that these might not be the players he wanted to align with. What if they were the bad guys, pretending to be good guys? Or vice versa? He grew more confused, pulled one way, then the other.

And he'd gone on like that, his hands moving over plates of food in robotic fashion, until suddenly his breath caught and lights went off and his gut sank under a deluge of knowing that Min was in danger and he lost all feeling in his limbs for a moment.

"Turn here," he commanded when Agnes reached the highway. "Take the north on-ramp."

Back at Avery's he had seen the full-fledged, golden glitter downpour, like in the rainforest. Now he ordered twists and turns according to their flashes and the knowing in his heart and stomach.

Agnes obeyed without question until, fifteen minutes later, they reached the SUV—smashed into a tree in a watery ditch beside a deserted back road that no one would take unless they had a remote destination in mind.

Garritt flew out of the truck and had his hands on Min's back within seconds. She lay on her stomach in the snow where she'd been thrown from the vehicle. Her legs were twisted and her arms tangled near her head.

"Are you all right?" he practically screamed—at least that's how it felt in his mind. In reality it was no more than a whisper. Dread caught the sound in a web at the back of his throat.

She moaned, pressed down on her hands, and tried to lift herself off the snow.

"No!" he commanded. "Lie still."

She collapsed back down, and from what he could tell, immediately lost consciousness. He didn't see any blood in the snow around her. He was afraid to move her. Agnes had called 911 the minute she stopped the truck. *So why aren't they here yet?*

"Agnes, come help her," he shouted, raising his head to locate the girl. That's when he saw the driver's body.

It lay deeper in the ditch, a few yards away, where the snow-melt rushed along in a steady flow. So much blood stained the melting snowbank, he could see it from where he crouched. Gently, he slipped his stocking cap beneath Min's face, careful not to move her too much as Agnes hurried over.

"Can you do that thing with your hands? I'll be right back."

He had to fight down the nausea that crept up when he got closer to the man's body. Squatting down, he felt he knew, and the flicker of gold that accompanied his thought told him it must be true, that life had already fled this shell. He recognized the Holland cop who tackled him at Burt's Crossing—the same man Juan claimed as his savior from Bobby Lee.

What was Min doing with Zacharia the cop? Did he work for Blackthorn? Did that mean it really was Blackthorn who arranged for police officers to kidnap Juan, and that she knew all along?

A surprisingly strong wave of indignation swept through him—not about the kidnapping but because this man probably saved Juan's life. Where was the justice in this, that he lay dead in a ditch now? Killed by a mere patch of shade, from the evidence of where the SUV had swerved. He thanked the Infinite God that Min still breathed and hurried back to her.

Not one but two ambulances arrived, lights flashing. He scrambled up to meet the first one, pointing, "She's alive but the other one doesn't seem to be."

The EMTs motioned the second crew to see to Zach, as they went to work over Min.

A deputy sheriff pulled up and got out to survey the scene.

"She's going to be okay," Agnes whispered at Garritt's side. They watched as the experts eased Min onto the first ambulance. She was still unconscious.

"How do you know?"

"Because I do," Agnes replied, with the confidence of a farm girl who'd seen a lot of life and death. Or one with supernatural powers. "Let's follow them," she suggested, and he eagerly agreed.

Garritt lied to the sheriff's deputy who stopped them to ask questions: They happened along after the crash. No, they didn't know anything more than what the deputy could see.

As Garritt watched the second crew lift Zach's body, he recalled Min's vision. She said it was a co-worker she saw lying in the snow, near water, with blood all around him. Garritt stared at the dark stain circling the body. So both of her visions were accurate and detailed, first Juan and now Zach, though she'd called him by some other name. Beyond that, Garritt's distressed brain refused to connect all the dots. How much of all she'd told him was true? And how much did she leave out?

"Come on, Garritt," Agnes tugged at him.

He hoped like hell he'd get another chance to ask her.

35

The Agreement

∞

The last thing Min remembered was asking Wade to slow down, then her body landing in the snow. She cursed him for screwing up her life again. Then blackness.

She thought she'd heard Garritt's voice for a minute but now she was sitting across from Reverend Ben. He suggested that she call him *Commander* Ben. That was too confusing, what with the Commander being the Commander for as long as she could remember, and what else could she call this tall man but "Reverend," because that's how he seemed to her.

"Where are we?" she managed to ask without using his name at all. "Did we catch him?"

"Bobby Lee?" His gentle eyes roamed her face carefully, as if looking for signs of mold in the shower. "Not yet."

"But I'm supposed to be on the starship, tracking him." Nothing here looked familiar.

"Minda, you've had another mishap. This time, not so serious," he oozed that chocolate fountain over her ears. "You'll wake up soon. Before you do, I need to tell you some things."

"What things?"

"Garritt—he's with you. And Wade—he's not."

"Not?"

"Min, the vision has come true. Only it wasn't a bullet. The car accident ..." He searched her face again—was he looking for cracks?

Then she felt his words settle into her chest. "You mean—?"

"Wade has left one life for another, yes."

She'd done nothing at all to stop it! Tears gathered of their own accord and fell freely from her eyes, while a wave of bitterness flooded up from her depths.

"So what *fucking* good is this so-called future vision of mine? Huh? *Tell me!*"

He sighed deeply. "You cannot stop energy from repeating itself, lifetime after lifetime. You can only alter its patterns when you have the opportunity. This time it was not your place. You did not hold the key, Min. You mustn't waste your time trying to open locks for which you do not hold the key, and you must not waste your energy mourning that which you cannot influence."

He laid a hand over hers and leaned in. "And you are wrong! It *does* matter, what you can do. You can help in the circumstances for which you do have a role to play."

"You can stop with the platitudes," she spat back. "I know you just have some mission you want me to carry out and you don't want me to give up."

She knew none of this was his fault but he was the only Supreme Being sort of individual present and *someone* needed to know how angry she was. Fury trumped grief.

"It's your mission, too, Minda." He leaned back, out of range of her intensity. "You swore to uphold it a very long time ago, so many millions of years ago, you wouldn't believe me if I were to tell you how long your personal history is. At least, not while you're alive on Earth—and you are, Minda. You are still alive, and you have so much to contribute! But," he admitted, "you are surrounded by people who think of themselves as nothing more than products of your twentieth or twenty-first centuries. That is only a random measurement of time, snatched arbitrarily from the eternal flow of the Infinite Intelligence that supports your lives. Time. It is the construct upon which the Earth people hang their security."

"What are you talking about? And what does that have to do with Wade being dead? And for no fucking reason!"

She was too furious to worry about words. What really burned was the fact that he died from stupid ice on the road—not chasing an artifact, or even confronting a criminal. *Ice.*

"Wade is in his eternal self now. When he reorients himself, I will let him explain it to you himself. He's done what he could with his life, and he's made an admirable job of moving our objectives forward. He is a protector of Earth, and so am I. And so are you. That never ceases, Min, no matter where your consciousness may be centered, whether in an earth body or out of it. And now, *when you return to your awareness on Earth,* you will introduce others to our humanitarian efforts.

"We work together in brotherhood, life after life, to aid the progress of the humanity that swarms the planet you currently call home. Today, that development is threatened by one lost fragment of a material that does not belong on Earth. It rests in the hands of a man who is rapidly losing touch with his sanity, and who is willing, for personal gain, to hand it over to people who may destroy what we've worked so hard to preserve: this planetary refuge for souls who need rehabilitation after thousands of years of interplanetary warfare."

He rolled this stuff out like he was reading a script, she thought. Tripe just pouring out of his blathering mouth. But a man's life was lost and she had seen it coming! She'd done nothing at all to stop it.

"Listen to me," he leaned closer again, coming down from his lofty heights to hiss, "you and your talents are needed. You must go back now and do what you can to help us stop this extraterrestrial interference. That is what will happen if Bobby Lee carries out his intentions. The destructive forces that pounce on the unsuspecting have found a willing victim in him. They are preying on the weaknesses of Bobby Lee's mind. Soon, they will have that artifact in the hands of their Earth minions—unless you help us stop that from happening. And what *they* do with it will have implications for eons to come—and not only for this one planetary speck in the hinterlands of a single, ostracized galaxy.

"*Resonance,* Minda. Remember how what you do here resonates out into the vastness of the multiverse and affects every linking harmonic throughout all of Infinity!"

She could only stare at him, eyes glazed from inner pain. In a distant part of her brain, she knew he was telling her the truth because she resonated with his words in the depth and breadth of her soul. As he went on, her own words—even resentful ones—gradually left her.

"Our plans have been temporarily disrupted but not halted. Do not forget that I am ever at your side. When you get stuck, think of me here," and he reached out a hand to place his palm gently against her forehead.

She felt soothing heat pour into her flesh—or what passed for flesh in this otherworldly state—and with it, calm and clarity.

"Teach those around you," he continued as he lifted his hand. "Ask for their help when you need it. We will support their efforts in our own way. They may become strong allies in our mission. But right now, they are still trapped in the psychic amnesia that afflicts your world as a whole."

Did he mean Garritt? Juan? Agnes?

His face started to warp and flicker.

"Wait!" she found her voice again, desperate to catch him before he vanished. "I can't do it! I can't make my mind linger in that starship like you taught me. I can't make it travel! And I keep falling through the floor…"

"You can do it, Minda. You only needed more reason to try. You will find Bobby Lee midair, if you focus your intention there."

And he faded with the words until he evaporated completely.

What then? she wanted to ask. What was she supposed to do when she found him? She didn't have Wade to follow up with land-based trackers. She didn't even know where Wade lived, so she didn't have any place to try this lunatic viewing method.

But inside, something had clicked. Reverend Ben's cryptic sermons finally rang in and she understood now. Not until the people on this planet are ready—and collectively they aren't—so not until then can they safely peer through the veil that protects them from knowing too much, too soon.

That made her terribly sad. It broke her heart, in fact. Why couldn't it be now? She wanted it to be now. She wanted to believe that people would be so awed over the discovery of other civilizations, they would suddenly know how to behave. Yet she knew Ben was right. She had no clue how to achieve it but her task was clear: Close the magic mirror. Do it fast.

And rely on the help of the Super Beings with whom she'd somewhere, sometime, somehow made a pact and alliance.

36

The Third Man Factor

∽

Bobby fought to stay awake. He'd landed twice now and was back in the air for only thirty minutes when his eyes began to close again. He jerked them open.

He couldn't afford to set down and take a nap, although he knew it would be wise. Clouds were moving in fast, scuttling and billowing out of the northwest with the jet stream. They were early. Weather reports had predicted this front wouldn't arrive until later this evening.

He took another slug of super-caffeinated Mountain Dew and reached for his bag of cookies. All gone. *Damn it.*

He should have gotten more at his last stop but the attendant was nosy. Too many questions. He'd hurried aloft as soon as the fuel tank was topped off.

What really bothered Bobby, though, was not the cold in the cockpit, nor the steady engine noise, which was actually a comfort. As long as he heard that sound, the plane would remain airborne. No; what kept him glancing nervously into the back seat was the flicker of movement that started up again as soon as he left Iowa.

Anxious to prove nothing was there, he reached back, twisting his spine to a dangerous degree. He teased at the shave kit with his fingertips until he could grab the edge of the black vinyl bag and yank it free. It popped out and struck him on the side of his face. Cursing, he lowered the kit to his lap where he carefully, lovingly unzipped it. He slipped corpulent fingers between the zipper edges. He could feel his treasure, safe and sound, protected in the red-cloth work rags he'd wrapped it in.

The temptation proved too much. He pulled the solid mass out of the bag and the cloth fell away to reveal the full radiance of the golden piece, so bright it stabbed his drooping eyes wide open. He stared into the mysterious material, transfixed, forgetting to scan the skies around him.

He'd been flying with the autopilot, which was fine as long as he didn't need to change headings. Below, nothing but farmland, a brown-and-green quilt of rectangles and circles, dotted here and there with white remnants from the recent snowstorm. A few scattered buildings or clusters of trees broke up the monotony. The only landmark that mattered now was the long, white rope of Interstate 80, which would lead him on a cross-country line from east to west. The steady engine hum, the unremarkable terrain, and the strong electromagnetic fields inside the cockpit all conspired to lull him to sleep but now, as he fondled the chilly artifact, the iciness of it struck his senses back into play. In every way, the piece spoke to him of other worlds.

The cold it carried wasn't like cold in the atmosphere. This chill bored into his flesh. Once it reached bone, it almost felt like heat. In fact, he wasn't sure that it wasn't heat. He couldn't decide.

And the patterns! Deep beneath the surface, he watched a constantly moving oscillation of—what? Some kind of energy. Shapes appeared and disappeared in the fluid movement. For a moment he thought—

No, that can't be.

He set the fragment down on the passenger seat, shook out his fingers, looked up and around to reassure himself that he still flew over the highway. When he looked back down at the fragment, shorter than a ruler, not much wider than his broad palm, he saw the thing again, unmistakably. A face.

He blinked hard, rubbed his eyes. Took another swig of the Dew. Belched. Looked again. The face had changed. The eyes were clear, but the rest grew distorted. He couldn't tell: male or female? He reached to pick it up and the fragment scorched his hand. He dropped it so fast, it bounced off the vinyl of the passenger seat and down to the floor of the cockpit, where it slid underneath the seat.

Damn it!

He wiggled himself over as far as possible given his girth and wrenched his right arm down to feel around the sticky, gritty surface under the passenger seat. Nothing. He hunched further to his right, tried again, twisted his wrist backwards to strain it further toward the back of the underside of the seat, in case the fragment had wedged there. His arching left side bumped the control wheel, which overrode the autopilot, and the plane dove right. He tried to whip his body back up to make a correction but he was stuck.

The Piper lost altitude—fast banking right and falling from the sky.

He grunted and twisted again.

"Shitfire and damnation!"

His curses echoed through the cockpit as he huffed and fought to maneuver his body upright again. He yanked back on the yoke to raise the nose, careful not to put her into a stall. Gradually, the Piper regained altitude and he leveled her off. But the damage was already done. Beneath him, no sign of the highway, and more clouds had moved in to obscure the vital ground features. He calculated that he'd veered north during the dive—but how far? He would have to guess.

He cursed again and gambled on a southwest heading, as he searched for signs of the interstate, which should lay somewhere off to his left.

Long, sweaty minutes later, he spotted flashes of water that gleamed up between the clouds below the plane. Was this the lake he'd seen on the map, where it lay north of I-80? It should be on his right. Now it was far to his left. Way too far.

He made some further mental calculations—mere guesses, really—and adjusted his heading again. The minute he intersected I-80 again, he planned to revert to his original course.

He would have to wait until his next stop to retrieve the artifact from under the seat. He didn't want to throw his back into a spasm, which it was too fond of doing after years of twisting around under tractors and cars.

Before long, Bobby's top lashes began to hit the bottom ones every few minutes. A couple of times he caught his head lolling to the side and he quickly righted himself. He slapped at his face, and when that stopped working, he splashed it with water from a plastic bottle he'd brought along, although he rarely drank water.

It was a last-minute concession to safety planning that made him think of it. He'd grabbed an old one he kept in a cupboard in his workshop as he loaded the Jeep. Now, as he stared at the plastic, wondering just how old it was, he thought he saw something reflected in it. He froze.

It didn't.

Don't worry, Bobby. Everything is going to be okay. We're with you. You have an important mission to carry out today. You can do it.

He could swear he saw a reflection of someone sitting in the back seat. His heart raced and he refused to turn around and look. Yet he felt their presence.

You're going to be just fine, he heard in his mind.

His breathing grew shallow as he ascended into a full-blown panic. He squeezed his eyes, then opened them quickly. Still there, reflected in the plastic bottle. He both saw and felt when it shifted from one back seat to the other, never mind that his overnight duffel sat wedged between them. The figure passed right through. He threw down the bottle.

He'd read about this, he told himself frantically as he willed his reasoning brain to take over from his emotional reaction. Nothing to worry about here. The Third Man Factor.

He'd read Sir Ernest Shackleton's memoir, *South,* where the famous explorer became the first to describe the unseen presence that arrived during his last-ditch effort, with two volunteers, to save the rest of his crew stranded in Antarctica as their ship slowly sank into the frozen sea. As the party of three trekked across a treacherous mountain range to reach a distant outpost and send rescuers back to the trapped crew, they each felt the presence of an additional man. None of them spoke of him to his companions, though the incorporeal figure inspired, encouraged, and kept them all alive while they achieved the "impossible" journey. They didn't admit to his ghostly presence until long after they'd survived the crisis.

Yes, Third Man, Bobby.

That's what they named the phenomenon when other adventurers came forward with similar stories. That had to be what this was. Wasn't he, too, on a mission to save souls, pushing his endurance limits? An unseen helper. (Yet in this case, he *had* seen it.)

Something squirmed behind him. Why didn't that feel comforting? Or benevolent?

He heard a sound that wasn't the engine. Like a moan.

Goosebumps skittered down his arms. He froze, eyes fixed straight ahead, afraid to move, stealing short gasps of air so he wouldn't stir the atmosphere around him. Nevertheless, all his attention riveted on the seat behind him.

Like the child who's been left alone, terrified, who sits immobilized on the couch for hours until his family comes home, Bobby's ears went into high alert for the slightest sound that didn't belong. Sweat trickled down his neck, ran beneath his clothes, streamed down his torso. All thoughts of the interstate, or his plan to change course the minute he spotted it, fled from his mind.

He wasn't alone in this plane, and there was nothing he could do about it.

37

Remote

∞

By the time Garritt and Agnes pulled into the emergency bay at Holland Hospital, the sun had fallen behind the trees. Glaring artificial lights blazed off the entrance awning. Beneath them, Garritt saw Min struggle against the ambulance restraints as they slid her gurney out.

"Get off me!" he heard her yell at the EMT. The poor woman probably had a protocol to follow but Min kept up her fight. As she broke free, Garritt thanked all the healing powers in the universe. Min would be fine.

He jumped out of Stewart's truck in time to hear her fume, "There's absolutely nothing wrong with me! This scar is months old!"

"But miss, you've been in a serious accident."

"I don't give a pollywacking hopdoodle," she fumed with a face serious as fire.

Then she spotted him. "Get me out of here—I've got work to do!"

"Min, you can't. You need to let them check you out."

"I do not." She pushed at a man in scrubs who'd come out to assist. "I'm perfectly fine. I don't have time for this!" She turned to Garritt as she hopped off the gurney. "Let's go," she commanded and headed for Stewart's truck.

What can we do, he shrugged at the frustrated attendants as he hurried to catch up with her. He offered her an arm. She refused it.

"Bobby Lee could be halfway across the country by now. He's probably two hours behind Michigan time, which means he's still got sunlight. He'll be airborne and I need to track him. "

"You *need* to take it easy and…and…" He didn't know how to tell her.

"Wade? Yeah, I learned about Wade while I was unconscious."

So that was his other name.

"Look, I don't have time to grieve. This is what Wade would want me to do. He'd tell me so himself."

She yanked open the door of Stewart's truck and ordered, "Agnes, take us to Garritt's house as fast as you can."

Garritt managed to squeeze in beside her, his leg and hip crushed against hers. Under any other circumstances, he might be pleased about that. His private hope was that Agnes would know what Min needed, whether she was okay or whether he had to drag her back to a hospital using bodily force. Now that he knew what she was capable of, he could probably manage that if he had surprise on his side, and by applying his greater height and bulk. Well, he'd have to try anyway.

He could feel Agnes hesitate. He caught her eye seeking his approval. "Yeah, do what she says. But why my house?"

"It's quiet, it's private, and it's the only place I know."

He wanted to ask her what else she knew, like whether she knew Zach and Wade were the same person, and that her own company had kidnapped his best friend and all that implied. For now, he thought it best to wait. Two could play the withholding game.

Half an hour later, he had her tucked under a down comforter in his navy blue armchair, close to a blazing fire.

During the drive, she managed to explain to Agnes about the remote viewing in a way Garritt never could have done. Once they got to his place, he had to insist, then show Min his ugly leg, in order to explain about Agnes. But that finally convinced her to let the girl sense into her state of health. Otherwise, Garritt said he wasn't going to "allow" Min to do any psychic probing "in my living room." (Weak, but it was the only card he held.)

Agnes ran her hand slowly down Min's spine, touched places on her head, then felt Min's fingertips.

"She's extremely stressed out," Agnes announced, "and she's had a shock—but she'll recover from that. I think she'll recover faster if you let her do her thing. I don't feel any major malfunctions. I'm not an x-ray machine, though."

"*Thank* you, Agnes. See? Told you I was fine."

He read something in Min's eyes that made him happy: she was secretly pleased by his concern—though she'd never admit it.

"Why can't they just use radar or spy planes or something? Drones?" Agnes asked.

"Yeah, they've got their helicopters and their fancy gear," he agreed, "why can't they just barge in and grab Bobby Lee?"

"Because he's not our prey. Not even the artifact, really. He's leading us to the prey. They want to know where Bobby Lee is going, and who he's going to meet—and other things the technology can't provide. Psychic viewing is the ultimate stealth tool."

She turned to Agnes, "I lost my phone in the crash. Can we use yours to text my bosses? We need to let them know where I am, what I'm doing, and then I'll need you to relay information once we've set up the link. Let me give you a number."

Agnes eagerly handed over her phone, proud to help.

Min typed for a long minute, presumably texting Blackthorn. She handed the phone back.

"Now both of you, please stop fussing over me and be quiet for a minute while I catch up to this fanatic."

She closed her eyes and Garritt wished he'd asked her about the Wade/Zach thing. Once again, she had ordered him around and told him nothing.

A gold light flashed near her temple.

Okay, so maybe that didn't matter right now.

She certainly confirmed what Juan told them. Bobby was in over his head with the wrong people. Blackthorn, with all its apparent knowledge of aliens and whatnot, believed that. They must consider the situation urgent to let their valuable and talented employee evade a doctor's examination. They did care that much, didn't they?

Did they? Did they even know she'd fled the hospital?

Min's voice sounded strange, slow and heavy-soft, as if she could barely move her lips. "He's flying over what looks like farmland. But there are a lot of clouds below him. He's not IFR rated."

"So is that bad?" Agnes asked.

Min opened her eyes. "Shhhh… don't interrupt. Just text what I'm saying to that number I gave you, okay?"

"Sorry. Right," Agnes blushed.

"And yes, it's bad. He's licensed for VFR only, according to Wade." She swallowed hard after she said his name, but explained, "That means, legally, he has to be able to see where he's going. If he can't fly by instruments alone, he just made a dangerous mistake by not landing that plane."

"Oh," Agnes said. "Before you go, um, back—what if someone answers the text, should I tell you what they say?"

"No," she snapped, then apologized. "Sorry, but here's the thing. Don't interrupt or touch me or move or make noise or speak to each other, okay? I'm not in a trance, although it might look like that to you. I'm acutely aware of you both, of every muscle you twitch, every sniffle and rattle. Every sound around me is magnified, and because I've stepped up my sensitivities, it can be extremely irritating or distracting. And if you touch me or bump me—it will jolt me back here with a terrible shock. In order to do what I do, my focus has to be intense and somewhat... *out of body,* you might say."

She'd shifted into a tone Garritt hadn't heard before, all business, the military side, he assumed. He held back everything he wanted to say, every worry about her welfare, every question she hadn't answered. Instead, he watched a light-show of sparkles around her head. When she went back into her altered state, the lights blossomed in colors he hadn't seen before.

"The plane is rising and falling, skittering all over the place. Steep left bank. Now right bank. Something's wrong. I can't see what it is." She opened her eyes and blinked a few times. "Garritt, we need Juan. Can you text him?"

"Juan? What for? He's working. And he's got no credit with the boss right now." *Plus, you guys already kidnapped him once; wasn't that enough?*

"Worse than that. He's been fired. Ask him."

"How would you know that?"

"It's the fragment. We both touched it. We connect at a new level. There was some confusion with the replacement worker Corbyn hired. Right now, Juan is on his way home, frustrated and angry. Although Bobby Lee also touched the artifact, I can't read the man for some reason. I'm hoping Juan can."

"He can read him. He told us so," Garritt said as he reached for his phone, trying to hide his surge of jealousy over the idea that she and Juan had a "special connection."

Juan answered immediately.

On my way

"He didn't even ask me why."

"Yeah. That's how it is. He knows."

Then another text came through.

Pendejo fired me

While Garritt typed a reply, Min got up to watch over his shoulder.

No worries bro you're too good for that job

Luciana's pregnant

We know

I'm screwed

Nope. Stop texting and drive

"Tell him the job I offered awaits, but he needs to hurry."

"But you didn't offer him a job. I was there, remember?"

"Oh yes I did. And he knew it the minute I shook his hand. It just freaked him out, is all."

"What's next? Hiring Agnes to perform faith healing?" He was pretty sure some of his bitterness leaked through the sarcasm.

She grinned at him. "You've got a lot to learn, guy. Your little Dutch world is about to be replaced by a frickin' universe of wonders you are not going to believe. Until you do. And then, just like me, there will be no turning back."

38

In the Aethers

∞

"He's lost," Juan blurted as he barged through Garritt's front door. He plopped three greasy bags down on the little brass table where she'd shared a pizza with Garritt. They smelled amazing. She hadn't realized how madly starving she was. In fact, if she had tried to continue her remote viewing, she would have failed completely.

This kid truly is telepathic.

What if this were the real reason Ben showed up on her psychic starship and told her to call Juan?

She swooped on the bags, pulled out containers, and deftly ripped off lids to reveal fresh green guacamole, expertly charred *carne asada*, and rolled chicken tacos. This was accompanied by steaming portions of refried beans and rice, fresh *pico de gallo* with lime, cilantro, tomatoes, and onion, and plenty of red and green pots of hot salsa. Full of promise, the spices burned at her nose as she inhaled.

"You are *brilliant*," she cooed at Juan as she pulled out paper plates, plastic ware, and both flour and corn tortillas.

"You can thank my uncle's bar," he fended off the compliment, although he looked smug.

She filled a tortilla with beef, added a healthy glob of guacamole, and shoved a huge portion of the steaming, fat tortilla into her mouth.

"I make no apologies," she announced, mouth half open as she sucked in air to cool the hot meat. It tasted like San Diego's best. Not Tex-Mex; this was Baja style, almost impossible to find in the Midwest. "Where is your uncle from?"

Juan laughed. "He owned a bar in Ensenada once."

Meanwhile, the others stared in astonishment, probably at her lack of manners. She swallowed. "I can't do this work on an empty stomach, and I mean that literally."

"My uncle would be proud. Dig in, you guys. My treat."

"No way," Garritt argued as he pulled out his wallet. "You just got fired."

"Yeah, but your lady friend here has a job for me. Right?"

She grinned at Garritt, faintly aware that she might have red sauce staining her teeth. "Didn't I tell you?"

As soon as they devoured every morsel, Min was ready to get back into her golden starship to figure out if Juan's proclamation could explain why Bobby was flying so erratically.

Ben was right. With her new sense of urgency, her starship viewing had improved. Now she would have Juan to supply reports about Bobby's state of mind, especially clues about his destination.

Juan didn't know about his friend "Zach" yet — and that was good. Keep the kid's mind clear. Neither had she figured out how to break the news to him that they would not be making the artifact public. She guessed how he might feel about that. In fact, she should stop thinking of it, or he'd pick up on her own disappointment. Strong emotions were like waving flags to a telepath.

Telepaths varied, though. Ben said he caught her thoughts when she was ready to launch them into words. But what else could Ben read that he kept to himself? She guessed that Juan's ability might be less accurate until he had better training, though Ben thought the kid had a special link with Bobby. Apparently, she could not read everyone who touched the artifact. She was glad. Maybe she could only hear Juan, whose thoughts weren't too repugnant, and Garritt—which made no sense at all because he'd never touched the artifact. After vividly sharing his jungle experience, she was only able to sense that Garritt cared about her well-being, which didn't require telepathy to surmise. Beyond that, no clue what he was thinking.

She settled Juan on a kitchen chair next to her recliner and gave him permission to speak during her visions. Since he would also be in an altered state, his voice wouldn't come as a shock. She put Agnes on her other side to relay texts of anything she or Juan said that seemed relevant. "Use your judgment," she told Agnes. That made the girl visibly nervous but how else would she learn?

Whoever was on the receiving end of the texts hadn't identified themselves. They'd sent one-word acknowledgments so far, typical protocol for the number she'd used.

Garritt sat across the room, watching them anxiously. Outside the dark windows, she could hear the wind blow through the surrounding pines but no snow fell to seal them in.

"Okay, let's do this," she announced and they all turned silent.

"He's in a bad way," Juan spoke first. "Something threw him off course and he can't find the highway. He's really worried." He stopped for a minute as if listening. "There's something else. I'm not sure what it is. His thoughts keep jumping around and he's spooked." He paused for a breath. "Oh, and he lost the artifact."

"What?" Garritt piped up despite her warnings. "How can that be?"

"No, not *lost*-lost. It's in the plane but he can't find it. Or he can't reach it…he's freaking out!" Juan jumped to his feet. "I had to bail, okay? I can't listen to that shit. It gives me a headache!"

"It's okay," Min encouraged, patting the chair for him to sit again.

Her affection for the kid had grown considerably after the feast he'd brought and she was worried about him. He could lose himself in this kind of thought-connection. It happened sometimes.

"Don't stay in his head when it gets like that. We only need to know about his destination so we can alert our ground team. Or anything about his buyer. Hop in and out if you have to."

She was keenly aware of her responsibility to these three. None had her years of careful training. Blackthorn wouldn't even ask for their help if the situation weren't critical, and time-strapped. She only hoped her presence was enough to keep Juan safe.

He sat back down, reluctantly.

"Do you think he knows you're listening in?" Agnes asked him. "I mean, can you tell by his thoughts if he hears you, as well?"

"If he could hear me, he wouldn't have left me to freeze to death in that fucking shed, would he?"

Garritt cleared his throat. "Sorry, Agnes," Juan said.

"Will you all please stop saying that? I grew up with two brothers. I'm the daughter of a farm wife, and a farmer dad who could cuss a blue streak would make your ears turn yellow! I don't know where you get these ideas about me," she huffed.

They laughed, which probably didn't help.

"Besides, none of this is about me," she added with such sincerity that Min wanted to hug her.

The girl probably didn't recognize her own wit. But she was right. This wasn't the time to coddle any of them.

Min closed her eyes again and was surprised to see Wade, looking fully alive. He stood before her inside the shimmering craft.

"I'm okay," he said, clear as a drill sergeant. "I'm going to take some rest and get some help, but I'm okay. Stop crying! You're doing a fantastic job, Blake, and you know I don't hand out compliments easily." He appeared just like he had in life, only more light-filled and etheric, exactly as one might expect.

"Wade—I'm so sorry! It's my fault—"

"Stop right there!" He held up a shimmery hand. "This was my mission too. We do what we have to do. Just like when I pushed you down that dune and I had no idea it would go the way it did. You and I have sworn our commitment to the consortium we serve. Nothing else matters. Bodies come and go, as you can see. And now, I'll be here to help from the other side. I can do more." He flickered in that way she'd become accustomed to. He would disappear soon.

She wanted to say something to him, something profound and meaningful, but she couldn't think of the words. Instead, she held out her hand and he took it.

The handshake was so much more than that. Gentle waves of energy encompassed her, as if he bestowed upon her the last bits of his Earth-energy, and as he did so, his image wavered and slowly faded. But they had shaped a new understanding: No grief necessary. They would meet again, when the time was right and her job was done. She would try to remember this when it came time to tell Juan what happened to his friend. Maybe it would soften the blow.

Min and Juan tracked Bobby Lee for a little while longer before the sky grew dark where he was.

"He's going to land," Juan announced. "He's pissed that it's not where he planned. He's north of where he expected to be by now."

"I can see it," Min agreed. "He's in the final approach and I can see a building sign that says 'Scottsbluff.' Where is that? Anyone?"

"Nebraska," Agnes whispered, texting the news.

"It's a big airport," Min observed. After a moment, "He's down."

"Cow town," Juan said after a long silence as they returned to the here and now. "He keeps thinking about this 'cow town.' Where is that?"

"Could be Colorado," Garritt offered, "or Wyoming. Or just about anywhere out west. Lots of cattle."

"Yeah? Well mostly he's freaked about something inside the cockpit. It's scaring the shit out of him."

Min had lingered long enough to watch Bobby secure the plane and catch a ride to a nearby motel before she joined their conversation. "Mosquitoes? Maybe a bee got in and he's allergic. That's weird though. Did you get the impression he'll meet his buyer in Scottsbluff?"

"No. And he's freaked about flying again tomorrow. He's not where he wanted to be. I think the cow town is far away. But …" He paused for a minute. "He's happy now; he found the artifact."

"They texted back," Agnes interrupted. "It says, *Sending in freelancer.* What does that mean?"

"That means it's time for us all to get some sleep," Garritt stood up. "We can meet here again at whatever time you insist."

He looked directly at Min and she felt a little thrill go down her spine. *What was that?*

"Meanwhile, Min, you're going back to the B&B with me—I mean, I'm going to take you there."

It was as if Garritt's whole body turned red. Min deliberately turned to Agnes so he couldn't see her own reaction.

"The text means they're going to keep surveillance on Bobby in case he makes a connection while he's on the ground. Garritt's right. Go home and get some sleep, you two. You've done a great job so far."

Until Garritt made his pronouncement about the B&B, she'd planned to ask if she could bunk on his couch for convenience. Clearly, he'd already thought that through. *Wise.* What shocked her was the deep disappointment she felt as they climbed into his truck to make the trip.

Garritt had to accompany her in and persuade the Petersons to let her stay. He swore there would be no helicopters, and that no, she was not a gangster, drug runner, or wanted by the FBI or CIA. She didn't hear everything he said because he pulled them aside to elaborate. She caught only a few words: "Friend of her family … Army surplus … likes to scare with that fake CIA gag … not her choice…"

As she finished a long, luxurious bath, she was still chuckling over the expression on Mrs. Peterson's face when she and Garritt first walked in together, so late at night. Had they really looked like *that*?

39

What Does Not Glitter

∞

Bobby squinted in the morning brightness, though the sun was rising behind him and filmy clouds drifted beneath him. He hadn't slept a wink last night. He shoved on his aviators and slugged down his Mountain Dew, one of the supplies he'd replenished at that shithole in Scottsbluff. Clearly a deal between the FBO and the motel's owner. Fly-ins don't have much choice, do they? One night—what should they care if the water never heats and the sides of the bottom sheet are smeared with rusty bed-bug stains?

He'd known enough to look for them before he turned on the overheads in the shoddy room. Sure enough, a prime infestation. Desk manager claimed he didn't have another room. So after the cold shower treatment, Bobby put on his morning clothes and lay gingerly atop the coverlet, hoping like hell the bugs wouldn't find him. After a few minutes, he got up and turned on the room light to discourage the little night predators from coming out to feast on his flesh. What else could he do? He lay down again for a few minutes, then realized he would never relax enough to fall asleep and decided to try the stiff maroon side chair near the window.

Sleep still wouldn't come. Every time he drifted off, he jerked awake again. He thought he saw things moving in the corner of the room. A dream? Or real? He spent the entire night weaving in and out of a drowsing state that wasn't restful at all.

Now that he was back in the air with some caffeine pumping through his veins, he felt a little better. He chewed once or twice as he gulped down a boiled egg he brought with him from the greasy spoon next to the motel, where he also scarfed bacon and toast and sausage before pocketing the eggs for later. The food filled his stomach, though it didn't rest easy.

He hit turbulence again and the plane bucked like a bronco.

Up ahead, the distant Rocky Mountains cast back the rosy sunrise and made him think of the old saw, "Morning red, sends the traveler back to bed." He'd be gone before the storm hit, he smiled, stretching his thick gray mustache tight against his teeth. Turns out his unplanned course correction was another stroke of genius.

His original route would have taken him over Denver, a massively crowded airspace, a hub for every major airline—military jets as well, what with the Air Force Academy and all. He would have had to contact air traffic control. He could lose his license for flying in instruments-required conditions. Worse, guiding the plane south along I-76 to pick up I-70 like he had planned would have forced him to skim over ski resorts and dodge around those fourteen-thousand-foot peaks. He hadn't thought it through when he was distracted by the need to hurry out of Michigan undetected. The dive that took him north instead? The work of his invisible guides, he decided, the ones clearing his path with synchronistic miracles. Divine intervention. More proof he was on a mission of great importance to humanity.

His new course would edge along southern Wyoming until he picked up I-80 again in Rawlins. He'd be farther north than he needed to go, but he wouldn't require oxygen, although he cursed himself for not having it on board. Would have been a simple thing to do. This new plan felt smart to him; smarter than he was. In a moment of gratitude, he gave credit to his invisible aides.

After an hour in rough air, he landed again to stabilize his innards at another look-alike airstrip in the middle of nowhere. He relieved himself, topped off his tanks, told a few lies to the lingering pilots who probably couldn't afford to fly too often. Private planes were an extremely expensive hobby, another reason he was eager to accomplish this mission. Those poor guys had to get their kicks from talking more than doing. Not him. He felt powerful for so many reasons this morning, including his new personal distance-flight record.

As he lifted off again, his spirit wanted to soar with the plane. Yesterday, he got too tired, he reasoned. He had started to imagine things. Today would be different.

But the voices in his head…they had pestered him all night, alternating between encouragement and worry.

You can't be late. Might miss your connection.
Sleep now—you need to get some rest!
Why aren't you sleeping? Your body needs it.
You'll be okay; you'll be fine. You deserve this money.
You are meant to have that fragment. After all, you searched for years. This was no accident.
Don't drop it again!
You are the right man for this job. You always have been.

At first, they sounded like his own thoughts. Now they felt like outsiders shouting in. His self-talk had never been quite so—*distinctive*.

Something flitted through his line of vision and for a moment he thought it was a bug inside the cockpit. He reached up to swat at it, a Michigan reflex. But then he saw it outside the windshield, larger this time. It glowed at him, an orangish light, and zoomed far out in front of the plane, hung there for a minute, then vanished from his sight.

"What the hell?" he said aloud.

A UFO? Did he just encounter a full-blown UAP? A thrill ran through him.

But another hour passed and he saw nothing more. The altimeter indicated that he had increased his altitude, although he had maintained the same distance above the ground. Must be over a plateau that he didn't notice as it rose up from sea level. Well, hell, he wouldn't go over twelve thousand feet. The FAA didn't require oxygen until twelve thousand five hundred feet. His mental advisers would alert him if his situation became unsafe. Right?

He grabbed one of his old charts. Cheyenne, Wyoming, sat at six thousand feet.

Damn. That was elevation enough to make some people on the ground feel sick.

But good weather surrounded him now as the clouds scudded south of his location. In the clear, dry air, he could easily track the few streams and lakes he had located on his laptop back in the motel. (He finally tried to buy new charts in Scottsbluff but the flight office operators laughed and told him to use his iPad like everyone else. Which he didn't own.)

You're doing fine, the voices sang to him. *You'll see us soon.*

"See you soon? See who soon?" His fingers tapped nervously as he scanned the world around him. He'd taken to speaking aloud; it broke up the monotony of the engine hum.

There again—the orange light, twelve o'clock high. He craned forward to look up through the cockpit window. Gone.

A commotion flared up in the back seat, like it had the day before. It moved, side to side, jostled the bag that once again held his precious fragment. Thank the Maker he'd found it last night! This morning he put the shave kit where he could see it and left the seat directly behind him empty.

Or it had been.

Hairs rose on the back of his neck.

You know we're here, don't you?

His right arm twitched involuntarily.

Don't be afraid! We're your friends, remember? We are the ones who've guided and helped you all along.

He couldn't argue about that. From the minute he stumbled into those agents out on the dunes, he knew he'd been guided. But he couldn't convince himself to turn around and look where he felt the movement, and where this single deep voice came from, directly behind his head. Cold seized Bobby's spine. He tried to keep his eyes moving, watching for air traffic, following landmarks.

There's nothing back there. I'm just edgy. Tired. Imagining things again.

A strange electricity suddenly charged the atmosphere inside the cockpit. With it came the sharp smell of…cheddar cheese? His gauges showed that the temperature hadn't changed, though he went from cold to boiling hot in his flannel underwear and winter coat.

He reached up to rip the Velcro at his neck but something stopped his hand. *Don't worry about that, Bobby. You will adjust in a moment.*

He grew frantic. His own voice burst out in uncontrollable spurts, peppered with gargled exclamations of pain. "Who—are—aggh!" Tight fingers squeezed his wrist, so fat and long, he couldn't feel a palm connected to them. The unseen force completely immobilized his arm.

"You know who we are, don't you?"

The voice resonated through the cockpit, no longer confined inside his head. His arm was released. He shook it madly.

"NO! I do not!"

He fought to move his legs, too, trapped in the cramped cockpit. His left hand gripped the control yoke so tightly his fingers turned to snow. He clung to this piece of airplane as if it were his last connection to reality.

"Just close your eyes for a minute, Bobby, and you will see us. Then you will know that you are perfectly safe."

"Us?" Sweat ran into his eyes. "How many of you…are there?"

"Oh, we are many, didn't you know? We thought you knew. You've been calling to us for a long, long time now. Don't you remember?"

He didn't remember any such thing.

The air he forced in and out of his lungs began to fail him. He glanced at the altimeter. Only eight thousand feet. Too low for hallucinations. He gasped again and nosed the plane down.

Trees zoomed up so he yanked back on the yoke, lifting her nose to miss the treetops but the steep upward angle cost him airspeed. Another degree up and the plane would stall and turn to plunge straight back to earth. He wasn't high enough to pull out of that before he hit the ground. He leveled the plane again in the nick of time.

"That really wasn't a very good thing to do, Bobby," the voice said smoothly. "Why won't you look at me?"

"Because you're just a figment of my imagination," he whispered. "You're a goddamn hallucination!" he shouted. He couldn't seem to control the volume of his words. Something about the lack of air getting into his lungs and the scarcity of oxygen reaching his brain.

"You know that's not true. We've been with you for years. Besides, you're not flying high enough for hypoxia. Although, it can happen to some people. Maybe you're one of those."

His stomach dropped to his knees.

"Although, I don't think so." A slash of movement sped around his head and the thing lingered before his eyes, like a giant snail without a shell. A horrifying, shiny, flesh-toned mass that spoke to him as if it were human.

"Oh, but I *am* human—or, I was. Long ago. But that doesn't matter now, does it? We are all here with you. You've been our friend for a very long time now."

It multiplied. Suddenly he saw dozens of them floating in the cockpit. They blocked all sight of the world beyond this claustrophobic enclosure.

The plane tipped violently. First right. He jerked in response, correcting the level. Then left, like in the turbulence over Illinois, as if gusts of wind threatened to capsize his lonely ship in this ocean of endless sky. *Are they doing this?* The plane rose back up to his cruising altitude.

The slimy creatures swarmed through the cockpit without gravity to hamper them. They spun around his head as if he were a Maypole and they were chanting children. They wove ribbons over his body, covered his eyes with colorless streamers. He clenched his lids shut and squeezed his face tight. The engine fumes he'd breathed for two days faded beneath the stench of cheese and his own body odor. He thought he might retch at any moment…

Desperately, reflexively, he fell back on prayers his mother taught him because that's all his failing mind could conjure.

"Our Father, who art in Heaven …"

He didn't even believe in that! What was he saying?

"Our Father…who resides in Heaven and who rules the Universe, I… pray…to you now," he tried again, spitting out the words in halting breaths.

He opened his eyes a slit. They were still there, only now the one before him, the first one, grinned with a round hole that appeared in the beige mass. Miniature green eyes glittered above it. The thing had grown.

He slammed his lids shut and the prayers came rumbling out between his lips in gibberish, a kind of sobbing whimper that made no sense at all.

"Now Bobby, you really need to calm down. Look, I'm going to sit here beside you. I promise I won't move. Open your eyes. See? I'm your friend—and you are mine."

He dared it. He didn't know how he found the courage, but he wrenched open his eyes—just a fraction—and it was true. The thing was as big as him now, filling the passenger seat with its slithering bulk. A short beige pyramid rose up from the top of its shapeless body. At its sides, protruding triangles where a human would have limbs. No legs at all. It rested its entire mass on the plastic seat cover, ugly as the color of library bookends, or the old file cabinet he'd dragged home from the dump—a nondescript shade of neutral banality, terrifying in its lack of definition. The color of sick, rotting, lifeless bodies.

The others, which had been swimming in the air around the cockpit like tiny airborne mollusks, had vanished, although he still felt a rustle in the back seat. Then he heard the zipper of the shave kit and a kind of squealing noise, like pigs in the pen when the slop was ready to be poured, as if they were fighting over the contents.

"Leave that alone," he tried to command. His voice sounded puny and weak. No one would listen to a voice like that.

"Bobby, be reasonable," the thing beside him turned to face him and it was more horrible than before. The green-glowing eyes had turned stinging yellow. The opening that should have been a mouth, situated near the bottom of the pyramid, was no more than a slash that opened to sooty blackness inside the creature. "You know you are bringing this shining treasure to our representatives on Earth, don't you?"

Bobby felt his head nod feebly. That wasn't what he'd wanted to do but somehow this thing had taken control of his body.

As if in response to his thought, he felt a thousand needlepoints plunge into the back of his neck, then around at the front of his throat. A great sucking sound erupted in the claustrophobic space.

"Then you won't mind if we admire it, will you."

It wasn't a question but a command. He knew that.

His spirit deflated, and as it did, he sagged against the plane's controls, ever so slightly. The plane lost altitude, so gradually, he didn't notice at all. He'd stopped looking out. His eyes turned glassy and the edges of his vision dimmed into blackness.

The Piper banked steeply. Some vague prompting urged him to make a correction. Remnants of his survival instinct? Or were the creatures protecting themselves, using him to steer the plane?

Why should they care? They weren't of his world. Real, yes. But no longer flesh.

His energy waned further, siphoned off through the needle-like proboscises they'd inserted. Soon, he wouldn't be able to control the plane at all. He wasn't ready to die. Not like this.

The truth settled over him like a shroud: these creatures wouldn't care. They only needed his plane to reach their minions on Earth, his buyers, so willing to offer a huge price. He should have known.

40

Too Far

∞

Juan jumped to his feet. *"Pinche cabrón!* He needs to land the fucking plane!"

"He can't," Min said. "I'm going in."

"What are you talking about?" Garritt interrupted, breaking all her rules.

He hated the way she'd behaved for the last few minutes, thrashing her head from side to side, jerking around like she was following sharp corners on a race track. At one point, she'd gripped the armrests and stretched her flexed feet out in front of her, as if bracing for impact.

"What's going on?" he demanded, as he saw blue lights flash around the room.

"He's totally fucked up, dude," Juan said.

Min stubbornly returned to her altered state. Her words came out in distracted bursts, like someone engrossed in television, or texting. "I can … hardly follow his plane …it's tossing …all over …" She clutched at the chair.

"Whatever you're doing, stop!" Garritt insisted, rising to his feet and moving toward her.

Agnes texted furiously, then held her breath, as if ready to leap up herself and…do something.

"No!" Min erupted. "I'm almost there! *Don't touch me!*"

∞

She'd been trying to keep her psychic starship out of Bobby's sight because more than once she thought he'd seen her. Juan said he was babbling about UAPs. This wasn't supposed to happen. Was she more connected to Bobby than she realized, because of the artifact?

The first time, Bobby stared directly up at her through his windshield. Instantly she relocated her ship.

When it happened again, she pulled herself all the way back down into her body in Garritt's living room.

Actually, she never left that body completely. This was all merely a matter of focusing her perspective, either into the third dimension where Garritt, Juan, and Agnes sat nearby, or out into the unlimited, multi-dimensional existence that ran simultaneously along with her life on Earth. According to Ben's ice-cream-cone analogy, what she experienced on Earth was the end result of what happened first in those higher-frequency dimensions and then spiraled down into her present moment. Nevertheless, it was all her.

Stay focused, Minda.

Juan was right, of course. Bobby had lost control of the plane, and maybe of his mind.

The Piper Cherokee dove. He pulled out of it but shifted his course south again. He was headed straight for the Colorado Rockies again, at a suicidal altitude. Was that his intention? Suicide? That made no sense.

If she could place her mind inside this ball of orange light that they were calling a psychic starship, then why not inside a small plane? She might learn something new about Bobby's intentions, or discover what caused this erratic flying. What if he'd had a heart attack or something? She didn't want to risk Juan's healthy state of mind by asking more from him. He had suffered from Bobby's distress for hours. Garritt was right to feel protective. It wasn't safe for Juan; he didn't have her training.

She tuned out the trio in the living room, drew in a deep, clear draft of the pristine energy inside her twinkling seashell craft, and imagined herself transporting into Bobby Lee's airplane.

Distantly, she heard Garritt protest.

Once she reopened her eyes, all she saw and smelled and heard took place inside that reeking cockpit.

Bobby seemed barely conscious. His wide eyes stared ahead but no one appeared to be home inside. And something else. The air inside the cabin was visible. Viscous, like engine oil pooled atop a dirty puddle. She reached a hand in front of her face and moved it aside. It swirled, murky-like. Suddenly she couldn't breathe. Then she calmed down, reminding herself that, in this state, she didn't need to. Did she?

Out the side of her eye—wait, where was she, exactly? Was she sitting in a seat? No. This was like a dream, where you're an observer but you're not really there, yet you know what's inside everyone's heads, one by one, as if you're zooming in and out of the dream-characters sequentially. She'd made it here, but she wasn't really. When she reached to touch the plane, just there, above the passenger window, she felt nothing. No tactile sensation whatsoever. Her head swam for a moment. By now, she should be more accustomed to this astral state of awareness. She waited for the sensation to pass.

I'm fine now. Everything's fine. Again in her peripheral vision—a flash of beige. Large. Massive, in fact. Amorphous. It frightened her deeply.

She felt the mass move toward her, blocking her view through the windows. Then it stopped and she couldn't see the thing anymore. The sky opened up again.

For now, the plane flew level. In the distance, she could see the high mountains that stretched across the horizon. She needed to get Bobby's attention, wake him up.

"Hey," she shouted at him.

Nothing.

Gingerly, she reached out to touch the staring figure.

He jerked his head up and instantly sucked in a deep, horrified breath like a man who'd seen his own body lying in a casket. His eyes were ribboned with red veins and they didn't connect to anything—not to her, not to the plane, not to the airspace beyond it. A trickle of snot ran into his mustache.

"Who's there?" he rasped as he swiveled his head blindly.

He can't see me. Has he lost his sight entirely? What could she say that wouldn't add to his terror? *It's me, the woman from the government agency?* She said nothing, hoping that at least she'd aroused him enough to notice where his plane was heading.

His empty eyes darted frantically around the inside of the cabin. Then he jerked his hands up to his throat, desperately scratching and pulling and clawing. His fingernails left long bloody scratches. She darted back to stay clear of flailing arms that moved like they were flinging leeches away.

She was having trouble herself now. She kept trying to breathe, then she would remember that she didn't need to. So why did she feel like she was suffocating?

Panic rose in her chest and she clutched at her solar plexus. Something was stabbing her there. She ripped open her blouse to see what it was. Nothing there. But she felt something pierce into her and plunge inside…

"Reverend Ben!" she screamed as the thing embedded itself in her solar plexus.

She could see it now, an enormous slug with a suction mouth big enough to cover her entire belly. The more desperately she clawed at it, the stronger that mouth became. Now it began to suck, to suck her life and being away from the center of her Self, from the place where her identity lived. She felt the energy run out from her middle like someone had opened a faucet.

She forgot about Bobby Lee. She forgot what she was doing here, on this plane where the floorboards were splitting open. She tried to step clear but there was nowhere to go. Dozens of vile-looking snakes appeared between the gaps, their glittery eyes fixed on her—all of them with the characteristic, triangular heads of poisonous vipers. Red ones, green ones, yellow ones, impossibly gaudy patterns. They slid rapidly from their hiding places to swarm over the floor, rushing toward her so fast, they collided into writhing Celtic knots at her feet and began to squeeze.

She screamed again.

∞

"She's blacking out!" Garritt exploded into motion.

The blue light that warned him swelled to the size of a man. The danger had grown extreme.

He broke the rules again and touched her arm. Giving her a shock strong enough to jolt her back to him was exactly what he intended.

"Min! Wake up!"

She didn't respond.

"Agnes!"

"I texted them five minutes ago. They said don't call 911. They're on their way."

Golden lights flashed and blue lights lingered and he knew Min needed help now.

Oddly, an incredible calm settled over him—just like it had in Peru. His surroundings blurred. Movements slowed. He cupped Min's head in his hands and began to whisper to her, words he didn't really plan to say, words that came into his mind as if from beyond it, as if the lights had dictated them. They came with a powerful clarity. He didn't stop to question but kept calling her back to her body in a steady stream of words he repeated, words that were nothing more than energy that swirled around them both, soothing, peaceful, inviting her back to her body.

In one of his books, he'd read about psychics who lost themselves while giving Spiritualist readings. One woman had tried to read for a family who wanted to know about their son, a sailor overseas during WWII. The moment she began, she found herself sitting in a chair on a bare church stage—and drowning. Literally drowning! A more skilled psychic rushed to her side, brought her out, and revived her. He said later that she would have actually drowned with that sailor if he hadn't been there to intercede. Psychics, remote viewers, psi experimenters—whatever you wanted to call them, Garritt understood their work was dangerous, both mentally and physically.

Min could die, right here in his living room.

She murmured something unintelligible.

"What? Tell me!"

She jerked her head back and forth a few times, then lapsed again. He felt her pull far away from him. He touched her forehead—icy and damp. At least she was breathing but this was all desperately wrong, not the relaxed state she'd been in before, when she did her "normal" remote viewing.

He began to feel her physical distress as if it were his own. She wasn't drowning—but something else. He couldn't define it; he only knew it would hurt her if they couldn't bring her out of it. Gently, he moved the hair from her face and stared at the brutal scar on her forehead. *Head injury.* He tried to recall anything he'd read about head injuries.

"Agnes," he shouted again, but she was already at his side. "Can you help her?"

Without a word, she dropped to her knees and placed a hand on the top of Min's head. She ripped it away. "This isn't right!"

"What's not right? I know it's not right!"

"I'm not sure …" Agnes hesitated, touching fingers to Min's cheek. "I've never felt anything like this before. Her face is cold; her head is hot."

"Try again," he insisted.

Obediently, she laid her hand on Min's gleaming hair, grimacing.

"What's wrong?" Garritt demanded.

"It's hot," Agnes answered, "but it's not really. Because it's so hot, it's also cold. Or it's so cold, it's also hot." Again, she pulled her hand back.

"It's not that it hurts me," she answered Garritt's exasperated look. "Every time I touch her, it's like someone shouts in my head to leave her alone. It feels so wrong for me to try…and if I go against that, I might injure her. Intuition—that's all I have, you know? I've never gone against it. The healing only flows because it's meant to be. I mean, it's like I help speed it up but it was going to happen anyway. This—this is different." She stood up. "No, Garritt. I can't interfere."

He stared at her. He wanted to panic but a sudden impulse reminded him that panic erased his intellect. This situation went far beyond his experience. Inwardly, he cursed that fact—and the lack of a user's manual. How do you bring back a psychic who's in trouble?

You ask for outside help. Like you did in the rainforest.

But he hadn't *asked* there! It simply arrived when he needed it because his motives were…humble enough to admit that he was far, far out of his depth.

"Where the hell is Blackthorn? Juan, call 911!"

"I don't think they can help," he answered.

"Why not?" Garritt turned on him. Juan's naturally tan skin had gone pasty gray.

"Because now I can hear both of them. All of them, in fact. To hear this, you'd think there were a hundred…uh, people inside that plane."

41

Authority

∞

The two men burst through Garritt's front door the second Juan opened it. The one in the lead had a head of bristly short hair, muscles to spare, and his shout for everyone to "Stand clear!" brought immediate obedience.

The tall Black man who surged in behind him pushed his way past Garritt and Agnes to reach Min's side. He purred at her in an extraordinary voice, "Your mind, Minda. Remember what I told you. Trap doors in your mind. You can do this."

His face said more than his words: he seemed as distraught as Garritt felt.

"You're Blackthorn? What have you done to her?" Garritt demanded.

"Commander, keep them out of my way," the Black man boomed.

"Yes sir. You three, this way."

GI-Joe advanced on Garritt first, then Juan, herding and pushing them back toward the kitchen doorway. When he spotted Agnes, who'd straightened her shoulders and looked about five inches taller than usual, he stopped and merely jerked his head at her to join them. She looked ready to take him on if she had to, which swelled Garritt's pride in the young woman. Instead of obeying, she moved across to the tall man's shoulder.

"She's alternating hot and cold. I would have massaged her feet to bring her back to Earth—you know, where she connects to it—but something told me not to interfere. Is she going to be okay?"

"Who are you?"

The tall man didn't take his eyes off Min, whose coloring looked hideous. Long moments before they arrived, she had stopped moving. Her eyes were glued shut and her breath came in uneven bursts.

"I'm Agnes. Her friend," she said defiantly. "And who are you?"

"That doesn't matter. Commander, we need to get her to Rose."

"But sir …" the Commander protested.

Garritt cut in, "Who is Rose?"

They ignored him.

"You heard me! Rose can help her. We cannot." He stood up—and up—massive, tall, and impressive.

"Don't you think …" GI-Joe tried again.

"NO. We have to get her to Rose NOW."

The fear behind his words made Garritt's own stomach coil. If *they* couldn't fix this…

"You shouldn't have done this alone," the tall man whispered down at Min, eyes full of regret. Garritt's ears picked up on the crack in his confidence, the held-back despair as the man castigated himself.

Garritt felt insulted. She hadn't actually been alone.

"I pushed you too hard…too soon," the man was saying softly, "Too fast." He dropped back down to his knees, pressed himself closer to Min. He touched her cheek with his fingertips. "I am so sorry! So very sorry. You have to come back to me, you hear?" He stroked her face and his features twisted into the agony of a lover facing the death of his beloved. "I cannot lose you. Not this time!"

Only the depth of the man's grief stopped Garritt's tongue as the man stood again and bellowed, "All of you—you're coming with us. Commander—"

"You two," the Commander burst into action, "help me lift her."

None of them hesitated. They eased her onto the portable gurney GI-Joe had carried in, carted her across Garritt's yard, and lifted her into the dark, military-style helicopter that idled on the cul-de-sac where the street ended. It was three times the size of the one that took Min away from him the last time.

Garritt found his voice again. "Who is this Rose person?"

"You'll see. Secure those straps," their "commander" ordered.

They situated her gurney in the center of the helicopter. Rough seats lined the edges, faced inward. "You." The Commander pointed at Garritt. "Sit across from me and use your feet as a brace. We'll keep her stable. This ship isn't outfitted for medical transport but we don't have time to wait. If that gurney moves, you and I move to stop it at all costs, hear?

"This is precious cargo, folks. We protect her with our bodies and our lives, got it?"

The big boss meanwhile settled behind the pilot. He spoke rapidly into his headset.

Garritt assumed he was giving orders, maybe contacting this Rose person to let her know they were coming. He wondered what kind of expertise she had. What was Min's ailment, exactly? He wracked his brain to think of which military hospital might be closest. It failed him.

Neither Juan nor Agnes spoke a word of protest, or anything else, as they obeyed these orders. Personally, Garritt would have insisted on coming if they hadn't offered. Juan, seated next to Garritt, still looked pale, and he was unusually quiet. Agnes sat across from them, next to GI-Joe, the one the tall man called Commander, which was confusing because the tall man was definitely in charge. He watched the Commander show Agnes how to use the headsets he distributed.

Between them, Min lay deathly still. A sheen of sweat glossed over her troubled expression.

The helicopter lifted off with a deafening rumble, nose down. They swooped up and swung out in a gut-dropping move not designed for newbie passengers. Garritt prayed this would be a short trip, for Min's sake. God grant this Rose woman would know the way to bring her back to him.

From the look on her boss's face, the prognosis was dire, and that slashed through his chest like a sword, even as he wondered about her relationship with the man who seemed so overcome by this threat to her life.

The Commander remained all business. But the tall man seemed to vacillate between panic and irritation, guilt and heartbreak. This was not the attitude of a mere boss.

42

Rose

∞

The helicopter sped northwest as they gained altitude. Garritt glanced across at Agnes. Her eyes shone and her face glowed, not with fear but excitement. What an extraordinary experience this must be for her. Juan, seated next to him, looked seasick. So much for the space-travel junkie.

"*Güey,*" Garritt teased over the headset, "you look like you're about to heave."

Juan lifted his middle finger to scratch his temple. "Don't forget I've seen you worse, *putillo!*"

Garritt laughed.

If Juan could read people, he wouldn't have boarded this helicopter if these men intended harm—would he? He twisted to see that they were flying north, no sight of Holland, which they should have reached by now. Instead he recognized the slash of highway I-96, then a clutter of buildings that looked like Zeeland.

"Hey, why aren't we landing? Holland Hospital is closest!"

"You need to stay calm. Your panic won't help her," the Commander advised.

"But she needs urgent medical attention! Where is this Rose person, anyway?"

"Garritt, these men know their job," Agnes interjected. "Min trusted them. Whatever's wrong with her, it's not the ordinary thing a hospital could treat. Rose must be some special kind of expert."

The Commander gave her a nod of respectful agreement, as if he couldn't have said it better.

Soon they also passed the opportunity to land in Muskegon, instead slicing straight north across the Dutch Triangle until a vast forest stretched below.

Without warning, Juan let out a sharp gasp and clutched at his throat. His eyes bulged. He was trying to speak but couldn't seem to get enough air.

Garritt reacted but the tall man—*Ben*, the Commander called him—materialized on Juan's other side with blinding speed. He settled a massive palm on Juan's forehead, another on the back of his neck. He spoke soft words of comfort or instruction, Garritt couldn't tell which.

He too wanted to reach out, grab a hand or an arm or something, but knowing Juan that would only make things worse. Instead he asked, "What's wrong with him?"

Juan sucked in a huge inhale and struggled to speak again. Garritt overheard "snow-blind" but the rest was lost in the helicopter's roar.

After a moment Juan's breath returned but in awkward rasps. His eyes shone like unnatural mirrors.

Ben soothed and quieted and called him steadily back to the here and now, as Garritt had done for Minda. Then he barked an order into his headset and the pilot dipped the helicopter's nose to gain speed.

Min's gurney careened forward.

Garritt cast off his seatbelt while the Commander did the same and they threw their body weight against the sliding contraption.

Agnes leaped up to help at the same moment the helicopter made a sharp bank. That threw her back into her seat and twisted the gurney into Garritt's knee, which at least stopped the contraption from tipping. Finally, the pilot leveled off and they wrestled the gurney back to center. Garritt and the Commander braced it between them and buckled back into their seats.

Throughout all this, Min never stirred. Her face never changed, which brought Garritt a new surge of worry.

Then Juan, half-conscious, let out a few pungent words in Spanish, followed by phrases new to Garritt. He translated bits of them in his mind. Prayers? Shared repugnance for all things church-oriented had formed a strong foundation of their friendship. If Juan was praying the prayers he learned as a kid, he must fear for his life.

The Commander looked, if possible, more stern than before, while Ben once again cupped Juan's forehead in his broad palm. He uttered gentle phrases, like a mother soothing a sick child. Except this time, Garritt saw golden lights surround them both.

The sight of the twinkling rescuers combined with the pitch of Ben's voice caused some recognition to rise up from deep oceans of Garritt's past, followed by waves of gratitude and some pure form of love that crashed over him and left pools of moisture in his eyes. He quickly cleared his throat to cast off the emotional debris before anyone else noticed.

As Juan's distress visibly dropped a level, the side of Garritt's body closest to him began to tingle. Distracted, he didn't notice the helicopter losing altitude until they stopped and hovered a few hundred feet above the treetops.

"You might want to close your eyes for this next part," the Commander suggested over the intercom, "especially you, Agnes."

"Why should I? I'm not afraid of anything. I've got two older brothers," she proclaimed, as if that explained everything.

The Commander gave her such a look of admiration, Garritt felt like a wimp for even considering the man's advice. So he kept his eyes open, then suppressed a holler of protest when the helicopter fell straight down toward the looming treetops. Shocked back to memories of falling from the sky in Peru, he pulled back from the window as they plunged through a dense forest of trees packed too close for a helicopter to fit. He squeezed his lids tight for impact.

It never came.

He opened his eyes.

The helicopter hovered in a rosy light that burst up around them. For a long moment, Garritt believed he might have died. Was the transition to the afterlife so quick? He heard Agnes gasp, "Oh my God," something she would never say. What if it were literally…

No. Couldn't be.

He peered out.

Beneath them gleamed a massive crystal rose in full bloom—the size of a civic building—surrounded by five crystal rosebuds that glittered in sunlight to create the rosy glow that bathed the helicopter.

As they slowly descended toward a landing pad, he realized that the petals were actually tall architectural sails, curved and glazed in graduated shades of reds, oranges, and pinks. A strong latticework of deep green, leafy swirls and arches further concealed the buildings within their embrace, a total of six. The open blossom stood at the center, largest of all, surrounded by five, five-sided wings disguised beneath the rosebuds. The entire complex consisted of a cleverly-concealed pentagon surrounded by five smaller pentagons.

Biomimicry.

He'd read something about this architectural trend but never expected the illusion could create a structure so dazzling it looked like a massive cluster of crystal floribundas, suspended in the center of a lake that stretched out toward exquisite gardens, with woods that beckoned just beyond the grounds. The nature-lover in Garritt rejoiced at the sight. But how had this majestic complex remained so completely invisible from the air?

"What just happened?" Agnes asked breathlessly.

"We've passed through the dome of concealment," the Commander replied.

"Are we still on Earth?"

"Most definitely."

"How on Earth, then…" Garritt began.

He glanced at Juan, who hadn't seemed to notice. Ben still held him, and he looked semi-conscious. Two people who meant so much to him were both in some bizarre state of psychic illness and they'd just plummeted into fairyland.

"New materials, advanced engineering," the Commander shrugged off the question. "State of the art invisibility tech…you'll understand later."

As they settled on a helipad ingeniously fitted into the design of one roof, Garritt took a closer look at the formal gardens beyond the lake. Artfully curved bridges and walkways wove out over the water, then wound back into the surrounding forest. Marble statuary gleamed in the afternoon light.

In summer, with living roses in bloom, the fragrance must be overpowering, he imagined, although the buildings alone were enough to inspire out-of-body transcendence. Patches of snow lingered beneath evergreens and places where the green latticework cast deep shadows.

Whatever concealment they passed through must be entirely porous to the elements, he decided, which might explain how the lush gardens could thrive.

The moment the rotors died, a handful of what he assumed to be orderlies rushed out to whisk Min and Juan away. Ben hurried after.

Before Garritt could follow, the Commander took him gently by the arm.

"We go this way." He guided them to a different door, holding it open for Agnes. "And welcome to ROSE."

His face lit up in a smile—the first to break across that steadfast jawline.

∞

As soon as she screamed his name, Min saw a faint outline of Reverend Ben's face. But the creature sucking on her life energy pulled harder. The pain spread from her stomach where it was attached, quickly encompassing her entire body. The sounds that erupted from her became unintelligible.

Seconds later, she lost the power to move her mouth or even hold up her head. She slumped, lifeless, on the back seat of Bobby Lee's small plane.

Then, softly at first and quickly increasing in grip, she felt huge fingers clutch her upper arms and lift her through the roof of the diving aircraft and straight out into the open sky.

"Minda, come back to me."

She could hear him as if from a hundred miles away.

"Min!"

But she couldn't respond and the sound grew further and further distant until it faded completely.

A long time later, she felt as if she were being propelled through the air but the sensation went away quickly and she drifted again in a timeless emptiness. Any will to form thoughts left her.

"Minda, look at me." The words were harsh, cruel even. "Look at my face."

She wanted to bat them away.

"You must come back to me. That is the way, Min. It is the way out of this stupor. You are not dead, darling girl. You are here with me, as I am with you. Now open your eyes!"

She tried to ignore him but with the words came a compelling force.

"Your *mind*, Minda. The trap doors. You went too far into Bobby's world. Now come back to your own. Follow my beacon!"

Before she could think of a way to resist these demands, her eyes were squinting at a rivulet of sweat streaming down his forehead. Then a broad crease formed across his cheeks as he smiled at her, eyes ablaze with love. Behind him she saw clouds, streaming vapors in rainbow colors.

Ben?

It was the first complete thought she'd had in an eternity.

∞

"It's like those plans for the Hanoi Lotus that I saw online," Agnes gushed.

They'd stepped onto a second-floor gallery that opened to an enormous atrium.

"I saw pictures of it, only I don't think they've built it yet. But instead of lotus blossoms—roses!"

"Good call," the Commander said. "The same Australian architects participated in this design, along with a guy named Eugene Tssui, who consulted on materials and energy efficiency. Everything is based on nature, especially the five-sided pentagons, which is why the pentagram is such an ancient symbol. Ask Dan Brown," he winked.

This Commander was definitely not the man Garritt first assumed him to be.

Agnes looked more shy than usual as she asked, "Is the architect, Sway…is he…*an alien?*" Her eyes opened wide enough to accept it if she had to.

"Eugene Tssui?" The Commander chuckled. "Not exactly. Although some people might argue that. No—he's an architect from Northern California."

"So," Agnes pointed up through the high glass ceiling, several stories above their heads, beyond which the rosy petals soared, "are those solar panels?"

"Not exactly. These are more environmentally prudent. Next generation, you might say. Less polluting. That was one of Tssui's insistent contributions. But we are self-supporting here and they do supply energy."

From this angle, they could also see the steel honeycomb that braced the glassy panels.

"So how did—what did—" Garritt didn't know how to describe that helicopter descent.

"The dome uses light reflection principles and projected imagery to deceive overhead surveillance," the Commander replied. "Beyond that, need to know only."

Agnes nodded gravely, a look of unmistakable admiration passing over her sweet face as she gazed up at the man.

Garritt had to admit, the place was stunning both inside and out, and worthy of many more questions. But he had his priorities.

"Where did they take Juan and Min? I need to stay with them."

The Commander eyed him for a moment, as if weighing the level of his distress. Probably figured that anyone who could ignore the magnificence of the atrium surrounding them meant business.

"Come with me."

He set off at a brisk pace along the open gallery.

The atrium was oddly deserted, though Agnes made enough commotion for a crowd. She kept exclaiming over its extraordinary features, such as the long streamers of glittering crystals suspended from the roof at its center. Or the waterfalls that flowed down from upper stories into pools full of swirling koi fish. Garritt couldn't help but stare up at the massive hanging planters.

Must have special cranes for watering and feeding, he decided. He looked down. *Plus a huge crew of caretakers.*

Tropical plants in full bloom and potted trees in radiant health dotted the atrium's marble expanse. As their heady perfume reached his nostrils, something gave way in Garritt's nervous system and he craved more. He always found comfort in green, growing things. By the time they reached an elevator that took them to the ground floor, much of his anxiety had floated away. Coincidence? Or architectural planning?

Agnes found new fascination in the koi ponds, which served as curved waterways that wound like small streams through the atrium before they disappeared into the building's five appendages. "I've heard that people pay a lot of money for these carp and I never understood why until now," she marveled as she watched the colorful beauties glint their brilliant orange, silver, and red combinations. "They aren't like the ugly ones my brothers spear from the river, are they?"

The Commander actually smiled at her. "Not quite."

This unapproachable man seemed have developed a fondness for Agnes's forthright manner.

"So this *is* a hospital, right?" she asked him.

"It's complicated. But trust me, you are going to like this. Especially you, Agnes."

When did he learn her name? Garritt wondered.

The Commander led them along one of the waterways and into a separate wing, where he opened a door into the most incredible greenhouse Garritt had ever seen.

At its heart grew a massive hickory tree. Despite the season, it still bore leafy branches that stretched up to a high glass dome, then fell like green fireworks all the way to the floor around the edges of the room. Beneath this living umbrella? Juan and Min, sitting on reclining lounges, looking as strong and vibrant as the tree.

"Dude!" "Garritt!" "Agnes! Come in!" "Isn't this amazing?"

Min beamed like she'd just opened the best present ever.

Juan's black eye had vanished and his color had returned.

Agnes rushed forward, trailing her fingers through the tree's lush leaves. "Oh my gosh! Whoa…Garritt, come and touch this."

Glad for something to hide his spinning emotions—gratitude, love, embarrassment for feeling either—he obeyed.

"Hey!" He'd never felt a plant so vital—and he'd felt many.

"Like it's talking to you, right?"

"This tree healed us," Juan proclaimed.

"Well, not entirely," Min corrected. "We had some other help—"

A door opened on the far side of the circular room, behind a draping of branches.

Through it entered a slender Asian woman. She wore a lavender gown covered with crystal embellishments that sparkled in the softly-lit room. She bowed slightly in their direction.

"I am Naranatha," she said in a voice like tinkling chimes. "Welcome to our healing room."

Garritt's knees nearly buckled as the blast of her delicate voice hit his face, arms, and chest. All he could do was blink, the power of it was so overwhelming.

Juan and Min jumped to their feet. It looked like an involuntary show of respect and Garritt completely understood the feeling. If he weren't already standing he would have done the same. Meanwhile, Agnes's hand froze on the leaf she'd been caressing.

"I see you have discovered our secret," the woman smiled. "You must be Agnes, the healer." She came closer and raised an alabaster hand to Agnes's cheek, probing the girl with her fingers. "You sense our special tree's gift?"

Agnes nodded dumbly, though she remembered to let go of the leaf and lower her arm.

"No, no, you are correct. Draw all that you can from that leaf, while you can. I know you will share it generously later, when called upon. It is I who must thank you for all that you have done."

Agnes turned scarlet. "But—"

"Never underestimate your abilities, dear." Her shimmering eyes bored into Agnes's own. "Yet you must also trust your inner promptings. Just as you did when Minda fell into trouble a few hours ago. You were right not to interfere with methods you have learned thus far. I hope that you will accept the opportunity to expand on that knowledge. The healing power of this tree is a small reflection of the Infinite Intelligence that pours through all of nature, including each one of us."

As she turned her attention to Garritt, he felt thought-needles probe at him, up and down, examining, inspecting his very soul. He feared he did not measure up.

To him she said only, "That doubt will not serve you, young man." And she turned sharply away.

Young? He was nearly forty! And, what doubt? But his tongue was suddenly glued to the roof of his mouth.

In mere seconds, this woman deflated his ego more than any parent or boss or coach or dominee or personal failure had ever done. Not even Min's take-down felt so crushing. This slip of a woman…who was she? And why did her disregard make him instantly feel like he'd been disemboweled?

To Juan, she granted nothing but smiles and praise. "My dear boy, you are very brave. You gave of yourself, you risked your sanity for our cause. We will not forget your eager willingness to sacrifice." She patted him. "I am very proud of you. You have quite the future in store!"

Juan beamed.

"Now don't you worry about what happened. You are free of all of that now. You will learn better ways in the future."

His face sobered for a moment.

The experience must have been incredibly traumatic for his friend, Garritt realized, and he longed to ask but instinct told him this was a time—if ever there was—when he needed to keep his teeth closed and his voice silent.

She moved to Min next, and the embrace they shared was not one of strangers.

"It has been a long time, my dear. Yes, you may tell them."

Min grinned. "Meet my teacher, my substitute mother. She means more to me than you will ever understand, unless you experience it yourself. Everything I know about what I do, I learned from her. You could say she raised me up from my psychic infancy. And I'm very sorry, Naranatha. I made terrible mistakes back there. I never should have gotten so close—mentally, I mean…"

"That's all right, dear. It's how we learn."

The Commander, who had disappeared when they entered the room, reappeared.

"Ma'am? It's time."

"Thank you, Commander. I know you all have questions but I'm afraid they will have to wait. If you will accompany the Commander?"

Garritt couldn't hold back any longer.

"But what happened to Bobby Lee? And why are you all so calm? These two nearly died chasing after him!"

Naranatha turned from the hidden doorway where she was about to exit. She took him into her cool gaze. "Yes. It is as I said. Your doubts feed that temper you must overcome."

He felt himself turn an ugly color, more humiliated than angry. That didn't stop his tongue. "I have a right to be upset! No one has told us anything."

"Patience. Add that to your list of requirements, if you wish to meet your full potential," she added, as if he were nothing more than an untimely breeze, or an equation to be solved over an eternity of time. Her complacency made him feel worse about his own lack of control.

Min, to her credit, shot him a sympathetic look as Naranatha disappeared the way she'd come.

"What the fuck," he groused.

"You also need to learn some manners," the Commander practically growled at him. "And respect for your superiors. Do you know who that woman is?"

"Hell no! And no thanks to you!"

"Güey!" Juan broke in, grinning at his friend's distress. *"Putillo!* She *runs* this place. And what it is…you're not going to believe."

He seemed so overjoyed, Garritt had trouble accepting the darkness of the cloud that flickered over Juan's face mere seconds later as he added, "Bobby Lee is dead, *compa*. He died. Crashed the fucking plane into a mountain."

Snow-blind. Now it made sense. Juan must have been in Bobby's head when it happened.

43

Connection

∞

"Did you hear what she said to you?"

Min hurried to catch up with Garritt before he made a complete ass of himself as the Commander led them back to the atrium. Bad enough he'd already found himself lacking under the beam of Naranatha's scrutiny.

"What?"

"It's your bad attitude."

She knew exactly what it felt like to be called out by her teacher. She'd certainly experienced it enough times. Naranatha could turn you inside out and put you back together again, all for the sake of shaking up your ego so you'd be more open to education. It meant she had high hopes for Garritt, or she wouldn't have bothered. He would come out shining in the end but it could feel like a gut-punch at first.

"She does that. She takes you in hand and shows you what you're not seeing about yourself."

"You've been to this place before?"

"No—never. But I've been her student for, um, let's just say longer than one lifetime. Just…not *here.*"

She finally looked up and around. She was unconscious when they wheeled her into that amazing room.

"Spamoly-oly!"

Garritt laughed. "Now that's the woman I remember."

"You mean all I have to do is make up words to get you to lighten up? Come on, they're leaving us behind."

Juan, Agnes, and Garritt hustled to match the Commander's swift stride among the fish ponds and dazzling crystals but seconds after she told Garritt to hurry, Min wanted to stop and stare. She had visited plenty of places around the world, some of them pretty spectacular, but a building like this? In Michigan? She wouldn't believe it if her eyes weren't confirming it.

"Wait till you see the outside," Garritt called back to her.

She scuttled to catch up. "When was the last time you saw your golden lights?"

All around them, people were flooding out of the building's five wings toward a glass wall at the back of the central atrium. Some wore clothing that hinted of foreign cultures and beliefs. She caught Garritt staring, as if he'd never seen Southeast Asians, or Arabs, or Persians—wait, what if he hadn't?

Does he even know the crucial difference between Arabs and Persians? This Dutch dude from a community that prides itself on cultural isolation?

Maybe not, she realized. *In person* was not at all like *on a screen*, where your prejudice can distort what you're seeing to suit your bias. But in her experience, when she stood before a person whose heart beat like hers, whose breath went in and out like hers, whose eyes told stories of pain and love and confusion and heartbreak and need … *Yeah. That's when things begin to change.*

The people streaming by were old, young, and in between. A few smiled warmly as they passed or mumbled a hello, but most were focused intently on a far opening through which they all thronged. Min felt the outdoor chill blow into the atrium and wondered why they would swarm outside on such a frigid afternoon.

She had grown suspicious when Naranatha first appeared. Now speculations churned up from her memory banks. She'd heard rumors… *Are we where I think we are?*

Garritt stopped suddenly and pivoted toward her, light breaking in his eyes. "Wait, you're saying—?"

"Exactly. You only see your glitter friends when you're thinking positive thoughts, right? So if you were worried or angry or fed up or, in this case, deflated—"

"Then I don't see them. I know this. I'm so stupid! "

"No—you're so human. Your negativity—that's what she sensed. Self-doubt. That's one of the most vicious forms of negativity because we never think of it as that. It's like a black hole that sucks in any compliment, or success, or achievement. It turns them all to *shite*, as Alex would say, and you just go back to beating yourself up with insecurity.

"Now come on. If I'm right about what's happening here, it's going to knock your Dutch brain out of its isolation once and for all."

Without thinking, she took his hand to drag him forward.

The jolt of personal connection felt extremely intimate. But too late. She'd made the move. No taking it back now. She pretended not to notice the extraordinary feeling and kept her hand locked into his.

Can he feel that?

∞

Not *now,* Garritt told himself. *Not here.* Yet not for all the light in the world would he pull his hand away from hers, not even when they caught up with the others.

"Why can't I text Luciana?" Juan complained as they hurried along.

"It's a health thing," Min said. "You won't even find Wi-Fi in a Blackthorn building. Right, Commander?"

The Commander grunted, intent on that mysterious glass wall they were rushing toward.

"So this is Blackthorn?" Garritt's head swiveled. He'd expected paramilitary austerity, not the ice palace from *Frozen*.

"No, this is Blackthorn's biggest client. For all my years with them, I thought this was just a rumor."

"And you'd better keep it that way," the Commander warned her. "Need to know."

Even here among the flowers and the dangling crystals, the man carried himself as if an enemy might lurk behind the next potted tree, special ops embedded in his sinews and bone. He moved soundlessly, tense as a leopard. Garritt was impressed.

Min let her hand slip away.

He felt a keen sense of loss. Depression started to move in. Almost immediately his thoughts swung back to Naranatha's scolding and Min's

explanation. But how the hell was a person supposed to walk around full of "positivity" all day? *Never going to happen.*
And there, I just proved it. Negative thinking.

A smarter part of him argued, *Maybe it's not about suppressing emotion versus letting your temper fly. Maybe it's about knowing the consequences.*

He thought of what happened at his father's house. If truth be told, the rage that came over him was so intense, he'd felt his muscles tense for a physical attack before he made himself turn away. That toned it down a notch, until pity took over. But that moment—he could easily have killed the man.

He knew the truth of that, deep within his soul, although no one else would ever believe him. So close, he'd been. He'd heard a chorus within, urging him to do it. Just like Juan said, to wrap his hands around the man's throat and squeeze the hypocrisy right out of him. Thank the Infinite he walked away before he forgot who he was and turned into the thing he reviled most.

But I'm human. We're nothing if not wild in our emotional swings. That's how we learn.

Fall down, scrape knees, get back up again, try some new tactic. Pain is the great motivator; everyone knows that.

A golden flare loomed before his eyes, confirming his assessment. He was grateful to see it again.

The light unspooled another perspective: *Can you control where you live in your head; your resting state? Bottom of the scale, versus top side? Selfish, versus selfless? Greedy, versus generous? That will determine the company you keep,* the luminous visitor seemed to say.

So his own temper brought him the only real form of "demonic" influence this world knows, he realized, the one that chimes in on negative impulses, impulses we generate and we feed. Until we cut them off and become free.

Scary business, being human.

Their little group exited through one of two nearly invisible breaks in the massive glass wall.

Once again they emerged on an enormous, high platform, this time hanging over an open-air, outdoor space. He could see the lake twinkling below, the gardens beyond, and he wondered fleetingly if the lake formed naturally or if the builders dug it out from springs, which were abundant in this part of the country.

The place their group stood was decorated like a ceremonial stage. The Commander led them to a far corner of it. Half-circles of stadium-style seating curved beyond and below them, cupping the airy space. Stairs at either end of the platform led down to the seats, which were nearly filled.

What happens here, quidditch?

He chuckled, then considered that his life had turned so strange, he shouldn't be surprised if competitors swooped into the empty space on flying broomsticks.

Overhead, wispy clouds scurried by, probably coming off Lake Michigan, which he judged to be far to the west of them. The air was brittle, devoid of the floral scent inside the atrium. From where they stood on the decorated stage, he saw no sign of the "dome of concealment" but it must be up there, invisibly protecting this strange gathering.

He stared out at the crowd, cast in a rosy glow from the sunset-tinted petals soaring above them. They looked eager, chatting in a subdued rumble. Where did they all come from? The atrium was completely deserted when they landed. Things didn't add up.

He thought of the building's designers. The Commander said they "participated" in its creation. With whom? And how did they keep this place secret from surrounding communities while they built it—because people would post photos all over the internet if they could see what he was looking at right now, freezing in a chill wind. Like the others, he pulled on the coat he'd held bundled under his arm.

As if from a cue, the crowd suddenly fell into eerie silence, every face focused on a central point in the open space.

When he turned to ask the Commander why they hadn't been ushered down to sit in the bleachers with the others, the man gave him a curt signal to be silent, to do as the others were doing. Juan shrugged at Garritt and did as he was told, directing his vision into the empty space. Min, Agnes; they were already staring. So Garritt joined in.

Instantly he felt plugged in, as if he'd joined a chorus of chanting monks. As soon as he thought it, he flashed on a memory of exactly that. Another lifetime? Chills of recognition ran over him, tickled his nose, and made him sneeze against his coat sleeve.

"Psychic sneeze," Min whispered. She slipped her hand into his again. He really liked that. "I remember those monks, too."

"Then why aren't you sneezing?" he whispered back, trying to leaven the thrill of her touch.

"Shhh," she scolded and said no more.

The uplifting energy swelled, filled his lungs, took over his heart, deleted everything else from his thoughts.

That's when the glitter flickered into his vision: golden twinkles of countless number, multiplying, brightening in the space before them. Did the others see? He didn't want to divert his sight, break his contact, so he kept eyes forward and soaked up what the lights gave back to the crowd of people who might have called them.

The tiny lights danced and sparked until their mass grew, and expanded, and turned solid. Slowly, they morphed into the shape of a cosmic seashell, pointed above, wider at the middle, pointed at the bottom like a spinning top. It glimmered and shimmered and oscillated like a living biomass.

Fully materialized, the starship hovered at the height of the platform where they stood. Garritt's grip on Min's hand grew so tight, she wiggled her fingers free and shook them out. But she slipped them back in again, much to his delight. He couldn't decide which was more exciting, the sensation of her skin on his, or the fact that he was watching an alien ship materialize from another dimension.

To their left, Naranatha emerged from another door in the glass wall and took up a station near the front of the suspended stage. She wore a different gown; this one twinkled gold from head to toe. The tall Black man—"Reverend Ben," Min whispered—filed out to stand just behind and to the right of Naranatha, looking regal in ivory and gold robes. Another equally magnificent figure, a woman Garritt had not seen before, emerged to stand beside him, also in finery fit for royalty. Behind them, four more emerged from the atrium, then eight, and so on, until they formed a triangle of glittering dignitaries, all in vibrant colors, representing cultures from all over the world. With Naranatha at its apex, the assembled triangle of officials faced the hovering ship.

Garritt, Min, Agnes, and Juan had been left alone and forgotten at the back of the stage—because the Commander was nowhere in sight.

Intuitively, they pulled back as a group into a rear corner, hoping for shadows in which to hide.

Garritt's pulse ran faster. He wanted to disappear, slip down those stairs and meld into the crowd. He might have tried it, if not for Min's proud, upright posture and warm hand linked to his own.

She looked up at him, her face suffused with joyful expectation.

"I'm so glad you're seeing this! One less secret I'll have to keep!"

A swirl of color began to spin on the side of the ship. None among the spectators uttered a sound, their communal breath held in anticipation, as a crystal-clear walkway extended toward where Naranatha stood waiting.

After long moments that threatened to send Garritt into the stratosphere, a lone figure stepped out of the ship…

"Wade?!"

Min's shout sliced through the ceremonial silence.

"You *mother*—"

Garritt managed to get his hand over her mouth before she could finish the word, though he was equally astonished. The last time he'd seen this man he lay dead in a snowbank.

He wasn't the biggest shock, though.

That was reserved for the two men and two women coming down the clear gangplank behind him. The shortest one must have been at least seven-and-a-half feet tall.

44

Elevation

∞

A cheesy grin spread across Wade's face, which blossomed with self-satisfaction.

That did nothing to quell Min's indignation. He'd lied! In the astral, even! She'd been played.

That son of a...

She struggled out of Garritt's grip and marched to the edge of the platform. She didn't give a hoot where she was, who she stepped in front of, or the fact that she'd been waiting for this grand starship entrance her entire adult life. He'd ruined it! She would have it out with him right here and now, and she didn't give a flying ...

"Minda!" Ben's booming voice cut through her plans and echoed out over the proceedings.

She hesitated. Turned.

"Do not humiliate yourself," he hissed at a level she hoped only those on the wide stage could hear. "You will have answers soon enough."

That promise wasn't sufficient to quell her resentment but she paused. This, from the man who rescued her when she called out to him on Bobby Lee's airplane.

Ben had arrived in his astral form right before her mind and her energy failed completely. He talked her out of Bobby's head and into harmony with his own shining vibration. He told her the snakes were conjured by her personal phobias—another trap door in her consciousness. But the leeches were real, he said, an aspect of this new enemy Blackthorn faced: a highly effective, sub-astral organization that they would undoubtedly meet again. The enemy they'd sought to discover. So, in a sense, her disastrous mission had nevertheless succeeded in their quest for information.

Without Ben, though, she might have perished from the task.

She wavered long enough for Garritt to reach her at the front of the platform and lead her back to the others, who stood with their backs against the glass wall as if to melt out of sight, though they were all on display before the assembled crowd.

She didn't care what anybody thought of her outburst. Wade had twisted her guts out with his phony death scene! It wasn't the first time he'd played her, and she renewed her vows of revenge, never mind the fricking spaceship grandstanding entrance he'd just performed!

Wade reached the stage and inclined his head respectfully toward Naranatha. Four individuals trailed behind him, faces she didn't recognize. In fact, at a second glance, they were so extraordinary she had to avert her eyes to keep from staring. Were they…?

"Welcome back, brave souls."

Naranatha's amplified words resonated across the airy stadium, though to Min it was the near and dear sound she knew, the one that could drop a man at twenty feet—or with equal ease, elevate him from a personal gutter.

Wade beamed and took a knee before her, bowing his head again.

Min rolled her eyes. An entirely unnecessary display of showmanship! Naranatha did not command that kind of obeisance, Min scoffed, even if that's how she made you feel.

"My Golden One," he intoned, "I present you with the missing item we have retrieved."

And what happened to your southern drawl, butt kisser?

He reached inside the strange fitted coat he wore and pulled out a slender package, placed it in his leader's outstretched hands. Naranatha passed it to Ben, who gave it to the woman beside him. Then Naranatha reached to help Wade to his feet.

His crew of four had followed him onto the stage. They stood together on the other side of the triangle of officials, though she could still see that when they moved, they moved in unison, as if they were one. They turned to face the crowd below, who applauded raucously. All four stood taller than Ben. Wade turned to the audience and held up a hand for silence. "We cannot accept your applause. It does not belong to us but to the four individuals who stand behind me."

She thought he meant the four crew members but then he said something that hit her like a gunshot.

"Minda Blake, Juan Talamantes, Agnes Crump, and Garritt Vanderhoeven, will you please step forward?" He sounded now like a Shakespearean actor who owned the stage with his commanding vocal presence.

The shock of hearing her name subsided but the dance in Min's stomach did not. Anger might lead her to make a spectacle of herself in public, but don't ask her to stand in front of a crowd voluntarily! No way. She hung back.

Until Naranatha turned, smiled, and beckoned with an outstretched hand. That, she could not refuse. Meekly, she moved to accept it. Naranatha's eyes shot beams of strength into her. The spectators melted away.

The others followed reluctantly, standing behind her as Wade and his crew slipped to the far rear of the platform.

Naranatha's voice echoed out over the assemblage. "This member of our collective gave of herself, when she bravely offered her services to track the criminal who stole this vital artifact. She risked her life and mind, placed herself in great danger, and all without hesitation. She understood the need to protect this planet from dangerous interference. She gave no thought to her own well-being."

What a terrible lie!

Min cowered inside as cheers rose up from the crowd. She'd meant to steal it! To expose their secret! To violate all the vows she'd made to this group—even though at the time she didn't know the group existed. Worse, she turned out to be too cowardly to carry out her own defection, so *she* was the reason the artifact became lost in the first place. If she'd followed protocol and notified her team as she'd sworn to do…

The crowd's approval might have been the most supportive sound she'd ever heard, and yet she didn't deserve a single decibel.

Naranatha dropped her hand.

She must know what I'm thinking. She always sensed more about me than I knew myself.

Her teacher reached for Juan and pulled him into the forefront. "And this young man, without prior training, used what the artifact gave him to support our cause. He knew deep within himself that it was the right thing to do. When we called, he responded without question. He also risked his life and sanity for the greater good. In his true self, he understands where his future lies." She winked at him.

Oh my gosh, she knows about him, too. And she knows he *knows she knows! He's the one who first intentionally stole the artifact.*

She could read it on Juan's face, the same guilt and shame she felt. Oddly, that lessened her misery, to know that she wasn't the only fraud who might have accidentally done something right.

Leave it to Naranatha. She always found the cleverest ways to lead you to self-improvement.

This whole ceremony is a sham she cooked up, Min realized, *designed to encourage us to level up, to see where we've failed, yet also to glimpse our potential. We'll never feel whole again until we earn her praise, now that we've tasted it. That is, after we recover from the ego deflation she's managed to dish out simultaneously. She is so brilliant. Never misses an opportunity to teach.*

As the crowd cheered and Naranatha beamed Juan, too, with her unconditional Love-power, Min could see the change fall over him. No one would ever deter this young man from serving whatever objective these individuals, this place, these aliens might ask of him. She couldn't help but smile at him, the most encouraging smile she could manage. It was true for her too. No turning back now.

Naranatha next led Garritt and Agnes forward, taking their hands so they had to stand on either side of her tiny figure, facing the crowd.

How would they weather this exposure? Garritt, with his insecurities and his senator father and his cold-hearted mother who'd weaned him on insular, outdated biases, and Agnes, in her relative innocence about the planet she lived on, let alone the universe in which all these people claimed citizenship. *What must she think?*

From Min's vantage point, both looked shell-shocked. They'd wake up tomorrow wondering if they dreamed it all.

Naranatha's oratory quieted. "These two brave individuals have come to us of their own free will. Through kindness, compassion, selfless giving, and that vital component of curiosity, they have made their way against strong odds to this moment, to our haven on Earth, to the greatest opportunity they have ever faced."

She turned her back on the crowd to focus on Garritt and Agnes, although her words were still amplified for all to hear.

"My dears, I know you have many questions. That is good. Never, ever stop asking those questions. But we are offering you a chance to speed your evolution exponentially, to leave behind lifetimes of trial and tribulation that you would normally suffer, in order to learn what our beautiful training center here can teach you now. If you choose to join our ranks, you will become one of the Golden Ones. Together, we are working to form a bridge between planet Earth and the countless other civilizations that surround this lost world. But this connection must be built slowly and carefully. We must both protect your innocence, and help you raise yourselves up to achieve a new place in the universe."

Min feared Agnes would ignite in the blaze of embarrassment that erupted on her face. Garritt, for the first time, looked as if his resistance had finally collapsed. He drank in Naranatha's promises like a thirsty man and seemed to grow a little taller with each one. His fair hair shone with new brilliance, and his eyes—oh, those eyes…

Naranatha spun to gesture across the assemblage. "Each of the individuals you see seated in our pavilion—they have all earned their places. Their acts of selfless humility, their heroism, their kindness, their willingness to let go of the past, and their open-minded eagerness to learn have brought them, slowly, over the course of countless lifetimes of struggle, to this time and place, this unique opportunity in the history of your planet. Just as you have done.

"They are all ambassadors now. When they return to their homes, they serve as examples. Whatever their occupation, they are leaders in thought and deed. They help us bridge the gap between the present Earth human—and the evolved humans you will all become. They work to break through barriers of hatred, prejudice, conflict, and ignorance, each in their own fields of endeavor.

"Some of their accomplishments are small—tiny, even. Some are grand and spectacular, like the discovery of new planets that surround you, or the development of technologies that don't harm their human counterparts. They are demonstrating how to solve ecological problems, or how to unite diverse populations with insight into the science that binds us. Together, we are transforming this world into the better world that will be prepared to join the universal collective of humanity."

A joyous sound of approval went up. Agnes's eyes shone like emeralds. Garritt stood tall, like the Golden One he must have become for a time in that rainforest; she was convinced of that. This would be permanent. He had clearly made his decision. A trill of love and respect for him passed through her.

"We will not ask you to decide at this moment. But if you choose to join our family, our unified efforts, we will be most pleased to have your company and your abilities in support of our Earth mission."

Naranatha dropped their hands and reached her own to the sky for a moment, as if to invoke and receive the support of all civilizations throughout the multi-dimensional universe, the multiverse. The energy in the place amped up to a point that made the top of Min's head buzz with new vibrations.

And then it was done. Naranatha and Ben and the other officials made a quick but gracious exit.

The ship vanished with nary a flash.

45

Clarity

∞

"*You roofied* me!"

"Nothing so primitive. Similar, though. I heard you almost took out an EMT when you woke up," Wade laughed.

"You mother…fucking…*asshole!*" Min slammed a fist into his shoulder, one punch for each word. Garritt suspected Wade might feel that bruise later. She was no slouch. And so much for her elaborate attempt to give up profanity.

They'd stepped back into a private alcove as the crowd filed by. Most looked as if they'd had their systems flushed and their spiritual gears lubed. He felt the same. If it weren't for Min's outburst, he'd be floating right along with them—unless he could find the aliens who slipped out of sight when the ceremony ended. He was terrified of them—and desperate to meet one. He wished she would get this over with.

"Min," he said, "he's explained it three times: the latte was drugged. He carried you into the snowbank to look like you'd been thrown out and knocked unconscious." That deception didn't please Garritt, either. His heart barely survived it. But he wasn't going to say that out loud.

"Then he tricked *all* of us into believing he was dead."

"How'd you do it, *güey?*" Juan's voice carried only admiration—and relief.

"The drug I took only mimicked death long enough to convince Garritt and Agnes. And we have friends in the ambulance business," Wade grinned. "Listen, Min—we had to do it."

"Oh yeah? And what happened to your accent?" She punched him again. "You were a phony from the beginning! A plant! Mother—"

"So what sent me after you two?" Garritt cut in. "Was that part of the plan?"

Wade danced away from the question. "We needed you all to do exactly as you've done. If it weren't for your efforts, we wouldn't have located the crash so quickly. How else were we going to get you all in one spot, working together? We didn't have time for subtle persuasion, but we needed you to make these choices yourselves. I confess, the fast way was my idea. It worked pretty well, I think."

"Fucker," Min hit him one last time, hard.

"It was a test, get it? And you all passed with flying colors! You should be proud. Look where it's brought you," he gestured at the spectacular surroundings.

"If you want to stage a deception, this is your man," Juan said. "Way to go," he gave Wade a high five. "Now I owe you twice. Once for my old life and now for my new one."

"Any time." They hooked fingers, knocked knuckles, touched elbows, a ritual they must have developed during Juan's "interrogation."

Agnes hadn't said a word since the ceremony, though Garritt could see her eyes flicker with curiosity as she stared at the passersby. Any minute and she'd be chatting up someone wearing a sari.

Garritt's first priority lay elsewhere. "So when do we get to meet your crew?"

"My crew? No, man, you've got that wrong. I was their passenger. They only needed me to retrieve the artifact because, as some of you may know, they cannot make themselves visible in public. Not yet. That's the whole point here."

"And where is here, exactly?" Agnes spoke up. "What is this 'Rose' we're in?"

He considered for a moment. "When I first came here, my understanding was that ROSE stood for *Restoration of Spiritual Energy*. Then I saw it as a *Regional Outpost for Scientific Expansion*. Later, as my studies progressed, it became a *Respectful Outreach to Space Entities*," he chuckled, "and more recently I've viewed it as a

Resource Observatory for Speeding Evolution. Get it? You can call it whatever you want."

"But who pays for it," Garritt wanted to know. "This place must be worth a fortune—the real estate alone! I mean, since we're speaking freely now, right?"

"Good question. The graduates of this training center usually do quite well in their respective careers. They are very generous, because after all, they've pledged themselves to a cause like none other on the planet. Well, except for the other training centers emerging around the world."

Just like that, he dropped another bomb on them.

"I don't understand, though," Agnes said. "I see some women wearing head scarves, and men in turbans and prayer shawls and orange monk's robes. Isn't this some kind of church school or…cult, maybe? I mean, Naranatha said we could 'join the family,' which sounds like church to me."

Wade smiled at her, "We're a resource center for evolutionary advancement. You know, religion is like any other tool: it can also be turned into a weapon. Some people use their outward piety to deceive and conceal—ask Garritt."

He winced. His own father.

"Some use it politically to manipulate the masses, using people's innate spiritual drive to convince them to wage wars, while their leaders solidify a power base over piles of dead bodies."

True, sadly.

"But most people come to a church, temple, or mosque because they want to understand their place in the universe. They want to be better people, to take a step up on a path of self-enlightenment. No one who chooses to study here has to give away the progress they've made on this path. Whether they are churchgoers or leaders or scientists or artists or bricklayers, we teach them a science that expands on what they've learned so far, what the planet as a whole has known in the past but lost. When they go home, they take this knowledge with them.

"Some of the people you saw in religious garb might become the visionaries who lead their cultures forward, who change religious institutions from within. We are all changed by the knowledge we acquire here. There's no going back."

"So if I study here, I don't have to stop going to church with my family?" Agnes wanted to know.

"Of course not! You are free to pursue whatever course of life you choose. And when or if it stops providing you with meaning and opportunity, we hope you will have learned enough about how evolution works that you will quickly move up to the next rung." He smiled kindly at her again, as everyone who encountered Agnes seemed to do—especially the Commander. "This isn't a cult, or a religion, or a club. This is a training center for visionary leaders. Every option you undertake here will be of your own choosing. If you qualify for it, of course."

A happy radiance spread over her face.

Listening to Wade's perspective, Garritt thought maybe he'd been too hard on religion as a whole. Having it shoved forcefully down his throat certainly killed any enthusiasm, though. He was glad to hear ROSE wasn't yet another form of institutionalized belief system.

"But what about Bobby Lee?" Min interrupted. "Tell them what you told me a few minutes ago. They deserve to know."

"You're right. Thanks to your excellent work, we located Bobby's plane quickly and found the artifact wrapped in old rags, inside a bag buried in the wreckage. My colleagues had no trouble pinpointing its location. It's possible that Bobby also tried to find it. We found evidence of his search."

"What? I thought that *pendejo* died! I mean, I heard him…when the plane went down—" Juan choked off at the memory.

Agnes laid a comforting hand on his shoulder. "It's okay. Don't go there. We know."

Garritt recalled how it felt on that cliff in Peru, expecting to die moments after his feet left the ground.

No, that was different. On the edge of that precipice, in the steaming heat, he still had a choice. Bobby Lee had already made his choices, whether he realized that or not. His shock and horror, suddenly knowing he'd lost control, seconds from death—Juan must have felt like he faced death too. Juan's prayers on the helicopter made sense now.

"Bobby Lee didn't die in the crash," Wade explained. "I followed his tracks until they disappeared into a rocky gully. He was probably looking for shelter from the wind and pelting snow. My colleagues sensed no signs of a living being, and I found no body. If he remained on site but hidden, he had already succumbed to either his injuries or exposure.

"No, Juan—don't try," he cautioned. "It's too dangerous. When Ben pulled you back during the crash, he probably saved your sanity. If Bobby *is* alive, he's too far gone mentally for you to risk the connection. By the way, Vacaville—that's your cow town. Apparently you automatically translated the Spanish. Located in Northern California, near an Air Force base."

"Damn. I should have gotten that!"

"No, you did a great job," Min consoled him. "Go on, Wade. What aren't you saying?"

He sighed. "Since Bobby never made it there, we can envision several possible scenarios. One is that the astral entities led Bobby as far as their physical buyers needed him to go. Then he became expendable. By the time he crashed, the humans knew where to retrieve the artifact, without any multi-billion-dollar pay-off. Except thanks to you and the speed of interdimensional travel, we got there first. That suggests we have technology these buyers don't."

Juan's eyes lit up, probably at the prospect of moving between dimensions, if Garritt knew anything about him at all.

"Under orders, we left the vicinity immediately to avoid a battle over the artifact, since we don't know what technology they do have."

"So it's not the civilization whose drones we've been shooting down?" Min asked.

"No. That world's interest in Earth is more curiosity than avarice. But their clumsy approaches threaten Earth's protective shield of ignorance. Hence our mutual, alien/human efforts to conceal their existence until they can be convinced to cease and desist."

He directed this startling news to the three who'd never heard it before.

"Bobby's buyers, on the other hand, appear Earth-based. We can't be sure at this stage but they might possess either re-engineered or borrowed alien technology. We need to know more about their alliances and capabilities before we engage."

A few days ago none of them, except Min, fully believed in the existence of extraterrestrial civilizations, let alone the idea that we might already be involved in interplanetary conflict over weapons or resources. Garritt knew that even Juan, for all his enthusiasm, daydreamed only about the glamour of alien first-contact.

Garritt needed a minute to mull the magnitude of Wade's words but the man pattered on, "Another possibility: these buyers are minor players. Maybe they stumbled into this, completely unaware of the fragment's more esoteric properties. Or they knew just enough to be dangerous. Either way, the sub-astral interference is clear, thanks to your work, Juan, and Min's, um, aggressive approach." He gave her a scolding look, which probably wasn't the best idea.

"What do you mean, minor players?" Garritt cut in. He was thinking of his father's industrial friends, always eager to develop new weapons of mass destruction. "Private corporation? Foreign government? Are you saying that you don't know who was in charge, the astral beings or the Earth buyers?"

"Something like that. Bobby also crashed very near a site where the U.S. still houses nuclear ICBMs, intercontinental ballistic missiles, although the exact location is highly classified, of course. This might be a factor. We know there are factions within the government that have their own agendas. That's a possibility—one of the worst."

He paused, as if weighing whether to burden them with the whole truth or not.

Finally, he added, "Depending on how much the buyers know, they might realize that possession of Bobby Lee himself could provide them with an unexpected research opportunity. The fact that we never located his body gives us some concern."

"You mean they could use his mental impairment to study the effects of the fragment," Min surmised.

"That is a possibility we must consider."

"Any others?"

Wade nodded. "Believe it or not, a best-case scenario would be that Bobby Lee merely found someone online who wanted to own a piece of 'a real UFO.' Some super-wealthy fanboy. And the astral beings you saw, Minda—which Ben assures us are a real, organized society, so to speak—they might have acted as opportunists. They took advantage of

Bobby's open channel of egotism and greed and had no desire for the artifact itself and no connection to any buyer."

Garritt felt ill.

"Such creatures thrive in the astral bands surrounding this world. They also wouldn't care if their host died, like the sub-astral entities who work their way into the heads of mass shooters. They feed off of the energies of hysteria and terror and gore. In that case, when the shooter dies by his own hand or a police take-down, they simply find a new host they convince to recreate the crime. Which is why it keeps repeating. Gruesome as that is, we hope that's what this was—and not some sophisticated operation determined to create new weapons, with astral and alien support."

"You're giving me nightmares." Agnes's face had grown pale.

"Rightly so. Even so-called aliens must guard against this type of mental invasion from the lowest of the low. Except that they're usually better educated and thus better protected against it."

Garritt's stomach churned. He'd made himself vulnerable back at his father's house. For some reason, his psychic connections went both ways, from the highest frequencies to the lowest. Ironically, that's also what saved him. "So what do we do now?"

"We give you an opportunity to make a phone call," Wade smiled. "This problem isn't going to be solved today. It's as old as the cosmos. And wouldn't you like to meet my shipmates?"

Of course they all quickly agreed that meeting live "aliens" would be highly agreeable.

Wade led them to an outdoor gazebo designed for all-weather use. He called it a communication cubicle. Behind airy marble embellishments of French or Italian design, a nearly-invisible membrane kept the interior warm and inviting. The flowers inside bloomed as cheerily as if it were a summer's day.

Wade doled out precise instructions:

"Let your people know you'll be home tomorrow. Juan, two calls: Tell Luciana that you might be contagious and can't go out. Tell your parents that you're with Garritt, same story. Garritt, tell Corbyn your ankle's not healed yet. Agnes—you're staying with a friend. Minda—well, it's up to you; Amrita isn't expecting to hear from you. Whatever you do, no texting or photographs, and do not tell them you're in the company of individuals who are not of this planet. Got it?"

Wade clearly relished giving these orders. But how had he known what mattered most to each of them?

46

Luminosity

∞

Garritt brushed off the sadness that rose up when he realized he had no one to call except Corbyn. He owed his boss much. Yet the restaurant that had given him wings now felt like an anchor.

He glanced over at Min, holding a phone to her ear and smiling at something her friend must have said.

His life in Veenlanden, so important to him until now, suddenly felt incredibly empty.

And if he understood the invitation correctly, he'd just enrolled in this training center. So how would he make a living? What about Juan, with his pregnant girlfriend?

Agnes burst out laughing.

"Nathan quit his job with my dad," she announced. "He's going to backpack through Portugal with Sam!"

They all agreed it was the perfect match.

Wade led them back inside, to a room where his starship crew stood regally awaiting their arrival, as if pre-warned. Straight and slender like Maasai warriors but with gleaming golden skin, their heads nearly touched the ceiling, while their sleek garments reached the floor of the well-appointed reception room. As Wade introduced them one by one, the two women and two men stepped forward graciously. For the first time in his life, Garritt had to look up to catch one of the women's eyes.

Here were human beings, no doubt about it. No weird extra limbs or crinkly green skin. A beautiful golden tan, yes, but no bizarre, buggy black eyes. No earless heads.

Human. Breathing oxygen. Kindred spirits. He *knew* these people, and they knew him.

Min and Agnes smiled and nodded politely—except that Min had a look in her eye that echoed his own thought: *Where have we met before?* He saw a trickle run down her gleaming cheek. Exactly the way he felt.

Wade spoke their language and he translated for most of them. But Juan was able to communicate by standing close and listening—or so it appeared.

With one of the men, Juan exchanged a few hand gestures, facial expressions—and sounds, bits of English and Spanish, laughs, grunts, giggles, clicks like you'd hear in Africa, and what must have been the crew members' own language, which sang and danced over Garritt's ears in a pleasing way and made him long to learn its intricacies as soon as possible. Within moments, Juan and the man were exchanging words in each other's languages.

Wait—was Juan teaching him macho vulgarities in Spanish? Garritt laughed. *Typical.*

Overall, the greetings were joyous. Oraylians, Wade called them. *So familiar!*

In the midst of all this happiness, Juan suddenly broke away from these beautiful beings. He kicked a wall so hard he could have broken something, swearing in two languages.

"Dude, what is it?" Garritt followed him across the room.

"Fucking impossible, that's what it is!"

Wade went on alert. "What's the problem?"

"I can't do it!" Juan's face contorted.

"Do what, man?"

"What's wrong?"

"I can't leave Luciana to raise my baby alone! And this is so…it's… it's what I've dreamed…" He lost it.

The choice did seem cruel.

Wade let out a short laugh. "Is that all? I thought you were tweaked about talking to aliens!"

Juan spun to face him, throwing his arms around in despair, yelling, "No—what the fuck? Don't you get it? I can't choose this! I can't give up Luciana and my family and my unborn child! I can't fucking do this.

Wipe my brain so I can forget all this! Or let me tell the whole world the truth right now. Bobby Lee was right. People deserve to know!"

Wade snatched one of the flailing arms and led Juan to a chair, sat him down, and crouched before him so his face loomed close.

"Juan, listen to me. First of all, this isn't Hogwarts. It's not some chauvinistic Shangri-La. It's a university. No one who's earned a spot here has to leave anyone."

"Oh yeah? So why can't we just open the doors and let everyone know that aliens are real—and they look a lot like us!"

"I understand why you're upset. We've all been there. But we have good reasons for all of this."

Min interrupted. "Juan, just think about this planet you're living on. How well was your father treated when he first moved into the Dutch Triangle?"

That hit a chord, Garritt knew. They treated him with scorn and hatred, like anyone who wasn't Dutch—only worse, because Juan's father was born in Mexico.

Wade went on, "To study here, you will have to give up one thing: your old self. You won't be the same person. And you'll learn many things you can't share—but not because you are forbidden to. In fact, ultimately sharing them is what this training is all about—*but not until the time is right*. We come here to learn how to help prepare people to bridge the deafening gap of silence between Earth and other cultures, off-world cultures. We're training to become intermediaries of a sort."

"You mean liars. Because we can't tell anyone about this place, can we." Juan wasn't going to budge.

Across the room, Min made a face.

"Do you know why? People you love will think you're crazy."

"She's right," Wade agreed. "Try to tell them about the interdimensional flow of life-energy, the same science that makes us breathe, the science that makes interplanetary travel possible, and their eyes will glaze over, it will be so far beyond them. They won't hear a word you're saying. Trust me. I've tried it. You, Min?"

She nodded, sadness in her eyes.

Wade stood up, gesturing to include Agnes.

He must think I'm a shoe-in, Garritt thought. *He's right.*

"You will both *feel* like you've left everything and everyone you've known—except for people like us, and your new friends," he nodded toward the Oraylians who looked confused, probably wondering how they'd offended Juan. (Or did they read minds like Juan could?)

"The places that right now support your entire life? You might feel alone in them. So yes, for now you'll have to keep some secrets from your new wife, Juan. But you won't have to leave her."

"You mean those aren't dormitories?" Agnes interrupted. "The rooms on the upper floors?" She meant in the five wings beneath the architectural rosebuds.

"Not entirely. Most are classrooms. People come here from all over the world to take classes, but only a very few students live here." He glanced at Garritt briefly and Garritt caught the implication.

Right. What else do I have?

Min cut in, "No one took my family life away when I started working for Blackthorn, and I've got the idea now that Blackthorn is just one form of outreach for this place."

A little of her glare returned as she shot a look at Wade.

"But the price of knowing even as much as you do now is very high. If you agree to stay, you must carry this burden. We all do. Here, you're going to learn more than most people are capable of believing. Christmas and holidays won't be the same for you. Or if someone in your family gets sick—you might know things about their illness that you can't tell them. The most you can do is hint, or steer, or try to guide them. And they probably won't listen."

Sounded to Garritt like she'd faced this.

"You might have to watch them make bad choices—some that might kill them—and you still can't interfere. We all get one life at a time to screw up any way we choose. It's our birthright. So, non-interference—like *Star Trek*. That's the vow you'll make, am I right, Wade?"

"Yes."

She moved closer, searched Juan's face—as if seeking the spark that brought him this far.

"But which would you choose—to live in ignorance? Or to know how incredibly far life extends, and how far we, as human beings, can improve ourselves, individually and collectively?

"I realized today that our job is not to protect a lie. Exactly the opposite. We are protecting the opportunity to tell the truth—*at the right time*. We're telling it already, in a million tiny ways, so that one day, when the whole picture emerges, people will just shrug and say, 'Well, of course. How could it be otherwise?'"

Garritt saw Agnes lean in to listen. She was so close to her family; she probably harbored the same doubts.

"There's a bonus," Min added. "Here, in this place, we can serve. We can play an active role in the most incredible development this world has ever seen. The little social deceptions you might need to carry out for a while—won't they be worth it? You've already played a huge role, didn't you hear Naranatha? How did that feel?"

Wade interrupted. "Dude. You *will* get a few chances to help speed up the process. It's not all secret-keeping. Sometimes we do things to make people think. I'll never forget my first night in the crop-circle class." He grinned, waited for that to sink in.

"What?? Are you serious?" Juan wiped at his eyes. "Okay, okay. Stop, both of you. But how am I supposed to sneak off and not tell my family what I'm doing? I mean, where are we? How far from Veenlanden? I'll spend all my time driving to and from, and then how will I earn a living to support my kid?"

Wade's face erupted with absolute delight.

"You haven't seen our big yellow school bus." He winked broadly.

"No way."

Wade nodded, grinning. He must realize that this was a gift beyond all gifts for Juan.

Juan's eyes ignited. "No...No. Fucking. Way."

"Way, *güey*. You'll meet up at the rendezvous point—after you've trained and adapted to interdimensional travel, that is. It does take some getting used to. But it's very fast. Your family will only know that you're taking business classes. You know how good we are at deception when it serves a noble purpose, right? Oh—and we give scholarships for worthy beneficiaries."

Juan laughed and put up a hand, his eagerness rekindled into a roaring fire. "Sign me up, *compa*. What else am I gonna do?"

Agnes sighed.

"What happens to us if we don't choose to attend? I mean, Naranatha did say the choice is ours."

Garritt saw Min shoot Wade a dark look. What was she thinking? He remembered well her earlier fears about Blackthorn.

"First of all, anyone who sees this place has already been screened for integrity," Wade replied. "We trust you would try to keep our secret. For a time."

"Yeah, that would be tough," Juan agreed.

"Fortunately, it's easy to forget a thing you barely believed in the first place. It takes a lot of repetition before new things sink in. So, over time, you're likely to think you dreamed or imagined ROSE, especially when it shows up in your real dreams later. With a tiny bit of hypnotic suggestion when I put you on that helicopter," Wade shrugged, "I can help you quickly forget this place. Your friends can watch me do it, to be sure I don't mess with your head where I shouldn't."

Agnes shuddered and Garritt had to agree. Why would anybody want to forget this?

"Well, it's a good thing I've decided I want to learn more," she breathed, and a huge smile broke out across her face.

Garritt caught her eye, happy they'd be taking this journey together, but her return smile was unlike any she'd given him before. Distracted? Or—? Something was missing.

After Wade successfully explained to the Oraylians what had overcome Juan, that it was not their fault, food arrived on carts from who-knows-where and they all realized how famished they were. Especially Min, who ate with the kind of gusto Garritt loved to see, although he was startled when the Oraylians joined in. They seemed to relish Earth foods, especially the veal piccata and mashed potatoes. He flashed back on photos of mutilated cows he'd seen decades ago in sensationalized UFO stories. He might have laughed—if he weren't still new to all this.

Juan and his new Oraylian friend soon went back to making up their own language. When the others grew distracted by their antics, Garritt took his blueberry cobbler to a cushioned chair in a corner. He toyed with it thoughtfully as he conducted his "quiet sit," the kind you do in the forest when you want to observe wildlife, or think over where your own life is going.

One of the Oraylian women—he'd caught her eyeing him earlier—followed him. He'd been told her name, which he couldn't pronounce even if he remembered it.

He looked up and she leaned down to touch his cheek, lightly, with two golden fingers. Her face erupted in a stellar smile and her arm began to glow. Quickly, an aura of luminous gold encompassed her, until she disappeared inside it, until nothing more than a magnificent golden light stood before him.

47

Alien

∞

"Looks like you've fallen in love with an alien," Wade whispered.

"What?!"

Min turned in time to see the golden aura flare up around Garritt, so intense she could barely make out his features.

"Ho-ly flambeau…"

She shot a look around the room. Agnes, Juan, and his Oraylian friend were laughing and dancing around, mimicking the foibles of Earth people, from what she could tell. But the other two Oraylians, man and woman, had their eyes fixed on Garritt and their female comrade, more flame than form now.

"Ben says Garritt's existence was rather, um, unexpected. Not part of the plan, you might say."

"Maybe it's part of a plan we're not privy to?"

She'd let Wade's remark about "falling in love" pass. Pretty much true. The falling part, anyway. She hadn't landed yet so she couldn't say how that might feel. But this…

"Above our pay grade," Wade considered. "Quite possible. Coming from a *lot* higher up, if you know what I mean."

"But Naranatha—"

"You know how she is. The brightest stars must be taken down a notch or two. Personal ego inhibits their shine. That business in the tree room was all part of integrating him into the training here."

Wade is a telepath! Of course! How else would he know what she felt? Or what happened in the healing room?

The fact that he'd hidden this skill answered so many questions, she didn't need to ask if it were true. No wonder Juan couldn't read him!

Sure enough, reading her mind again, he added, "It's kind of a shame. You'd make such beautiful babies, the two of you."

"Why don't you just go suck a lollipop," she hissed at him but her face grew hot and she couldn't stop herself from exploring the idea of it. And if that were ever going to happen, she'd have to pry Garritt away from the golden goddess who had just extended a glowing hand to elevate Garritt to his feet.

"But he looks so human," she whispered, as if to herself.

To Wade, who hadn't gone away, she added, "He can't be entirely Oraylian, can he? Mixed? Or can they shape-shift? His skin isn't gold, though. No, you have to be wrong. If he's an alien, then he's like Ben—born of Earth woman this lifetime."

"Not sure. The Oraylians don't tell us everything, you realize. That would constitute interference. Garritt's physical appearance is only part of the mystery. As time goes on, Ben hopes we'll learn more, because the Oraylians have remained firmly silent on the subject."

She watched in astonishment as the golden aura of the Oraylian woman expanded and merged with Garritt's, fueling it into a flame large enough to encompass them both. Garritt's shoes began to lift ever so slightly from the tiled floor.

"Nope, I think they're just having Oraylian sex."

Min sent a blow to Wade's nearest body part. He feigned a reaction that quickly turned into a quiet laugh at her expense.

What if they are?

They hovered, oscillating in perfect golden harmony.

What else could that be? Some kind of mind-meld? Even Agnes and Juan noticed.

"You know, if it weren't for that plane crash and the little girl from Ecuador who forced him to bring his skills out into the open, we might never have discovered Garritt's existence. He could have died in that rainforest and no one would have realized his origin or that he possessed certain special qualities."

"But what about him? Have you told Garritt any of this?"

Wade shook his head. "Ben says his psychic links are broadband. He can reach the highest of the high—a rare feat on Earth. Yet he also picks up the lowest if he's not careful. He was brainwashed into his parents' religious cult, for one thing."

"That monstrous senator he grew up with."

"And he's got a bad temper habit he hasn't broken, which can put him in the same danger as Bobby Lee. No one's taught him psychic discernment or mental maintenance yet. Although I suspect he's getting quite an education at this moment."

Even Wade raised an eyebrow as Garritt and the Oraylian woman remained poised in silence, gazing into one another's countenance, lips not moving. Min felt their energy spark around the room. At the very least, they were sharing information. Then she remembered Wade's telepathy.

"Can you hear what they're saying?"

"Can't understand it. It's not in the Oraylian spoken language. Apparently, they've linked at a frequency that's beyond my abilities." He turned back to her. "You keep this all to yourself, hear? Orders from Ben."

Sure, she was going to obey that one. Not for one minute.

"I'll take care of Juan and Agnes." He indicated the two standing side by side now, mouths agape.

When Juan turned to his new Oraylian friend with a quizzical look, Wade leaned in to Min so that only she could hear, "Ben wants you to stick close to Garritt. Be his friend, become his study partner, whatever you need to do to explain your presence. But he also asked me to convey a warning, and I am truly sorry about this."

He caught her eye deliberately, as serious as she'd ever seen him.

"*Stay out of his bed.*"

∞ ∞ ∞ ∞

Acknowledgments

So many thank-you's:

To my Cosmic CoAuthors who, as always, pulled me in directions I never would have dreamed of pursuing.

To Joseph Downey for reading it a million times, who offered his keen wit and insight as usual but especially about Baja food and profanity, along with his endless support and encouragement and love. He's the guy who made this book happen.

To Roslynn E. Moore who was willing to speak to a nutty stranger that day in the Target store when I besieged her with rude questions, resulting in what I hope will be the continuation of a lifetimes-long friendship. And to her mother, who generously but roughly steered me away from egregious pitfalls and misunderstandings that would have ruined my intentions.

To my social media friends who participated in a character-naming contest so many years ago, and who are always willing to cheer and laugh and support.

To my brave and persistent beta readers, Nancy & Janna Sipes, Chelle & William Doetsch, and to Linda Jo Hunter who read it twice! To Dale E. Graff and Eugene Tssui for their generosity and kindness to me, and their ongoing work for the world. And to Jonathan Maberry and the San Diego Writer's Coffeehouse for proof of possibility.

To the state of Michigan—to the good people, both the friendly neighbors and the hostile strangers, and the new friendships with students who came out to hear us talk about energy medicine and past lives ("California ideas") when Joseph and I were feeling like fish in a sandlot in West Michigan. It was my youthful experience in the friendlier southwestern part of the state that drew us back to Michigan for a few years, to its natural beauty and long history of hosting a different sort of human. So I also owe a debt to the tradition of crazy tales and stories Michigan's wildness has always inspired—of shipwrecks and ghosts and UFOs—along with my brother Bill who told them to me, even when his intentions were purely for the fun of frightening his little sister. (You can thank him for the horror elements in this story.)

To the reckless ex- who shall remain nameless, who decided it would be a good idea to fly a small plane over the Rocky Mountains even though he didn't have a license to fly on instruments that weren't installed, and even though his youngest daughter was also aboard and at risk. We made it, further convincing me of the existence of "Lighted Ones," those spiritual guardians and teachers who make sure we don't die before we've completed our individual missions on this planet.

And especially, to Ernest L. Norman and Ruth E. Norman, who taught me everything I've managed to retain about the cosmic energy principles woven into this book. My debt to them is incalculable.

About the Author

Lianne Downey has spent decades exploring, teaching, and writing about the outer reaches of her own broadband perception. Books include her YA fantasy *Cosmic Dancer* (NIEA Finalist), her channeled space opera, *The Liberator: A Psychic-Spiritual History of the Orion Empire*; and her self-help psychic awareness manual, *Speed Your Evolution: Become the Star Being You Are Meant To Be*. She holds a BA in Mass Communication from UC Davis, and served as a theater critic for *The Los Angeles Times* and the *San Diego Union-Tribune*. She is a lifelong student of the works of Ernest L. Norman, and names his widow, the late Ruth E. Norman, as her most influential spiritual mentor. When not writing or reading, you'll find her ballroom dancing with her husband Joseph, playing in their San Diego garden, dabbling in watercolor, or watching movies. For more about her exploration of past lives, energy medicine, interdimensional science, or book news, visit her website at **liannedowney.com** and sign up for her newsletter.

Milton Keynes UK
Ingram Content Group UK Ltd.
UKHW051914300624
444825UK00001B/47

9 781953 474087